SHADOW'S END

SHADOW'S END

END

A *Novel by*

Sheri S. Tepper

BANTAM BOOKS

NEW YORK   TORONTO
LONDON   SYDNEY   AUCKLAND

BEHOLD NOW BEHEMOTH

which I made with thee. . . .

He is the chief of the ways of God.

The Book of Job

SHADOW'S END

CHAPTER 1

D awn on Dinadh.

Deep in the canyonlands shadow lies thickly layered as fruit-tree leaves in autumn. High on the walls the sun paints stripes of copper and gold, ruby and amber, the stones glowing as though from a forge, hammered here and there into mighty arches above our caves. Inside the caves, the hives spread fragrant smoke, speak a tumult of little drums, breathe the sound of bone flutes. Above all, well schooled, the voice of the songfather soars like a crying bird:

"The Daylight Woman, see how she advances, she of the flowing garments, she of the golden skin and shining eye. . . ."

I do not speak with Daylight Woman. I revere her, as do all Dinadhi, but it is Weaving Woman I plead with, am pleading with. Origin of all patterns, I pray, let my shuttle carry brightness!

Each morning before first light, songfather comes to the lip of our cave, where it pushes out, pouting above the darkness below. There he stands, hearing the far faint sounds of daysongs from the east, raising his voice when first light touches the rimrock above, using his song to coax the light down the great wall. Today I stand unnoticed in the shadow beside the hive, listening as the song flows north and east and west into a dozen canyons, past a hundred hives, stirring reverberations and resonances, joining a great warp and woof of sound that follows Daylight Woman's eternal march westward. Dawnsong, so the songfather tells us, endlessly circles our world like the belt that runs from the treadle to the wheel, and thus Dinadh is never without welcome to the Lady of Light.

One time we had another lady. One time we had another father, too, but they were relinquished long ago, when the terrible choice was made. Though the songfathers assure us we were made for that choice, we people, we women, sometimes I grieve over it. Sometimes in the night, darkness speaks to me, and the stars call my name. Saluez, they cry, Saluez, look at us, look at all the mysteries in the night. . . .

But still we have appropriate and sufficient deities. We have Weaving Woman and Brother and Sister Rain, and many others. And Lady Day. In darkness, one could step into error. In cloud or fog—rare enough anywhere on Dinadh—one could stray from the right path. Led by Day-light Woman, we walk only the chosen trail, the wise way, and each morning and evening the songfathers celebrate her shining path.

"The lighted path, the chosen way," intones Hallach, in the words I had anticipated. I hear those words coming back from farther north, where the canyon rim is lower and comes later into the light. Though it sounds like an echo, it is being sung by the songfather of Damanbi. From where I stand I can hear light welcomed not only from Damanbi but also from beyond it, from Dzibano'as and Hamam'n. When the wind blows from the east, we hear the song from Chacosri, around the corner in Black-soil canyon.

I am not the only listener. Inside the hive everyone is gathered behind the doorskins listening, waiting the time of release. Children jitter impatiently. Some men and women paint their faces to ready themselves for the day. Old people with many tasks confronting them stand stolidly, wishing the welcome finished.

And I, Saluez? I wish it could go on forever. I wish the moment could stand frozen in time and not move at all.

"See her rise," sings Hallach. *"See her dance in garments of fire. See dark withdraw, exposing the world to her grace."*

It is planting season, a time to consider fecundity; so songfather sings now to Brother Big Rain, begging for storm upon the heights, and to Sister Deep Rain, begging for long slow drizzle that will wet the canyons and fill the springs. He mentions the top spring and pool, the lower spring and pool, the waterfall that spreads its moist lace over the rock, the wetness of the bottomland where the summer crops will grow. He sings to Weaving Woman of the pattern of foods eaten at different seasons.

No doubt songfather is eager for summer food, as we all are. We are all sick of winter-fungus, life-bread, grown in the hives during cold time, using the warmth of our bodies, the waste of our bodies to feed itself. It has no taste. It keeps us alive, but it gives no pleasure. During winter, all the pleasurable food must be saved for others, for there are worse things than mere tastelessness.

But soon the time of winter-fungus will be past. First-water has already been carried to the fruit trees, to wake them from winter. Now songfather sings of damp soil, the feel of it, the perfume of unfolding blossoms, continuing this litany until light falls on his face. He opens his soft, fleece outer robe and his patterned cotton inner robe, exposing bare flesh to the light, closing his eyes as he feels the warmth move from chest to belly to thigh. When it reaches his knees, he looks downward through slitted lids, not to miss the moment the sun touches his feet. The final words of the song must be timed properly.

". . . even as she has commanded, step into her day! Go forth!"

The song ends as all morning songs end, when light lies on the feet of the singer. Hah-Hallach, songfather of Cochim-Mahn, turns and steps forward onto daylight, seeing the way clearly. The musicians on the roof of the song-study house have been waiting for this. The bone flute shrieks, the panpipes make their breathy sound, the gongs tremble, the little drums, with a final flourish, tum-te-tum into silence. Only then the poisoned doorskins are set aside by careful hands, and people pour from the hive, the sound of day voices bubbling up like water in the spring. Now are talking voices, voices for the light, stilled since dark came. They speak of planting maish and melons. They ask who left a water bowl outside all night. They rise in annoyance at children, and children's voices respond after the manner of children.

And I? I wait until songfather sees me standing there, where I have been since before light, my head bent down, trying not to tremble, for it would not be fitting for songfather to see me tremble.

"Songfather," I murmur.

"Girl," says Hah-Hallach, who until yesterday called me Saluez, sweet Sally-girl, who until yesterday was Grandpa, who until yesterday would have put arms about me, holding me.

Am I different today from yesterday? I am still Saluez, granddaughter of his heart, so songfather has said to me, manytime, manytime. Am I changed? Am I not still myself, the self I grew to be? Until yesterday, I knew who Saluez was. Until yesterday, when Masanees told me it was certain:

"You are with child," she said, gripping my shoulders to help me control my shaking.

I cried then. I was too proud to scream, but I cried, and Masanees wiped my face and cuddled me close as only women will cuddle me close now, only women who know. I had not wanted to be this way. I was not ready for this. Some say there are herbs one can take, but such things are only whispered. The songfathers do not allow it; they say we were made for fecundity, such is the purpose of the pattern, so the Gracious One has spoken. They tell us how all nature is made the same, every tree with its fruit, every blossom with its bee. So every girl must take a lover, once she is able.

I said no, no, no. My friend Shalumn said no, no, no. We were enough for one another, she and I. But this young man said yes, yes, yes. And that young man said yes, yes, yes. And Chahdzi father looked at me beneath his eyebrows, so. So, I picked the one who was least annoying, and it was done. I had a lover. If all went well, soon I would have a husband. When the seed sprouts, Dinadhis say, then the gardeners join their hands and dance. Their hands, and other parts as well. I take no great pleasure in that thought. First loving is, as the old women say, fairly forgettable. Nor is there any pleasure in the thought of what comes between.

So, now I am with child and am no longer favorite anything to Hallach, songfather. Now I become part of the promise, part of the covenant, part of the choice. For this time between the planting and the dancing, only that. Nothing more.

"A day has been appointed for you," says songfather, not looking at me.

I feel myself shake all over, like a tree in wind, like a newborn little woolbeast experiencing the coldness of air for the first time. Is it fear I feel, or is it anger at their pushing me so? "Soon you will be old enough. Soon you will have a lover. Soon you will have a husband. It is the way of Dinadh." I learned these words when I was first able to talk. Now it is all I can do to stand until the shudder passes, leaving me chilled beneath the sun.

"You are prepared?" It is the ritual question.

"Songfather," I say, "I am prepared." The words are the correct words. I have been trained since babyhood to say those words, but no amount of training has made them sound sincere, not even to me! What is it I am supposed to be prepared for? No one will say. They whisper. They hint. But no one ever says!

"You were made for this," he says solemnly. "As the Gracious One has told us, you were made for the giving of this gift. Who will go with you?"

I say, "Masanees, sister-mother." Masanees has done this thing before, several times, successfully! She is of my mother's generation, though my mother is gone.

Hah-Hallach knows all this. "She will watch over you," he says, approvingly.

"Yes, songfather." I suppose she will.

"Attend to the day. Soon you will go and our songs will go with you." He strides past me, toward the song-study house.

So. The Gracious One has been mentioned in passing. I have fulfilled my destiny and said my words. The songfather has said his words. Sweet-Sally and Grandpa have said no words at all. The thing is resolved upon, whatever the thing is, and all Dinadhi know their parts in the pattern. They are they, and I am Saluez, who turns and goes back into the hive, for there is much preparation to be made.

Still I cannot keep my head from going back, far back to let my eyes look high, there, among the rimrock, among all those piles of stones where stands the House Without a Name. It has stood there since the Dinadhi came to this place. One stands above every hive. This was the choice we were offered by the Gracious One. This is the choice we made, so songfather says. We people of Dinadh.

But deep inside me I say no! No! This is not the choice *I* made. I had no part in it. You songfathers made this choice for me, and I have no part in it at all!

Songfather spoke to me at Cochim-Mahn on Dinadh. In another place another man spoke to another woman. That place was the city of Alliance Prime on the world now called Alliance Central. The world had once been called earth, when Alliance Central was only a department, a bureaucracy, that grew and grew until all the earth was covered by Alliance Central and no one called it earth anymore. So I have been taught, as all Dinadhi children are taught, for Dinadh is a member of the Alliance.

The powerful man was the Procurator himself, and the woman was Lutha Tallstaff. She was part of a happening thing and I was part of the same happening thing, a branching of the pattern, as we say, though she and I knew nothing of one another at the time. While we live, say the weavers, we are only the shuttles, going to and fro, unable to see the pattern we are making, unaware of other shuttles in the weft. After years we can look back to see the design we have made, the pattern Weaving Woman intended all along. A time comes when one sees that pattern clear, and then one says, remember this, remember that; see how this happened, see how that happened. Remember what the songfather said, what the Procurator said.

What he first said was, "You knew Leelson Famber."

It was a statement of fact, though he paused, as one does when expecting an answer.

Lutha Tallstaff contented herself with a slight cock of her head, meaning all right, so? She was annoyed. She felt much put upon. She was tired of the demands made upon her. Anyone who would send invigilators to drag her from her bath and supper—not literally *drag*, of course, though it felt like it—to this unscheduled and mysterious meeting at Prime needed no help from her! Besides, she'd last seen Leelson four years ago.

"You knew Famber well." This time he was pushing.

Skinny old puritan, Lutha thought. Of course she had known Leelson well.

"We were lovers once," she replied, without emphasis, letting him stew on that as she stared out the tall windows over the roofs of Alliance Prime upon Alliance Central.

A single ramified city-structure, pierced by transport routes, decked with plazas, fountains, and spires, flourished with flags, burrowed through by bureaucrats, all under the protective translucence of the Prime-dome, higher and more effulgent than those covering the urbs. The planet had been completely homo-normed for centuries. Nothing breathed upon it but man and the vagrant wind, and even the wind was tamed beneath the dome, a citywide respiration inhaled at the zenith and exhaled along the circumference walls into the surrounding urbs with their sun-shielded, pallid hordes. Lutha, so she would tell me, had a large apartment near the walls: two whole rooms, and a food dispenser and sleeping cubicles and an office wall. The apartment had a window scene, as well, one that could create a forest or a meadow or a wide, sun-drenched savanna, complete with creatures. Lutha sometimes wondered what it would be like to actually live among other creatures. Came a time she and I laughed ruefully about that, a time when we knew all too well what it was like!

On that day, however, she was not thinking of creatures as she remained fixed by the Procurator's expectant eyes. He was waiting for more answer than she had given him thus far.

She sighed, already tired of this. "Why is my relationship with Leelson Famber any concern of yours?"

"I . . . that is, we need someone who . . . was connected to him."

Only now the tocsin. "You knew Leelson Famber," he'd said. "You *knew* him."

"Why!" she demanded with a surge of totally unexpected panic. "What's happened to him?"

"He's disappeared."

She almost laughed, feeling both relief and a kind of pleasure at thinking Leelson might be injured, or ill, or maybe even dead. So she told me.

"But you were lovers!" I cried in that later time. "You said you were made for each other!"

So we believe, we women of Dinadh, who sit at the loom to make an inner robe for our lovers or our children or our husbands or ourselves, beginning a stripe of color, so, and another color, so, with the intent that they shall come together to make a wonderful pattern at the center, one pattern begetting another. So people, too, can be intended to come together in wonder and joy.

So I pleaded with her, dismayed. "Didn't you love him? Didn't he love you?"

"You don't understand," she cried. "We'd been lovers, yes! But against all good sense! Against all reason. It was like being tied to some huge stampeding animal, dragged along, unable to stop!" She panted, calming herself, and I held her, knowing very well the feeling she spoke of. I, too, had felt dragged along.

"Besides," she said, "I was sick of hearing about Leelson! Him and his endless chain of triumphs! All those dramatic disappearances, those climactic *re*appearances, bearing wonders, bearing marvels. The Roc's egg. The Holy Grail."

"Truly?" I asked. Even I had heard of the Holy Grail, a mystical artifact of the Kristin faith, a religion mostly supplanted by Firstism, though it is practiced by some remote peoples still. "Practiced," we say of all religions but that of the Gracious One. "Because they haven't got it right yet." It is the kind of joke our songfathers tell.

But Lutha shook her head at me, crying angrily, saying well, no, not the Holy Grail. But Leelson had found the Sword of Salibar, and the Gem of Adalpi. And there was that business about his fetching home the Lost King of Kamir. Well, we knew what came of that!

Perhaps the Procurator understood her ambivalence, for he lurched toward her, grimacing. "Sorry!" He chewed his lip, searching for words, his twisted body conveying more strain than the mere physical. "I perceive the fact of his disappearance does not convey apprehension."

"His disappearance alone does not make me apprehensive," Lutha drawled, emulating his stuffy manner. Though it annoyed the Fastigats, who claimed intuition as a province solely theirs, even laymen could play at inferences. "I gather from *your* obvious distress, however, that his disappearance does not stand alone."

Seeming not to notice her sarcasm, he gestured toward the wide chairs he had ignored since she entered the room. "Sit down, please, do. Forgive my rudeness. I haven't had time for niceties lately. Let me order refreshment."

"If it pleases you." She was starved, but damned if she'd let him know it.

"I hope it will please us both. Today . . . today could use some leavening of pleasure, even if it is only a little fragrance, a little savor."

She seated herself as he murmured rapidly into his collar-link before scrambling into the chair across from her, a spindly lopsided figure, his awkwardness made more evident by the skintight uniform. When in the public gaze, draped in ceremonial robes or tabards or togas or whathave-you, even elderly bureaucrats could look imposing enough, but without the draperies, in official skinnies with their little potbellies or saggy butts fully limned, many of them were a little ridiculous. Even the Fastigats. So she said of him.

He, peering nearsightedly at her, saw wings of white hair at either side of her face, stark against otherwise char-black tresses, a bed-of-coals glow warming the brown matte skin at lip and cheek: forge lights, comforting or burning. He saw her square, possibly stubborn jaw. He looked into her eyes, a dark warm gray, almost taupe, showing more anger and pain than he had expected. No doubt the Procurator saw it all. If he cared about such things, no doubt he thought what I thought: how lovely! Though perhaps he had less reason than I to value loveliness.

So he looked at her but did not speak again until the almost invisible shadows had fetched fragrant teas and numerous small plates of oddments, something to suit every taste. Lutha averted her eyes from the food items that were still moving or all-too-recently dead and concentrated on the tray of small hot tarts set conveniently at her elbow. The aroma and taste were irresistible.

"You have some problem concerning Leelson Famber?" she prompted, brushing crumbs from her lips with one of the folded finan skins provided as napkins, soft and silky to the touch. On its own world, the finan is rare, almost extinct. Using its skins for napkins would be a conceit had the animal not been made for that purpose, as the Firsters aver. They are the hierarchs of homo-norm, of whom there are many, even upon Alliance Central. Besides, the finans' genetic pattern had been saved in the computers at Prime. So Lutha told me.

Instead of answering, the Procurator asked, "Are you familiar with what is now called the 'Ularian crisis'?"

Familiar, Lutha thought. Now there was a word. The crisis had been when? Almost a century ago. And on the frontier, to boot. Why in the world would a linguist like herself—a document expert, yes, but withal a mere functionary—be expected to be "familiar" with such distant and ancient history?

She put her mind in neutral and stared at the table, noticing the foods she found most attractive were now closer to her and the disgusting dishes had been removed. How did the shadows know? Was her face that easy to read? Or were the shadows taught to interpret the almost imperceptible twitches and jerks most people made without realizing it. Were they empaths, like Fastigats? Perhaps they actually were Fastigats, turned invisible as penance for some unseemly behavior. Fastigats were great ones for seemliness.

What had the old man been talking of? Of course. "Ularian crisis," she said. "Around twenty-four hundred of the common era, a standard century ago, give or take a little. Alliance frontier worlds in the Hermes Sector were overrun by a race or force or something called Ularians." She paused, forehead wrinkled. "Why was it named that?"

"The first human populations that vanished were in a line, a vector, that led toward the Ular Region," he replied.

She absorbed the fact. "So, this something wiped all human life off a dozen worlds or systems or—"

The Procurator gestured impatiently at this imprecision.

She gave him a half smile, mocking his irritation. "Well, a dozen somethings, Procurator—you asked what I knew and I'm telling you." She resumed her interrupted account, "Sometime later the Ularians went away. Thereafter, briefly, occurred the Great Debate, during which the Firster godmongers said Ularians didn't exist because the universe was made for man, and the Infinitarians said Ularians could exist because everything is possible. Both sides wrote volumes explaining Ularians or explaining them away—on little or no evidence, as I recall—and the whole subject became so abstruse that only scholars care one way or the other."

The Procurator shook his head in wonder. "You speak so casually, so disrespectfully of it."

She considered the matter ancient history. "I shouldn't be casual?"

He grimaced. "At the time humans—at least those who knew what was going on—feared for the survival of the race."

"Was it taken that seriously?" she asked, astonished.

"It was by Alliance Prime, by those who knew what was happening! All that saved us from widespread panic was that the vanished settlements were small and few. Publicly, the disappearances were blamed on environmental causes, even though people vanished from every world in Hermes Sector—that is, every one but Dinadh."

She shrugged, indicating disinterest in Dinadh. She who was to learn so much about Dinadh knew and cared nothing for it then.

The Procurator went on. "My predecessors here at Prime could learn nothing about the Ularians. The only evidence of the existence of an inimical force was that men had disappeared! Prime had no idea why they—or *it*—attacked in the first place."

He leaned forward, touching her lightly on the knee. "Did Leelson ever speak to you of *Bernesohn Famber*?"

She was suddenly intrigued. "Oh, yes. Leelson's great-grandpop. One of the greatest of all Fastigats, to hear Leelson tell it. A genius, a biochemist."

"Do you remember the name Tospia?"

Lutha smiled. "Bernesohn's longtime lover. A Fastiga woman, of course." She frowned. "A diva in solo opera. Leelson played some of her sensurrounds for me. Very nice, though I think the senso-techs were owed as much credit as Tospia herself. To my taste, one person's performance sensed six times, however differentiated and augmented, does not have the interactive passion of six separate actors. I've yet to experience one that has true eroticism."

The Procurator peered at her over the rim of his cup. "But Leelson never mentioned Bernesohn and the Ularians?"

She gave the question to her subconscious, which came up empty. "I recall no connection."

He settled himself with a half-muffled groan. "I beg your patience:

"A century ago, there were twelve human populations on planets in Hermes Sector. Eleven of these were only settlements, six of them homo-normed, the other five at the survey stage. The twelfth world, Dinadh, had a planetary population. Dinadh is a small world, an unimportant world, except that it is near us in a spaciotemporal sense, though not in an astrophysical one. Everything into and out of Hermes Sector, including information, routes through Dinadh and did, even then.

"So, it was customary for freighters to land there, whether going or coming, and one did so a century ago, bringing the news that two of the settlements in Hermes Sector had vanished. Prime sent six patrol ships carrying investigative teams; two ships returned with news of further vanishments; the other four did not return. We sent more men to find the lost men—frequently a mistake, as in this case. None of them returned. Dinadh's government, such as it is, refused to consider even partial evacuation, which would have been the best we could do. Evacuating a populated planet is impossible. There aren't enough ships to keep up with the birthrate." He sighed.

"And?" she prompted.

"Dinadh is the only occupied planet of its system, the only one suitable for occupation. The Alliance did the only thing it could think of, englobing the system with unmanned sentinel buoys. We might as well have done nothing, for all the good it did. No one came out of the sector toward Dinadh. Every probe we sent into the sector from Dinadh simply disappeared.

"Ten standard years went by; then twenty, then thirty. Planets applying for colony rights were sent elsewhere. Then, thirty-three standard years after the crisis, the sentinel buoys picked up a freighter crossing the line *from* Hermes Sector into Dinadhi space! The holds were stuffed with homo-norm equipment. The crew claimed they had found it abandoned and therefore salvageable, after falling into Hermes Sector accidentally, through a rogue emergence. Later we checked for stellar collapse and found an enormous one about the right time—"

"Stellar collapse?"

"The usual cause of rogue emergences is stellar collapse. The dimensional field twitches, so to speak. Things get sucked in here and spat out there. Well, the crew was brought here, and more questions were asked. It turned out they'd picked up equipment from four worlds in the sector and had noticed nothing at all inimical. We sent volunteer expeditions to investigate. All of them returned shrugging their shoulders and shaking their heads. Nothing. No sign of what had happened to the human population thirty-odd years before, and no signs of aliens at all. We assumed the Ularians, whatever they or it had been, had departed."

"So there were no survivors?" mused Lutha.

He shook his head. "Oh, we looked, believe me! We had no information about Ularians, no description of them, no actual proof that they existed, which gratified the Firster godmongers, you may be sure, for they'd claimed from the beginning there were no such things as Ularians. Since government is always delicately poised vis-à-vis godmongers, we were extremely interested in what survivors might tell us, but we never found a thing in Hermes Sector. Oh, there were some children who turned up on Perdur Alas around twenty years ago, but they were probably emergence castaways also."

"Unlikely they'd have been there for eighty years. They'd have had to be third or fourth generation."

"Quite right. All this is mere diversion, however."

"You started by asking me about Bernesohn Famber," she said impatiently.

"The *relevant* fact is that Bernesohn Famber was on one of the ships that went into Hermes Sector right after the vanishments."

"One of the lost ships."

"No! One that came back. Bernesohn was erratic and secretive. A genius, no doubt, but odd. Sometimes he didn't appear outside his quarters for days and days. His colleagues didn't expect to see him regularly, so they didn't realize he was gone! When the ship got back here, they didn't have any idea where or when he'd gone. We couldn't find him."

The Procurator leaned back in his chair. "Imagine our discomfiture sometime later when we learned he was living on Dinadh."

"How did you find that out?" Lutha asked.

"Well, a year or so after Bernesohn disappeared, Tospia, his longtime companion, gave womb-birth to twins. In Fastiga."

Lutha knew where Fastiga was. It might be called a suburb of Prime. Leelson's mother lived there.

The Procurator went on. "Tospia's twins were entered in the Famber lineage roster, but nobody at Prime made the connection."

She said impatiently, "You intend to make the point, I presume, that the twins were conceived after Bernesohn's disappearance?"

The Procurator assented. "Years later a sensation sniffer for one of the newslinks did a so-called biography of Tospia—unauthorized, need I say—in which he alleged that Bernesohn Famber could not have fathered the twins. Tospia threw a memorable and widely publicized tantrum and sued the sniffer for misprision of media freedom, asserting that Bernesohn had been living on Dinadh and that she had visited him there."

The Procurator set down his cup and went on:

"Enormous consternation, as you might imagine! Alliance officers were sent to Dinadh immediately to debrief Bernesohn about the Ularians."

"And?"

He shrugged, mouth downturned. "And the Dinadh planetary authorities turned them all away, saying that Bernesohn had bought a hundred-year privacy lease, that even though he was no longer at his leasehold, his lease was still in effect and no one could be admitted but family members, thank you very much. His 'family members' were notably uncooperative, and since our only reason for questioning Bernesohn was the Ularian threat, which was seemingly over, we couldn't demonstrate compelling need. In the absence of compelling need, we had no authority to invade a member planet, and that's what it would have taken."

He nodded to himself, then resumed in a thoughtful voice: "Of course, we drew what inferences we could. We assumed Bernesohn had gone there because he expected to find something on Dinadh, but if he'd come up with anything useful, he hadn't told Prime about it."

"You said he was no longer at his leasehold?"

He sighed, turning his cup in his hands. "All Dinadh said about the matter was that they 'had welcomed him as an outlander ghost.' "

"Which means?"

"We presume it means he died. And there the matter has rested until now. . . ." His voice trailed off disconsolately.

"But?"

"But, now they're back."

Lutha stared at him, disbelieving. "The Ularians?"

He nodded, swallowed, shredded the finan-skin napkin between his fingers. "Almost a hundred standard years! Why not fifty years ago? It was then Prime decided it was safe to open up Hermes to colonization once more. There are three populated worlds and several colonies in there; there are homo-norm teams on half a dozen other worlds, and survey teams everywhere worthy of survey."

"And?"

"And two of the colonies are gone. Like last time."

Lutha turned away from his distress, giving herself time to think, holding her cup over the table and feeling it grow heavier as it was filled with tea by an almost invisible shadow.

"What has all this to do with Leelson?" she asked.

"Now we're desperate to know whatever Bernesohn Famber knew. As long as Bernesohn's privacy lease has any time to run, however, the only people Dinadh will allow to poke about among Bernesohn's belongings are family members. Family is a very big thing on Dinadh. Since Leelson is descended from Bernesohn, Leelson is Bernesohn's 'family,' so far as the Dinadhi are concerned."

Now Lutha understood what they were asking of her. "You need Leelson, but Leelson has disappeared." She tapped her fingers, thinking. "Did you think I might know where Leelson is? Or did you have some idea the Dinadhi would accept me as Leelson's 'family'?"

"I don't think you know where Leelson is, no. I know the Dinadhi will accept you as family. You are Leelson's wife as they define wife."

When Lutha told me this, I laughed. It was true, in a way. She was Leelson's wife as we on Dinadh define wife. Some of the time.

"Because we were lovers?" she asked him.

"Because you bore his child," the Procurator said.

She felt the blood leave her face, felt it drain away to disclose a familiar sorrow, an endless ache. "My son is a private matter."

He sighed. "Believe me, Lutha Tallstaff, under other circumstances I would not challenge your privacy. The Ularians give us no choice. Do you remember Mallia Stentas? From Keleborn?"

Lutha answered distractedly, "We were at upper school together. She became a manager for some agricultural consortium. . . ."

"You may mourn her now—she and her lifemates and all their many children—gone from Tapil's World. And the people on Updyke-Chel. They are not merely dead, but dust in the wind, vanished and gone, no stone to mark the place they were. Whatever the Ularians may be, when they come upon a world, they leave behind no monuments. . . ."

He stood, walked across the room to the wall retriever, and flicked it into life. "Tapil's World," he murmured. "Beamed by our recorders."

An empty town materialized before them. Everywhere evidence of interruption. A doll lying abandoned by a fence. A child's wagon, half-full of harvested vegetables, standing at the side of a fenced garden. A sun hat caught in a thorny shrub. A fuzzy native animal—either useful for something or a neutered pet, as it would not have escaped homonorming otherwise—hopping slowly along a hedge, crying plaintively. Kitchens with food half-prepared, rooms with tables still littered, desks still piled. The probe came down over one desk, focusing on a holo that stood there. Herself. Mallia and herself, young scholars, arms around one another, grinning into eternity.

"Damn you," Lutha said without heat.

"I want you to feel it," he admitted. "It could be your house. It could be you, and your son. It could be all humanity."

During our time together, Lutha described his voice, full of a sonorous beauty, like the tolling of a funeral bell. He was working Fastigat stuff on her, wringing her emotions like a wet towel, making her all drippy. Leelson had done that from time to time, worked Fastigat stuff on her, though he had done it for their mutual pleasure.

"Nothing like a romantic moon," she told me. "A little wine, and a silver-tongued Fastigat to make the worlds move."

"It does not take wine or a Fastigat to move the world," I told her, thinking of my own love.

"I am relieved to hear it," she said then, laughing as she wept. We had then a good deal of reason to weep.

But even then, during her meeting with the Procurator, she thought all that Fastigat stuff unnecessary. The memory of Mallia alone wrung her quite enough.

So, she took a deep breath and said to this old, conniving man: "You want me to go to Dinadh, is that it?"

The Procurator nodded. "We want someone to go, and the only people they will allow are Leelson, his mother, or you. Leelson's mother has refused to go. Leelson himself, we can't find. That leaves you. You're already proficient in basic Nantaskan. Dinadh speaks a dialect of Nantaskan. And I'll send a Fastigat with you."

"Please. No," she cried.

He reached toward her, pleadingly. "Lutha. Please. We'll pick someone who isn't . . . intrusive. Someone tactful."

She snorted.

"Some Fastigats can be," he said in an offended tone.

"The Dinadhi will allow me a companion?" She sneered. "Someone nonfamily?"

"If he goes as your assistant or servant, yes. You'll need some such to help with your son. You'll have to take the boy."

She laughed again, this time incredulously. "You're joking, of course." He knew how ridiculous the idea was. Even the invigilators who had summoned her to this meeting had been aware of the problem Leely presented. They'd brought a whole crèche team with them to take care of Leely while she was away.

He shook his head at her, leaning forward to pat her knee, an avuncular gesture. "Believe me, Lutha, I wouldn't ask it if it weren't necessary. The Dinadhi won't accept you without the boy."

"You expect me to drag a child across half a dozen sectors to . . ."

This child, she said to herself. This particular child, with his particular problems.

"Spatiotemporally, it's not half a dozen sectors," he told her. "I wish it were, quite frankly. We'd be safer!"

She made herself relax, slowly picked up the cup once more, finding it fresh, steaming hot.

"Will you go?" he asked.

"Do I have a choice?" she grated. "If I don't go, you'll—"

"Nothing," he assured her. "Really nothing. We have the power to compel you, but compelling you would be useless. We need your willing, intelligent cooperation. It's up to you whether you give it or not."

As though that old devil conscience would have let her say no! "You know me," she said angrily. "You knew I wouldn't say no. Didn't you?"

As he did. As Fastigats did. Lutha told me all about Fastigats. Fastigats get to know people very quickly, very well, very completely, as had this bald, quirky old empath across from her who hadn't come right out and told her he was one of them. Who hadn't needed to, any more than Leelson had, when they had been together.

"You're going to be fine," Leelson had said often during her later stages of pregnancy, soothing her in moments of dismay.

"I know," she'd snapped. "Women have been having babies for hundreds of thousands of years."

"Well, yes. But I don't regard that as particularly comforting, do you?" He made a face at her, making her laugh. "Stars have been blowing up into novas for billions of years, but that doesn't make their near vicinity desirable."

"If you intend a similarity, I am offended," she said. "Though I may have assumed the proportions of a nova, I have no intention of bursting. I merely scream when I stand up, because it hurts to stand up! This may sound like an explosion, but actually—"

"We are not Firsters. You could have—" he interrupted gently.

"Don't tell me. Of course I could have." Could have chosen not to be pregnant. Could have chosen to delay the development of the fertilized egg. Could have had the baby developed in a biotech uterus, given crèche birth. She hadn't chosen that. Why not? She didn't know why not! Why had he gotten her pregnant in the first place? Fastigats could control that if they wanted to! Obviously, he hadn't wanted to!

"Well then?" Leelson being reasonable.

"I keep thinking it must be boring for you." Great Gauphin, it was boring enough for her.

"A new experience is seldom boring. Womb-birth is becoming quite rare, and rare happenings appeal to the collector's taste. All Fastigats are collectors."

She didn't say what she was thinking, that the whole thing had been an accident. That she'd had second thoughts about it, but then Leelson's mother had said—Leelson had said . . .

The less thought about all that the better. Still, she was peevish when Leelson seemed more fascinated by the pregnancy than he was by her. She said this, laughing at herself.

"It's not true," he assured her. "I am passionately fond of you, Lutha Tallstaff. You are like a dinner full of interesting textures and flavors, like a landscape full of hidden wonders. I am not ignoring you in all this."

True. When one had a Fastigat for a lover, one could not complain of being ignored. One's every whim was understood; one's every mood was noted. For the most part, one's every desire was satisfied, or thwarted, only to make the satisfaction greater when it occurred. If a Fastigat lover was not forthcoming, it was not through lack of understanding. Sometimes Lutha felt (so she told me) she was understood far too well. Sometimes she longed for argument, for passionate battle, for a sense of her own self back again. Pride kept her from showing it, that and the fear that Leelson would accommodate her. Only a fool would take on an opponent who could block every thrust before it was made.

It was easier during those early months after Leely was born, for then Leelson switched at least part of his searching intelligence from her to the child, leaving Lutha to her udderish moods and mutters while he hovered over the infantender, forehead creased, feeling his way into that little mind.

"Like a maze," he'd said, almost dazedly. "All misty walls and dazzling spaces. Hunger or discomfort comes in like jagged blobs of black, and the minute he eliminates or burps or takes the nipple, he's back to dazzling spaces again."

"No faces?" she'd asked, disappointed. Babies were supposed to recognize faces. Like baby birds, back when there had been birds, recognizing the special markings of their own species. Eyes, nose, mouth: that configuration was supposed to be instinctively recognized by humans. Lutha had read about it.

"Well, I can't feel faces," he'd replied. "No doubt they're there."

Later he postulated that Leely recognized something else or more than faces. Some quality unique to each person, perhaps. Some totality.

"He's not one of us, I'm afraid. Not a Fastigat." Leelson had shaken his head ruefully over the four-month-old child. It was then Lutha admitted to herself what she had refused to consider before: Leelson was disappointed at not having a Fastigat son. Virtually all Fastigat sons were empaths, at least. If she'd had a daughter, it wouldn't have mattered!

"Hardly fair," she'd muttered, wanting to weep. "Sexist!"

He'd smiled charmingly, the way he did. Fastigats were almost always charming. "Not my fault, Lutha. I didn't design it. It's sex-linked, that's all."

"You'd think biologists—"

He hadn't let her finish. "Well, of course our women say attempting to make female Fastigats is meaningless, because any normal woman is a sensitivity match for a male empath, any day."

He'd made her laugh, hiding his own disappointment. Perhaps even then he'd known—or at least suspected—this disappointment wasn't to be the only one.

Time came soon enough, of course, when suspicion was fulfilled and Leelson went away. Unforgivably away. Without announcement or preamble. One morning she had wakened to find him gone. He'd left a note, of course, if one could call five words a note. Not much after their years together.

"You must feel abandoned. Betrayed!" This from Lutha's older sister, Yma, sector-famed, thespian absolute.

The accuracy of this made Lutha blaze hotly as she denied it. "I do not! Leelson's and my relationship lasted a long time. Neither of us is from a contractual culture, so why would I feel betrayed!" She said it as though she meant it. In fact, she did feel betrayed and abandoned, not that she could possibly admit it to Yma. How could he? She couldn't have left Leelson! How could he have left her?

Yma went on. "Perhaps not a contract, but still . . ."

"But still nothing, Yma. I had a child because I wanted a child." That was partly true. She kept her lip from trembling with considerable effort. After the initial shock, she had wanted a child.

"Well, of course you did, darling, but it was a genetic risk. With him."

"Fastigat men father normal children on non-Fastigat women all the time!"

Yma couldn't leave it at that. "Well, there are no aberrations in your family line."

"You don't know that!" Lutha cried.

"Oh, yes I do and so do you. Even though we've never met them, we know all about Papa's side of the family. They're all totally ordinary, ordinary, ordinary!" To Yma, nothing could be worse.

Lutha did indeed know a great deal about Papa's family, and his many siblings and half siblings out on the frontier. Frontier worlds began with a colony ship, a few hundred crew members, and a hundred thousand human embryos. Thirteen or fourteen years later the original embryos were boys and girls who began procreating on their own, using the crèche equipment on the ship. A few decades, the colony might number in the millions! Twenty children per woman was not uncommon, virtually all of them crèche-born. In a homo-normed world, there were few impediments. No dangerous diseases, little danger from weather, no danger from plants or animals—in fact few plants and no animals at all.

"Mama Jibia does go on and on about the kinfolk," Lutha admitted.

"She's never said anything indicating they're anything but boring. And Mama's family, we know all about, both sides, four generations back. Her mother is Lucca Fineapple, and we've met her. Remember?"

"The religious grandma," said Lutha with vague discomfort at the memory. "Who visited us on her way through the sector."

"Exactly. You do remember! We thought her very strange! Well, women who depilate and tattoo their entire bodies *are* strange. But that's simply attitudinal; biologically she's quite all right. And Mama Jibia is always telling stories about Lucca's mother—Nitha Bonetree, remember, the one who first ran away to the frontier?"

"Which is where Lucca was born, and Mama too. I guess I remember some of that. Mama Jibia always said we'd inherited our talents from Nitha's line."

"It isn't the detail that matters in any case! The only thing that matters is there's no problem in your family on either side back four generations. And Leelson should *not* have left you to provide the entire care for the boy, as though it were somehow your fault!"

Lutha felt herself turning red, felt the tears surging, heard the anger in her words. "I had always intended to be responsible for my child. It was *my* choice."

Was it? Was it indeed? Then why couldn't she remember making it! She asked me this and I laughed. I couldn't remember either. It had just happened. One couldn't really question it. Lutha said even Yma knew she'd gone too far. Wisely she let the matter drop.

Lutha never mentioned to Yma the credit drafts regularly deposited to her account from Fastiga. Fastigats did not father by chance. As a society, they fathered no unknown or unacknowledged children, and all children fathered by Fastigats received support from Fastiga. It was a matter of honor, one of the primary differences, so said Fastigats, between Fastigats and lesser men.

Fastigats didn't even sign certificates of intent. Their honor was so untarnished they were exempt from the requirement imposed on all other citizens of Central, to have five responsible, self-supporting coparents on record by the fourth month of pregnancy.

Lutha and Yma and Mama Jibia and two male cousins had signed for Leely. No one cared who had children, or how many, but one of the basic rights of Alliance citizens was not to be responsible for other people's. The penalties for dereliction of responsibility were severe, and the credit drafts from Fastiga were infuriatingly beyond the call of duty. Even more infuriating were the Fastigat uncles and male cousins who visited at intervals, observed Leely's growth and development, then went away again. Meantime, Leely grew bigger and stronger and older and Lutha became more tired and desperate.

"You ought to consider the alternatives," Yma said, every time they met. "Really, Lutha. You ought to. . . ."

The Fastigat uncles and cousins also urged her to consider alternatives. Santeresa's World, they'd suggested, where the whole planet made its living caring for the sick, the injured, the disabled. It was expensive, but Fastiga would pay for it. Lutha had refused. Her child was not an alternative. End of statement. End of consideration, no matter how her life narrowed around her day by day and even her necessary professional duties gave way to Leely's needs. She could not decide to let him go any more than she had decided to have him. Though she had. She must have!

For years now she had kept a fragile calm, slathering sentimental oil on every emotional linkage, making her life move like some old cog-and-belt-driven machine, creaking and wobbling from one day to the next. And now, here, all at once, this skinny old fart, this Fastigat servant of the Alliance, this bureaucrat, had thrust an additional duty among her gears, grinding her to a screaming halt!

She abandoned simile and summoned anger, making herself rage at being forced to do the Alliance's will. Was this a penalty, for having known Leelson? Another one?

The anger wouldn't hold. It was too hard to hide from herself the anticipation she felt at the promise of somewhere to go, the relief at the idea of someone to help her. The promise of succor and change.

So Lutha planned a journey, even as I, Saluez, planned a journey, though hers was far longer than mine. In a sense, at least, hers was longer, though mine wrought greater changes. For me a night soon came when Shalumn and I wept on each other's shoulders, I out of fright, she out of fear of losing me. The following morning I bent beneath the brow-strap of my carrying basket and went up the rocky trail with Masanees. High on a shelf above Cochim-Mahn, I panted, waiting for her to catch up with me. Masanees is not as agile as she once was. She has not yet received Weaving Woman's reward, that comfortable time of life when she need no longer fear conceiving, but she is no longer young. I am young. I am twelve in Dinadh years, twenty standard years. Too young for this, perhaps. But no. Women younger than I, much younger than I have made this trip. If a woman is old enough to conceive, she is old enough for this. So the songfathers say. "Soil which accepts seed is ready for the plow!"

"Whsssh," Masanees breathed as she came up to the stone where I waited. "Time for a breather. That path gets steeper every year."

"Have you come up before this year?" I asked, knowing the answer already.

Masanees nodded. "With Dziloch. And last year with Kh'nas."

"Imsli a t'sisri," I murmured. *Weave no sorrow.*

"None," Masanees replied cheerfully. "They're both fine. We did it right."

I tried to smile and could not. I was not reassured. Each year some did not return from the House Without a Name. Each year some went behind the veil, down into shadow. Each time the women no doubt thought they had done it right. Who would go there otherwise?

There was no point in saying it. Saying it only increased terror. I had been told one should, instead, sing quietly to oneself. A weaving song, dark and light, pattern on pattern. Turning away up the hill, I chanted quietly to myself in time with my plodding feet.

The House Without a Name stands on a promontory above Cochim-Mahn. One can see a corner of it from the shelf where the songfather stands, only a corner. One would not want to see it all. One would not want to look at it as part of one's view of the world. It is easier to ignore it, to pretend it isn't really there. One can then speak of the choice in

measured tones, knowing one need not fear the consequences. As songfathers do.

"That which we relinquished, death and darkness in the pattern.

"That which we took in its place, the House Without a Name . . ."

That's how the answer to the riddle goes, the one no one ever asks out
loud, the riddle my grandmother whispered to me in the nighttime, as
her grandmother had whispered it to her. "What is it men relish and
women regret?" Grandma asked, preparing me. Letting me know without really letting me know. Frightening me, but not terrifying me.

It's the way we do things now. We hint. We almost tell, but not quite.
We let young people learn only a little. If they never know it thoroughly
or factually, well, that makes the choice easier. If they do stupid things
because they don't know enough, that's expected.

As a result, ignoring the house becomes habit and I was able to ignore
my approach to it until we arrived at the stone-paved area outside the
door. Then I had to admit where I was.

"Shhh," whispered Masanees, putting her arms around me. "It's all
right. We've all been through it, child. It's all right."

Still I shivered, unable to control it. "I'm scared," I whispered, shaming myself.

Evidently I wasn't the only one to have said something like that, for
Masanees went on holding me.

"Of course you're scared. Of course you are. The unknown is always
scary. Sooner we get to it, sooner it'll be over. Come now. Be a good,
brave girl."

She pushed the door open. The house had a pitched roof, but there
were wide openings under the eaves where birds had flown in and out
and little nut-eaters had scrambled down to make their mess among the
other droppings.

"First we had to make all clean," said Masanees. The brooms were
lashed to her pack, and I followed her example as we gave the place a
good sweeping and brushing, including the tops of two low stone tables
that stood side by side. One table had a stone basin in its center. We
wiped it clean and filled it with water we'd carried up from below. Then
we emptied the packs at either side of the basin, and I exclaimed at the
sight of such bounty! Meal cakes, beautifully colored and baked in fancy
shapes. Strips of meat dried into spirals around long sticks of candied
melon. Squash seeds roasted and salted. Dried fruits. More candied
fruits. Masanees showed me how to lay it all out in patterns, varying the
colors, making it bright and attractive. There is always a store of such

foods kept in the hive, she said, even when we have nothing to eat but winter-fungus. Even when *we* hunger, these ritual foods are kept sacred so *they* will not hunger.

When everything was done on the one table, she cast me a look from the corners of her eyes, and I knew whatever was going to happen to me, Saluez, would happen now. She spread a folded blanket upon the other table and helped me lie facedown upon it. She gave me a ring of basketwork and told me to put my face firmly down in it. She shackled my wrists and ankles to the rings in the stone.

"Ready?" asked Masanees.

I jerked at the shackles. I could feel my eyes, wide. I knew the whites were showing, knew I was beginning to panic.

"Shh, shh. It's all right. Here. Drink this." She raised my head and held the cup to my lips.

"I'll be all right," I cried mindlessly, not drinking.

"You'll be all right," Masanees agreed, tipping the cup. "Come on, Saluez. It's easier so."

I made myself drink. My arms and legs jerked against the bonds. Gradually they stopped moving and lay quiet. I could hear. I could feel. I could breathe through the basketwork, but I did so quietly. The basket ring encircled my face, and beneath my eyes was only the stone of the table.

I heard the heavy door close as Masanees left. I knew what was outside, nearby, hanging from the branch of an ancient tree: a wooden mallet beside a gong. I heard her feet pause, heard her voice saying words I knew, heard the metal struck by the mallet, a slow series of blows that reverberated among the canyons, a long plangent sound, not sweet but seductive. One, two, three. Then a long pause. Then one, two, three again. The series went on. Triplet, then pause. Triplet, then pause. Then a responsive sound. Was it what she expected? It seemed very loud to me.

My limbs wanted to jerk, to pull free. They could not move. The sounds outside increased. . . .

I heard her feet hurry off. Somewhere nearby, hidden in the trees, she would conceal herself to wait, and watch, until she could return to let me go. . . .

I do not like remembering that time. Sometimes the whole thing comes back on me, all at once, before I have had a chance to shut it out. I cry out, then. I stand shivering. People pretend not to see me, turning their

eyes away until I have shaken the memory off and closed the door upon
it. I do not like remembering that time, so I shall remember something
else instead.

I shall remember when I was a child in Cochim-Mahn.

Dinadhi girl-children have much to learn. Clay between the hands and
the whirl of the wheel. Wool and cotton between the fingers and the
twist of the spindle. The weight of brush and broom, the long hours at
the loom. The feel of the grindstone under one's palms, the bend of the
back when dropping seeds into the holes made by the planting stick. The
setting of the solar cooker to gather all the sun's heat. The forward
thrust of the head against the tump line, bringing down wood for the
winter. A woman must be always busy if her family is to be clad and shod
and fed and kept warm, so a girl-child is taught to be constantly busy as
well.

Once each left-thumb day—it is how we count days: little-finger day,
lesser twin, longer twin, point-finger day, thumb day; right hand first,
then left, making a double hand; five double hands to the month; twelve
months to the year, plus the eight or nine extra days Daylight Woman
gives us at harvest time. As I say, once every left-thumb day, my mother
went to the sanctuary cells of Bernesohn Famber, taking me with her as
her mother had taken her. Famber was not there, of course. He had
become an outlander ghost a long time before, in the time of my great-
grandmother. Still, he had paid for a hundred-year lease, paid for cells
allocated to him and secured against intrusion or extradition for one
hundred standard years. The price for such a lease includes food and
cleaning. The food mostly came from off-planet, but the cleaning was
done by us.

Each tenth day we took brooms and brushes and soft old rags and
went into his cell, which is around the back of the main hive, on the
cave-floor level, in a kind of protrusion built out from the body of the
hive. We don't like outlanders stumbling about among us in the hive, so
our leasehold has its own entrance. In case an outlander needs help at
night, there is a corridor that comes into a storeroom of the hive, but it
is seldom used except by those who serve the outlanders.

The Cochim-Mahn leasehold is three cells built around a toilet place.
We don't use the manure of outlanders in our fungus cellars. There is
some feeling it might kill the fungus. Instead we buy these closet things
from the Alliance for our leaseholders to use, and when they get used
up, we trade for new ones. So Bernesohn Famber's place was a little
corridor with five doors in it, one to the hive storeroom, one to the

toilet, and three more to the three cells. The cell nearest the front, nearest the lip of the cave, had a door to the outside as well. All of the rooms had lie-down shelves around the sides. One back room was where Famber had slept, one he had used for storage, and the one with the door to the outside had his worktable and a comfortable chair and many strange devices and machines. These, Mama told me, were recorders and computers and analyzers, to help Bernesohn Famber with his work.

"What was his work?" I always asked, each and every time.

"Finding out about Dinadh," she always said, winking at me. Grown-ups wink like that when they hint something about the choice. Or the House. Or the other world we had, before we came here. Things we are not supposed to talk about.

"Did he find out?" I asked.

"Nobody knows," she said, marching back through the cells to the back one, where she started with the broom and I followed with the brush, sweeping down the smooth mud walls, brushing off the sleeping shelves, making a little pile of dust and grit that got bigger the farther we pushed it from cell to cell, until at last we could push it right out the door onto the floor of the cave. Then I took the broom and pushed it across the cave floor, farther and farther forward, until it came to the edge and fell over, all that dust and grit and sheddings of the hive falling down like snow on the canyon bottom.

Sometimes, while Mama was sweeping, I'd sit and look at the machines, longing to push just one button, just to see what would happen. It was forbidden, of course. Such things were not Dinadhi things. We had to live without things like that. We had *chosen* to live without them. We had *chosen* to give them up in return for what we were promised instead.

After we cleaned Bernesohn Famber's leasehold, sometimes we went down to the storerooms to pick something for supper. In summers, there are all kinds of things, fresh or dried melon, fresh or dried meat, different kinds of vegetables and fruit, pickled or fresh or dried. There is almost always grain, head grain or ear grain, eaten whole or cracked or ground for making bread. We have seeds for roasting, and honey too. We brought bees with us, from the other world.

In late winter and early spring, though, there's mostly fungus from the cellars, pale and gray and tasting like wood. The only good thing about fungus is that it's easy to fix. It can be eaten fresh or dried, raw or cooked. We usually put some salt and herbs on it to make it taste like something. Most all of our cookery is done in the mornings, when the sun is on the cave. We use solar reflectors for cooking. The whole front edge of the cave is lined with them, plus all the level spots to either side, and any time of the morning you can see women scrambling across the cliff wall to get at their own ovens and stewpots.

After food is cooked, it's kept warm in padded boxes until eating time. None of our food is very hot, except in wintertime. Then we have fires in the hive, and we sometimes cook over them. It would take too many trees to have fires in summer. That was part of the promise and the choice as well. We have to protect the trees and certain plants because the beautiful people need them.

Even though girls had much to learn, sometimes Mama would tire of teaching me and say, "Go on, go play," and then I'd have to try to find somebody else whose mama had said, "Go play," to them too.

Shalumn and I played together mostly. We played babies and we played wedding and we played planting and harvest, smoothing little patches in the dust and grooving them like ditches, and putting tiny rocks down for the vegetables. We had dolls, of course, made out of reed bundles, covered with cloth, with faces painted on. We didn't play with the boys, not once we were old enough to know who was a boy and who was a girl. Boys played sheepherder and songfather and watermaster, and they had games where somebody always won and somebody always lost. Shalumn and I played bed games together, and once Mama caught us at it and whipped us both on our bottoms. I still have a little line there, on one side, where the whip cut. After that we were careful.

I remember those as pleasant times, but I can't make them sound like much. Nothing much happens with children on Dinadh. We don't have adventures. If we tried to have an adventure, we'd probably die right away. Maybe better . . . better I think of some other story. Not my life or Lutha Tallstaff's life, but someone else's. Another person entirely, the third one of us. The one Lutha and I met together. Snark the shadow.

At the end of each workday the Procurator dismissed his shadows, allowing them to descend the coiled ramps that led from occupied areas to Shadowland beneath. There each shadow entered the lock as he was programmed to do.

"Strip off your shadow suit," said the lock.

The shadow stripped off the stiff suit with all its sensors and connectors, hanging it in an alcove in one side of the booth.

"Place your hands in the receptacles."

The shadow placed.

"Bend your head forward to make contact with the plate."

The shadow bent.

Light, sounds, movement. Snark stood back from the plate, shaking her head, as she always did, bellowing with rage, as she always did.

"Leave the cubicle," said the voice, opening the door behind her, opposite the one she'd come in by.

"Goddamn bastards," screamed Snarkey, hammering at the cubicle wall. "Shitting motherfuckers."

The floor grew hot. She leapt and screamed, resolved to obey no order they gave her. As always, the floor grew too hot for her, and she leapt through the door just in time to avoid being seared.

"It's the mad howler," said slobber-lipped Willit from a distant corner of the locker room. "Snarkey-shad herself, makin' noises like a human."

"Shut the fuck up," growled Snark.

Willit laughed. Others also laughed. Snark panted, staring about herself, deciding who to kill.

"Slow learner," commented Kane the Brain, shaking his head sadly.

Snarkey launched herself at Kane, screaming rage, only to find herself on the floor, whimpering, her thumb in her mouth.

"An exceptionally slow learner," repeated the former speaker, kicking Snark not ungently in the ribs. "Poor old Snark."

"Good baby-girl shadow." Willit sneered as he passed on his way to the door. "Play nice."

Snark sobbed as the room emptied.

"Have you quite finished?" asked the mechanical voice from a ceiling grille.

"Umph," she moaned.

"I'll ask one more time. Have you quite finished?"

"Yessir." The word dragged reluctantly from her throat, burning as it came.

"Then get up and get dressed. The locker room will be steam-cleaned in five minutes. Besides, you are no doubt hungry."

She was hungry. Procurator had hosted a banquet today, and shadows had served the food, seeing it, smelling it, seeing other people eat it. Shadows didn't eat. Shadows didn't get hungry or sleepy or need the toilet. Sometimes they got in the way of things and were killed, but if so, they did it quietly. Ordinary people didn't stare at shadows, it wasn't civilized, any more than wondering about them was. Shadows were a peculiar possession of bureaucrats in office in Alliance Prime, and that's all anyone really needed to know unless one was a shadow oneself.

The metallic voice preached at her. "If you'll make it a habit to eat just before you go on shift and immediately after, you'll feel less hunger and you'll be less uncontrolled. If you are less uncontrolled, you won't find yourself rolling around on the floor making infant noises and attracting the scorn and derision of your fellows."

"Damn motherfuckers ain my fellows."

"What did you say?"

"I said I feel little collegiality for those sharing my conditions of servitude."

In the sanctuary, when Snark was a little kid, the grown-ups had talked High Alliance. She could talk like that anytime. If she hadn't been able to remember back that far, she could mimic her fellow-shad, Kane the Brain. Kane talked like an official butthead.

The voice said, "You aren't required to feel collegiality. You are only required to behave as though you do."

Snark panted, letting the rage seep away. Each time she came off shift, it was the same. Everything that had happened to her, every glance that had slid across her without seeing her, every gesture she was supposed to notice, every need she was expected to anticipate, all of them boiled inside her all day, rising higher and higher, until the cubicle took the controls off and she exploded.

Which was wasting time, she told herself. Wasting her own time. She only had one third of her time to herself, as herself. One third she was a shadow, under full control. One third she was asleep, also under control. The rest of the time, here in Shadowland, she could feel however she wanted to feel, do whatever she wanted to do. She could eat, talk, have sex—if she could find somebody willing. She could read, attend classes, engage in hobbies. If she wanted to kill somebody, have sex with somebody unavailable, the simulation booth would accommodate her. The booth would help her do anything! Anything except kill people so they stayed dead.

If they didn't stay dead, what was the point! So she'd asked herself before. What was the point of living like this?

"You are at liberty to end it," Kane had told her. "The fourth human right is the right to die."

"Th'fucks that mean?" she'd screamed the first time she'd heard Kane on this subject.

Kane had explained it all. Kane had even escorted Snark to a disposal booth and explained the controls. "Simple, for the simpleminded," Kane had said. "Enter, close door, press button. Wait five minutes to see if you

change your mind. When the bell rings, press button again. Zip. All
that's left are a few ashes. No pain, no blood, no guts, no untidiness
whatsoever."

So said Kane, but the last thing Snark wanted was a neat disposal
booth and a handful of ashes. Where was the joy in no pain, no blood?
Who got anything out of that? That was no way to kill anybody, not even
yourself! God, if you were going to kill yourself, at least make it a real
mess! Make 'em clean up after you!

"Why you all the time wanting to kill folks?" Susso, one of her sometime sex partners, wanted to know.

"Get in my nose," she'd snarled. "Push against me!"

"Everybody gets in your nose," Susso said. "All the time. The only
way you could be happy is if you killed everybody in the world and had it
all to yourself."

It wasn't true. There'd been some good kids at the sanctuary when
they'd first brought Snark there. Snark hadn't wanted to kill them. She'd
liked them. She'd been what? Nine or ten maybe? Old enough to tell
them things. And to tell the supervisor as well.

"Where are you from, little girl?"

"From the frontier."

"Don't tell lies, little girl. Children don't come from the frontier."

"It's not a lie! I did so!"

"Don't contradict me, little girl. Don't be a nasty, contradictory little
liar."

Her name hadn't been Snark then. It had been something else. And
she hadn't wanted to kill people then. That came later, after they'd
named her Snark the liar, Snark the thief. Not Snark the murderer,
though. She'd never actually killed anybody, though she'd wanted to.
Just her luck they'd caught her before she'd done it.

The judgment machines were clear about that: "You are sentenced to
lifetime shadowhood because of your emotional need to breach the first
and second rights of man."

"They got no right," Snark had snarled to Susso. "They got no right."

"Why don' they?" he'd asked. "As much as you."

"They're machines," she'd told him. "On'y machines. I'm a person, a
human. The universe was made for me!"

Susso had shaken his head. "You been listenin' to some Firster
godmonger on the newslink, girl. Some belly-sweller. Some prick-waver.
Forget Firsters. They don't talk for this world. Not for Alliance Central,
they don't. Too many Fastigats on Alliance Central. Fastigats don't listen

to Firsters. This world is different. This world has shadows, and most of the time shadows aren't human. One third the time, shadows got the right to live like they want except they try an' hurt somebody. The rest o' the time, shadows got no rights. That's the way this world is!"

Snark knew that. When the invigilators had dragged her before the huge, unbearably shiny robo-judge, they'd read her the words printed across its front: EQUAL JUSTICE; THE SAME REMEDY FOR THE SAME CRIME, EVERY TIME.

"On Alliance Central, human rights are those rights our people grant one another and enforce for one another," the machine said in its solemn, mechanical voice. "There are four human rights universally recognized. The first of these is the right of all individuals to do what they choose with an absolute minimum of interference. Man is not required to meet any standard of behavior so long as he is not adversely sensed by any other human. The second right is that of choosing one's dependents. Persons may not be taxed or otherwise forced to support dependents they have not chosen, though they are absolutely required to care for those they have signed for. The third right is to be protected from those who would infringe upon the first two rights through interference or unlawful dependency. Thievery, of which you have been convicted, is a crime of interference and dependency. You have put others to inconvenience and you have supported yourself at others' expense. You may be brought into alignment with social norms if you so choose. Do you so choose?"

Of course she hadn't so chosen. And she never would! Which she'd said, not quite that politely.

Imperturbably, the machine had gone on: "If one chooses not to be aligned, the fourth human right is to die. Do you choose to die?"

She hadn't chosen that either.

"On Alliance Central, persons choosing neither to be aligned nor to die have only one alternative remaining—to become shadows."

Or, as Kane the Brain said later, "Spend two thirds of your time asleep or serving the bureaucracy so they'll let you think you're doing what you want one third of your time!"

Which is what Snark had ended up doing. No fix for her. No having her mind changed so she wouldn't want to steal anymore. No having her chemistry changed so she wouldn't want to maim or kill. No, better be herself one third of the time than never be herself at all.

"So go to the simul and kill somebody," Susso had yelled at her when she'd tried to damage Susso and found herself curled up on the floor, thumb in mouth. "Go to the simul and slap people around, kill people, that's what you want. Do it! But you can't do it out here!"

It sounded great, but nobody stayed dead in a simul! How could you get any satisfaction killing somebody who didn't stay dead? You wake up the next day, the same person is still walking around, looking through you. No matter you'd disposed of him in the simul, you'd still be smelling him. And even when Snark was in the simul, something inside her just knew the people in there weren't real, even though they looked just like the ones, sounded just like the ones Snark hated!

Sounded like Kane, talking like he did. Or looked just like that bastard Willit, egging her on that way, making her end up with her thumb in her mouth. Sounded like that bastard Procurator, him with his fancy tea parties. If Snark wanted, she could bring up the Procurator in the simul booth, or that black-haired woman he'd had with him the other day, Lutha Tallstaff. There she'd sat, hair perfect, face perfect, dressed in clothes you could kill for, holding out a cup to be filled, never noticing who it was that filled it! Never noticing who brought the food, who served it! Not a nod. Not a smile. Pretending Snark really was invisible!

Bitch! What she'd like to do to that bitch! She could tie her up and make her watch while Snark carved the old bastard into slices. Then, when it got to be her turn, let her feel what it was like not to exist! Let high-and-mighty Lutha Tallstaff learn what it felt like to be chopped up into bloody pieces, made into nothing!

Whimpering in eagerness, ignoring her hunger, Snark ran from the locker room in the direction of the simul booth.

The day I went to the House Without a Name, Chahdzi, my father, spent the morning cleaning the upper pool. In the afternoon it was his responsibility to carry food down into the canyon, so all day he kept an eye on the shadow at the bottom of the canyon, judging the progress of the day. If he was to return before dusk, he would need to stop work on the upper pool when the shadow touched the bottom of the eastern wall, or perhaps, for safety's sake, a little time before.

When the shadow was where he thought it should be, he went up the short ladders to the cave floor, took a sack of Kachis-kibble from the storehouse, put it over his shoulders, fastened it onto the carrier belts that crossed his chest, swung himself around the ends of the ladder, and began the descent to the canyon floor. Tonight he needed to speak to songfather about the old outlander ghost who was causing so much inconvenience. When he had done that, perhaps he could also discuss

certain conflicts in his own life that needed patterning. Had these conflicts been decreed by Weaving Woman? If so, could they be sung and
acknowledged? Could his annoyance be exorcised in song? Or must it
remain silent, part of the corruption inevitably incurred when the terrible choice had been made?

I, Saluez, know this, because I know how he thought. My father often
spoke to me of his troubles, of his confusions. He did not get on well
with Zinisi, his wife (who was not my mother). Always he resolved to
speak to *his* father, to songfather about it. Always he delayed. Sometimes he spoke of his ambition to become a songfather himself, a das-
dzit, a patterner, a seer-of-both-sides. I asked him once why, if seeing
both sides was important, only men could be songfathers? Did not
women have a side? He said he would ask songfather, but he never did.

There were two ladders leading down to the first spring, two ladders
more to the first pool, where he'd been scraping algae that morning. Six
more ladders led to the second spring and pool, the big one that was still
under construction, and then two to the bottom, where the orchards and
gardens and grain fields were. From there it was an easy walk down the
canyon to the feeding stones where the beautiful people would come to
feed at dusk. *Lovely on wings, the Kachis,* he hummed beneath his
breath. *Lovely on wings, both powerful and wise.*

"See them come on their wings of light," he sang softly. "See them
emerge from the shadows of the trees. Beautiful on wings . . ." Though
sometimes he wondered if he really wanted . . . No. That had been
decided long ago.

He muttered these same phrases to me, sometimes. Whispering as
though he didn't intend me to hear. Or, perhaps, intended that I should
hear without being certain he intended it. A hint, rather than a word.
Which is the same way certain other information was transmitted. No
one had really said it.

When he came to the level of the spring, he slowed his climb, taking
extra care. There the water falls into the first pool from such a height
that it is often blown onto the ladder rungs and into the carved climbing
holes, making the footing treacherous. Wetness spread beside him, dripping from the higher to the lower rocks, in some places running in tiny
moss-edged diagonals across the almost vertical surfaces of the stones.
This was rain that had fallen far from here, high up, soaking into the
flesh of the mesa to emerge at last like blood from a wound.

Arriving at the first pool, he stopped to ease the straps over his shoulders as he listened to the spring dripping musically into the shallow

puddle at the lip. From the shallow it runs back into the cavern where he'd been working. There the water glints, sending wavering glimmers of reflected light up the smooth vertical shaft that emerges before the hive. This is the household pool from which the people of Cochim-Mahn take water for cooking and hivekeeping. Several large round pots hung before him, tipped on their sides in their rope cradles, ready to be lowered into the water. As he rested, a pot dropped downward, filled, leveled, and then jerked upward, dripping and sloshing as it went. He could hear women singing, *Yeeah-mai, Eeah-mai,* as they turned the spool to wind the rope. Our water, our blood; our water, our blood.

Beneath the sound of their voices chortled the sound of the second spring, the larger one, so powerful at this time of year that it actually spurts from the side of the mountain, arching out between two chunks of green stone to fall chuckling into the big pool the people of Cochim-Mahn have been building for a long, long time. Generations of our people have carved out the mountain behind the waterlip, caulking the cracks to make a place for the water to rest away from the sucking wind and the thirsty sun. Huge stone pillars have been left to hold the mountain up, and among these monstrous trunks the water lies smooth as a mirror, stretching far back into the darkness, deep in some places as four or five tall men.

Between first pool and second, the ladders are shorter and quite dry. My father made quick work of them. The main water gate stands beside the second pool, where well-caulked wooden pipes lead downward to the tanks below. There, also, is the stone house of the seasonally elected watermaster, one who will assure fair distribution of crop water. This early in the year the house was empty, no water was being used except the bucketsful that had been carried to the fruit trees. From far back in the darkness, my father could hear the tap of hammers. There, behind a cofferdam, several of our kinsmen were cutting more stone away, making the storage pond even larger.

The last ladders are the longest, down to the canyon floor where a trickle of meltwater, all that had escaped the traps of the hives upstream, ran between green banks dotted with flowers. From here it is an easy trot to the feeding stones.

The stones are huge and flat. Later in the season, when true warmth comes, the people of the nearer towns spend a day here, scrubbing away the grease and winter-filth and scenting the place with fragrant smoke and fresh herbs. My father ignored the smell as he set the open end of the sack at the lip of the dished stone, then turned to spill its contents behind him. He left without looking back. It is not polite to look at other persons' food or at persons who are eating; so it is not polite to observe the Kachis either. Looking at another person's food implies that one has not had enough. Looking at another person's food is like begging. Only babies and dogs look at people eating.

He set out at a trot for the ladders. Behind him he heard nothing. He slowed. Stopped. Turned. Nothing. Usually there was a call from a tree-clustered canyon and an answering chirrup from somewhere nearer. Usually he had to hurry to be away from the feeding rocks before dusk.

But tonight, nothing. The Kachis were elsewhere. Unwillingly, my father turned his eyes where the rim of the canyon gleamed high and bright in the last of the light, toward the House Without a Name.

Dusk on Dinadh.

Below in the canyon was only darkness. Beneath the arch of the cave, shadows gathered. In the hive, nighttime quiet stopped the tongues of children, men and women began to whisper. The evening song was done. Chahdzi had returned from the canyon. All the doorskins were down but one. Of all the people of Cochim-Mahn, only Hallach still stood outside upon the lip of stone. Hallach and the two women of his family who had gone to take him food and drink.

"Songfather, this woman brings you evening food," whined son's daughter, my half sister, Hazini.

"Songfather, this woman brings you water for your mouth," hummed daughter's daughter, Shalumn. My friend Shalumn.

She remained my friend. Even afterward, she talked to me sometimes. Or, she talked to the wall, knowing I was where I could hear her. So I learned how things were, how things happened, how she read Hallach's face and his movements, seeing what he really felt written upon him.

So, she said, Hallach turned and held out his hands. Shalumn poured the water into them, murmuring rapidly as she did so. "Blessings upon the pattern of water, water that fecundates, that cleanses, that cools, that blesses, that heals, that becometh a tool in the dedicated hands of the Dinadhi."

He sipped from his hands, rinsing away the words of song so they would not be contaminated by mere food, then dried his hands upon the folds of his cotton inner robe. He approved of Shalumn's abbreviated litany. If Hazini had poured the water, she would have chattered out the entire water-blessing catalog rather than ending expeditiously with the all-purpose phrase *becometh a tool in the hands. . . .* And while Hazini had gone on and on, Hallach songfather would have had to stand hungry, which would not have bothered Hazini, who was bony as a lightning-killed tree and ate only so much as a small picky bird. Hazini did not understand hunger.

Hallach took the bowl Hazini offered, casting his eyes upward. There was light upon the height, still time to eat outside before real darkness came. He sat down, his back politely turned so the girls would not offend custom by catching sight of his food, an important courtesy in times of famine, though one not rigorously observed during the present days. There was no current shortage of food in Cochim-Mahn.

The women had raided the last of their winter stores to provide stew for tonight, stew full of the flavors of smoked meat and dried roots. A bright stripe of flavor among all those dark stripes of fungus! He scooped a mouthful onto a round of hearth-bread and let the softened meat pleasure his tongue.

"Songfather?" Hazini said in a self-important voice. "This woman has learned the rest of the rain names and would recite them for songfather."

"Umpn," Hallach said around a mouthful. "Not tonight, Hazini. It is not a proper time."

She made a disrespectful sound behind him, almost a rudeness.

He put down his food and turned to look at her. Her lips were compressed into that pinched line Hallach found so annoying. Just like Chahdzi's second wife, Zinisi. Pinch-pinch, whine-whine, never satisfied with anything. Pretty, though. The way she turned her head and looked at men under her lashes, with that half smile, letting that whiny little voice come out like a seeking tendril to wind around their loins. Songfather remembered how Zinisi had wooed poor Chadzhi, the poor widower. "Chaa-dzi. Can liddle Zinisi have the pretty feathers, Chaa-dzi?" Poor Chahdzi hadn't been able to resist her. Now look at him! With only Saluez to listen to him, only Saluez to . . .

Hallach felt sudden fury. He fixed Hazini with a songfather glare. "Girl, do not make that tightness with your mouth. You cannot recite sacred names from a mouth like that." Rage filled him. He dared not stop to question why. "Also, your voice is too whiny. It must be full and generous if you are to pray to Daylight Woman and Weaving Woman and Great Lightning Wielder."

Shalumn's mouth puckered as though she might laugh, but as Hallach turned toward her she bowed hastily, hiding her face. Hazini, shocked into movement, turned and ran back toward the great dark slab of the hive.

Hallach, ignoring Shalumn for the moment, turned back to his food. He did not ask himself where this rage had come from. He knew. Saluez. Feelings he was supposed to have put behind him. Affections a songfather might not indulge in. His anger was unworthy of him, but nonetheless, he felt no remorse at chiding Hazini. The Gracious One had decreed this conflict from the time they had come to Dinadh. Age must discipline youth. Men must teach women the proper way of things. Some must lose that others may gain. Cold against heat, dry against wet, life against death, every quality must strain to contain its opposite, the whole requiring songfathers to sing the pattern into balance.

Though sometimes it was hard to accept . . . what happened.

Hallach shifted uncomfortably. It wasn't wise to think about that either. Such thinking smacked of doubt, and of course he didn't doubt. She'd be fine. She was his . . . his son's daughter. Of course she'd be fine.

No longer at all hungry, he set the half-emptied bowl aside.

Shalumn saw all this and drew her own conclusions. She moved slightly toward him, her hesitancy reminding him she had not been dismissed. Hallach held one finger upright, stopping her where she stood.

"Saluez," he said, a mere whisper. It would not have been proper for a songfather to ask about a mere girl, but he had not asked. He had merely said a name.

Shalumn had seen Masanees return. Shalumn had seen her leave again, with two of the sisterhood. Then, in the dusk, they had returned again, a cluster of women who had carried someone, someone alive, perhaps, or dead, perhaps, but who had in either case gone into a side entrance to the hive and down into a shadowy place below, a place Shalumn could not go, where even songfathers could not go.

No one had mentioned this to songfather, and he could not ask. He had not asked, and Shalumn did not move or speak. She did not look up. Her eyes remained down. There were certain things a woman would never say to a man. Not any man.

After a moment Hallach waved the finger at her, letting her take the bowl and go.

It was many days later that I came upon Shalumn in a corridor. She knew me by the borders painted upon my outer robe. Had she not painted them? Had the robe not been her gift to me? Now she turned away, as she must, and began to speak to the corridor wall. She told the wall about songfather, and Hazini, and how songfather had looked and what songfather had said. She knew I was standing in an alcove just behind her. She knew I could hear.

"Songfather looked very sad," she said. "Songfather looked very strange. I went away then, stumbling a little. I wept. I miss my friend." She gulped, and I saw her wipe her face with her hand. "I miss my love. I will always miss my love." She walked away then, not glancing at me, but her cheeks were wet.

Shalumn's were the only tears I saw shed for me. Songfather could not show grief. Chahdzi could not show grief. Hazini would not grieve, nor Zinisi, nor any of the people of the hive. Weaving Woman sends the shuttles to and fro, light and dark, youth and age, good and ill, wisdom and stupidity. Belief and doubt, also. Belief and doubt.

Often the pattern is not as we ourselves would weave it.

CHAPTER 2

Masanees brought Saluez back to the hive and her story stopped. Time went by, yes, but Saluez did not care much about that. She did not hunger or thirst. The women around her forced her to eat and drink. Her prayers to Weaving Woman had not been answered. Her shuttle had not carried light. Her pattern was dark, only dark, and no one could see its end. There was no story of Saluez.

What was true of me was true also of Snark. During that time, she had no story. She was as she was, and little changed from day to day. We were stopped, our shuttles still, our colors waiting. During this time, the story was Lutha's story, the pattern was Lutha's pattern.

"My name is Trompe Paggas," the Fastigat said into Lutha's annunciator. "I've been assigned as your assistant."

She opened her door to the surging traffic. A hurrying passerby bumped her visitor hard enough to carom him into her, and clutching one another, they almost fell into her rooms. She stumbled to the door and shut it against the noise of the crowded concourse while her disheveled guest brushed himself off. He seemed more annoyed than the minor trampling warranted.

"How do you stand it?" he growled.

"Stand what?" She was puzzled.

"Living in all this mob!"

Her face cleared. It wasn't a mob. It was just the ordinary workaday crowd, but this man was used to Fastiga, where things were managed differently, or to Prime, which was, if anything, too sparsely populated. Trompe Paggas had even put on a coverall so he wouldn't be contaminated by rubbing up against people. Now, before he had even divested himself of this garment, he said, "You're ambivalent about me."

She laughed, the sounds fluttering up her throat like startled birds. This was so familiar, so like Leelson, this Fastigat habit of holding her feelings up before her, as though she didn't know how she felt unless he told her! Even his gently concerned tone of voice was the same, even his expression, kindly and questioning.

"Trompe, don't tell me. Please. Let that be a rule between us. Of course I'm ambivalent about you. I'm ambivalent about everything! About the trip. About taking Leely. About finding out something, or not finding out anything. About the Ularians wiping out humanity!"

"Ambivalent, even about the prospect of destruction?" he asked, shocked.

"Sometimes. Sure. Some days, doesn't it seem like a good idea we should all be wiped out? Some days, don't we make a royal mess of things?" As an official translator, she was aware of that mess, if he wasn't. Words of impassioned rage and raw desperation flowed through her workstation every day. Broken treaties. Misinterpreted promises. Endless renegotiation. Forged certifications. Lies and evasions. She laughed again, seeing his expression.

"No," he said soberly. "It does not seem like a good idea. All problems can be solved. It merely takes the will and attention to do so."

She shrugged, smiling: he was so very Fastigat!

"All right, I won't make problems. I realize you'll know how I feel. I'll tell you right now, you probably won't ever know how Leely feels about anything. Let's accept that. Your job will be to use your abilities to help me cope while we search for anything Bernesohn Famber might have left on Dinadh. You're not here to *tell me* how I feel or help me deal with my emotions or any of that Fastigat stuff. I've had that. I don't need it."

He shrugged, making a face like a Leelson face. Physically, he was as unlike Leelson as possible, being short and chunky and dark instead of tall, slender, and bright-haired. A man of gold, Leelson. A man of iron, this. In his favor, he had astonishingly alert blue eyes and was also quite young. Younger than Lutha, at any rate.

"Can I see the boy?" he asked.

She pointed. The door between the office room and the sleeping room was open. He went through it with her behind him.

Leely was standing naked before the window scene, which was dialed to *forest*. His clothes lay as he'd dropped them in the corner. He had decorated the wall near the window with a feces finger painting, an extraordinary impression of the blown trees in the forest scene. He turned toward them with a lovely smile and a lilting laugh.

"Dananana," he purred. "Dananana."

"Excuse me," she murmured to Trompe. "If you'll give me a moment."

Trompe nodded expressionlessly.

She was aware of him watching her as she keyed the room-bot, cleaned Leely, and got the clothes back on him. No matter where she put the fasteners, he managed to get his clothes off, little contortionist! And look at the skin of his chest and shoulders, all blotchy from chill. Well, no harm done. The room-bot had the floor and walls cleaned by the time Leely was dressed again.

"That's my sweet boy," she murmured, hugging him and putting him down once more, handing him the child-sized paint sticks she'd gone to such trouble to find.

"Dananana," he said, patting her face with one hand as he threw the sticks across the room with the other. "Dananana."

"How old is he?" Trompe asked from the doorway. His face showed nothing, but he knew the answer. He was only checking.

She stiffened. "Almost six." Leely was just past his fifth birthday.

"Big for his age." Trompe's voice held no emotion, but she could feel something. Disapproval? Or what? "He must weigh what?"

"He's heavy for his age. But, as you know, Leelson is tall and muscular, and my family also runs to size, so Leely will probably be a big man."

Now she knew what he was thinking. *How will she cope then? When he's a big man, what will she do?* His mouth opened, then closed again, the words unspoken. Well, at least he learned fast. And what right did he have to disapprove?

"What kind of treatments have you tried?" he asked.

She fought down her annoyance. Even though he'd been briefed, he wanted her to talk about it so he could feel what she felt, find his way into her psyche. Damn all Fastigats! Would he be more help if he understood?

She gritted her teeth and said in a patient voice, "I'm sure you were told, but both Leelson and I had a genome check early in my pregnancy. Both of us are within normal limits. Leely's pattern differs from ours only within normal limits. Physically, he's fine."

"And mentally?"

Had the man no eyes? She kept her voice calm as she answered.

"Well, sometimes he won't leave his clothes on. He won't learn to use the potty, though he does like to eliminate outdoors. He has no speech, obviously. And he doesn't seem to classify. He reacts to each new animal, person, or thing in pretty much the same manner, with curiosity. If one food chip is tasty, he doesn't assume similar-looking ones are. He regards each thing as unique."

"Really?"

"Give him a red ball, he'll learn that it bounces and squeezes. He may treasure it. If he loses it and I give him another red ball, he has to start from scratch. Though it looks identical to me, somehow he knows it isn't the same thing he had before."

"Strange."

She nodded. It was. Strange.

"I understand they've tried splicing him."

It wasn't a question, but she answered it anyhow. "The geneticists spotted a few rare variations that they thought might be connected to behavior, and they tried substituting some more common alleles. Among Leely's unique attributes, however, is a super-efficient immune system. Each time extraneous genetic material is introduced, his body kills it. It may take him a day, or a week, but he manages it every time. That means that even if we hit upon whatever variant might help, it would take him a very short time to get rid of it. And, of course, it may not be in the chromosomes. It may be elsewhere in the cells."

The geneticists had suggested a complete cellular inventory, but she had resisted that. Perhaps she didn't really want to know. If they found something . . . Well, how very final that would be!

Trompe said, "I imagine the doctors are very interested in him! The immune system, I mean."

"Extremely interested. Particularly inasmuch as he also heals very quickly. At first thought, these traits would seem to be extremely valuable—"

"But only the healing, the immunity."

"Right. If they could be separated from the rest of his pattern, but no one knows what particular combination of combinations has resulted in that trait."

"So, whatever's wrong, it can't be fixed."

She stiffened. "I object to the word. Leely is all right the way he is! You may as well know that Leelson Famber and I disagreed on that point."

He narrowed his eyes at her. "But . . . how intelligent is he?"

"I believe he has a different level of intelligence," she said belligerently. One of her most vehement arguments with Leelson had been on that subject. She tried to be fair. "Though it's hard to be sure because our idea of intelligence is so dependent upon the use of language. He scores quite high on some nonverbal tests, those that don't depend solely on classification."

"I don't understand."

"What I said earlier! He doesn't classify things. He can't look at a pile of blocks and pick out all the blue ones. Mere blueness isn't a category for Leely. Nor mere roundness, mere squareness, mere . . . whatever. Each thing is its own thing."

"With its own name?"

"Who knows? If he could talk, perhaps that would be true. He's past the age when most children either learn a language or create one." She heard the pain in her voice, knew Trompe heard it too.

"So?" He was looking at her curiously, figuring her out.

Lutha took firm control of her voice. She had to sound objective and calm. She would not start out on this arduous project with a companion who felt she was irrational.

"Since he's so very healthy, I've considered he might be a new and fortunate mutation. Perhaps he will learn language later than most children."

There was no legitimate reason for her to believe that, but she believed it anyhow, passionately, with her whole heart. Leelson had said that for every positive mutation, there were undoubtedly thousands of useless or lethal ones. Intellectually, she accepted that. So far as Leely was concerned, she could not. He couldn't be . . . useless.

She pulled her mind away from that thought. She didn't want Trompe Paggas to think she was—what? Deluded. A mother who was blind and fond to the point of stupidity? Speak of something else!

Trompe gave her the opening. "He didn't like those colors you gave him. Why was that, do you suppose?"

"A mistake on my part," she admitted ruefully. "He loves to paint, as you saw, and I thought the colors would be tempting. I was wrong. They don't please him for some reason. They have the wrong texture or smell. He does quite nice renderings in feces, as you've seen. Or in gravy, or mud."

"Organic media," mused Trompe. "Probably with organic smells."

"Perhaps he identifies by smell, categorizes by smell. I don't know. Maybe he has another sense entirely."

A superhuman sense, she didn't say, though she thought it. A more-than-human sense. She caught herself and flushed. She'd mentioned these thoughts to a few family members, a few friends, all of whom thought she was pushing the limits of reality. And sometimes—yes, sometimes she knew she would trade eventual superhumanity for a Leely who would learn to use the potty and keep his clothes on!

"No need to get upset, Lutha. I understand." Trompe was smiling at her, squeezing her shoulder. "Fine. I was briefed. I was just digging for some kind of overall understanding, but we've obviously said enough." He seated himself and adopted an expression that said he was getting down to business.

"It's going to be hard for you," he said.

She nodded, admitting as much.

Trompe tapped his front teeth with a thumbnail. "The Procurator wishes you to know you may have all the help you need, both in preparing to go and to keep your business alive while you're gone. Meantime, I made some inquiries of my own. I thought Leelson might be, you know, simply avoiding the issue, but he's truly gone. No one I spoke to had any idea where he was."

"Limia could go," said Lutha, referring to Leelson's mother.

"Easier than you," he agreed. "I wonder why she won't?"

Both sat silently for a time.

"Let's ask her," he said. "Let's go ask her!"

"Now?" she cried. "I can't leave—"

He interrupted her with a finger to her lips. "I'll call a crèche team to take care of Leely, and why not now? If Limia won't go, I think we both should know why. We'll run on over to Fastiga and find out."

South of Alliance Prime the enclave of Fastiga lay beneath its own separate dome, the towers of the men jutting aggressively above the sprawling domiciles of the women. Nothing separated them but multilevel sculpture gardens and fantastically ritualized behaviors, both well observed.

In the domiciles the languorous hours between the evening meal and the erotic observances of deep night were set aside for the reception of visitors. Fires were lit in the halls of lineage, dusty bottles were opened and decanted into elegant crystal, children were sent to their own quarters to bedevil their adolescent minders, womenfolk put on their most seductive draperies, and everyone gossiped about everyone else. Fastiga women were much interested—some said obsessed—by lineage. All Fastigats claimed common ancestors; they were all one clan; only the precise degree of kinship was subject to analysis, but of such minor quibbles nightlong conversations could be built.

Trompe brought Lutha up from clangorous, crowded traffic levels belowground to the murmuring quiet of a house she had visited once before. And had not intended to visit again, she acknowledged to herself as he fetched her a glass of wine and ushered her to a sheltered corner of the hall of lineage. It was a secluded niche mostly hidden from the other visitors.

"Leelson brought me here once," she said, aware of a sudden bellicosity, the flaring embers of old anger.

He nodded, as though he already knew. Well, Fastigats did know. They knew entirely too much.

"It may take me a while to get to Limia," he murmured. "Custom demands I work my way around the room. Don't move. I'll be back."

He left her. She settled into the chair, which was both comfortable and private. The wings on either side hid her from anyone who was not directly opposite, and there was more uninhabited room around her than in her whole apartment and three or four others like it. Behind her, she could hear two Fastiga women making conversation, unaware they were overheard.

"There's Olloby Pime, with her Old-earth friend," said one voice. "So hairy, Old-earthers. I had an earther lover once. Did I ever tell you, Britta? So relaxing. Such a treasure. Poor thing had no idea what I was feeling, and I can't tell you how refreshing that was."

Britta paused before responding. "I perceive your satisfaction, Ostil-ohn, but my own experience would lead me to believe such a liaison would be rather frustrating."

Britta and Ostil-ohn, said Lutha to herself. Ostil-ohn, who had had a terrestrial but non-Fastigat lover.

Ostil-ohn, who was saying:

"Oh, my dear, no. For example, if I wasn't in the mood for sex, instead of being coaxed and wooed and pestered for simply hours and having to heat up out of sheer inevitability, I could just pretend I was wild with desire to begin with."

"He didn't know the difference?"

"Not at all! He hadn't the tiniest flicker of perception, so he got on with it, and I sighed and yelped a bit, and shortly it was over, while meantime I'd gone on thinking what I was thinking about before he started!"

"But, Ostil-ohn, this implies . . . what if you were in the mood and he wasn't?"

"Ah, well, there are drawbacks to every relationship. It's true one gets in the mood much less often than with Fastigats."

Britta snorted.

"I wonder where Limia Famber is," Ostil-ohn murmured next. "I haven't seen her lately."

Lutha leaned back, listening intently.

"One assumes she has not been taking part in public life since her son disappeared."

"I shouldn't think she was surprised! What did she expect? Leelson was destined to disappear. Takes after his father in that regard."

"Ostil-ohn! You're being cruel. Grebor Two didn't disappear purposely. Any more than *his* father did!"

"Listen, when three generations of Fambers stick around only long enough to father one child, then take off and are never seen again, one may be forgiven for assuming a genetic tendency toward vanishment!"

A pause indicating that Britta was considering this. "Three generations?"

"Actually four, if you count uncles. Leelson; his father, Grebor Two; his grandfather, Grebor One; and his great-granduncle."

"Who was his great-granduncle?"

"Paniwar Famber, son of Bernesohn and Tospia. That's five generations, because Paniwar was an only too."

"Paniwar was *not* an only. Paniwar had a twin sister, Tospiann. Boy and girl—"

"I meant only *son,*" interrupted Ostil-Ohn.

"—and Bernesohn had flocks of children with other women!"

A moment's silence. "That's right. I'd forgotten."

"Paniwar had more than one child, too, though it was a scandal! He got some little tourister girl pregnant when he was just a boy. She wanted him to marry her, can you imagine! When he told her Fastigats *don't,* she went to some remote place and had the child secretly, making Paniwar guilty of improper fathering! The talk went on for years!"

"My dear, it wasn't a little tourister girl. I remember now. It was someone famous on the frontier! He was only a boy, she was twice his age, and that's what the talk was about!"

Ostil-ohn murmured, "Whoever. I'll modify my statement. When four generations of Fambers stick around only long enough to father one *acknowledged son* and then take off never to be seen again, one may be forgiven for assuming it's genetic."

Britta said, "Limia would argue with you. She doesn't acknowledge the boy Leelson fathered. He had it out of that translator woman he took up with. You know. We met her once. Lutha something. Tallstaff. Basically earthian stock."

"Did I meet her?"

"But of course you did," Britta insisted. "Leelson brought her here. Then Limia went to see her!"

"Oh, yes. To warn her off, don't you suppose? Limia was furious! And what is it about the child? Something not right?"

Lutha's face flushed. Damn them. What right had they to discuss Leely!

Britta went on. "It isn't Fastigat. It's not even normal earthian. I haven't seen it, though some of the men have. Oh, look, there's someone who'd know. Trompe Paggas. Trompe knows everything!"

Lutha looked up, saw Trompe moving toward her, gave up any attempt at concealment, and rose to her full height. She turned to the matrons she'd been eavesdropping upon with a pleasant smile and a nod.

Both had the grace to flush, though only Ostil-ohn was capable of speech. She murmured politely as Lutha moved to join Trompe, and then the two woman put their heads together once more, to share the full delicious horror of what they'd just done.

Leelson Famber's mother was in no mood to talk with Lutha Tallstaff. When Trompe insisted, she made them wait a discourteous amount of time before inviting them to her private quarters. During that time she dressed herself with some care and prepared herself mentally for what she supposed would be a request on the Tallstaff woman's part for additional help with her idiot child.

It turned out, however, that Lutha Tallstaff had something else in mind.

"I've been asked by the Alliance to go to Dinadh," Lutha announced. "With my son."

Limia sat back, surprised both at the announcement and at the propriety of Lutha's language. "My son," she'd said. Many women might have said "Leelson's son." Or "our son." "Leelson's and my son." Or even, courtesy forbid, "your grandson."

Limia sat back in her chair, feeling an unintended frown creeping onto her forehead. "Yes," she said, smoothing both her face and her voice. "What has that to do with me?"

"I don't want to go," said Lutha. "I've agreed to do so only if no other way can be found."

"Other way?"

"The Dinadhi will allow entry to you. The Procurator says you've refused to go."

"Yes."

"I thought perhaps you didn't understand how important the matter is and how very difficult the trip will be for me."

"I am an old woman. You are a young one." Among Fastigats, with their reverence for age, this was all that needed saying. Seemingly, it was not enough for the Tallstaff woman.

Lutha explained, "In order to be allowed to investigate Bernesohn Famber's life there, I have to be connected with his lineage. This means I have to take my son with me."

Limia's gorge rose at the word *lineage,* but she kept her voice calm. "Surely that is not onerous."

Lutha threw a glance in Trompe's direction.

Smoothly he said, "Lutha Tallstaff correctly assesses that the visit to Dinadh will be more than merely onerous, mistress. It will be extremely difficult."

Limia rose and stalked across the floor, her long skirts foaming around her ankles. With her back to the younger woman, she allowed herself a bitter smile. "Leave us, Trompe."

"Mistress . . ."

"Leave us!"

She waited until she heard the sound of the door sliding shut behind him. "I came to call upon you," she said, turning to Lutha. "At your office. Remember."

"Of course."

"When I first heard you were pregnant. I believe I told you then something of the family history."

"I respect the meaning lineage has for you, madam, but as I said at the time, family histories are most interesting to members of the family in question. You'd made it clear you would never consider me as any part of your family."

"I told you of the saying among Fastigats? Do you remember?"

"I remember it, madam. 'Mankind, first among creatures. Fastigats, first among mankind. Fambers, first among Fastigats.' "

Lutha thought it unbearably arrogant, then and now. "I thought it hyperbole, madam. Fastigats are not known as Firsters."

"Ninety-nine percent of all Firsters are vulgar, but even they may occasionally assert a truth. It is a truth that the universe was made for man, not as Firsters exemplify man but as Fastigats exemplify man. Evolution moves in our direction. It is our pride and our duty. You would have been wise to respect our history and traditions, though you were outside them. I mentioned to you that Leelson's line is composed of only sons."

A fact that seemed to be generally known, considering what Lutha had overheard downstairs.

"I thought that interesting, but not compelling, madam. At best it is a statistical anomaly."

"I asked you—no, I begged you not to go on with your pregnancy."

"As I told you at the time, it was not something I had planned." She hadn't, and she had no explanation for not having done so. None at all. Against every tenet of her rearing, against every shred of her own resolution, it had simply happened.

Limia went on implacably: "You chose to ignore what I had to say. I explained that Leelson's child would have a better chance of being valued by his father and by me if born to a Fastiga woman and, if a son, with the Fastigat skills. I spoke from conviction, from concern. As you now admit, you felt my reasoning was not meaningful, not compelling. Why, now, should your conviction be compelling to me? Why, now, should your difficulties or problems be my concern?"

Lutha stared out the window behind the woman, not wanting to look her in the face. Everything she said was true. The only omission from Limia's account was Leelson's reaction when Lutha had told him of his mother's visit. He had been angered, infuriated. Let Limia keep her opinions to herself. If he wanted to father a child on Lutha, that was his business! At that moment Lutha had loved him most, for he had not spoken like a Fastigat but like a lover.

One could not say to Limia Famber, however, that the child had been Leelson's choice. Limia Famber wasn't interested in what her son had wanted. *Had* wanted. Then.

Very well. There was still one final question she needed to ask. Lutha breathed deeply, counting the breaths, holding her voice quiet as she said, "There is an additional possibility. Leelson himself could make this trip far easier than I, and he would have no reason to refuse. Do you have any idea where he might be?"

Limia laughed harshly. "Don't be a fool, woman! Do you think I would be so grievously upset if I knew where Leelson was? If I knew he was anywhere, alive? If I knew that, I could assume he has time yet to beget another child. If I knew he was still among the living, I would not despair of his posterity."

The sneering tone made Lutha tremble, only partly with anger. She could actually fear this woman!

"It is early to despair of his posterity," she said at last. "Leely is only five."

The older woman regarded her almost with pity. "Leely! Your misbegot provides no posterity, not for our line, not even for yours, if you cared about such things. My kinsmen have seen your *Leely,* at my request. Believe me, it is because of your Leely that I despair!"

Some weeks after I returned from the House Without a Name, a veiled woman stopped me in the corridor, asking that I meet her behind the hive that evening. I knew her voice. From her veil, I knew she was one like me.

I did as she asked, leaving the hidden quarters in the bowels of the hive and encountering her near the back wall of the cave, whence she guided me through a hidden cleft and along a narrow trail that led downward to a turning behind a rock where there was a dark crevice.

"Puo-toh," came the whisper from the crevice. *Who goes?*

"Pua-a-mai etah," my guide replied. *Goes a newly wounded one.*

"Enter," said the whisperer, lifting a foliage curtain from within the crevice. "Follow."

My guide held the foliage while I went beneath. It fell into place behind me as I went down a path that twisted among great stones. This was a water path, smoothed by the rains of a thousand years, dimly lit by occasional candles on metal spikes driven into the stone. I wondered if the lights were there for my benefit, for my guide did not seem to need them. She moved as easily in darkness as she did in the infrequent puddles of light.

We came to a blanket door, the two blankets slightly overlapping.

"Remove your veil and come in," she said.

She raised both hands to the flap of her veil, loosing it and thrusting it aside as she went through the blanket and around the draft wall that stops the outside air from blowing in. Behind it was the cave itself. It was dim inside, lit only by the small fire burning upon the central hearth under a metal hood. It was also warm, which meant it was well plastered, with all its holes and crevices stuffed with stone and covered with a layer of mud. As I looked around I realized the walls had been not only sealed, but smoothed. Walls and benches had been painted with white clay to reflect the light, and there were designs drawn there, ones I had never seen before. The mortar chimney that led the smoke away went beneath the lie-down bench, curved with it, and came up against the far wall, where a little door gave access to the shelf where the start-fire is built, to get the warm air rising. Once air is going up the straight chimney, one shuts the start-fire door, and the heated hearth air is pulled under the bench, warming the place we sit or sleep.

It was a warm cave, carefully planned, carefully built, as carefully as any hive cell I had ever seen. The air was fragrant, scented by spices stewing over the fire. I knew there would be breathing holes somewhere, a few at the bottom of the cave, beside the fire, to suck new air in as the warm air rose. We do the same in the hive.

On the curving bench sat a score of women, all with their hoods pushed back, their veils down. Only once had I seen my face in a mirror since my day at the House Without a Name. Once had been enough. Now I stared as though into fifty mirrors, seeing my face again and again, with variations. Here was a missing eyelid, there a ragged lip, there nostrils chewed at the edges. There were ears missing, cheeks pocked and scarred and riven. Foreheads and scalps and jaws with only skin across the bone.

When I had wakened in the hive, the bandages had already been in place. Veiled women had told me what had happened. No one knew why. It happened sometimes. It was no fault of Masanees or any of the other attendant women. Every detail of the ritual had been reviewed, again and again. Did you do this? Did you do that? Did you lie with your face firmly in the basket ring? Was there plenty of food and drink? Yes and yes, everything had been done as it was supposed to be done, as it had been done over and over for generations of years.

"Welcome," said an old woman. "To our sisterhood."

The others bowed and murmured. Welcome. Welcome.

"Are you still with child?" asked the eldest.

I nodded. So far as I knew, I was. I was no longer about to be married; I was no longer considered marriageable; but I was still with child.

"When your birthing time comes, you will come here," said the woman.

This was a surprise! I looked around the circle, seeking some reason. Those who could, smiled comfortingly at me.

"We have all had the experience," one of the women said. "Most of us are from Cochim-Mahn, but some are from Dzibano'as and Hamam'n and Damanbi. When the moons are full, we delegates come to offer comfort to our new sister, walking in the day from hive to hive, staying overnight with our sisters who then join our travels the following day. Tonight we have with us women even from Chacosri, around the canyon corner. We all know what you are suffering. Many of us have had children. When your time comes, come here."

"We are a sisterhood," said another to me, kindly. "We are a sisterhood of wounds. We must care for ourselves, for the others are afraid of us."

"Afraid!" I cried. I knew it was so. Walking veiled in the corridors of the hive, I had seen it on their faces, even on Father's face, Grandfather's face. I had seen it on Shalumn's face, though her fear was outweighed by pity. I did not want to believe it. "Why afraid?"

"Because we do not fit the promise made by the Gracious One," whispered another. "Because we seem to cast doubt upon the choice. Because they are afraid we will bring the abandoned gods among them again."

And then they put their arms around me, and I wept, and they said soft words and let me weep, and the singing began and went around and around the fire, old songs to fit the designs upon the walls, songs so old the ordinary people of the hives had forgotten them, songs of our former father, our former mother, songs of the time when the shadows had welcomed us and we did not go in fear or hope of the Kachis or the ghosts.

It is time to introduce new color into the robe we are weaving. I have woven Lutha and Leelson and Leely, Saluez and Snark. Now I will fill a new shuttle with heavier threads than ours. I will weave the King of Kamir.

I had never met a king before, and when eventually I did, at first I thought he did not look like much. Still, his pattern would be rich and vivid, a storm design set against our simple stripes of joy and pain. While Lutha Tallstaff was traveling toward our meeting, while I sang in the cave of the sisterhood, he, the King of Kamir, thought mighty thoughts and made the fabric tremble!

*   *   *

Jiacare Lostre, the King of Kamir who had been lost (who had tried desperately and unsuccessfully to stay lost), sat cross-legged on the chalcedony throne of Kamir-Shom-Lak considering with measurable satisfaction the demise of Leelson Famber and all his lineage. Famber's siblings and their children and all their children. Famber's parents and their siblings and all their children. Beginning, however, with Leelson himself, with Leelson's wife or mate, if any, and his offspring.

Despite the burdens of kingship, which had piled up during his absence, Jiacare had found time to recruit and dispatch an appropriate assassination team: Mitigan, a professional killer from Asenagi, a Firster who saw no dichotomy between profession and religion; Chur Durwen, another Firster, a talented youngster from Collis who was well on his way to high professional status; plus the brothers Silby and Siram Haughneep, the king's own bodymen, sworn servitors to the royal family. Oh, definitely a four-assassin target, the family Famber, all of whom would learn painfully and lengthily that "finding" lost kings who did not wish to be found was not the wisest of occupations.

Words penetrated his preoccupation.

". . . and so, Your Most Puissant and Glorious Effulgence, it is no longer possible to reserve the forests of Tarnen, though they are Lostre-family possessions, since they are needed by Your Majesty's peasantry in Chalc as pastures for their cattle."

The Minister of Agriculture lowered his databoard and peered over the top of it at His Royal Highness, who stared rigidly past the minister at the tapestries behind him.

"This is a serious question," murmured the Minister of Agriculture, as though to himself.

"I'm sure," said His Effulgence from a tight throat. "Too serious to be delayed for my benefit. Why didn't you just get on with it?"

"The Scroll of Establishment of Kamir-Shom-Lak requires that all matters concerning the general welfare be presented to the king for his approval or advice."

"Since my advice is invariably ignored, I don't advise," said the king.

"The Great Document does not require that Your Effulgence advise. It merely requires that matters be presented in case Your Majesty might choose to do so," said the minister, with an unsympathetic yawn.

"Take it as written that I do not choose. I neither advise nor approve. Nor will I ever approve of any matter brought before me. Certainly I do not approve of cutting the forests of Tarnen. They are the last forests remaining upon Kamir."

"As Your Majesty knows, the removal of forests is one of the necessary steps in homo-norming a planet. Kamir has delayed far longer than most planets. Why, on Kamir, we still have animals!"

The king became very pale. "We have a few, yes. There are fifty species of birds in the forests of Tarnen, including the royal ouzel, whose feathers grace our crown, whose image is graven upon our planetary seal. There are numerous species of insects and animals. There are ferns, orchids—"

"None of which is required by man," the Minister of Agriculture interrupted. "We have been over this, Your Majesty. In accordance with Alliance regulations, before we may establish outgrowth colonies, our home planet must be homo-normed at least to Type G. That means—"

"I know what it means! It means no trees, no birds, no animals. Why don't we skip over a step? Why don't we save the forests by eliminating the cattle, which we will do sooner or later when we set up the algae farms required by Class G."

"We have preserved the patterns of the forest species, Your Effulgence. They are in our files as required by the homo-norming laws."

"They won't be alive! No flutter of wings, no plop of little green bodies into water, no silver glitter beneath the ripples. There will be only men and the crops to feed men!"

"The stored species can be enlivened whenever there is sufficient space and food for them. Just now, however, there is widespread hunger in the area of Chalc. As Your Majesty is aware, food and medicines are already stringently rationed everywhere on Kamir."

"Except among the aristocracy."

"Your ministers cannot be expected to govern if they are hungry or worried over the welfare of their families."

"Suggest that the peasants of Chalc restrict their fecundity."

"Humanity comes first. Fecundity is the blessing of the universe, which was made for man."

"What universe is that?"

The Minister of Agriculture flushed, slightly embarrassed. "One gets into the habit—"

"I am not one of your Firster constituents, Minister. I am a faithful son of Lord Fathom, ancient and enigmatic, god of the Lostres." He took his eyes from the tapestries and looked directly into the minister's eyes. "Listen to me for a moment. You have traveled. You are a sophisticated man. You have been to Central, as I have. What do you think of it?"

"Your Effulgence . . ."

"Be honest! What do you think of it?"

"It seems a very efficient place."

"Did you feel at all crowded?"

"Well, one does feel a bit—"

"Did you go to the Grand Canyon of Old-earth?"

"Yes. I confess, I didn't see what the fuss was about."

"You rode down in a transparent elevator. Through the glass you saw the strata, each one labeled as to age. At the bottom you experienced a sensurround of the way it used to be, a few centuries ago. You were told that the canyon now houses over a billion people. Do you want that for the forests of Tarnen?"

"But it's inevitable, Your Effulgence! There will be frontiers for our great-grandchildren, perhaps, but for us, now, there is still space to fill! So long as there is space to fill, we must go on having babies. So Firstism teaches us."

The king sighed deeply. "Save the teachings for the fecund masses, Minister. Why don't you give the peasants some land in the Orbive Hills."

"There is no arable land left in the Orbive. There has been widespread erosion. . . ."

The king nodded slowly. "Oh, yes. Because your father chose to allow firewood cutting in the Orbive instead of providing solar stoves. Because his father permitted unlimited herd growth among the Chalcites to woo their votes. Just as his father, your great-grandfather, first Kamirian convert to the Firster cause, defeated the attempt by the Green Party to limit human population upon Kamir. And so sealed our fate forever."

The minister flushed angrily. "As Your Majesty says."

"*My* grandfather told *your* grandfather that the herds would die and the people would die."

The minister's mouth twisted into a half smile. "Your Majesty's grandfather is remembered for his sagacity. Now that the herds are dying and the people are dying, however, there is a public outcry which will not be stanched by mere laying of blame on persons long dead. Hungry people do not care what our grandfathers did. So long as one inch of Kamirian soil remains, the people will believe that using it will solve their problems. Only when all the land is gone and destroyed will they permit the next step in homo-norming, and Your Majesty knows it as well as I."

The king uncrossed his legs and put them flat upon the throne, his hands flat beside them, wondering if by will alone he could sink into that stone, obliterate himself, become nothing. He said, sighing deeply, "Do as you will. I do not approve. Take that as written, and let me abdicate."

"The Scroll of Establishment of Kam-Shom-Lak specifies a hereditary king, Your Majesty, and it has no provision for abdication."

"I have a younger brother. Several, in fact."

"So long as Your Effulgence is alive . . ." The threat in this was implicit. Kings might die, but they could not run away. Kings had died, as a matter of fact, under more or less mysterious circumstances. He did not mind dying. He did mind what they would no doubt do to him first, to make him say something they could use for a reason. Conspiracy against the welfare of Kamir. Kamir, that he loved as some men love women!

"How many more of you are there today?" asked the king. "How many more ministers out there in the anteroom, crouched slavering over the few remaining fragments of our planet."

The minister stiffened. "Seven, Your Highness."

"Tell them they may go. I don't approve of anything they're doing."

Angered, the minister growled: "The Firster godmongers pray for you daily in your blindness, Majesty. Man is meant to procreate! We were given the universe to fill. What are a few animals, a few trees in the face of our destiny?"

"Tell the rest of them to go home," the king said desperately. "Tell them in future they must condense their reports to something less than five minutes. In future, I will listen to nothing longer. I will set a timer."

"But Your Highness can not possibly comprehend the ramifications of the problems from a condensed—"

"Why should I comprehend?" he cried, pressed past endurance. "I don't comprehend. I will never comprehend. I see a different world than you ministers see. On ascending to this throne, I took an oath to rule the world of Kamir. That world, though much diminished, still had seas and forests and animals. You are destroying that world. Greater comprehension would only increase my sense of futility." The Lost King rose from his throne, turned his back upon his minister, and stalked to a nearby window that stood open to let in the fresh breezes of early spring.

He had escaped on a day much like this—it had been late fall, not spring, but on a similar day—slipping out this very window in the darkness before dawn, across the velvet lawns, into the trees. Once Tarnen was gone, this royal park would contain all the trees left on Kamir. He had thought of that as he had walked through them that day toward his cache of clothing and money and documents, hidden away bit by inconspicuous bit over a long, long time of preparation. He had emerged on the far side of the trees dressed as an Elithan, and he had slipped into the crowd that always stood there, staring at the palace, to stand for a time himself, staring at the palace, before he went away.

He had taken ship for Elitha, unremarked, unnoticed, calling himself Osterbog Smyne, a common Elithan name. He had reached Elitha. Oh, with what eagerness had he taken up a new life as a nobody on Elitha. If not for that damnable Leelson Famber, Osterbog Smyne would be on Elitha still, keeping a fruit stall, taking his holidays in the forests, watching birds, maybe even going fishing, far from ministers and reports and briefings and the whole irrelevant, endless fal-de-rol of kingship.

"Your Majesty is so deep in thought, one assumes he is considering marriage and the production of an heir," said a pontifical voice from behind him. So. The Minister of Agriculture had called for assistance, and here was Lord Zhoun, the Prime Minister, the quintessence of boredom, the paradigm of duty undesired.

Jiacare Lostre murmured, "I've told you, I've no intention of begetting a child to carry on this charade. The planet is within a year or so of being Class G. Soon you'll be directing the aristocracy to turn in their pets for euthanizing. Soon will come Class-J domed cities, which will grow, and grow, until they make a glittering ceiling over the final convulsions! You know how it will end, how it always ends. The Scroll of Establishment contains no requirement that I be part of the process."

"Common sense would indicate—"

"Common sense, hah! Focus on one of my no-doubt-eager brothers or nephews. Groom half a dozen of them for this thankless ascendancy."

"Your Majesty, please . . ."

"Prime Minister, please!"

"You used to call me Uncle."

"You used to call me Jickie, Lord Zhoun, and you used to tell stories of adventure and mystery. You used to like to go riding. Remember horses? You even took me fishing once. When father was alive, you were quite a nice fellow."

"When your father was alive, he attended to his duty."

"In a manner of speaking, Uncle. My father, though beset by uncontrollable and inappropriate affection for small girls, was in most respects a very good king. He had no convictions to confuse him. He was impressed by ritual and dedicated to traditions. He complied with them well, but then he had certain talents I do not."

"Jickie!"

"It's true, Uncle. Father was quite open with me. As I had four older brothers, he felt free to tell me things he would never have told the heirs. First, he had taught himself not to care about anything but sensation. Then he taught himself to sleep while sitting bolt upright, eyes wide open. He could do this either while upon the throne or upon horseback, and he was invariably asleep while you and the others read your interminable accounts of continuing destruction. He told me this, enjoying his cleverness, without realizing the effect it had on me. Of course, he never thought I'd ascend the throne.

"Unfortunately, I lack his simplicity. My existence is entirely symbolic, yet I am expected to behave as though my thoughts and acts had significance. My office could be filled by an android. Indeed, an android would do my job far better. It could be programmed, as my father was. It could smile gently and pay no attention to the destruction going on around it."

"I thought when Leelson Famber found you—"

"You paid Famber to bring me back!" the king snarled. "You paid him!"

The Prime Minister shook his head, confused at the vehemence of this reaction. "Actually, no, Jickie, we didn't. We were worried about you! We paid Fastiga a fee to ascertain what had happened to you. They assigned him to the task, that's all."

"Ah." The Lost King turned on his minister with an expression both wild and strange. "You didn't mention that when I returned. Nor since, come to that."

"You never asked," said the Prime Minister, astonished into a loss of aplomb. "You never asked, Jickie."

The king turned back to the window, unable to hide his emotions: anxiety, rage, regret, what? All those Fambers, even now being disposed of! Well, few enough of them compared with the population of a planet. And were they not foremost among Firsters? And were not Firsters his enemies, now and forever?

The window beside him reflected his pale face, a ghostly image superimposed over the distant trees. That long Lostrel nose. That triangular Lostrel mouth. The very face of dynasty hiding the person of . . . whom?

Who had he been, there on beautiful Elitha? Who might he have become? Famber the Fastigat hadn't actually forced him to return. Once found, however, he had thought . . . Or had he thought?

"Why?" asked the Prime Minister in a concerned voice. "What difference does it make who hired him, or for what?"

After a moment the Lost King shrugged. "None, really. The free agent is as culpable as the director of that agent. That's Kamir law, isn't it?"

"Yes. With certain reservations. What have you done?"

The king turned, a vague and rather nasty smile on his face. "Nothing, Prime Minister. Nothing that is not entirely traditional for kings."

Shortly after that, in the office of the Procurator, Snark the shadow stood immobile against the wall, alert to any need expressed or unexpressed on the part of the Procurator's guests.

There were three of them, ponderous all, two Fastigats and a non-Fastiga woman, counselors to Alliance Prime, heavy with the weight of years and experience, heavy with cynicism and doubt, heavy, at the moment, with anger and despair.

"Two more worlds," said the oldest of them, a gnarled tree of a man. So Snark thought of him, Twisted-tree. Shadows were not introduced, and the three knew each other well enough to have needed no introductions among themselves. In the absence of other names, Snark labeled the two men Twisted-tree and Thunder-man. The woman's name she knew: Chief Counselor to Prime for Planetary Management Poracious Luv.

Thunder-man rumbled, "The latest communiqué came just this morning. Two more worlds wiped clean in Hermes Sector, yes."

"Survivors?" asked Poracious Luv.

"We're not looking for any. Except as they may show up on the monitors."

"Weren't there survivors last time?" she asked.

The Procurator murmured, "No proven survivors. Some children were found."

"Didn't they say?"

"I don't know. I don't think I ever read the report." The Procurator waved his hand impatiently. What had happened last time really wasn't germane. "What's being done?" he demanded.

Thunder-man went on. "Last time, a century ago, there was only one populated planet in Hermes Sector, Dinadh. There were also a few outposts and colonization teams. This time there are four systems containing a dozen worlds, most of which have been homo-normed to Class D, basic treefarm grass-pasture biome, with all native life eliminated except for a few tough but relatively unimportant species. Yes."

"And?"

"And Dinadh, the single world of its own system, doesn't want to be involved. They've refused intervention. The other populated systems are cooperating in what we call an evacuation. It's purely symbolic. We can't really evacuate the population; we couldn't even keep up with the birth rate. We're giving first priority to people who have friends here in Prime. In addition to the symbolic gesture, we've actually removed advance teams from several worlds." Thunder-man referred to his notes. "From planet Mandalay and the first moon of Cabal in Jerome's system; and from a planet in Goan's system, Perdur Alas."

"Where the hell will you put evacuees?" asked the Procurator in a whisper. "Every habitable world is full to the shores!"

"There's a used-up planet a bit nearer in, across the space time border in Janivant Sector, yes. Borthal's World. The original population on Borthal's colonied out a couple of generations back, shortly before it hit crit-popple and ah . . . perished."

"Crit-popple?" Poracious Luv murmured, her lips quirking.

The Procurator cleared his throat. "Some of the younger administrators have their own jargon, Madam Luv. We used to say things like, 'absolute carrying capacity,' or 'sanity limitation.' Lately it's become critical population level, crit-popple."

Thunder-man went on: "As I was saying, there's no flora or fauna left on Borthal's, but we've seeded the seas with resistant photocellulars for oxygen production, and we're stockpiling foodstuffs there now. Practically speaking, there won't be that many evacuees. Most of them will be children, and we can only get a few tens of thousands off."

The three visitors sat in gloomy silence.

Poracious Luv murmured, "How long is the Alliance going to go on promising a continually expanding frontier?"

"Don't talk dirty," boomed Twisted-tree. "You talk like that, somebody'll hear you."

"Somebody's already heard me," she snorted. "The Celosians don't care if I talk population limitation for the Pooacks. The Pooacks don't care if I talk population limitation for the Schrinbergians. So long as I don't mean them, they don't care. Sometimes, late at night, I have these dreams about all the animals. . . ."

"Animals?" asked the Procurator. "What animals?"

"All of them. The ones in pattern storage. In the files. Whales. Elephants. Grampuses. Winged things, some of them. I have these dreams. The souls of all the animals are speaking to me, condemning mankind as the greatest beast of the field. They make a kind of hollow roar, like the sound of the sea."

"This is no time to be fanciful!" Twisted-tree announced. "Besides, I find your words offensive. Man is not an animal."

She made a rude gesture. "You Firsters have been top-aheap ever since you came up with that 'universe made for man' claptrap."

Twisted-tree snarled, "Fastigats are not Firsters, madam, any more than kings are commoners. As kings and commoners may share pride of identity while being otherwise unlike, so we and Firsters share certain opinions. Neither they nor we are the first to have those opinions, and the Firsters are saying no more than we have always said. The universe was made for man."

The Procurator said, "Firsters are oversimplifying, of course. 'Humanity first' leaves certain refinements unaccounted for. Still, their numbers are growing."

The big woman grumbled, "They're making their politics senseable, that's why. Have you seen their sensurrounds?"

The Procurator shook his head, making a little moue of distaste.

She went on: "They portray exciting journeys to newly homo-normed planets where the senser lives happily ever after with no shortages, lots of room, plenty of food, and a couple of dozen live, healthy children."

The Procurator laughed knowingly. "Sensing is believing!"

Poracious Luv gave him an indignant look. "Once they've sensed the Firster version, they don't want to hear anything about your so-called refinements. They don't want to know the ordinary Firster has about as much chance of going to the frontier as he has of surviving once his world hits—what did you call it?—crit-popple? And, of course, you Fastigats may continue in your ivory-tower opinions because it won't happen here."

Twisted-tree flushed slightly. Thunder-man looked offended. The Procurator, through long practice, ignored what she had said. Alliance Central wasn't officially a "world." It was a government. Freedom-of-procreation laws that applied to Alliance worlds could not apply here. The administration would not remain in power if Alliance Central ever hit crit-popple. There were ways to assure that it did not. Required emigration for larger families. Shadowhood for overactive males. A little something in the water supply. A little something else in the air.

Poracious Luv's hand twitched toward her cup. Snark moved like invisible lightning, taking away the used cup, filling a clean one, putting it where the avid hand could fall upon it. Poracious drew in the hot fragrant brew as though breathing it, half emptying the cup. It was time to change the subject.

"Is there any news from Dinadh?" she asked.

"Lutha Tallstaff is on her way there now," said the Procurator. "It will be some time before we hear anything from there. How about the recorders we had hidden all through Hermes Sector? Did they function properly? Did we get anything useful?"

Twisted-tree growled, "They functioned well, yes. We have excellent records of thousands of colonists going about their business. Then we get deterioration of the audio segment, then brief exclamations, drawn breaths, yes. We see people staring fearfully around themselves. Then we see a gray veil, and the next moment we have good views of a planet without human life."

"That quickly?"

"More quickly than I can tell it. Subsequently, the recorders stop functioning."

Twisted-tree said gloomily, "They stopped functioning on Mandalay and Jerome's System, yes."

Silence once more except for the almost surreptitious inhalation of tea.

After a time the Procurator offered, "If they are taking the people first, perhaps some kind of device implanted *in* the people themselves would give us useful information."

"Political suicide," hissed Poracious. "If it were ever found out we'd used workers or colonists . . ."

"What if they were volunteers?" asked the Procurator.

The woman shook her head. "Even so. There are populated worlds out there, worlds with representation here at Prime. Those representatives are already giving us hell because we didn't start evacuation the minute we knew the Ularians were back. Never mind that it's impossible to evacuate a settled world. We take off a thousand; the same day they have a thousand and ten babies! They don't want to hear we can't do it, even though that's what we've told them right along. Blind faith in somebody stepping in to fix things eliminates a lot of emotional stress, so blind faith is what most people have!

"Now that they're facing the fact nobody can fix things, they're on the screaming prod; and if they found out we'd put recorders into people we knew would be taken, they'd have us for breakfast, broiled."

"But we need information," the Procurator murmured.

"Well, we can't use colonists." Her eyes came to rest on Snark, seeming to see her through her garb, through her shadowhood. Poracious

Luv's gaze went past Snark, on to the several other shadows in the room, resting briefly on each. "Not colonists, Procurator. But . . ."

His eyes followed hers. "Shadows?" he asked in a hushed voice. "You mean shadows?"

"Why not?"

"Why not? Because it denies the first right of man! As shadows, they can live part of their lives normally. But on a frontier world . . ."

"How do we know they wouldn't be better off?" Poracious asked in a silky tone. "We don't know what the Ularians do with them. Maybe they transport them to other, more suitable worlds."

"Tchah," he snorted.

"We could always claim we believed so, and who could prove we didn't?" asked Thunder-man. "Besides, in a time of war, there have to be sacrifices. Whom would you rather sacrifice?"

"The first rule of governance is never to choose who to sacrifice," snarled the Procurator. "Or, at least, never to be seen to choose. Death and dismemberment must always be . . . inadvertent. Everybody's fault or nobody's fault!"

"What are you suggesting?" Thunder-man asked the woman, ignoring the Procurator's words. "Replacing a real preliminary team with one made up of shadows?"

Poracious Luv nodded thoughtfully. "Exactly. If I heard you correctly, we took preliminary teams off three worlds. One of them was Perdur something?"

He glanced at his notes. "Perdur Alas," he confirmed.

Twisted-tree drummed his fingertips on his chair arm, scanning his databoard. "The team there was only a few hundred strong. How many shadows are there?"

"I'm sure there will be enough," said Poracious significantly. "By the time we get them ready to go."

The Procurator folded his hands in his lap and stared at his guests. Was he capable of this? He murmured, "You'll recall we use simulation booths to control the shadows, to vent their hostility. The booths are a modified form of sensurround. Shadows are accustomed to the satisfaction they get in the booths. There are no simul booths on Perdur Alas."

"No, and you can't put any there," said Poracious. "The Firsters would have a fit."

The Procurator shook his head slowly, considering.

"There aren't that many Firsters," said Twisted-tree.

"There are altogether too many," whispered the Procurator. It was true. They had an influence that was out of all proportion to their numbers, and those numbers were growing.

Thunder-man said, "Firsters have enough trouble accepting sensurround. They'd have a fit if they knew about simul booths."

Poracious nodded. "You're right. We may get away with sending shadows, but we'd never get away with the other. Someone would talk. Some shipping coordinator or installation tech."

"Then you're talking about deep conditioning," the Procurator objected. "The very conditioning the shadows have rejected!"

"How much can be accomplished with deep conditioning?" asked Poracious. "Can we make anything much of them?"

The Procurator mused, half aloud. "Look around you, madam! Half the people on the streets have been conditioned to some degree, though they've done it voluntarily. Most professionals are educated at least partly through deep conditioning. The only difference between them and the shadows is that they've asked for it and the shadows have vehemently rejected it."

"Forget that for the moment," she urged. "Just tell me what can be realistically expected."

He mused. "We can't make a master mathematician out of a discalculic, but we can enormously multiply natural aptitudes. It has always been interesting to me that many shadows are very bright. We could assign them jobs in accordance with their aptitudes."

"Advance teams are mostly bio-generalists anyhow," muttered Thunder-man.

"But it's got to look natural, and the group must include women," said Poracious. "I suppose there are women shadows."

"There are." The Procurator sighed.

"You don't like the idea?" she asked.

"It may seem foolish to worry about a few lives, about depriving people of their guaranteed human rights, or about the appearance of impropriety when we're threatened with extinction, but I am sworn to uphold the rights of man," protested the Procurator, somewhat stiffly. "I can't just—"

"It seems to me the rights of man include the right to go on living," growled Twisted-tree. "If we're wiped out, it won't matter what we do now, yes? To protect ourselves, we need information, and this is one way, maybe the only way, to get it!"

"We could be open about it," the Procurator said plaintively. "People would understand. . . ."

"No, they wouldn't." Twisted-tree grinned without humor. "They'd jump at any excuse to depose us, because that's what people do. Yes. During a crisis, people pull together; they're afraid rocking the boat will dump them over the side, but still, crises make people fearful, which makes them angry, which makes them hostile. When the crisis is over, the opposition decides to see what was done that might be called illegal. Yes. Then executions happen. Exile happens. If we survive this, it should not be to face such a fate! Therefore, we do whatever offers the slightest hope, but we protect appearances while we do it, yes."

"He's right," mused Poracious. "Later, when survival is assured, the little opposition scholars will start digging. Make sure there are no records of this, Procurator. And damn few recollections!"

The Procurator sighed. It was true. What they said was indisputably true. "Shadows, then. On Perdur Alas, as soon as we possibly can."

"Strip off your shadow suit," said the lock in its metallic, impersonal voice.

Shadow stripped.

"Place your hands in the receptacles."

Shadow placed.

"Bend your head forward to make contact with the plate."

Shadow bent.

Light, sounds, movement. Snarkey stood back from the plate, shaking her head as she always did, bellowing with rage as she always did, though this time with more reason.

"Leave the cubicle," said the voice, opening the door behind her, opposite the one she'd come in by.

"Goddamn bastards," screamed Snark, leaping from the cubicle, turning to shake her fist at it.

Behind her someone laughed, and she grew abruptly cold as she turned and glared.

"The mad howler back once again," said Willit. "Good day, old Snarkey-shad."

"I nominate you," growled Snark with a toothy smile.

Willit laughed, uncertainly. Snark went on smiling viciously as the laugh dwindled.

"Whaddayou mean, you nominate me?"

"The name Ularians mean anything to you, shad?" Snark sneered.

"Monsters," said a voice from a corner. "From outer space." The speaker giggled.

"No game?" muttered Willit disbelievingly. "Monsters?"

"Monsters," said Snark. "And they wiped out most of the frontier."

"That's history," said Willit doubtfully.

"That's today, buttface. They're back. And the bureaucrats want to find out more about them. So they're gonna put people on a frontier planet, people with chips in 'em, so the skinsuits can tell what happens to the people when the Ularians eat 'em or blow 'em to forever. And guess who, shitheads?"

Silence. Snark glared at them with satisfaction. That had shut the crawlers up. She screwed up her mouth and yowled, "I nominate all of you."

"Who the fuck's gonna listen to you naming anybody," muttered Willit. "Ma Ugly herself! Who're you, the Procurator all of a sudden?"

Snarkey laughed. "Who you think they're goin' to take? They need a few hundred men and women. How many of us you think there are down here?"

"I never counted." Willit, suddenly apprehensive.

Snark didn't answer. Let the bastards stew. Look at 'em. Every one of 'em trying to think up reasons it wouldn't be him or her.

The hell it wouldn't.

In the simul booth, Snark lay snug, the flexible carapace enclosing her, the multiple loops and feedbacks pulsing gently. This time, this one time, she hadn't come in with murder in mind. This time, this one time, she hadn't come in with anything in mind at all except running away, the way she used to run away when she was little. Sometimes she thought her whole life had been running away from things or places or people to other things or places, and it was one of these she dreamed of now, maybe the best place ever, from a long time ago, somewhere far.

There was grass. The grass was important, the smell of it and the feel of it. There were thickly needled evergreen trees and shrubs growing close and tight along a wall. There was an earthen half tunnel burrowing beneath the scratchy branches, a tunnel that could be hidden behind her, and in the heart of the shrubbery lay a nest thickly carpeted with dried needles and soft ferns where a bit of film stuff was wrapped around a dirty old blanket to keep it dry. She could lie wrapped in the blanket with the film stuff outside that, warm and dry no matter if it rained, peering through a tiny hole in the leaves almost like looking through a telescope. Out there the big stone building loomed over the fields and garden plots and barns, and she could watch what went on: the young ones doing their work, the grown ones walking among them, smiling their dangerous smiles. They had their hands hidden in their pockets, holding weapons, just waiting until one of the kids did something wrong, the way Snark always did something wrong.

The journey always started here, in this hidden place, with her looking out. The people out there might even be looking for her, calling her name, but they couldn't find her. Even if they told the kids to find her, they couldn't. Long delirious moments would go by, with Snark relishing her safety, feeling the warmth around her, the contentment. Her eyes would close, finally, shutting out the world, the people, the stone house. Her breathing would slow. Her heart would slow, too, into quiet, purposeful *bump, bump, bump*. Then even that noise would fade and she would be . . . elsewhere.

To begin with, she was always on a moor. That's where the journey started. It didn't matter how she got there; the dream didn't bother with that. She was simply there, on an almost flat highland covered with low, scrubby-scratchy bushes between aisles of softer bracken that were interrupted by shallow, moss-surrounded peat-dark ponds. When she thought about the place at all, she thought perhaps it was a place she had been once, a place she had seen, smelled, walked in. Maybe it was the place she'd been born to, where her own people were. She never thought she'd made it up. It was too real for that.

Sometimes she found herself standing there almost naked. Other times she had stout boots and a rain cape with a hood that covered her, and when dressed like this, she could lie well hidden on the moor itself, her body shadowed by the brushy growths or obscured by the bracken. Still, if she did that—and sometimes it seemed someone told her it would be all right if she did—she knew she could be tracked eventually. They could smell her. They could come whistling through the evening air, seeking anything warm-blooded, calling in those tempting voices that always seemed to know her name. No. Even though the moor was safe in comparison to most other places, it wasn't safe enough.

So she never gave in to the relief she felt when she arrived. Relief was only a momentary feeling, not enough by itself. She had to cross the moor, had to dodge along the folds in the ground, following the bracken aisles, keeping her feet out of the ponds, staying as dry as possible as she worked her way toward the horizon, where the world ended against a gray span of featureless sky. Later it might change to blue or even violet, it might glow with sunset or darken to lapis night, but when she arrived, when she crossed the moor, it was always the same: gray and clear, without depth or measure.

At a certain point on her journey she would hear the sea. A murmur only, a soft susurrus against the rattle of the bracken and the squodge of her footsteps. The whisper would grow louder, though never really loud, until she reached the edge where the world fell away in rooty edges above cliffs of gnarl, where the seabirds made screaming dizzy clouds beneath her as they wheeled wildly out, spiraling from their precipice perches over the hammered surface of the sea.

Then panic came, always. Even if she wasn't closely pursued in the dream, even if she had lots of time to walk slowly along the sheer drop, noticing the sparkle of the waters and the whirling gyre of the birds, panic always overcame her. She wouldn't find the right place! It would be better to jump now, jump before they caught up with her. Otherwise they might catch her, and that would be worse. Every time she came here she had to fight down the urge to jump, shut it out, stop thinking about it. She had to turn to her left to walk as close to the edge as possible, eyes hunting for landmarks, putting her feet carefully onto stone and pebbly places, leaving no track to be seen, knowing all the time that her smell remained, floating on the air, hanging there for the hunters to find!

Eventually, long after she'd become convinced she had missed it, she came to the curiously twisted rock looming at the edge of the cliff. It was always there, alongside a shrubby tree with an outflung trunk.

Then she had to be agile and quick. Once, long ago, someone had carried her. Then, she'd locked her arms around someone's neck and that someone had made the jump. Now she was old enough to jump by herself, out from the edge of the cliff, catching the protruding trunk, holding on tightly as it sagged below the level of the rim, and then . . . then she had to grasp the rooty growth that extended from the cliff face and pull herself in!

In was through the narrow entry of a cave, a little sandy-floored crevice not much bigger than two or three Snarks, where the floor was softened with dried bracken and flat stones lay piled near the opening. The stones were for stacking in the entrance until only tiny airholes remained. Soft animal skins waited to be pulled around her. Someone . . . someone had given her the skins, but she could not remember who. It didn't matter. When she was curled there, wrapped there, she was warm and completely safe. No one, not even the trackers, could find her there.

From her position of warm safety, she sometimes heard them coming, their voices keening over the sound of the waters, louder and louder until they were wailing into the ocean wind from just above the place where she lay. They had smelled her as far as the edge, but they smelled her no more. She had flown away like a seabird. She had vanished. Her hole was not visible from above. When the stones were stacked in the opening, it was not visible from the sea below or from the gulf of air. So far as the flying things knew, she was gone.

The spray blew gently into her face. The sound of the seabirds came softly to her ears. At night she could see the stars through the hole in the stone. Sometimes it was enough merely to be there, merely to be safe, and it was tempting to lie there, not eating, not drinking, letting life go away somewhere else, letting herself wither into nothing, quietly, contentedly, safe. Being dead was safer yet, she knew that, but life still pulled at her. Besides, the cave supported life. At the back of the crevice, water leaked down onto a hollowed stone beside a tight chest full of hard bread and dried fruit and strips of smoked meat. She could stay in safety for days and days at a time, without dying. It was a good place.

Later, after she was . . . found, picked up by . . . whoever it had been; later, after she was somewhere else, after she was at the stone house with the wall; later, when she burrowed into the shrubbery to be safe, to be hidden, it was the moor she dreamed of. Rather than go back to the stone house, sometimes she stayed in the dream for a very long time. It didn't matter how long she stayed. When she came back eventually, they still had to feed her, even if they didn't want to. Any child who was sent to the stone house, they had to take care of. They had to feed her. They weren't allowed to kill her.

That still left a lot of stuff they could do if they felt like it, if you broke the rules, if they caught you. It was always Snark who got caught, even when it wasn't Snark who'd done it. When a matron asked who did it, who bloodied the nose, who ripped the shirt, who broke the chair, somebody always giggled and said, the Snark did it. The Snark hit me. The Snark pushed me. The Snark bit me and bloodied my nose. Always when she had and often when she hadn't.

So she figured she might as well. If they were going to say she did, she might as well. And she might as well do it right, once and for all. Might as well use something sharp or heavy, so afterward they couldn't point fingers, couldn't name names, couldn't go running to the older ones yelling Snark, Snark did it.

In the simul booth, she groaned, heaved, grew red with fury at her persecutors.

Peace, whispered the booth. *It's all right. You don't need to kill anyone. Don't need to hit anyone, hurt anyone, bloody anyone. Peace. No one can find you here. You're safe here. It's better here than where you were before.* . . .

Here. Here at the edge of the cliff it was. Everywhere else the two feelings were all mixed up. Scared-hate. Threat-anger. Fear-rage. She couldn't separate them. They were one feeling. What she feared she hated, what she hated she would kill. . . .

Peace, whispered the booth.

If she could just kill whatever-it-was, whoever-it-was, so it would stay dead forever. Then, then . . .

Peace, the booth insisted.

Peace. See the jar your mother put there, in the niche. See the pictures on it. There is Father Endless and Mother Darkness. There are the peacemakers, the peace bringers. Here, with them watching over you, you needn't kill or harass or bother. Here, with them watching over you, you are safe.

Eventually, the booth had its way. Snark quit fighting and slept. There in the simul booth, safe in the carapace, she slept, dreaming she was in the shrubbery at the sanctuary, wrapped in her old blanket, sleeping. And in that dreamed sleep, she dreamed she was in the even safer place at the edge of the moors. Sleep within sleep within sleep, dream within dream, she dreamed of becoming safer and safer still.

CHAPTER 3

Lutha, Leely, and Trompe arrived upon Dinadh at our only port, Simidi-ala (the Separated Place), which stands in an area of desolate coastland beside Dinadh's only sea. This is the one place on Dinadh where there are garages for vehicles, where complicated things brought from off-planet may be repaired, where foreign wares may be housed. The stretch of coastline including the neighboring bay is called Tasimi-na-Dinadh, that is, the Edge of Dinadh, and visitors are told that when they came "across the Edge" and "through the Separation," they have left behind them, symbolically at least, those things eschewed by Dinadh.

What things are eschewed by Dinadh? All those things that might draw us nearer other worlds. All those things that might make others look at us more closely, that might cause curiosity or speculation. These we eschew in favor of duty, gravity, privacy, knowing our place. Also beauty and order and reverence for . . . our chosen ways.

Lutha and Trompe were informed of this, there at Simidi-ala. Lutha looked over the head of her sleeping child as the latest of several informants departed, fretting over the time already spent in fruitless waiting. It is Dinadh's way to make people wait and spend time and fret a little. Let them decide at first whether they wish to come to Dinadh at all. Let them think long about spending all those years with us. If they cannot stand a little frustration in Simidi-ala, they will never stand a winter in a hive!

"Why do people keep coming by and looking at us and then going away again?" Trompe demanded.

"You're the empath," Lutha breathed. "You figure it out!"

"They're curious about us," he said. "About why we're here. And they're very curious about Leely." He sighed and rolled his head onto his shoulders, trying to ease aching muscles. He blinked sleepily and sat up straighter. Someone was coming.

The approaching Dinadhi was dressed as we all are, as Lutha and Trompe and Leely themselves were, in robes of fine, creamy cotton, high shoes woven of thin leather strips and soled with the durable, flexible wood of the paran tree, and over all a robe of soft leather—in summer, thin and light; in winter, heavier, with the wool still on—with bright patterns painted down the front and around the cuffs of the sleeves. These patterns are one's own, painted by the wearer, so even veiled women may be identified by their specific patterns. I have learned from Lutha and Snark what women wear on other planets, frilly thises and lacy thats, but we have no stockings, no intimate undergarments. Lutha tells me that all the time she spent on Dinadh she felt she was walking around in her night clothing. I told her we do not wear night clothing. Wool and leather we have. Cotton we have. That is all that we have.

Lutha said they were surprised to find our garments exceptionally comfortable. Even Leely objected to them less than he did to his ordinary wear. They had managed to keep him dressed during most of the trip out.

"Sorry to have kept you waiting," murmured the official, seating himself beside them and setting his feet squarely together. "There've been several someones here looking for you, and when you arrived, we thought it wise to have a small conference and share our perceptions of the matter."

"Looking for me?" asked Trompe, sitting up straighter and opening his eyes wide.

The official shook his balding head and stroked his beard from the point where it was gathered into a carved bone ring below his chin, down the glossy tassel to his waist. All our men who work at the port wear their beards like that so we will know who they are, so we will pray for them, exposed as they are, to the influences of outsiders.

The official said, "Two were here yesterday, looking for the wife of Leelson Famber, and Leelson Famber's children. They said they came to seek peace and ultimate truth upon Dinadh and wished to meet with Leelson Famber's family while they were here."

"While they were here seeking truth," said Trompe heavily.

"Who?" asked Lutha, suddenly wide-awake. "And what do you mean, children?" She indicated her sleeping son. "To my knowledge, this is the only child Leelson ever fathered."

The official smiled again. "We leasehold officers are accustomed to applicants of many kinds and degrees of fear or fervor, gush or melancholy. The two I speak of are of another stripe. Though Mitigan of Asenagi and Chur Durwen of Collis make proper application for right of residence, neither their desire for sanctuary nor their wish to learn from the songfathers rings true. Instead of a manner either fervid or meditative, both men display an attitude of aplomb, of alert disinterest, of customary unsurprise."

Trompe slitted his eyes.

The official shrugged. "We are parochial, but we are not naive. To our eyes, they have the appearance of mercenaries."

"What did you tell them?" demanded Trompe.

The official smiled. "Nothing except that the wife of Leelson Famber was not here. That no children of Leelson Famber were on Dinadh. As was true at the time."

"Did they accept that?"

"No. They wanted to see our records."

Trompe snorted.

The official smiled. "As you are no doubt aware, there are no such things on Dinadh. We don't record things. We remember them. We don't have files or archives or libraries, we have rememberers. We don't have maps, we have guides. We don't write books, we tell tales. We don't even have money, as you understand money. The only reason we allow outlanders on the planet at all is to get hard currency credit for off-planet purchases."

"Did you remember anything for them?" Lutha asked.

"Nothing. But neither did we discourage their remaining upon Dinadh. Hundred-year leases do not grow on trees."

"I don't suppose you found out what they're really here for. Or where they're from?"

"We watched them, we listened, trying to find out why they were really here, but they spoke a language we have no record of. A secret language, our translators think. An assassin's tongue."

"So, where are they now?" Trompe demanded.

"Across the port. In one of the other hives. We thought we'd let you get on your way before we send them anywhere else."

Lutha sighed.

Trompe said, "How much will you charge to tell them nothing?"

The official shook his head chidingly. "We don't play games of that sort, Outlander Paggas. That leads to a pattern of darkness, and we try to avoid such. The only reason for our mentioning these people is that we thought you might know of them, know who they are, why they are here. Seemingly, you do not, so they will not be allowed to infringe upon your privacy—or, I should say, the privacy of Bernesohn Famber, whose lease has still two standard years to run."

"You'll send them away?"

"They have the same privilege as any other applicant. If they wish to buy a lease, they may buy one. The only cells available at the moment are in hives some distance from Cochim-Mahn, where Bernesohn Famber dwelt among us."

"You're saying we won't encounter them."

"I'm saying it would be extremely unlikely. Now, your other visitor presents a somewhat different situation."

"Other visitor?" Lutha raised her brows.

"Thosby Anent. Supposedly he is a broker in craft items, of which Dinadh creates a small array. He pretends to be a broker, and we pretend to believe him. He is actually a spy for the Alliance, and he was here yesterday, asking for you."

"But we are here for the Alliance," Lutha erupted, spontaneously and unthinkingly.

The Dinadhi beamed at her. "Of course you are. How nice of you to admit it. It relieves us of the burden of fiction! Old Anent is harmless, but I may not force him on you. Will you see him?"

Trompe shrugged assent.

"Rest here. I'll send him along, and then the vehicle manager to start you on your way."

"And your name, sir?" Trompe asked.

"Merely a humble patterner, doing his duty." He went away, leaving Trompe and Lutha to stare at one another, and then at the elderly man making his way across the floor toward them. He was somewhat gray and dried-out looking, with pale watery eyes of so light a blue they seemed almost white, when they could be seen through the wreath of smoke around his head.

"Thosby Anent," he murmured, taking the pipe from his mouth and peering over his shoulder even as he cupped his hand beside his lips, a perfect parody of conspiracy. "Covert agent of Alliance Prime, at your service."

"What do you mean, covert agent?" asked Lutha. "Why would the Alliance have a covert agent here?"

"Why, why," he stuttered, "to receive information. To forward it to Alliance Prime. They sent me because there's some conspiracy here. Something going on. They needed someone of my experience. I knew you must have been sent to . . ." He made an inclusive gesture.

"I see," said Trompe fretfully, pinching the flesh between his eyes into a ridge as he felt for what was actually going on inside the oldster's mind. He seemed perfectly sincere, feeling a little outraged dignity, a little pomposity. A minor functionary living on dreams of glory. "How did you know we'd been sent to . . . ?" He aped the other's inclusive gesture.

"The ship," the man whispered. "It was an official ship."

As it had been, without question. Well. Trompe bowed formally. "Thank you for your offer. If we learn anything at all, we will bring it directly to you."

"I thank you sir. I will keep my, ah . . . *network* in readiness. Should you, by any chance, happen upon something urgent, the code word is *vigilance.*" He pursed his lips and nodded rapidly to himself several times. *"Vigilance."*

"I see," said Lutha, trying to keep from laughing.

Leely chose that moment to stroke her face and mutter his customary polysyllable.

"So this is the young man," Thosby said, peering at Leely like a squirrel peering at a nut, as though wondering where to begin nibbling. "They were speaking of him in the corridor. So this is he."

"He is," said Lutha. "And we've come a long way, and we're tired. If you gentlemen will excuse us." She stood up and took Leely away with her to what was called on Dinadh the female privacy facility.

Trompe bid Thosby Anent farewell, though it took several more conspiratorial exchanges to do so. As Thosby went the vehicle man arrived.

"Are you the last one we have to deal with?" demanded Trompe in a weary voice.

"The last person here at the port, yes," the man replied. "I am about to rent you a vehicle at an exorbitant price, and sell you a guidebook, also quite expensive, by which means you may reach the hive where Bernesohn Famber had—or, I should say, has—a lease on a certain number of cells. On Dinadh, leases survive the lessees. Kin may claim them as inheritance and may sell the remaining rights, with our approval, of course. So, Famber's place is still there, undisturbed, his belongings as they were the day he left, in the hive of Cochim-Mahn, where the songfather has been told to expect you."

"How long a journey to Cochim-Mahn?"

"It will take you several days. There are hostels along the way."

"It seems a long time. Why can't we fly?"

"Flight is permitted only in certain, well-defined cases of emergency."

"And why is that?" asked Trompe.

The vehicle man shrugged. "Have you seen persons sitting at their ease in the afternoon, drinking, perhaps, or talking with one another, when an insect comes suddenly buzzing and darting about their faces? Have you seen how they slap at it, wave it away, how it plagues them? Or in the evening, beside the lamp, when one is reading, and a flapping thing comes to the light?"

Trompe nodded.

"So our mother world feels about unnatural flying things buzzing about her face."

"But she doesn't object to unnatural things crawling on her?" Trompe exploded.

"On her clothing," corrected the vehicle man. "We can all put up with a few tiny things crawling about in our clothing. So long as they do it quietly and do not bite!"

"Which pretty well put us in our place!" Trompe remarked to Lutha when she returned. "In effect, we're mites in the seams of Dinadh's garments. Harmless ones, of course."

Lutha went to one of the porelike openings in the outer wall and stood looking out. "Several of the female port workers came in to use the facilities while I was there. They were curious. Mostly about Leely."

"Trying to talk to him?"

"Just watching him. He did a portrait of one of them on the wall."

"In what medium, dare one ask?" He allowed himself a hint of distaste, hoping she would look at him, speak to him, Trompe, rather than to the air over his shoulder as she seemed always to do.

She ignored his tone. No Fastigat would use such a tone unless he were eager for argument, and she was not interested in argument. "In some pinky-colored dirt he found in a flowerpot in there. He peed in it to make mud."

Trompe turned away, frustrated. "They were impressed?"

"They seemed to be." She fell silent for a moment. They had been impressed. More than merely impressed. Awed, perhaps. "There was a great deal of discussion about Weaving Woman. . . ."

"A goddess, as I recall," he said distantly.

"A goddess, yes."

"One they feel rather guilty about," he said.

"Guilty?"

"Hmm. I note some who, when they speak of her, brood with a sort of self-reproach."

"Then you note more than I do. All I know about Weaving Woman indicates she's an indwelling spirit of art and craftsmanship. The women using the facilities spoke of Leely as her child."

"Which means?"

She shrugged. The women's concentration had been a little frightening, but she chose not to mention that. Instead she gestured vaguely. "From what I recall of the culture chips I reviewed on the way out, Weaving Woman is pattern, which probably includes portraiture and sculpture, portrayal of any and everything."

Trompe turned the idea around, seeing if it had any focus for him, then let it go with an impatient grunt. It was time to get moving. They had already wasted too much time.

At the garages below, the manager of vehicles gave them precise instructions. The vehicles were economical, but of low performance. They could not be driven off the roads, which the hives kept clear of overhanging foliage by cutting winter firewood along them. If visitors traveled without a guide, the route would be programmed into the vehicle before departure and could not be deviated from thereafter. The doors of the vehicle would be locked before they departed from Simidi-ala and would not unlock until they reached the first hostel. The same would apply between hostels. One did not get out of the vehicle between destinations.

"What if we have a mechanical breakdown?" Trompe asked.

"Press the alarm button in the vehicle and wait. The time will afford an excellent opportunity for meditation. Eventually someone will come to fetch you."

"We can't hike to the nearest village?"

"All worlds have their threats. We make rules to protect visitors from the threats present on Dinadh. Outside the vehicle, you might be injured, or even killed. Then your world would bring a complaint against our world. And our world would have to defend the complaint before the high Alliance courts. We would have to hire experts qualified to present cases before that court. We are a poor people. We cannot afford the expenses of litigation."

Trompe muttered about this exchange to Lutha, concluding, "So much for exploration! Even though the route is programmed in, the vehicles aren't automatic, oddly enough. Evidently we can stop to rest or admire the view wherever we like, we just can't get out!"

"You rejected the idea of a guide?" she asked curiously.

He made a face. "The people here want us to hire a guide. They want it so firmly I feel we'll find out more without. During the trip we'll get a feel for the place, enough to be well acclimated when we arrive at Cochim-Mahn."

"So be it, then." She smiled, indicating acceptance. She would have preferred to go quickly and get the matter over with, but it didn't really matter. They could go without a guide.

The vehicle, though clumsy looking, was commodious, with both a sanitary compartment and a well-stocked food-service console. The food was off-planet, Lutha noted, prepackaged elsewhere and imported. Every meal they'd been served at the Edge had been off-planet food. Which made one wonder if planetary food was tasty enough for off-worlders. Or if there was enough of it. Of course, at the price they had paid to rent the vehicle, they could have been fed on ambrosia with enough left over to pay a year's expenses on Central!

"Now if Leely will just leave his clothes on," Trompe remarked.

His slightly sarcastic tone reminded Lutha of Leelson. Though she understood it, it angered her nonetheless. Fastigats could always empathize, always understand, except with Leely. They had no idea how or why he felt as he did. They were offended, as though they had reached out and been rudely rebuffed. She bit back an angry response. If Leelson himself had felt frustration, then Trompe was certainly entitled to a similar feeling.

"Pity you have to be bothered with all this," she said, thinking it a pity she herself had to be.

He made an impatient gesture. "Sorry. This is my job after all. You really couldn't have managed alone."

"No," she said, mimicking his tone and surprised at the depth of her furious agreement. "I really could not have managed alone."

Though their destination was a considerable distance north, they had first to go eastward from the coast, up a series of switchbacks on the face of a more or less vertical cliff until they reached the level highland that we, who live here, call the skylands. At first they were relieved to have reached the level road, but soon they found they made no more progress than previously as they traveled first eastward, then westward, then eastward again between the deep gorges that interdigitated the skylands from either side.

"This is ridiculous," Trompe muttered, making yet another hundred-sixty-degree turn.

"Dinadh at one time had a great deal more water than it has now," remarked Lutha. "These canyons must have been cut by sizable rivers."

She peered down at the threadlike trickles glittering in the depths among clean-edged patches of green, letting her eyes move upward to the mesa tops, all of them like the one they were traversing, covered with low forest broken by occasional grassy glades.

"Trompe. Stop!"

He stopped obediently. "What?"

"Animals." They were approaching an open glade where a group of small, woolly, long-necked animals grazed under the watchful care of herdsmen. "What are they doing?"

"Eating grass," said Trompe. "Haven't you seen an animal before?"

"I never have. Oh, sensurround, of course, but not a real one. What are the herdsmen doing? Twirling those things?"

"Spindles. They're spinning thread from wool, or perhaps from wild cotton. It's in the chips I gave you."

She nodded as Trompe started the vehicle once more, as they went slowly by. The herdsmen had a stout little wain with shutters at either end and head-high sections of woven-mesh panel racked at its sides. As they passed the group Lutha waved, receiving only the barest of blank-faced nods in return.

"Was Dinadh this arid when the first settlers came?" Trompe asked as he maneuvered the vehicle along a road uncomfortably close to a sheer drop on one side. "Or did it change after?"

Lutha let her subconscious seek the information. "It was as it is now. The first Alliance scholars to visit the planet were told the Dinadhi had come from another world and they 'remembered' emerging onto this world from their previous one through a hole in the ground. It's not an unusual origin myth. Other cultures have similar ones."

"They were probably on one of the fabled 'lost ships,' " Trompe conjectured. "There've been enough of those to go around."

She shrugged. "There have been 'lost ships,' but this is the only unidentified colony. I looked it up before we left Central. Except for the population on Dinadh, the Alliance ethnologists have always been able to identify the planet of origin, and that's true even when populations have ended up far from their original destinations."

"But not here."

"According to the stuff the Procurator gave me. No one knows for sure how the Dinadhi got here."

"No missing ship with a Dinadhi-like society?"

"No record of one."

"No similar societies from which this could be an unrecorded off-shoot?"

"One theory had it they came from a frontier society beyond Hermes Sector. The world was called Vriat or Breadh; something like that. The colony on it disappeared."

"The Ularians?"

"Nobody knows what happened. They just disappeared, that's all."

"There have been a lot of Nantaskan-speaking worlds that colonied out. Arriving from any of them makes more sense than this hole-in-the-ground story."

She glanced at him sidewise. "There is a real site for the supposed emergence, Trompe. As a matter of fact, it's in a wide valley not many days' travel from Cochim-Mahn. Or so the maps say, at any rate."

"A sacred site, no doubt," he said flippantly.

"Oh, very sacred! It's the omphalos. Extra-special rites every third year, a Dinadh year being six hundred and a fraction days. Every third year they draw an additional day out of the omphalos, the navel of time. That doesn't quite do it, so every sixtieth year they have to pull two days. Tahs-uppi, the ceremony's called."

"Meaning what? You're further along with the language than I am."

She mused. "Tahs-uppi. Tasimi means the edge or the border. Well, actually it means 'our borders',' plural possessive. Tahs probably means something like end, or limit. There's a word . . . uppas, uppasim, up-pasimi." She fell silent.

"So?"

"I was trying to figure out the ending. It has something to do with selection, I think. Part of the litany of Weaving Woman gives her the name of K'loch mahn uppasimi. Selector of our patterns. Well, not quite that. Chooser, intrinsic."

"I don't quite get that."

"Well, in our language we wouldn't say the rain chooses to fall. It just naturally falls. Weaving Woman *is* pattern, she doesn't choose it."

"So the name means what? The end of pattern?"

"The crux, the fulfillment. That would fit. Every hundred standard years, more or less, they reach the fulfillment of the pattern, pull out an extra day or so, and start over."

"With feasting, I suppose. Processions."

"More likely fasting and prayer. Actually, I don't know. The chips you gave me merely mention Tahs-uppi and gave the date for the preceding one. When a ceremony is very holy, taboo, it's hard for an outsider to learn the details." She stared down into the abyss they were skirting. "The pattern is due to end fairly soon. Maybe we'll get a chance to ask about it."

"I wonder what would happen," Trompe mused, turning the vehicle away from the canyon and toward the forest, where the road disappeared around patches of thorny growths, "if they didn't find one."

"Find one what?" she asked, startled.

"An extra day. When they went to fish one out of the navel hole."

She laughed. "You're an idiot, you know, Trompe. What an idea." She chuckled, thinking about it, a kind of black joke on the Dinadhi. The high priest, or whoever, dipping into the omphalos with his what? His wand? His day hook? Slowly withdrawing it to the sound of drums and flutes, only to find it empty. No extra day. Gradually, as she thought on it and considered the implications, she stopped finding the idea at all funny.

Toward evening they arrived at the hostel, the first one between Simidi-ala and Cochim-Mahn.

"And not a moment too soon," Lutha muttered as she parked the vehicle and heard the doorlocks make a solid thunk as they disengaged. "I'm exhausted."

Leely was sitting up, looking around himself with some interest.

Lutha got out, sniffed the fragrant air, sighed, stretched, held out her arms to the boy, who came slowly into them, head turning as he tried to see everything at once.

They were at the top end of yet another of the endless canyons, its branches and ramifications receding into the distance: carved buttes, slender pillars and towers, stepped ziggurats of stone, vertical walls pocked with caves, some of them occupied by busy hive communities or by the lonely bulk of abandoned hives, all thrown into brilliantly colored contrasts of fire and shade by the level rays of the setting sun. Sound came softly from the canyons, voices and drums, the high shriek of a bone flute, the hissing rainsound of rattles.

"Evensong," Lutha said. "Farewell to Lady Day. And that, too, is about time."

"We're more tired than we should be," said Trompe as he slowly removed their belongings from the vehicle. "The trip wasn't that arduous."

She agreed with a weary brush at a lock of hair that dangled at her forehead. "Indeed, Trompe. We are scarce begun and I am so weary I can hardly see. What is it about this place?"

He considered the question soberly. "I think it's the fact that we have no sense of distance traveled toward our goal. It's been like a maze. One goes and goes, then comes a turn, and one goes back almost the way one came. It takes hundreds of lateral marks back and forth among these canyons before we make much progress toward the goal. I'm conscious of frustration in myself. I can certainly feel it in you."

"That's it," she said, almost relieved to have identified her feelings. "Trompe, you're right. It's all the same—mark after mark of thorn forest and herds of woolly beasts, then the road emerges onto an utterly astonishing prospect. We look out on marvel, complete with rising song and smoke from the occupied hives and mysterious silence from the abandoned ones—"

"More abandoned ones than I expected," he interjected.

"—then we turn back, almost the way we came; mark after mark of thorn forest once more, another astonishing prospect, then turn again, like a shuttle in a loom. Back and forth. Back and forth. After a time one's sense of astonishment wanes."

"But the landscape demands astonishment, nonetheless, so one is left feeling naughty to be so ungrateful." Trompe grinned wearily at her. "At least, that's how I felt! One more breathtaking view and I would gag. Especially considering we could have flown the distance in an hour or so."

She sagged under Leely's weight as the boy gripped her more tightly around the neck, murmuring his usual "Dananana," moistly in her ear.

"He's hungry," she said.

"How do you know?"

"I just know. Or perhaps I assume he is because I am. Let's go in and see what the menu offers."

What the Dziblom-nahro offered was a flavorful stew of grain and peppers, flat polygons of unleavened bread served with a dish of salted herbs and another of a fruity sweet-sour-hot sauce, plus a small helping of roasted meat, no doubt from the same woolly, deerlike creatures they had seen in flocks along their journey.

"Not bad," Trompe murmured.

"Should be quite acceptable," Lutha murmured in return. "It's the basic menu for human diets on most nonocean worlds. Grain. Vegetables. Fruit. A little meat. Evidently this is a nondairy cuisine. No milk. No cheese."

"The flocks we saw on our way here today had tiny udders between the front legs. Milk animals need more nourishment than animals raised for meat, wool, or hides, and Dinadh probably doesn't produce enough grain to feed animals." He leaned forward and poured another cupful of the beverage that accompanied their meal. "Water or water flavored with mashed dried fruit as a drink. There's probably no grain or fruit left over for fermented or distilled drinks, either. Definitely a subsistence diet, trembling always on the edge of famine."

"Which might explain the Dinadhi dependence upon their gods," she commented softly, casting a look across the empty room at the yawning young woman who had served them while politely averting her eyes. "They need to feel they have done all the right things to assure their continued well-being."

"You draw this conclusion from the language?"

"The use and frequency of religious words and phrases helps place the culture."

"How?"

Lutha made a little moue. "The precept is that consistent and frequent use of a limited lexicon, oral and gestural, denotes the presence of a rigorous sect, possibly one with a well-defined canon of positive and negative observances—"

"Thou-shalts and shalt-nots?"

"Right. Add to this adversarial language—"

"Adversarial?"

"Adversarial or exclusionary language—words that mean 'them,' as opposed to 'us.' I don't mean simple reference to identity. I mean trash words. Like the words the Firsters apply to non-Firsters—animal-lovers, ape-people, tree-worshipers, greenies. . . ."

He laughed. "Those are the mild ones."

"Well, you get the idea. Fearful people develop their religions as protective devices, ways to manipulate hostile environments, formulas for identifying and defeating their enemies. The more fearful people are, the more enemies they have, the more adversarial language they use. My race is proud; yours is uppity. My people are the elect; yours is damned. My religion is true; yours is false. I worship god; you're possessed by demons."

"Surely that's very common?"

"Of course it is! Only very secure people are able to think nonadversarially. As a linguist, I have to keep in mind that fearful people are dangerous. When backed into corners, they bite! Before I start translating some document, I need to know what words and phrases might be heard as corner-backers."

"So you look for trash words and adversarial and exclusionary language. How?"

She nodded thoughtfully. "If possible, you lay hands on transcriptions of meetings, observances of public holidays, special religious services, any session where the people aren't talking *to* outsiders but are talking about them. You run those records through a content analyzer looking for god words. You also want to know how manlike the god is. Fearful people prefer manlike gods, deified humans, or gods that take human shape or do human things, gods they can imagine being friends with, or asking for a favor."

"People don't go into battle shouting the name of the Ethical First Principle?"

"Not usually. Also, the god often resembles his followers in behavior and feelings. Angry people have angry gods and vindictive people have vindictive gods, and so forth."

Lutha indicated the serving woman who leaned against a doorpost, eyes half-closed. "When our serving woman spoke of the gods, however, she wasn't talking about deified humans. During our supper she mentioned Weaving Woman and Brother Corn and the Fruit Maidens and half a dozen other deities, none of them manlike, none of them adversarial. *But,* finally, when she left us to our dinner, she said, 'May the Gracious One hold us all in beauty,' and by using the word for 'us all,' she excluded the mentioned being."

"Meaning she wants the pattern to benefit her and her family and friends, but doesn't want it to benefit us?"

Lutha frowned. "No. The only creature specifically excluded was the other creature mentioned, the Gracious One. The language is adversarial by omission!"

He laughed. "Sorry, Lutha, but I don't get that."

"Listen. There are a dozen Dinadhi words for 'all,' or 'us all.' For example, there's a word that means us all, everything living in the universe. There's another word that means all us Dinadhi, and still another word that means all us humans here in this room. When you use an 'us all' word, if you mention anyone in particular in the same phrase, it means that person is excluded. You can say, 'Simidi-ala and *us all* Dinadhi are faithful worshipers,' and actually mean, 'Except for Simidi-ala, we on Dinadh are faithful worshipers.' Or you can say, 'Martha and *us all* were laughing at the jokes,' which actually means, 'We were all laughing except Martha, who has no sense of humor.' "

"If you use any word that means 'us all,' but mention someone by name, that person is excluded?"

"Right. If you want to include that person, you don't mention him, her, or it by name or you use the other set of words that just means 'all.' What our serving woman actually said was, 'May the Gracious One allow all other persons to continue in beauty.' "

"The implication being . . . ?"

"By the Great Org Gauphin, Trompe, I don't know! Either that the Gracious One is unbeautiful, or that the Gracious One can't appreciate beauty, or that the Gracious One is not concerned with beauty. How did she feel when she said it?"

"I wasn't paying attention," he said, slightly shamefaced.

Lutha shook her head. "Whatever it is, it doesn't concern us!"

"We're not the scapegoat, in other words."

"Right. And that's remarkable, Trompe. Outsiders are almost always suspect."

They rose from the table as the servitor bestirred herself to collect their dishes. Lutha gathered Leely into her arms and started for the porch outside the window where they had been sitting.

"Lady . . ." The woman spoke from behind them. "Are you going out?"

"I had thought it would be pleasant," Lutha replied in careful dialect. "Should I not do so?"

"If you go to enjoy the air, do not leave the porch. Stay behind the grille. Such is the proper pattern of dusk behavior."

Lutha bowed, thanking her, then murmured a translation for Trompe's benefit.

"This time I was paying attention. Her emotion had something to do with safety," he mused, when they were outside, looking through the grille into the clearing and past it to the thorn forest. "Or a taboo of some kind. One of those negative commandments you were talking about?"

"I have no idea. Suppose we sit awhile in these comfortable-looking chairs and enjoy the evening. I'm weary, but not sleepy yet."

"Can I take the boy? He looks very heavy."

"Leave him. He's all right, aren't you, Leely-baby? Of course he is, all snuggled down on Mommy's shoulder. Sit, Trompe. As the girl says, enjoy the air. One thing we will have to say about Dinadh; it has wonderful air."

They sat, breathing the resinous fragrance of day-warmed trees, the cool water-scented wind that came up from the canyons. The sky was pure lapis, not yet black, with several large planets pulsing in the last glow at the horizon. Empty planets, Lutha told herself. With a few abandoned mines. And beyond this single system, everything else wiped clean by the Ularians.

"Dana," whispered Leely, pointing with one chubby hand. "Danana."

"What is it?" whispered Trompe.

Lutha shook her head. She couldn't tell what it was. Something emerging from the forest: flowing draperies, melting mists. A wraith? A ghost? A creature oozing from among the trees into the clearing, seeming almost to glow in the dusk. Soon it was joined by others, half a dozen, ten, beings that lifted on their wings, circling.

Ethereally slender, androgynous in form, fairylike in effect. As Lutha's eyes adjusted to the dark, she could see more clearly the delicate arms, the twig-thin fingers, the pearly membrane of the wings. They danced at the edge of the forest, arms beckoning.

"Tempting to get a closer look," murmured Trompe. "If we hadn't been warned off."

The young woman who had warned them stood in the window, watching as they were watching.

"What are they?" Lutha asked.

The girl replied softly. "Kachis. Sim'midi-as-yah."

"Them, the beautiful people," Lutha translated in a whisper as the girl turned abruptly and went back into the building. "Which doesn't tell us much."

"Which tells us a good deal," said Trompe soberly. "Her voice didn't betray it, but her feelings did. She's . . . awestruck. And . . . hopeful. And . . . afraid."

"Frightened?" Lutha asked. "Surely not."

"I'm a Fastigat, lady. Remember?"

Lutha regarded the slowly circling forms, pale against the shadows of the forest. Their eyes were large, seeming almost to glow, though it was more likely they simply reflected ambient light as did the eyes of many nocturnal creatures. The forms were almost human, the faces those of smiling children, though they all seemed to be male, if the long, semi-erect organs paralleled earthian forms. They called and beckoned, their delicate feet prancing upon the grasses. Ridiculous to be afraid of these, Lutha thought.

"Perhaps she was afraid of something else."

Trompe shook his head. No, the girl had not been frightened of anything else. Whatever that strange mix of feelings meant, it had been occasioned by these, these beautiful people.

"Well then," said Lutha, intensely matter-of-fact. "She is awestruck because they are taboo. That is why she told us to stay upon the porch, behind the rail. To prevent our contravening some local custom."

Trompe nodded soberly. "If she prevents our contravening something, it's something more than mere custom."

Chur Durwen of Collis, who had without the least concern dipped deep into the King of Kamir's coin to pay for a hundred-year sanctuary lease-hold on Dinadh, now considered whether he might not have been cheated on the deal. After three days' travel, he seemed no closer to his goal than he had been in Tasimi-na-Dinadh. Now they were stopped at yet another hostel, and Chur Durwen carried his belongings into the place in sullen silence.

"How much longer?" he demanded of the guide when he returned to the vehicle for another load.

The guide shrugged. "It depends how much sun on the car. It depends how fast we go. It depends whether all the bridges are passable."

Chur Durwen turned to Mitigan and made an angry face, hiding it from their guide. "They ought to homo-norm this world!"

"Have you noticed that the herds are almost the only animals on Dinadh. I'd swear this place has already been homo-normed, despite the denials of every Dinadhi I've asked. What hasn't been done will no doubt be done, in time."

"In time! Everything's in time! Forever time!"

"There, there," soothed the man from Asenagi as he removed his belongings from the vehicle. "We'll get there when we get there, col-league."

The other snorted. "When we get there, we won't be any closer to where we want to be than we are now!"

"Patience! Eventually, we'll learn where Bernesohn Famber had his

leasehold, which could be where Leelson Famber is or was, if the
Haughneeps haven't killed him elsewhere already. That place will probably be where Famber's child or children are."

"We should have picked up some rememberer and shaken the information out of him."

Mitigan shook his head with an amused smile. "How would we know
which one to pick up, which one had the 'files' we're interested in? Ah?
They don't all remember everything, obviously."

"Surely the ones who remember were there in the port, where we
arrived. I mean, Famber had to come through there, just as we did."

"I have no idea. We're not sure Leelson ever came here! Our infor-
mant at Alliance Prime said Leelson's family was coming here, but we're
not sure when. We're sure Bernesohn Famber came, but that was a hundred years ago. One pleasant thing about this rememberer system of
theirs is that it is self-limiting. Old stuff gets weeded out as rememberers
die."

"If Leelson Famber or his son came here, it was recently. He wouldn't
be weeded out! If he's here, these people would know where!"

"Right. So we pick one at random and ask him? Without being discovered? Without any suspicion attaching to us? And with one carefully
guarded port the only way off Dinadh?"

"Not a good idea," admitted Chur Durwen.

"Not unless we want our exit slammed in our face. No, if we want to
ask a rememberer, we'll have to go to their central place, their capital or
holy city, where their so-called index men dwell. Of course, we have no
idea where that is. Assuming we can find out, assuming we can get there,
then we'll need to abduct one of the index men, hoping he's the right
one, one who can lead us to the rememberer we need. He might only
lead us to a local subindexer. It might take as many as four or five steps
to get us where we want to be."

Chur Durwen grimaced.

The other said, "I think it's simpler just to do as we planned. Go
where they send us, keep our ears and eyes alert, ask questions. When
we've got a clue, we'll leave. These canyons will be easy to get lost in. We
know how to live off the country. Nobody's going to find us unless we
want them to. Eventually, we'll find who we're after. King Lostre set no
time limit. We're being paid for our time as well as for the job, so we're
in no hurry. It's always safest to take one's own sweet time."

Their guide went stumping off toward the hostel, shouting something
unintelligible.

"As the zossit flies, we'd have arrived two days ago," muttered Chur Durwen.

"As the zossit flies on this planet, we wouldn't. It has no zossits. It has no large flying creatures at all, only tiny ones." Mitigan picked up his pack and settled it on one shoulder.

From inside the hostelry came the clangor of a gong, a disruptive sound, quickly smothered, like a cough at a concert.

"Food," Mitigan said, turning toward the gray building.

From the forest behind them came a voice, an interrogative note, a questing, almost human cry.

Their driver appeared beside the door.

"Come in," he called. "Now."

"Such a hurry," Chur Durwen muttered to himself. "The usual nonsense. Hurry up and wait."

Mitigan had not moved. He stood staring into the trees. "I heard something . . . wings. Didn't I just say there were no large birds?"

"Now!" insisted the guide peremptorily.

The man from Asenagi turned and trudged after his colleague, hearing behind him the flutter of wings coming purposefully through the trees.

Perdur Alas was a celestial anomaly, a planet on which life had stuck at the level of fish, bird, and shrub without any obvious cause for the lack of further diversification. Currently the planet held a limited variety of sea and land plants, enormous schools of a few varieties of fish, and sizable flocks of even fewer scaled bird forms that seemed to have evolved directly from air-breathing flying fish without intermediate land-dwelling stages. Biologically speaking, Perdur Alas was extremely simple. So far as homo-norming went, simplicity made the job easier, which explained the small size of the preliminary team recently evacuated from the planet.

When the pseudo-team of ex-shadows arrived, they were set down beside a new encampment, raw as a wound, just beginning to scab over with ferny and brushy growths. A thousand or so paces to the west a pallid sea swooshed gently onto a rocky shelf at the base of the cliffs. A little north of west the cliffs sagged onto a scanty crescent of graveled beach, the only beach a day's journey in either direction. Farther north, ranks of east-west ridges cut the sky, the nearest jagged, the more distant sparsely freckled with prototrees. Brackenlike and furzelike growths covered everything not covered by blue or purple mosses, making a moorland that stretched unbroken to the eastern and southern horizons.

When the preliminary work was done, the birds and plants would be gone. The planet would have trees suitable for lumber and grasses suitable for pasture. It would have grains, edible root, leaf, and fruit crops, plus at least one draft and one dairy animal and perhaps—if the colonists were not Firsters—one or two animals from the category "small-furry-dociles" or pets. There was no need for insects or birds in Class-C homo-norm. All plants were designed to be wind-pollinated, and Perdur Alas was windy enough.

The arriving team knew this without needing to consider the implications, though bio-assay tech Snark surprised herself shortly after landing by thinking that a million things could be added to Perdur Alas before it had the same complexity as most untouched Class-A planets. Her next thought was one of recognition. This planet, in all its simplicity, was entirely familiar to her.

"Quarters this way," announced team leader Kane, hoisting an equipment case onto his shoulder and stumping off toward the team housing at one side of the encampment.

The pseudo-team, though differing from the original team in physical appearance, was identical as to numbers, sex, and functions. Now most of them straggled after Kane without comment. Each of them had a role to play. Kane's was to keep everyone else working. Snark's was to compare current organisms with those included in Class-C category, using an automatic inventory device, to determine which species should be adapted or eliminated and what others should be introduced to make the world suitable for man. A few members of the team had been conditioned as tank-farm workers, assigned to grow and process food. Others were assigned as housekeeping staff, while others yet would provide maintenance duties and staff communications.

Each of them would occupy the same work space and sleep space as his or her counterpart on the former team. Each of them knew the routine for each day's labors. They knew what the departed team had known about the work already done. In addition, they knew, and had had it proved to them on the way out, that they could not injure one another. As in Shadowland, if one formed any intention toward violence, one found oneself curled into the fetal position, thumb in mouth, just as formerly. They knew who they were. They also remembered what they had been, though that matter did not seem relevant and was often forgotten for quite lengthy periods. Each of them had almost invisible scars behind which implanted devices made records of everything seen, heard, smelled, tasted, felt. The devices did not intrude upon thought. Their thoughts, though rare, were their own.

As the team moved off toward the camp the pilot and engineer of the vessel stood at the foot of the loading ramp watching, not noticing Snark, who had stopped to pick up a replacement filter for the bio-assay machine and now stood just inside the open cargo bay.

"Funny bunch," the pilot said. "You ever notice their eyes?"

"How could you help but notice. You listen to their mouths going on, this that, this that, all sounding pretty good, then you look at the eyes and see these wild animals glaring at you."

"Crazy people? With implants, maybe?"

"I dunno. One thing sure. They're out here on the edge of nowhere and the Ularians are coming."

"Hush," said the engineer. "We were told—"

"We were told not to talk. I'm not talking. Hell, how far is it back to where anybody can hear me!"

"I hear you," said the other, stiffly. "And both of us could get asked what we saw, what we heard. From anybody."

Snark read the look on the engineer's face to mean, "And if they ask me, I'll tell them you were shooting off your mouth!"

"Yeah, well," said the pilot in sudden discomfort. "We'd best get started back. It feels pretty exposed here. Like somebody might be watching us."

Snark slipped out of the cargo bay as they went up the ramp, then stood below, watching them. She was remembering another ship, like this ship. Herself going up a ramp just like this one.

Before the lock closed, the pilot risked one more look at the humans moving among the graceless buildings below and mumbled a final comment. To shadows, reading lips was nothing at all, and Snark read the words clearly.

"Bait! That's what they are. Bait."

Lutha and Trompe discovered their vehicle could not actually "arrive" at the hive of Cochim-Mahn. It could be driven to a point roughly opposite and above our hive, where the road ended at the edge of the cliffs. A flat triangular chunk of metal hung from the roof beam of the vacant guest house, and before doing anything else, Trompe struck it several times. They both waited as the resultant resonance trembled above the depths, seeming to hang interminably before fading into the daysounds of wind and creature.

We heard it, of course, though songfather hadn't waited for it. He knew when they were coming. I hadn't waited for it either. Despite what had happened to me, it was still my duty to clean the quarters of Bernesohn Famber, which I had done, along with airing blankets and sleeping pads for those who were expected.

After a brief wait, Lutha shrugged at the lack of response and carried Leely into the guest house. It had two cramped rooms, a sanitary arrangement added on the back, and a food dispenser wedged into a corner, all very dim behind tightly closed shutters. She stretched and bent, working out the kinks, then lay down on the padded bench, Leely beside her, and fell into a doze. She might have opened the shutters in order to admire the carved and crenellated canyon, the effect of shade and sun as the occasional clouds came sailing over, but both Lutha and Trompe, so she told me later, were sick unto death of canyons.

"I think someone's coming," Trompe said after a considerable silence. He lay as he had thrown himself down, in a posture of exaggerated exhaustion, and did not remove his forearm from his eyes as he spoke.

"How do you know?" asked Lutha.

"Hmm." It was a doubtful sound, as though he didn't know himself how he knew. "I'm picking up put-upon feelings. Someone out there is feeling overworked and irascible. Angry or aggrieved about something, too. Not us. Or, not us specifically."

"Ah." She rose and went out back to consult the sanitary system, returning brushed and furbished. "Still not arrived? When will he get here?"

"Now he's standing among the trees. Politeness, I think. Waiting until we notice him."

"If you weren't a Fastigat, that might take some time."

"I think his next step may be some throat clearing or modest coughs, growing louder with time."

Indeed, as she opened the door, the sound she heard was an apologetic cough that seemed to ask, "Was I wanted?"

"I am Lutha Tallstaff," she said across the clearing. "Mother of Leely Famber, direct-lineage son of Bernesohn Famber. With me is my assistant, Trompe."

"And your son?" asked my father, Chahdzi, who stood beneath the trees.

The upper part of his face was painted blue, the line running horizontally just below his eyes and across the bridge of his nose. Lutha tried to recall anything she might have read about that. Nothing. A local custom, she thought, which was accurate. Persons undertaking dangerous tasks paint their eyes yellow, asking others to pray for them. Persons who must deal with outsiders paint their faces half-blue, so we will watch and listen carefully, in case they show signs of deviance. And so on.

"Leely is in here, asleep," she said.

My father stepped from the shade of the trees and came forward. "I am Chahdzi, son of the songfather of Cochim-Mahn. It is my assigned task to serve you as guide to the leasehold of Bernesohn Famber." Without invitation, he came across the shallow porch and into the room, where he took a long look at Leely, to make sure he was a real, living person. "We have to walk and climb a long way," he said in explanation. "The boy will be heavy to carry."

"He can walk," said Lutha. "He can run and climb." Like a little goat. "Most of the way, at least."

"Partway. But of such complexity, interesting patterns are made," he said in the falsely cheerful tone one adopts for reassuring children.

"I suppose it does," she said doubtfully. Certainly this whole business was complex enough. "When do we go?"

"Since you were expected today, I left Cochim-Mahn this morning. It took me all of today to get here to meet you, and now it is late. Soon Lady Day departs with all her blessings and the time of whispering comes. When the Lady comes again, we will go."

"Shortly after dawn tomorrow then," commented Trompe.

The man shivered, almost undetectably, and nodded. "I will sleep in here, or perhaps in your vehicle."

"Because," said Lutha, moved by an obscure impulse, "because it is better not to be out in the dark?"

Again that shiver, almost unnoticeable. "Because of the pattern, matron," he said in a dignified voice. "Which alternates dark and light, activity and quiet, whisper and shout, sleep and waking . . ."

"Do I offend in asking about the night?" she asked. "I am curious about . . . the things that go about in the dark."

"Bernesohn Famber was also curious, or so I am told by the rememberers. Outlanders are often curious about Dinadh and the Dinadhi. Why do we paint our faces and sometimes our bodies? Why do we sing all the time? Why do we do this, or that? We tell you all the same things. All is part of the pattern; the light and the dark." He gestured vaguely. "If one wishes to learn details, one must consult a songfather who is schooled in such things. I am a simple person, a mere yahsdi' imicha dimicha'a."

She translated mentally. One-who-is-assigned-to-do-what-needs-doing. A man of all work, perhaps. A handyman. She started to ask him how far they would have to go on the morrow, the words drying in her mouth as she saw his face, suddenly alert, listening.

She cocked her head. There was a sound, distant, but not faint. A song, rising from the canyon.

"Forgive me," said Chahdzi. "I will return shortly."

He left the room and went out into the open, where he threw his arms open to the sky and began a breathy song, evidently addressed to thin air.

"What's he doing?" asked Trompe.

"You're the empath," she said.

"All I can pick up is a feeling of concern, a desire which he is repressing."

She listened, translated, nodded. "He's singing to Weaving Woman, begging her to keep the patterns clear and straight."

Afar, the song faded into silence, only the echoes remaining for a moment more. Chahdzi stood with bowed head. In a few moments he turned and came back to them.

"How far do we have to go then, tomorrow?" Lutha asked.

He shook his head, as though reminding himself of where he was. "A day. A long day spent in going quickly. Which is why I look at the boy, to see how fast we can go. Climbing down the walls is not easy."

"Perhaps we won't get there in one day," she said casually.

"One must," he said. Impersonal imperative. One must, that's all.

"Dangerous to be out after dark, is it?" Trompe's head was cocked, picking up all the little signals.

Chahdzi smiled, ducking his head slightly. "Danger has a place in the pattern, surely. And pain. Slidhza b'dasya a yana chas-as imsli t'sisri."

Again Lutha translated to herself, fumbling with the word order. *A wise person doesn't use his own shuttle to weave sorrow.* Or perhaps, a wise shuttle won't weave grief.

"I do not understand," she said.

He shrugged again, a habitual gesture. "It is foolish to create dark patterns for ourselves, matron. Weaving Woman will include enough darkness, whether we wish or no. Let us hope for a bright pattern tomorrow, if we are her beloved children." He pointed to the child. "That one is. Everyone says so."

"Now, why is that?" Trompe asked, amazed.

"He knows." Chahdzi smiled. "Everyone says he knows."

"Knows what?" asked Lutha, wonderingly. "Knows what, Chahdzi?"

"Knows," he said softly. "What is. Patterns. What comes next."

Though his words were not unlike other comments the Dinadhi had made about Leely, they were no more explanatory. The boy himself showed no signs of knowing what needed doing, unless sleeping was it.

"Will you eat with us?" asked Lutha.

"I accept your generous offer of food," he said, looking away from her in obvious discomfort.

His tone made her realize that he would have gone hungry had she not offered, and also that one did not say "eat with us" on Dinadh. Damn! She hadn't given sufficient thought to some of the stuff she'd found in the culture chips!

"Since I do not know your taste," she said carefully, "will you do us the courtesy of choosing for yourself?"

He went happily to the food unit, where he stood for a long time in contemplation of the listed menu, mumbling to himself.

"I like very much the taste of cheese," he said, pointing at a certain item and using their own word, *cheese,* which evidently did not exist in his own language. "But I cannot eat of it unless . . ."

She came to his assistance, reading labels. "It's all right. Everything in here is dosed with the necessary enzymes. Trompe and I have commented that you have no dairy beasts on Dinadh."

"It is said we brought milk creatures from our former world," he murmured. "But here, Weaving Woman could not permit them. Here our pattern changed."

"Human-owned flocks of grazers and browsers have ended a good many patterns," grunted Trompe. "Once man killed off the natural predators and let them multiply."

"So it is said," agreed Chahdzi, glancing at Lutha from the corner of his eyes as she manipulated the food-service unit. Something light for herself and for Trompe. She would feed Leely when he wakened. As for Chahdzi, who was obviously apprehensive that they might watch while he ate, she would make the matter simple.

She handed him the warmed packet of cheese and cereal-food, saying, "Perhaps you would enjoy your meal on the porch?"

"Indeed." He bowed gravely and took it away with him, leaving Trompe and Lutha to eat their own selections in silent company. Chahdzi might be out of sight, but he was not out of earshot, so Lutha did not mention her annoyance at the thought of a long climb on the morrow and Trompe did not remark upon the feelings he picked up from Chahdzi: awe, hope, terror, anger. The same feelings he'd detected in the serving girl at the hostel. The same strange combination.

As they ate, Lutha dug out a handful of culture chips and scanned the indices, muttering to herself.

"Nothing there on the subject?" Trompe asked, sotto voce, elaborately nonspecific concerning which subject.

"Not a . . . nothing," she replied. "You'd think—"

"The language chips I gave you were prepared by the people at Tasimi-na-Dinadh," he murmured thoughtfully. "All properly indexed for use by possible leaseholders and no doubt somewhat edited . . ."

"A sales pitch, in other words," she muttered.

He nodded. "They were the most recent chips the Procurator had, though he also gave me some old ones made by independent researchers. I didn't pass them on to you because they looked like heavy going. They're really old, and they aren't indexed at all."

"Please," she said. "Are they in your pack?"

"Finish your food," he said gently. "I'll get them in a minute."

After Chahdzi had thanked them again for food and sequestered himself in their vehicle, after Leely had had his supper and fallen asleep once more, Trompe dug out the chips he had promised: old ones, nicked at the corners, their labels faded.

"You say the Procurator gave you these?" she asked doubtfully.

"Well, he gave me the Dinadh file, and they were in it. He did remark that the newer chips were more up-to-date."

"They're so up, all usefulness has been edited out of them," she snorted. "They're completely superficial. All the taboos are avoided, so we can't tell what we should or shouldn't say, may or may not do! For example, we've seen the beautiful people are ubiquitous, but the chips don't even mention them. These are the ones I should have studied."

"Maybe," he said soberly. "But they seemed very ponderous to me."

Peevishly, she disregarded this as irrelevant. Fastigats weren't researchers. They didn't spend their time making laborious correlations from ancient records; they didn't sift history for nuances. They drew their conclusions from the here and the now, from whatever or whoever was feeling and emoting in the vicinity. Well, nonetheless.

She accessed one of the chips at random and began plowing through it, realizing after some little time that Trompe had been right. It was heavy going. This researcher had come to Dinadh as to virgin territory and had weeded nothing out. He or she had included everything uncut, every branch and twig and tangled root. Who knew what was alive and important, what had died long ago or had compacted into impenetrable peat?

She yawned, tried to focus, forced herself to concentrate, and finally gave up in disgust, no longer annoyed at Trompe. He was right. This was ponderous indeed. She would seek nuances later perhaps, but not tonight. Leely and Trompe had the better idea. One should sleep when one could!

CHAPTER 4

The first night on Perdur Alas, Snark bedded down in the dormitory with the other shadows, waking frequently, listening for some unusual sound, but hearing only breathing, snores, restless movements, and sighs. She herself slept little. The chip within her recorded her wakefulness. Someday, somewhere, someone might review these feelings, experience her perceptions. Everything the chip detected was beamed to a tiny satellite hidden beside a moonlet, and from there was relayed to the nearest occupied planet—Dinadh, probably, where the hated Lutha Tallstaff had gone—and from there to somewhere else and somewhere else again, all the way back to Alliance Prime and the damned Procurator. Perhaps even now someone on Dinadh was monitoring what had been done today on Perdur Alas and wondering why this particular shadow was awake.

Snark tried to care and could not. They had no right, she told herself, quite correctly. She knew it and they knew it: they had no right. The words were familiar, but the rage they usually evoked would not come. Those sent to Perdur Alas had been conditioned against rage, against rebellion.

No one had thought to condition any of them against childhood fantasies. On the third night, Snark lay down among the others as before, but when they slept, she rose and went out into the night. All day she had been smelling the moor. The smell had filled her to the exclusion of other perceptions, had preoccupied her with feelings long dreamed and totally familiar. Perhaps these woody and ferny growths had come from

the same place as the ones she had smelled as a child. Perhaps this moor
had been designed to be like one she had seen long ago, her dream
moor, complete with tea-brown pools and rustling bracken. Perhaps that
world and this one had shared a common designer or a common heritage.

Even as she said to herself, *perhaps, perhaps,* she knew there was no
happenstance involved. Similarity didn't matter. Only this place mattered, its odors that smelled like, its growths that looked like, its moor
that felt like the moor she had dreamed. This could be the actual refuge
she had found as a child—or dreamed she had found. If one went west
across this stretch of rolling ground, one would come to cliffs above the
sea. They would be the same cliffs, the same sea. During the workaday
world of daylight there had been no opportunity to explore. Now in a
dark relieved only by the pearly glimmer of tiny moonlets, shining
through the night like so many lopsided paper lanterns, she would find
the old cliff, the old sea, the old place she knew so well.

Every step of the way could have been dictated from memory! Surely
she had seen a pool of this shape before! Surely she had caught her foot
on just such a root and been sent sprawling in just this way, with this
particular herb crushed beneath her cheek to surround her with identical
pungency. Surely the sound of the sea had come at just this point and no
other, the swelling and sighing of the surf as it rolled small stones on the
rocky shelf below. Surely all of this was the same, her own childhood
place, wherever and whenever it had been, come here again.

She wasn't even surprised. However astonishing similar things might
be, identical things were not. One could be astonished at the close re-
semblance of brothers but not at that of identical twins. So she couldn't
be astonished at this moor, for it was not merely like. It *was* the one she
had known, and that was all there was to it. The two, though they
seemed separate in time and space, were the same place.

So musing, believing herself half dreaming, she came to the edge of
the cliff at last, feeling a familiar panic, a fleeting urge to jump. Why?
Why the panic? Why . . . because there was something following her.
Something seeking her. Now? Or then?

She puzzled over this as she turned left along the rimrock. This was
the way she had always turned. The cliff was as she remembered, and
the soughing of the sea. She wandered slowly along the precipice,
around this stone and that twiggy growth, searching, believing she had
missed it, as she had always believed—

Only to come upon it suddenly: the outcropping of stone, the branch extending into space, the bare, pale, polished place upon the wood where her hands, someone's hands, had rubbed the bark away to make a smoothness. Without thinking, without decision, she leapt out, hands extended to grasp, the springiness of the wood coming as a shock to the muscles of her arms as she bounced pendant beneath it like a toy jerking upon a string. No hole, she told herself in sudden panic. No hole in the cliff. Nowhere to go from here.

The fear was only momentary. The entry was there, a darker crevice among the striations of the cliff face. And a protruding stone where she needed to put her foot. And a ropy rootlet hanging down . . .

She didn't really remember this part. In her dream, she felt the details of the cave rather than smelled or heard or saw them. This cave felt sandier; it had no bracken bed. It felt smaller, too, but then, it would have seemed larger to the child she had been when she had dreamed it first. The trickle of water was there at the back, making a modest puddle on its hollowed stone, seeping away down a mossy crack. She remembered caches of food. There were none in this cave. She remembered warm animal skins, and they, too, were missing. She could bring food. She could bring blankets and armfuls of cut bracken to cushion her rest. From this time forward, she would go to bed with the others, but when they slept, she would sneak away to spend the dark hours here, in this refuge above the sea.

Now she lay down on the sandy floor, her body taking the curved form so often imposed upon it, knees up, thumb in mouth, hip seeking a familiar hollow. The stones beside the entry were piled as she had left them in dream. She reached with one hand to stack them, the larger ones on the bottom, the smaller above.

Moving the stones disclosed a niche. In the niche was a painted jar with a lid. Snark's eyes drifted across it, hardly seeing it. Though she hadn't remembered the jar before, hadn't recalled its presence or patterns, she did so now. The jar had always been there, its egglike shape of white clay covered with dark swerving lines, wings, and faces. She even knew the names of those portrayed. Father Endless and Mother Darkness. Mother had put the jar there. Someone . . . someone named Mother had put the jar there. And inside were the bones of . . .

Whose bones? Why there?

She fell asleep before she could answer the question.

Just before dawn she had a momentary panic when she prepared to leave the cave and realized she didn't know how. She remembered coming here, yes, time after time, escaping here, yes, finding refuge here, cuddling down warmly, nose to the gap in the piled rocks, smelling the sea wind, hearing the birds when they woke before dawn to plunge out in their screaming spirals above the sea. She could remember eating here, jaws moving in slow mastication while the birds screamed and dived. She could remember sucking up the slow seep of water as it accumulated on the hollowed stone. She even remembered squatting on the minuscule ledge, skinny butt jutting over the gulf as she peed down the face of the cliff, her own tiny stream joining the vast ocean below, but she had no memory at all of ever leaving this place.

So, how did she get out? The branch that had dropped her down had sprung back to its position above, out of reach. The cliff overhung the ledge. Above was invisible, unreachable. She sat, fighting panic, thinking it out. She needed something to draw the branch down. Once she had hold of the branch, she could pull herself up. So, she would use her belt, with a stone tied to the end to give it weight.

She tried this, but her belt was too thick, too inflexible. She took off her shirt and tore strips from it, braiding them together for strength, succeeding at last in drawing the branch down, close, where she could reach it. As she bounced and juddered, working her way up to the rim of the stone, she resolved next time to bring a strong line with a weight affixed so she would have the proper tool to get out. She must have had such a tool before. She could not imagine why she had forgotten it until now. Unless perhaps, before, someone else had drawn the branch down for her. Unless, before, she had been only a child.

She returned to the dormitory complex just in time to get into bed before the others woke. Perhaps the watchers on Dinadh knew she had been away, but none of the Shadowland people did. Certainly Snark did not tell them.

The shadows had been given the knowledge they needed to act as their roles required, and for some of them this had been the equivalent of an advanced education in biotechnology. Though the information had been imposed, they could use it, fumblingly at first and with more assurance as time went by. They had not been given a course in morals and ethics. No one had thought to prevent their stealing. What was there to steal on Perdur Alas?

Snark stole food and blankets to start with. Over the next dozen nights she equipped her refuge. She stole food enough for a lengthy stay. She made her bracken bed, a blanketful cut each night on her way to the cliff, a new blanket carried there each night until the entire floor of the cave was cushioned and comfortable. Though she remembered animal skins from the time before, the blankets were as warm and they smelled better. She brought two lengths of line with weights at one end, keeping one in her pocket and one in the niche next to the opening—just in case she lost the one she was carrying.

She did nothing that significantly changed the original dream until she had fulfilled it meticulously. Only then did she add other supplies, things the adult Snark thought might be useful: night glasses for spying, an emergency beacon, a box of vegetable and fruit seeds from the agricultural lab. Suppose, she told herself, suppose I get left here all by myself! Suppose the Ularians get all the others, but I'm hiding and they can't find me. Suppose they don't get me! I'd need the beacon so humans could come rescue me. I'd need to grow food. I'd need to stay alive!

The words, the very tone was familiar. Someone had said the same to her once, long ago. Fleetingly she realized the idea of rescue was ridiculous. Why would they come to rescue a totally dispensable shadow? A shadow who had been put here as bait in the first place? Does the worm on the hook expect to be rescued simply because the fish have eaten all the other worms?

Perhaps, she told herself. Perhaps, if the worm had information about the fish. Perhaps then. Suppose she *saw* the fish, the Ularians. Then there'd be reason to pick her up. The monitor would sense what she sensed, but he couldn't read her mind. The monitor might think she'd found out something important! Whether she did or not, she could say she had. If she said it out loud, the monitor would hear what she said.

So, she would try to see them, if they came, and whether she did or not, she would say loudly that she had found out something. Dangerous, that. How did one find anything out except through one's senses. If she merely deduced, it would have to be from evidence. From things seen and heard. Could one pretend to see? Pretend to hear?

Such questions preoccupied her. Rarely she thought about men. Susso had come with the other shadows. Maybe she ought to tell Susso about her cave. Invite him to come along.

The idea was transient, the motivation unconvincing. Sex was pleasurable, sure, but survival was sweeter still. Susso wouldn't keep his mouth shut. Then the others would get involved. They'd interfere. They'd stop Snark leaving. Stop her coming here. Better not say anything to Susso. Who needed men anyhow?

"Inventory's almost done," said Kane, when they had been on the planet thirty or forty days. "Tomorrow we'll start the ag-study."

"I'm missing supplies in ag-lab," one of the women said plaintively. "One whole carton of vegetable seeds is missing."

"They probably miscounted," said Kane carelessly. "They probably did."

They were the predecessors, the other team, the real team, acknowledged but unconsidered. They had been here. They had gone. Now *we* were here. No one ever said, "When we're finished and gone." No one ever said, "When the job's done." They had been conditioned against such expectations. The job was interminable. The task was lifelong. And though lifelong might be short indeed, they were conditioned against anxiety.

"You got enough seeds left to do the job?" Kane asked. "That's all that matters."

She had enough for the job. No one paid any attention to her earlier comment. They went to their daily tasks with perfect gravity and understanding, though it was all accomplished in dreamlike slow motion. Even eating was slow. Every movement, every task was set for them. Go from 1 to 2; 2 leads to 3; 3 leads to 4. Nothing was done because they wanted to or thought of it themselves. They didn't worry; they didn't fight. They scarcely spoke. Sometimes two of them would couple in the night with spurious urgency, but even such brief convulsions were muted and soon forgotten.

Very occasionally Snark remembered the simul booth back in Shadowland, but she couldn't bring herself to want it much. She sometimes remembered raging, remembered shouting, remembered fighting—or trying to. It was all another dream, not unlike this dream of being on Perdur Alas. Each day took care of itself. And now that Snark had found her own place, which was real and remote from dreaming, each night took care of itself as well.

Deprived of his shadows, the Procurator had not yet grown accustomed to pouring his own tea. Often more liquid slopped onto the table than stayed in the cup, on this occasion giving him reason to swear gustily as an underling entered, one Mikeraw.

"Sorry, sir," the underling murmured.

"You didn't do it," grouched the Procurator. "I did. I am clumsy and incapable! We had grown too dependent upon shadows, Mikeraw. Far too dependent!"

Mikeraw, who was lowly in rank and non-Fastigat, had never been served by shadows. He contented himself with a murmured agreement as he helped the Procurator mop both himself and the tabletop.

This accomplished, Mikeraw bowed, murmuring, "I thought you should see this, sir. It seems to impinge—"

"What? What is it?" He reached for the proffered document.

"An agent upon Dinadh, sir. Reporting rumor, sir."

"An Alliance agent?"

Mikeraw flushed slightly. "As a matter of fact, no, sir. We have an agent there, but he doesn't report much. This is from a Gadravian agent."

"The Gadravians take a lot on themselves!"

"They insist they are loyal members of the Alliance and are merely providing us with appropriate redundancy in intelligence matters. As in this case."

"This case? Case of what, man?"

Mikeraw cleared his throat. "It is rumored the King of Kamir has sent assassins to Dinadh to eradicate the Famber lineage, sir."

The Procurator sat down with a thump.

"Famber? Leelson Famber? Why in the name of all that's holy and intractable . . . ?" The King of Kamir was a joke, of course. Everyone knew of the King of Kamir. He was proverbial. "Useless as the King of Kamir." Said of lackadaisical students and lie-about workmen, as well as of tools that didn't function or equipment that fell apart. For the first time the Procurator considered that the king might rather resent this reputation. Might have resented it enough to have wished to put it behind him.

He gaped unattractively while thinking. Suddenly aware of this, he gave his mouth something to do, asking, "It was Leelson who found him, wasn't it?"

"Yes, sir. When the king disappeared, the government of Kamir retained Fastiga to investigate, and Fastiga assigned Leelson Famber."

"Excrement," muttered the Procurator. "Oh, excrement."

"I thought, inasmuch . . ."

"Quite right. Quite right. Good man. Well, it puts Lutha Tallstaff in the broth, doesn't it? And any Fastigat with her. On behalf of the boy, of course. The assassins might not bother him, and maybe not her, but they will the boy. Unless Trompe Paggas gets in the way!"

"I've consulted the relevant documents, sir, that is, the laws of Kamir as they might apply in this situation. I came up with the thought that we might approach the king himself to obtain a royal writ."

"Calling the assassins off, you mean?"

"Yes, sir."

"And then what?"

"Send the writ to Dinadh . . ." His voice trailed off, and he shifted from foot to foot, uncomfortably.

"Assuming one could get such a writ, who would deliver it on Dinadh, and to whom?" asked the Procurator.

The underling shrugged. He didn't know.

The Procurator sighed. "Fastiga," he murmured. "Whoever goes to Kamir can't be from Fastiga."

"Why not from Fastiga, sir?"

"The bureaucrats would suspect a Fastigat. They do, you know."

"Perhaps we could send another assassin, sir?"

"You say?"

"Send a corsair to catch a corsair, isn't that the saying?"

"Not in my language, it isn't."

"In mine, sir."

"And where are you from?"

"Far Barbary, sir."

"Well, that explains it. All pirates there, aren't they?"

"Not much anymore, sir. Once were, of course. My own great-grandfather, in fact."

"And how did you end up here?"

The man stared at his boots, reddening.

The Procurator accurately read his embarrassment.

"Government is merely another kind of piracy, is that it?" The Procurator guffawed, tears welling in his eyes. "I take no offense. It's true, my boy. Politicians are pirates, of a sort!"

"I wasn't going to say so, sir. Though my father does."

"And your grandfather, too, no doubt. Well. You could be right. Send a corsair to fetch a corsair, an assassin to fetch an assassin. In which case, who's our assassin?"

"We'll need to ask the King of Kamir, sir. He seems to have an inexhaustible supply."

It was, as a matter of fact, Councilwoman Poracious Luv who went to Kamir on behalf of the Alliance. She demanded an audience with the king and received it without delay. Jiacare Lostre, King of Kamir, was so enervated by his day-to-day life, he didn't even make her wait. He would have consented to meet with an offal-eater from Hapsobog to break the tedium, and he found little fault with this wallowing bulk, this monstrous bosom heaving at him, even though she insisted on boring him with a brief history of the Ularian crisis, which he cared nothing about.

His kingly prerogative allowed him to tell her so, yawning.

"I don't think Your Majesty understands," she said, growing quite pink about the jowls as she held out a pleading arm from which the quivering flesh hung in braceleted rolls.

"My Majesty does understand quite well," he said. "I just don't give a damn if we're condemned a wee bit sooner than our present course will equally condemn us."

She chewed her lower lip, wondering why in heaven's name the Procurator had picked her for this mission.

"There are those who feel differently," she murmured.

"Not I," he said. "Not while I'm pinioned here!"

"Are you?" she asked, suddenly interested despite herself. "By what?"

Her obvious interest caught him by surprise, and he became expansive. "Tradition, madam. And the force of law. I am coerced in many divers ways, by suasion horrible to contemplate, by threats against the comforts of my kin, of whom, despite my boredom, I am fond. My mother's life is hostage 'gainst my own, and so my sister's—who, in happier times, was very dear to me."

"You did have happier times, then?"

He snorted. "I had four brothers older than myself, all four of whom aspired to mount this seat. Efficiently they entered on the task of murdering each other, leaving me to sit upon a throne I much despised."

"So much so you ran away from it."

He flushed. "I planned escape, achieved it! Ah, but then I was dragged back to duty as bad boys are driven to their books by masters' canes. Like them, I swot and grimace and complain. . . ."

She gnawed at the inside of her cheek, a habit that gave her the look of some ponderous ruminant.

"Would you be more sympathetic if I could arrange for your . . . release?"

The king actually smiled. "Oh, madam, how my sympathy would wax, like moons grown fat on light. Away from here, my lips, most eloquent, would speak your cause."

"My cause, as you put it, is simply to stop your assassins, Majesty. My ultimate cause may be something else again, but for the nonce, it's only that. The Famber lineage must not be worried by threats of assassination, not, at least, until we've found what we need concerning Bernesohn Famber."

The king regarded his fingernails with gravity. "From all that lengthy tale you bored me with, it seems rather too late to look for him."

"For Bernesohn, yes. For whatever information he had, possibly not. We pray not."

"How would you think to get me out of this?" He gestured widely, including his kingdom, the planet, all the clutter and cumber of the monarchy of a dying world.

Poracious Luv shook her head. "I don't know yet. I'll have to think on it, perhaps seek some advice. We have excellent counselors. Sometimes they can be quite Machiavellian. Assuming we can think of something that will work, you'll give me the writ?"

"Oh, Madam Luv, I'd carry it myself."

She brightened with sudden inspiration. "Would you, now? Then, sir, that may be the answer you are seeking! Consider. It is likely the assassins will be turned aside only by you, true? It may be no one can save our desperate inquiry except yourself? It may be, therefore, that the saving of humanity is in your hands? Including the lives of all those upon Kamir? All the mamas and sisters and children of your ministers, for example?"

He stared at her from beneath swollen lids, startled once again from his ennui. "That would be true if ministers had kin. Reason declares that such men come from eggs abandoned by the deadly cockatrice, that they hatch forth among the desert sands, the word *tradition* peeping from their beaks e'en as they crack their shells. Myth has it that they strike their prey to stone, and that is true. This world will be but stone when they are through."

She regarded him quizzically. "Your Majesty exaggerates slightly. When humans use up a world, there are usually some bacteria left, even some hardy plants. In any case, your ministers are not free agents. They are responsible to a larger constituency—to all the people of Kamir who lust for life, who have encumbrances of kindred and friendship. Such people will not willingly accept extinction, no matter how traditional it might be."

"So much is true. I've heard that even weighty governors are wary of the people they abuse."

"So! Use your people to gain your freedom! That is, if you're truly resolved not to return to kingship. Our Procurator says the same man who will hail a leader in time of crisis will kill him once the crisis is over."

"Again, true," said the king with appreciation. "For though he'll play at resolution when death hangs upon a hair, once danger's passed, all his anxieties, like vicious fleas, do burrow bloodily. An itchy man is prey to discontent; he'll suage his flea bites with the blood of kings."

"Surely the common man wouldn't want that!"

"What common men want most is beer and sex, without disturbances."

"So if it were necessary for *you,* yourself, to leave Kamir in order to save the people from disturbance . . ."

"It is unlikely that the counselors would fight to keep me here. When all Kamir is threatened with despair, a king may make a kingly sacrifice!"

"One hopes such sacrifice may be relatively painless," murmured Big Mama.

"Even pain," said the king, with no intention of being prophetic, "even pain is preferable to dying of unrelieved ennui."

"She has who?" the Procurator asked Poracious Luv's messenger, believing he had misunderstood her.

"Jiacare Lostre, the king himself," the messenger replied. "He and Poracious went before his ministers and told them Kamir was in danger. The council pooh-poohed the idea. The king told them that in that case they wouldn't mind if he told the people of Kamir all about the Ularians being just next door in Hermes Sector. Poracious said the Alliance would help him publicize the matter."

"Somewhat exceeding her authority," murmured the Procurator.

The messenger muffled an undiplomatic snort. "As Madam herself said, it got the job done. The ministers knew there'd be widespread panic, possibly insurrection. They've let the king go. He and Madam were to have left for Dinadh the day after I left for Alliance Central."

"Amazing."

"Actually, the council of ministers didn't fight as hard as Madam Luv thought they might. She felt they'd really wanted an excuse to get rid of Jiacare. He has a younger brother, Fenubel, who's much easier to get along with. They've already installed him as regent."

"Interesting," the Procurator murmured. "You're rejoining Madam Luv?"

"Yes, sir."

"Talk to my adjutant outside. Make whatever arrangements are necessary. Things are getting complicated. I think I'd better go with you."

In the hostel above Cochim-Mahn, Chahdzi woke Trompe very early, before it was quite light.

"It is not good to move before the daysong has been sung," he told the Fastigat soberly, emphasizing his words with peckish nods, like an anxious hen. "Still, we must go all in one day, and we must leave now to accomplish that."

Trompe got Lutha and Leely up, and they made a hurried meal before taking up their packs and moving toward the canyon trail, arriving there just as the sun peeked over the farther canyon wall. They heard the dawnsong as they had heard it before during their journey, a rising smoke of melody, wavering, expanding, until all the world could hear it.

The narrow trail led them on a winding way downward among forest trees, coming out of the trees again and again to make hundred-eighty-degree turns and move into the trees again. At the beginning of the journey, on the outer edge of one curve, they saw far off across the canyon a strange house rising above the rim, barely distinguishable from the natural rock around it. The house was laid with dry stone, without mortar, and had a pitched roof with openings beneath the eaves. It resembled several other such structures Lutha had noted on their way toward Cochim-Mahn. She put glasses to her eyes and watched an elderly woman approaching the building, head down.

"What do you call that building?" Lutha asked, pointing it out.

"A House Without a Name," said Chahdzi, his tone forbidding further questions.

Lutha, who was looking back at the elderly woman, merely grunted. The woman moved in an unusual way. As though apprehensive. As though fearful. Fearful of what? What was inside?

Trompe, picking up on her perception, followed her gaze back along the road, too late. They had come around a curve and could see the place no longer.

Chahdzi spoke as though continuing some former conversation. "You see how this trail winds back and forth, into this side canyon and out again, each time a little farther down the great canyon but requiring much time in the walking. If we could go across, it would take only a little time, but there is no way to go across safely."

Lutha fumed silently. If the Dinadhi were sensible and efficient, they could go across, but the Dinadhi weren't sensible or efficient, so every-thing was done the long way, the slow way, the laborious way.

The patterned way, she reminded herself, cautioning against impa-tience. She settled the padded straps on her shoulders. When they stopped next, she would arrange the retriever at the top of her pack, set it on audio only, and listen to one of the grimy old language chips Trompe had given her the night before. No sense wasting the time en-tirely!

It was noon before they came halfway down the great wall, stopping on a promontory from which they could look directly south, across a spacious canyon bottom where a lake gleamed, and into the mouths of four other canyons. These four plus the canyon in which they stood made the five points of a star, with themselves at the northeastern point. They could look down the southern arm, a little way into the eastern and western arms, but they could see only the far wall and opening of the canyon to their right.

As they took food from their packs to make a hasty lunch, Chahdzi told them the lake was called "the Gathered Waters," and was neither deep nor lasting. Present in spring and early summer, it dwindled to almost nothing in fall or early winter when there was not enough water to fill the declivity.

The sun stood at its zenith, lighting the southmost canyon to its bot-tom but leaving those at either side still shaded. The sun also lighted the great stone cave eaten into the western wall of the canyon across from them, making the hive within it glow like gold.

"There is ba h'din, the hive, of Cochim-Mahn," Chahdzi said. "There is the leasehold of Bernesohn Famber. Below, stretching toward the Gathered Waters, is the greenblessing, the farm and fruit lands of our people. And now we have rested long enough. We must walk again."

Though Lutha saw a glimmer of water along the canyon bottom and in the shallow lake, she saw no green, blessed or otherwise. Her glasses brought it within vision: a soft fur of trees and vegetation nestled in a wilderness of red stone. Narrow ribbons of greenery, at some places only a few paces across. It seemed scarcely enough to feed the people of the looming hive.

Wordlessly, they got the straps of their packs across their shoulders once more. From this point on, the trail was much grown up with small thorny shrubs and tough grasses, and Chahdzi led the way.

"No one uses this trail much, do they?" Lutha asked.

Chahdzi took time to reflect before answering. "When Bernesohn

Famber was there, people came again and again, as he chose, to bring equipment and supplies that were unavailable in Cochim-Mahn. Once his wife came here to him, also. The animals go up in spring and come down in fall. Other people come, now and then."

Chahdzi seemed to feel this explained the situation fully, for he offered nothing more. Lutha soon found this understandable. The way had steepened; the footing was intermittently treacherous. It was sensible to avoid conversation in order to give all one's attention to where one stepped and what one was holding on to.

During the morning and for the first hour after their noon stop, Leely scampered along behind them or between them, interrupting his journey to stare at a flying bird or the shape of a cloud. In early afternoon, however, he sat down with a sighing "Dananana," and refused to move farther.

"Here's where I earn my fee," said Trompe, picking the child up and placing him on his shoulders.

"I will take him when you are tired," said Chahdzi. "We cannot stop for him to rest."

Light now came from the west, glaring into their eyes as they wound their way down and down.

"Some of the canyons don't get enough light to be habitable, do they?" Lutha asked, suddenly aware of differences among the various chasms.

"They must be wide enough to let the sun in," agreed Trompe. "Best of all are the wide east-west canyons with a sloping southern wall. Worst are the narrow north-south ones, with steep walls. In those the evening song would follow hard upon the song of morning. In those Lady Day finds little pleasure and shadow breeds."

Lady Day would take little comfort from the canyon beyond the Gathered Waters, south of them. Already its western wall threw heavy shadow halfway up the eastern precipices, leaving the depths in darkness. Each day it would be lit for a short time at midday. The rest of the time it would be a dim and forbidding region. Lutha stared into its shadows and shivered, turning her attention elsewhere.

"Trompe and I saw many abandoned hives on our way here. Why so many?"

Chahdzi cleared his throat. "H'din ha'disha. Empty hives, yes, they become . . . vacant when the Dinadhi move about. From one place to another."

"Why?"

He shrugged. "Perhaps a spring dries up." His tone shut off further discussion.

Trompe cast a quick glance at Lutha, pursing his lips, shaking his head. Chahdzi was uncomfortable with the question.

She read his expression and let the matter drop, turning her attention to the landscape below her, where the delicate green of new leaves sprouted beside the transient water, a silver shoestring of oasis in this rocky land. They were close enough now that she could identify fruit trees, the branches almost hidden behind a flourish of blossoms.

When they stopped to drink from their flasks, Chahdzi took Leely, who was by now asleep, fastening him to his back with crossed belts that might have been made for the purpose. They went on, more quickly as the day waned and the sun fell, climbing downward until Lutha thought she would drop from the pain in her legs where the muscles rebelled at every step. She told herself another thousand steps and she would rebel, danger or no. She began counting, storing up her pain against the explosion she intended. She had reached eight hundred and something when the trail leveled and they debouched upon the level gravel soil of the canyon bottom.

"Now"—Chahdzi sighed—"it will be easier." He was sweating and pale.

"Let me take Leely," said Trompe.

"Let Leely walk," said Lutha. "He's awake. He's just being lazy."

The boy screamed at being put down, and when the three adults started ruthlessly off without him, he ran after them, raging incoherently. Lutha stopped his mouth with a cookie, which occupied him until they were almost at the stream. The sun had sunk below the rim of the canyon above them, and the great cave with its hive was deep in shadow.

Chahdzi took a small stoppered bottle from his pack and directed them to take a small mouthful each, even Leely. Then, while they sputtered at the acrid taste, he said, "Take a deep breath and go fast. Only a little more now, but the darkness comes swiftly."

"I'm ready to drop," said Lutha.

"You may not," he said softly. "Not yet. Only a little more. Quickly."

They pushed themselves into an exhausted stagger that accelerated into a heart-pumping plunge, fueled by Chahdzi's stimulant, as they splashed through the narrow stream, tending a little southward to a place immediately below the great cave. Now they were in shadow. Now they could see the hive itself, see the few people assembled upon the lip of stone, peering down at them.

"Ladders!" said Lutha, disbelievingly.

"Only a few," said Chahdzi, gesturing her to climb first. "Go, rest, go, rest. Keep moving."

They climbed. They climbed forever. Leely screamed. Lutha cursed under her breath. One ladder led to another, led to another yet. A few were slimy with spray. And then they were on the flat, sagging with exhaustion.

A high tenor voice soared:

"See our Lady depart. See her dance westward, upon the rock-rimmed mountains, beautiful her feet among the trees. . . ."

A tiddle of bone flutes, a rattle of little drums sounded from the wide-windowed loft of a tower nearby. Seemingly the rush was over. People were moving about purposefully, with no appearance of panic, men and women both, difficult to tell what sex they were in the loose robes, their hair cut alike, their faces painted this way or that. Some wore only the underrobe, the back hem pulled between their legs and up over the belt in front. Others' robes flowed free. A few had put on leather outer robes, these evidently for ceremonial reasons, for the singer and the musicians were among those so clad.

"Now what?" breathed Trompe.

"The leasehold of Bernesohn Famber is at the back," said Chahdzi, sounding more cheerful than he had at any time during the day. "Only a few steps."

He led them along the south side of the great hive, past numerous pore windows and a few skin doors, each made of a drum-tight hide lashed to a frame of poles. Then there were no more windows and doors in the walls, and they entered upon Bernesohn Famber's private space: limited on the north by the featureless wall of the hive, on the south by the curving wall of the cave, on the west by his own living space, a small, single-story wing extruded from the hive: mud-colored, dome-roofed, softly rounded. Unlike the doors of our people, the annex door was made of planks, heavily strapped, hinged, and latched. The door had a lock. The single window was shuttered from inside.

"Is there a key?" Trompe asked, trying the door.

The latch rattled beneath his hand, and I, Saluez, opened the door from within.

They stared at me, Lutha and Trompe and the child.

I stood before them, my face veiled, holding a broom.

"What in hell?" demanded the tall, golden-haired man who came up behind me. "What in the hell are you doing here?"

"Dananana," cooed Leely.

"Leelson," gasped Lutha, surprise warring with fury on her face. "Leelson! Damn it all to hell, what are *you* doing here!"

We expected these people. We had been told to prepare for their arrival, so I had been inside the leasehold, cleaning it. I had fetched extra sleeping pads, extra blankets. I had brushed down all the walls and benches and had swept all the dust into a pile just inside the outer door. I had my hand upon the latch when it rattled, so I opened it. Lutha stood there, with Trompe and her child. I knew at once who they were, for we had been expecting them and I had seen them on the trail across the canyon earlier in the day. My father, Chahdzi, stood with them, but when he saw me, he turned and went away without speaking.

I stepped out of the way, drawing my pile of dust aside with my broom.

"What the hell *are* you doing here?" demanded Trompe, moving aggressively toward the man, who had been with us for some time.

Lutha scooped up Leely and came inside. Her face was twisted with effort; she was trying to scream or curse, but her voice would not come. She managed only a snarling croak, only a step or two inside the door, before she slumped against the wall, her face going blank. I knew at once they had been given the emergency drink, the one we carry when we are out in the world and need to reach the hive before darkness. The drug does that, when it wears off. It leaves bodies limp and minds shut down. I took her arm and helped her sit down, and behind us the darkness came, as though a blanket had been dropped across the light.

I had a pot of tea already prepared as a restorative. I filled a cup and held it to Lutha's lips. After a moment's hesitation, she drank.

"Let's get the door shut," said Leelson, suiting his action to the words before opening the inside shutters to let the last of the dusk seep in between the bars.

Across the canyon, on the trail they had descended by, pallid forms were gathering.

"You arrived just in time," said Leelson from the window.

Trompe shambled over to stand beside him, staring at the sight. I turned my face away.

"My god," said Trompe. "How many of them are there?"

More white forms streamed in from the darkness of the southern canyon, a constant milky flow, a torrent of wings and fluttering membranes.

"Well," Lutha said in a gargled whisper. "Was this the reason for our hurry? This assemblage?"

Since she spoke in my own language, I took it she was asking me. I bowed, murmuring, "On this world we do not talk of the things of night. Not in daytime voices. It is not wise."

"Would they do us harm?" she murmured between sips.

"Darkness is inimical to light by its very nature," I whispered. "All the beings of darkness, also. Living man may dream or hope as he will, but he must walk in the light. The wise man chooses his way and does not thereafter put himself outside his own pattern." This is the kind of thing the songfathers say, words to make one think one has been told something when, in fact, one has been told nothing at all. These are words to comfort children and strangers.

She barely nodded, the last effects of the drink draining away into exhaustion. "What you're saying is . . ."

She would not accept mere allusion. I bowed my head and spoke sense. "In the dark hours, a man should be at home beside the fire, speaking softly. See how all the animals and birds of day go to rest and to quiet; see how they lie hidden, how they whisper in their lairs. Are we less wise than they? Have we no hive, no hole, no cavern to hold us? And why would we choose to be elsewhere than in our homes?"

"We might choose for curiosity's sake, perhaps," said Trompe, in my language, though awkwardly. "A desire to know."

"We become what we know," I said bitterly. "If a woman wishes to stay alive, she must be careful what she knows."

"Enough," breathed Lutha in her weary voice. "I'm afraid we're all too tired to appreciate the finer points of Dinadhi philosophy. What's your name, by the way?"

I bowed. "Saluez," I said. "Saluez of the Shadow. Your servant, madam."

"Assigned to me? Us?"

"To clean the Famber leasehold. To fetch what you may need, any of you."

She dismissed me with a gesture, as though I had not even been there. I did not know then that there were shadows on her world, too, that because I had used the word, her reaction was to treat me as one of them. One took no notice of them. Both my words and my veil confused her, mostly because she was so tired. She dismissed me and turned to the others, and for a time thereafter it was as though I did not exist.

Leelson existed, however. Leelson Famber had been with us on Dinadh for some time. She had things to say to him!

"As for you, Leelson Famber, I think you owe us an explanation! Me, particularly!" She spoke our language as though, once started on it, she lacked energy to change.

"My presence is more explicable than yours," he said in his own tongue. "I came as legitimate lineage son of Bernesohn Famber—"

"You came without bothering to tell anyone at Alliance Prime!" Trompe exploded.

"Or your mother!" snarled Lutha. "Who is very busy just now advancing your Firster cause by despairing of your posterity and blaming it all on me."

He looked at them, astonished, his expression gradually changing from irritation to understanding.

He sat down, drawing Lutha beside him onto one of the cushioned mud benches along the walls. "On my way from Kamir back toward Central, I overheard some crewmen talking of the vanishment of a homo-norm team in Hermes Sector. It reminded me of the last time that had happened, the Ularian thing a century ago. I knew great-great-grandpop had been looking into it; and I knew he'd disappeared here on Dinadh. It was, in a sense, on the way, so I decided to make a brief stopover on the chance he might have left some information here. It was a spur-of-the-moment decision, and I thought I'd be back before anyone got in an uproar. . . ."

He made a gesture of annoyance. "And it certainly never occurred to me the Dinadhi would accept Leely as . . . as lineage son."

Across the valley the forms swarmed, swirling outward from the cliff face. They would not be content with the far side of the canyon for long. I moved to the shutters and closed them, returning to my former place. The people in the room did not notice me.

Lutha made an impatient gesture to Trompe, as though saying, "There! See!"

"I didn't perceive the threat as imminent!" Leelson said emphatically.

"I don't know what you call imminent, but the world you heard about was only the first. Several more Hermes Sector worlds have been wiped clean," snarled Trompe.

Leelson looked up in astonishment. "When?"

"Just before Trompe and I were sent here," Lutha said. "One of the colonists was an old friend of mine. The Procurator used her death as a goad to move me on this journey. God, Leelson! If I'd only known you were here!"

She fumed, her face set and hard, her anger—which had hottened with Leelson's reference to the boy—warring with her exhaustion. I wondered which god she had invoked. We do not consider it polite to call upon a god as one would a servant. We are careful to use the correct names and polite address.

As for Leely, he had climbed onto the wall bench nearest me and lay there staring at the ceiling, murmuring over and over, "Dananana, Dananana." I sat down beside him, drawing no attention to myself. We members of the sisterhood learn to do that.

"Did it never occur to you," Lutha snarled, "that Alliance Prime needed to know where you were?"

"If this attack followed the same pattern as a century ago, there'd have been plenty of time to advise Prime."

"And what pattern was that?" Trompe demanded.

"The first thing that went then was a supply facility on a moon near the far side of the Hermes Sector. It was a standard year before anything else happened, and another year went by before populations were removed from anywhere farther in."

Trompe snarled, "Well, the Ularians didn't follow the previous pattern. They've completely destroyed or transported colonies on three of the worlds closest to Dinadh. That's what alerted Prime." He sighed, running his fingers through his hair. "I suppose your intentions are understandable, though it would have saved a good deal of trouble if someone had known where you were."

Leelson nodded glumly, accepting this assessment.

Trompe asked, "Since you've been here awhile, I suppose we should ask if you've found out anything useful."

Leelson darted his eyes toward me and did not reply.

I rose and bowed, saying politely, "I will leave you now. Food stores have been augmented in anticipation of your arrival."

"You knew they were coming?" Leelson demanded in outrage. *"You* didn't tell me?"

"If you had asked, you would have been told," I replied, turning away from him toward Lutha. "Other supplies should be adequate for your stay."

I swept my pile of dust before me as I went out of the room and through the little hall to the door that connected with the hive. It, too, was made of wood, with a lock upon it. I swept my way through, shut the door loudly, then opened it a crack. No one noticed. I was able to hear everything they said.

"Damn them," Leelson was muttering. "Insular, taciturn, withholding information like that! I could have forestalled your journey. . . ."

Trompe said, "Calm down, Leelson. We're here now and we're on the same mission you are, so there'll be no conflict. Forget I asked any questions. We're too tired to think about it now. I hope there's space for all of us to sleep."

I heard Lutha murmuring agreement, then scuffings and murmurs as they moved about, exploring the cells. There were plenty of wall benches, plenty of cotton sleeping pads. Bernesohn Famber had used one room for storage, but the other two rooms were large enough for all of them. In the hive, they would have housed a dozen of us, but evidently outlanders needed more privacy than we Dinadhi.

"Leely and I'll take this room," said Lutha from the back room where Leelson had been sleeping. "I presume there's other sleeping space for you men."

"Plenty of sleeping space," Leelson murmured, moving in and out.

Though the dispenser could deliver hot food, I had cooked food for their evening meal and left it in food boxes on the shelf. Someone found the boxes, for I heard the sounds of their opening, the little homely noise of spoons and bowls. Those who were eating did so slowly and silently. Perhaps they were too tired to have appetite or enjoy flavor.

Through the door, I watched while Lutha took Leely into the room she had chosen and Trompe retreated to the storeroom where he'd made up a bed for himself. By opening my door a little wider, I could see into the room where Leelson was. He had spread his own bed on the bench under the window and had opened the shutters a crack, to let in the evening air. I drew in a deep breath and held it, forbidding myself to go in and close the shutters once more. Not while he was awake. He lay for a long time, eyes open, but at last he wearied, closed the shutters himself, and settled to sleep.

My own sleeping place was near the door, near the outlanders, where, without moving, I could see through the crack. Something was going to happen, because of them or to them, so I had brought my pad and blankets from below. We veiled women have few enough amusements, few enough stories to tell one another. We need to see and hear everything!

The sound of someone moving about woke me in the mid hours of the night. I saw Lutha come out into the little hallway, where she stood looking in on Leelson. Though I could see only his hand, his sleeve, it was enough to tell me he had, as usual, slept only a little before rising to busy himself with Bernesohn's equipment. Often he spent the night so, muttering to himself and making notes. His back was toward Lutha, and she spent a long time staring at him, fury and longing battling on her face. Later she told me her feelings for him were like surf, love and lust pounding at her, only to recede, leaving pools of chilly, clear anger behind.

I grew weary watching her silent battle, and I had shut my eyes when she spoke at last:

"I can't understand why you didn't tell someone!"

The legs of the chair scraped on the floor. It was Bernesohn's chair, the only chair I had ever seen except in Simidi-ala. We do not use chairs in the hives.

He growled, "You can come in, Lutha."

She bit her lip as she went into the room to join him. Though I could not see them, I could hear them clearly.

He said, "What I can't understand is your bringing the child out here."

She blurted, "I wasn't given a choice, Leelson!"

"I'm sure the Procurator didn't force you."

"He gave me to understand my doing what he asked might have something to do with human survival," she snarled. "Which would move most of us, even those of us who aren't Fastigats or Firsters." She came back into the doorway, half in, half out of the room.

He spoke from behind her. "Your coming, I understand. I said I couldn't understand your bringing the child."

Her expression was disbelieving. "Listen to yourself. Damn it, Leely is Famber lineage—"

"No," said Leelson firmly. "He is not Famber lineage. Not according to Fastigat custom."

"Your own people are supporting him!"

"Fastigat responsibility is one thing. Famber lineage is another. Each has its own parameters."

"You only say that because he's not . . ."

"Normal? Of course. Fastigat lineage, under Fastigat law, requires a basic condition of humanity. That's where we separate from the Firsters. They would accept Leely, we won't. Humanity, under Fastigat law, has a specific definition."

She glared at him. "You're saying your own son is not human!"

"Lutha—"

"Leelson!"

They fell silent simultaneously. I thought at first they were concerned about being overheard, but perhaps it was only to get control of themselves that they stopped when they did.

"My belief concerning the child is at least as sensible as yours," he said at last, rather sadly. "You're trying to hope him into superhuman status, into some new avatar of humanity. We Fastigats, on the other hand, say simply he does not meet our definition."

"You don't think he's human!" she charged again.

"No."

"Even though you and I are—"

"Lutha, we've said this—"

"I don't care. . . ."

He sighed deeply, wearily. He said:

"Genetic programming sometimes goes awry and produces a nonreplica. At the cellular level, such mistakes are eradicated. We remove warts; we cure cancers. At a slightly higher level, we remove extra limbs resulting from incomplete twinning. We do all this without great emotional hurricanes. But when the mistake is at a neurocortical level, when the body looks human, or even rather human, emotions get mixed in—"

She interrupted him with an outthrust arm, rigid and furious.

"Let's not discuss it," he suggested. "We won't agree, Lutha. We can't. Let's agree to accept each other's position. If you had to bring him, you had to bring him. I'll accept that you believed it was necessary."

She moved into the room and out of my sight. I sneaked into the dark hallway and stood where I could watch them. She was facing the closed shutters, her arms crossed, her hands clutching her shoulders, hugging herself, perhaps cautioning herself. He had gone back to the table and was sorting through the record chips Bernesohn Famber had left strewn about. My mother had gathered them up and put them in boxes, but some of them had already been nibbled by cornrats. Cornrats can survive only because we have made hives safe for ourselves, making havens for them in the process.

"Bernesohn didn't believe in labels," Leelson murmured. "I've been going through chips for the last three days, and I've yet to find anything that's identified. He also didn't believe in filing categories. Some of these chips have a dozen different things on them."

Lutha wasn't willing to give up the former topic. "The people here in

Cochin-Mahn knew you were here, didn't they? Chahdzi knew you were here. Hell, probably the people in the Edge knew you were here!"

"Of course. Chahdzi brought me here, just as he did you, and I came through the Edge, just as you did. I was surprised that the housekeeper did not tell me you were coming."

"Why didn't they tell us? I could have been partway home by now!"

"Well, it's the same question I asked Saluez, isn't it? You didn't ask them if I was here. I didn't ask them if someone else was coming." He shook his head at her. "If they'd volunteered the information, you'd have left without paying for the hover you no doubt rented, and the guides, and the supplies. Dinadhi don't do anything that discourages custom. They need hard currency too much."

He inserted a file chip into the retriever and pressed it firmly home.

A woman stood in the center of the room, her voice making a fountain of sound, lovely as falling water in an arid land. Then another woman stood beside her, singing, a voice joined to itself, a duet of pure wonder. The scent of something flowery and spicy filled my nose. I tasted wine. My body ached with wanting. . . .

It was only a fragment, over in a moment. Sensurround, they call it. Magic. Oh, to think of that being here all these years! If I had only known!

"Tospia," breathed Lutha. She took a deep breath, then another. She was trembling. I could see it from where I stood. But then, so was I.

"You played that one for me a long time ago," she said, her voice yearning.

He did not answer for a moment, but when he did, the words came crisply, without emotion. "Since there are no labels, I never know whether I'll find an aria, a shopping list, a lubricious monologue, or something significant."

He removed the song chip from the retriever and began clicking other chips into it, one by one. Voices muttered. Vagrant scents came and went. I tasted herbs, mud, smoke.

"You've found nothing so far?" she asked. She had gained control of herself and her voice was as impersonal as his own.

"One fragmentary memorandum. I marked it. It's here somewhere. I'll run across it in a moment."

I got out of sight as she wandered back into the bedroom where Leely lay sprawled, running her fingers along the walls, along the small, barred air-vent openings. At the storage cubicles, she began a meticulous search. Top to bottom, left to right, missing none, scamping none.

In the third compartment of the second row, she found a set of holograms and a display stand. I knew what they showed. Herself. Herself and Leelson. Different places. Different times. None of them with Leely.

In the next compartment below, she came upon clothing she evidently recognized, for she held it up, smiling, shaking her head. A rainbow-beaded vest. A belt of iridescent leather. Shirts and trousers and a long, warm coat of rare earthsheep's wool. At least Leelson had said it was earthsheep, though none of them existed on earth—Alliance Central—anymore.

I disappeared into my storeroom when I heard Trompe moving around. He came to Lutha's door, demanding, "What?"

"Looking for anything Bernesohn may have left, but all this stuff belongs to Leelson," she replied.

In the next room, Leelson inserted a chip that whined and scratched before speaking clearly and plainly. During the past several days I'd heard it more than once. The voice was scratchy and a little cantankerous. At hearing it, both Lutha and Trompe crossed into the room where Leelson was.

. . . 'fore leaving make record of . . . following significant findings . . . Ularians . . . reason for Dinadh's immunity . . . oldest settled world in the sector . . . only one, here or elsewhere, where the present inhabitants are mumble-mumble as to origin.

"Is that the memorandum you mentioned?" asked Lutha while the chip made scratchy, whining noises.

"This is the only one I've found that says anything about the Ularians," said Leelson. "Unfortunately, there are only a few clear places. Something has chewed on the chip."

He fiddled with the machine; it repeated the last phrase several times, *to origin, to origin, to origin.*

. . . narrowed field of inquiry . . . taken steps to . . . remedy situation . . . considering factors that seem . . . Dinadhi omphalos and abandoned gods . . . tell Tospia . . . rejoinder of my lineage . . .

The reader went on blurting fragmentary words and phrases interrupted by harsh scratching and stretches of gibberish.

Leelson, Trompe, and Lutha stared at one another.

"I've played that one several times," said Leelson. "I've jotted down the clear words and phrases, here. Any ideas?"

"It's enigmatic at best," said Lutha at last. "Was he anticipating legal action? Rejoinder is a word I've only run across in legal documents."

Leelson shrugged. "The bit about rejoinder to the question of his lineage may refer to the court action Tospia brought against the news sniffer over the paternity of the Famber twins. Did you know about that?"

Lutha said, "The Procurator mentioned it. Tospia visited Bernesohn here, returned to Central, had twins, and their parentage was questioned."

"Questions of lineage, as you've discovered for yourself, would have annoyed Bernesohn no end. His voice sounds annoyed. Also, there's a good bit of frustration and weariness, but no real excitement. Possibly because he's tired. As though he'd been digging and digging for something."

"The answer that wasn't here, perhaps?" Lutha sighed. I knew what she was thinking. To have come all this way for nothing.

"Or because he'd found out what he needed to know," said Trompe thoughtfully. "He could have learned what he needed to know and done something about the Ularians. He says he took steps to remedy the situation."

"The record didn't say he took steps to remedy 'the situation,' " contradicted Lutha. "There's a pause there. . . ."

Trompe paid no attention. "My god, Leelson. The only *situation* was the Ularian business. If he had a remedy . . ."

Lutha sat down, murmuring, "He speaks of abandoned gods. I've heard nothing of abandoned gods while we've been here on Dinadh."

Oh, but I had. Whispered by grandmothers to granddaughters, mentioned in old songs sung by sisterhoods.

Lutha went on: "He also speaks of the omphalos. Had he any maps of Dinadh?"

Leelson nodded. "Here? A whole file of them. But why maps?"

"Place-names often survive while language changes around them. Sometimes the names of places give us the only evidence of languages that have otherwise disappeared. God names are sometimes applied to places, therefore a place-name might be a clue to what he calls an abandoned god."

She ran her hands through her hair, pressing her fingertips into her forehead. I could feel her ache in my own forehead as she said:

"The only other thing that comes to mind is that Bernesohn disappeared from here, where we are. We know hover cars can't get down into the canyon. We know the Dinadhi use fliers only for emergencies—kind of emergency unspecified. So, wherever he went, he probably had to go on foot. Since he mentioned the omphalos, is it credible that he went there?"

I heard the rustle as Leelson unfolded the maps. I myself had seen them, had unfolded them, studied them, all the wonderful maps. Printed upon them were all the roads, lines of green; the ocean, a blotch of blue; the endless twisting edges of the canyons, black squiggles; and the names of places in curly lettering. The omphalos was shown there, too, shaded in violet and crimson, important colors, sacred colors. When duty had required me to tend to this place by myself, after Mother departed and before Leelson came, I had many times sat at that table and traced the way, how I would go if I were going to the omphalos. To Tahs-uppi. To the renewal. To say good-bye.

I could feel the map in my hands, soft from handling. I could visualize it, much fingerprinted, bearing many notations in a microscopic hand.

Lutha saw what I had seen.

"Somebody's used this," she said. "Bernesohn. He's annotated it."

"Used it a lot," said Trompe.

"If Bernesohn Famber went somewhere on foot," Lutha persisted, "how did anyone find out he was gone?"

Leelson replied. "They told me the housekeeper came in here to clean or bring new supplies. She found the last supplies hadn't been used, so the hive was told to keep watch. When no one saw him for a year, they named him an outlander ghost and said he was wandering among the canyons. They invited him to join the people of Cochim-Mahn."

"What does that mean?" asked Lutha.

"I asked the same question. They told me they invite all the ghosts to join them, and furthermore, that most of them do so. They wouldn't clarify the matter, so don't ask. I don't know and I can't pick up anything clear from their emotions."

He could have picked up a good deal from mine. I got up from the place I was hiding and went to the door. I wanted to hear what they were saying about the omphalos.

They stood around the table, looking down at the map. Lutha's fingers traced wandering lines of canyons and the tips of mesas, all ramified like the branches and twigs of trees, pointing off in all directions. Canyons run down all the sides of the mesas; mesas limit all the edges of the canyons. Except at the sea. And at the omphalos.

"Look at this," said Leelson softly as he pointed to the southward leading canyon. "What does that mean? 'Simi'dhm'a.' "

She raised her head. Later I was to learn what that posture meant, that alertness. Her mind was searching, searching.

"Separated," she said. "Separated something. What would the root word be? Dhuma?"

"Could be."

"The word for songfathers is hahm-dhuma. So this would be what? Separated father?"

He thought about it. "Ghost?" he suggested. "A parent who's died?"

She shook her head. "That doesn't have the right feel to it. I need a lexicon. Either that or I need a lot longer with the old chips. Tomorrow we'll ask Chahdzi. Maybe he'll tell us."

"I will tell you," I said from behind them.

They turned as one, surprised, perhaps a little hostile.

"There is a dark canyon, where the sun scarcely touches. It is Simi'dhm'a, which now means lost and lonely, though once it meant abandoned ones. Importances left behind."

"Left behind where?" whispered Lutha. "Where, Saluez?"

"On the other world. Before we came here. On the world of Breadh. It was there we left Mother Darkness and Father Endless."

They looked at me. I could feel the two men probing at me, trying to feel as I felt, feeling as I felt but not knowing why. Lost, they were. Not understanding.

"Why?" Lutha breathed. "Why did you leave them behind, Saluez?"

"Because of them," I whispered, gesturing at the shuttered windows.

Leelson moved to the window. I hurried to turn off the lamp, an outlander lamp, one that runs on stored sunlight.

They watched as Leelson shifted the lever that controlled the shutters, opening them only a crack.

"Careful," I whispered. "Oh, be careful."

Fragile fingers slid between the slats. Luminous eyes peered in at us. Teeth as delicate and sharp as needles bit at the edges of the slats. My flesh knew those teeth. I cried out.

Lutha turned to me, reached for me, catching my veil with the bracelet she wore. My veil dropped. They saw my face. Lutha hesitated for only a moment, then drew me close to her and held me.

Leelson closed the lever.

From the darkness outside came the cries of petulant children, denied a treat. It was the sound I had heard after Masanees had sounded the gong. I had not heard the sound of wings, one or two approaching quietly, as was customary, but these same cries, the noisy approach of many, talking among themselves. And when they came in, they had not gorged themselves on the banquet prepared for them before settling on my back to do what they had come for. No. Instead they had grabbed my hair, pulled at me, raised my head, insisted upon getting at my face.

"They!" said Leelson with certainty. "They did that to you!"

They had, yes, but I did not reply. Instead I stood with my head on Lutha's shoulder and let myself cry. I had not seen the beautiful people since the House Without a Name. Perhaps I had hoped never to see them again.

On Perdur Alas, Kane the Brain came in from the day's labor in the fields, where they'd been planting various food and fiber crops for the ag-test. He was carrying a bundle on his shoulder, something wrapped in his own jacket, and he put it on the table in the lab, saying to no one in particular, "We found this thing in a cave out there."

Snark was filing germination records, but she put the pile down and came over to see what it was. A jar, not unlike the jar in her cave.

"That's Father Endless," she said, tracing the pattern. "And Mother Darkness. And these are the horizons of sleep."

"How do you know that?" Kane demanded, not too urgently. "You've never seen it before!"

"I've seen them before," said Snark, remembering all at once that this was true. "My mother told me about them. On Breadh our people believed in them, but then our people listened to the words of the tempter and put their gods aside. My family was of the T'loch sdi, the old order." The words came of themselves. Labels. An identity, for herself, for her mother, for certain other children, certain other mothers and fathers. The old order.

"What does that mean?"

She quoted what she had been told:

"We were faithful to our beliefs. Faithful to Father Endless, to Mother Darkness. When we died, we died into their keeping, for that was part of the everlasting pattern. We did not allow the tempter to sway us. Even after many generations on the new world, we remained faithful. And at last we ran away from the new world, fled from the new commandment. We came here. That is, my parents came here."

"You weren't born here." Willit sneered. There was no real venom in his voice. The challenge was only habit.

"No. I think I was only a baby, though. I grew up here. Keeping away from the scourges of the tempter, until the ship came and took us survivors away."

"Survivors!"

She rubbed her head fretfully. "Me. And the other children. Five of us. All the adults were gone by then." Gone to Father Endless and Mother Darkness. Gone into the womb between the worlds. To the place where everything dwells in timelessness.

Willit started to say something sneery, but Kane stopped him. "Snark. Why did they call you survivors?"

"Because they didn't believe we had lived here. They thought we'd survived a shipwreck, taken off in a survival pod, got twisted into a wormhole, and ended up here. They thought we were castaways. I knew we weren't, but they said the five of us couldn't have lived here otherwise.

"It was on the ship they said we were survivors. Then, later, they put me in the home. But the people at the home didn't know . . . who I was. They said I was a liar."

"Right," barked Willit. "They knew you, kid."

"I wasn't lying," she said.

"There's no world called Breadh," said Kane. "Not in this sector. You were probably sent here from one of the other worlds, when the Ularians came. If you were the only ones left, what happened to the others?"

Snark thought about it. Part of it was clear and close. Scourges. They'd had to stay away from the scourges. And from something else, too. She shrugged. She couldn't really remember.

"Survivors from Ularians. I be damned," said Kane.

"And what are these damned Ularians when they're not hiding under a rock?" asked Willit.

"Nobody really knows." Kane looked at the jar he'd found. "Nobody knows who they are. There were no survivors. Not unless Snark was one."

"You mean she really could have been? A survivor?"

It was all very casual, not very meaningful, and everyone went back to work without agonizing over it. In Snark, however, the discovery of the jar began a chain of recollection. She remembered faces, voices. She remembered things people had said. She remembered words. The returned ones. The faithful.

That child Snark: How long had she been here, before they found her? Had it been only a few days? A few seasons? Had it been years? Whether born here or not, certainly she had grown here. Someone had provided clothing. There had been the animal skins, the fleeces in the cave, the clay jars. Where had the skins come from, with their woolly fleece? There were no animals like that on this world.

No. They'd been wearing the animal skins when they came! But they had brought no tools, no food. Who had told her that? Someone had. How had they grown food? Had they grown food?

How much was reality? How much was dream? That night, curled in her blankets in the cave at the edge of the sea, she asked herself that question again and again, finding no answer. In the niche in the wall, the patterned jar kept its enigmatic silence. There were bones in it, she was sure of that. Whose bones they were, she did not really want to remember.

CHAPTER 5

O n Dinadh, Leelson and Trompe asked me questions until I could answer no more questions. "Saluez? Saluez?" they begged, until at last I wept. All the pain I had refused to feel, all the tears I had stored away, everything came flooding out, drowning me.

"Leave her alone," Lutha said angrily to the two men. "Later on we'll find out what we need to know. We're too tired now. We will talk when it is light."

Everything was easier when it was light. Perhaps she knew that better than they. I let her lead me back into the entryway, through the door I had left ajar, to my bed in the storeroom of the hive.

"Do you sleep here?" she asked, her tone saying what her words did not, that it was a poor place for a woman to sleep.

"It is . . . private," I whispered. "And it is closer to my duties than the other place, below, for women like . . ." For women like me.

"Why, Saluez?" she begged, her voice a whisper. "Why did they do this to you?"

I choked, thrusting her away, trying to put her off, noting the way she had said it. Not "What happened to you?" but "Why did they do it?" How could I say why? How could I tell her when I did not know myself? She caught herself up, becoming very quiet before she laid her fingers upon my mutilated mouth. Tender fingers. Gentle hands.

"Never mind," she said. "Tomorrow."

Tomorrow would offer no more explanations than tonight, but I let it be.

She left me. I lay down upon the shelf, pulling the woolen blanket over me, turning my head upon the cotton pillow to find a certain position in which my face was mostly hidden but was not thrust hard against the fabric. I didn't want anyone to see my face if they happened upon me sleeping, but actually covering it brought pain. There is a venom in their teeth, and any touch can set it afire. The pain sometimes lasts for years, so my sisters say. If I find exactly the right position, the pain diminishes almost to nothing; I can fall asleep and, sleeping, forget, and sometimes even wake without remembering, believing for a few blessed moments I am as I used to be. . . .

The man who was father to my child is Slozhri T'ri. Turry. In Lutha's language, his name means Worrier. He worried at me from the time we were children together. His mother is . . . was a second mother to me. My only mother after my own was gone. Poor Chahdzi father. He has had little fortune with his womenfolk. Saluez, his first daughter, now come into this shame. And my mother, his first wife, long since gone into the night and returned as our departed kindred do. She left human form while giving birth to my little brother. I was only a baby then. So, after a time father took another wife, Zinisi, a s'mahs, which is to say a screech bird, one who has made his life a misery. His second daughter . . . Well, if any man can bear being close enough to Hazini to get her pregnant, the beautiful people will likely let her be. Likely her flesh is bitter as her tongue.

Even so, perhaps she is the better daughter. Perhaps she will be the better wife to someone. Someone will be a better wife to Turry, too, and he can worry at her for a time.

He has not asked to see me. Sometimes men do ask, so the sisterhood says, advising against it. Better not to see, not to be seen. Better to have one's child among one's sisters, better to nurse it and wean it and send it up into the hive to be reared by its father's people or by one's own people. Better never to let it call you mother. Better watch it from corners, from behind doorskins, seeing it grow, praying that Weaving Woman will do better for the child than for the mother. Better to take all one's joy in the sisterhood. In the special food and drink, stored by the sisters selfishly, for themselves, for their own pleasure and no one else's. In the special songs and stories one hears only there, the special weavings made only among the sisterhood. In the special herbs gathered and dried only there so the sisters may have peace . . .

Small pleasures, stored against the darkness of despair. Taste something savory. Smell a little sweetness. Let a sister rub your shoulders where they ache, or brew a special pot of tea, or even join in making bodily delight as some of the sisters do, as I would do if Shalumn were among us. That is the greatest loss. Love is the greatest loss. We make a life of remnants, of details, and so each hour's shadow is delayed, another day, another day. But, oh, the nighttime is hurtful when you lie down and your body longs for the body of the beloved. When your breasts tingle and your nipples get hard and you taste the beloved's skin on your tongue and between your legs, you are on fire. Even being pregnant does not stop that. Animals have more sense. They do not go on rutting and mating once the female has kindled. They do not stand knee-deep in sweet grass and long for apples. But we, we people do. We go on longing and longing and longing, and all the beautiful people and all their teeth and talons do not change that!

So I lay breathing like a bellows, panting, trying to imagine I was as I used to be and she was beside me, we two moving together in the bed dance.

All . . . all for nothing.

I sat up, tears flowing, unstoppable, as though another dam had broken. There was a water pitcher in the corner. I put my head over the basin and poured the cold water through my hair, gasping when it ran around my ears and into my eyes. Beside the basin was the packet the sisterhood had given me. At first I had taken it, thanked them, told myself I would not use it, but more and more I did use it. Now I took one of the leaf rolls and lit it at the candle, drawing the smoke deep into me.

"Say, 'Mother Darkness, come to me,' " the sisters had said.

"Mother Darkness, come to me."

"Say, 'Father Endless, come to me.' "

"Father Endless, come to me."

"Say, 'Mother and Father of peace, come to me.' "

"Mother and Father of peace, come to me,

> *Tomorrow will be easier.*
> *And the day that follows easier yet.*
> *And I will grow to age in tranquillity,*
> *In contentment approaching you,*
>   *whom my kindred have forgot."*

After a time my body went away somewhere, flying, as though lifted by a blessed wind. I lay down on the bed and nothing hurt. Oh, when I was a child, I would never have dreamed the pleasure that comes from the mere absence of hurt. Such a sweetness was, for the time, enough. I set the rolled leaf in the covered, spouted bowl beside the bed and turned my nose into the braided skein of smoke. I breathed and breathed, watching the guttering candle dwindle into dark. And I slept.

On Perdur Alas, Snark made her way toward the sea. Her hands were empty, for all the things needful for her survival had long since been stored in the cave. The stealing was over. The scurrying and sneaking were over. Behind her in the camp the other shadows slept, weary at the end of a tiresome day spent weeding the test gardens. The seeds of a sedgelike native plant came floating on every breeze, sprouting in mere hours to form a network of thick stolons in which nothing could grow but themselves. They had to be sprayed, early and often. They had to be cleared by hand from around the food seedlings. Despite this annoyance, the ag-tests were coming along. They knew now what would grow, or at least what would germinate and sprout, though it would still be some time until the harvest. A small victory among workers who did not care enough to count victories. The planet could be homo-normed. It would support human life.

There were other coups that had been counted, and these were Snark's own. Though technical knowledge had been forced upon her, it seemed to fit her mind as mate fits mate, making a comfortable fullness instead of an aching vacancy. It was like being transported from a barren desert into an orderly jungle, where every byway was lined with interesting bits of information, where techniques and processes grew on every tree, like fruit. She had been moved to create a microorganism to fixate nitrogen on plant rootlets. She had grafted genetic instructions for a flavorful grain onto the basic stock of one of the furzelike plants of the moor. There had been excitement in these experiments, in thinking of them and finding within herself the knowledge to accomplish them. She had felt elation, a hen cackle of victory at each successful outcome.

Tonight she was late in her journey, delayed by a stack of report forms. She had been tempted to stay in the dormitory with her fellows, but the retreat to the sea's edge was habit now. Let it go on. Whatever changes the day might bring, let comfortable habit sustain each evening.

"Sustain," she said to herself, as though quoting. Someone else had said that. "Sustain each evening with comfortable . . ." No. Not comfortable. Essential. Essential habit.

Whichever it was, she went through moonlit darkness toward the sea, past the tea-dark pools and the marshy places, through the rustling bracken, toward the roll of stones upon the sea shelves, the incessant grinding of gravel beside the waves. Which was, tonight, making a curious sound.

She stopped, confused. A curious sound. Not the usual one. This was flattened, muffled sounding. As though some enormously thick bandage had been pressed down upon the world.

She crouched, making herself as small as possible, then crept silently into a nearby tangle of bracken from which she peered out through slitted eyes. Near on her left, she heard a *clack-chitter-chitter-clack* as a small shelled creature made its laborious way across an outcropping of stone. From some distance to her right came the shrill cries of the seabirds in their spiraling gyre above the hammered sea. She was not far from the rim of the cliff. Not far from the cave itself. Perhaps a few hundred yards, all told. Still, better not move. Better merely wait to see what this oddness portended.

Whatever-it-was went on being odd. She turned her head seaward. The bird cries piped without resonance. Even the sound of the waves was wooden and flat, reaching the ear as a single impulse, a slap with no following susurrus. Everything seemed damped. And then, moving to the left, between her and the sea, a wallowing darkness, a silent, heaving immensity.

The thing had no edges! She could not see its shape. Though it swallowed stars, they were not thickly enough strewn to show an outline. At the advancing edge, a star winked out, then another, and at the trailing edge one winked into being, then another. Huge it was. Like a building. Yet moving . . . moving soundlessly. Invisibly.

She burrowed her face in her hands and did not look up for a time. When she did so again, the darkness had turned inland, toward the camp. Before her the stars winked out, one by one.

She could run, perhaps, and warn them! She could sneak quickly along under the bushes and get there in time to tell them . . . what? That a monstrous shadow was coming?

Her flesh tingled, as though an electrical field had been generated around her. Her hair stood on end. Her breath left her lungs in a sudden rush as the air pressure increased, more, and more, and more, then was suddenly gone, leaving her gasping into her cupped hands, desperately achieving silence.

The shadow was between her and the camp, approaching it from the south. She squirmed silently, turning so that she faced the camp. Everywhere, shadows.

Shadows. Immensities.

One approached from the north. And another yet, from the southeast. Wallowing darknesses, with no distinguishable features, no identifying characteristics . . .

Except the taste coating her tongue. Like carrion and cold and something hideously oily-rancid. She held her nose. It was not smell. The taste flowed between her teeth, making her salivate profusely, a copious, mucilaginous spit that trailed sickeningly from the corners of her mouth and refused to be spat away. The taste of moldy mastodon. The flavor of Behemoth. The savor of absolute immensity.

"Are you getting this?" her shadow mind mocked the distant observer, the monitor on Dinadh, the evaluator at Alliance Prime. Despite terror and discomfort, her rebellious ego thumbed its nose at that distant watcher, wherever, whenever it might be. "God, I hope you're getting this. This is them, fellows. The Ularians. Just taste them!"

She almost screamed, for she felt it then. A vibration in the soil beneath her. Perhaps she heard it too. So deep a sound. Once and again. And again. The sound of earthquake breeding but not breaking. The sound of unimaginable hooves, slowly treading.

A shriek from the direction of the camp, only momentarily human. More surprise than pain. Cut off in midhowl. The darknesses gathered thickly there, around the camp.

And at this evidence of purpose concentrated away from herself, Snark scurried silently on all fours toward the sea, toward her landmark stones and her polished branch, throwing only one terrified glance behind her when she arrived there, seeing nothing toward the camp but the absence of stars, hearing nothing, smelling nothing, but tasting . . . oh, that foul grizzly smell, that flavor of old fur, long and matted, of bloody hooves and a hugeness past belief.

She dropped into the cave in one frenzied movement, then thrust her head outside to spit into the ocean far below, scraping her tongue with her fingers, taking out her knife and using the back edge of that to scrape with, only then able to stop retching. The taste was still there, but diminished. Here it was diluted by the sea air, by its salt tang and chill cleanliness.

She crawled under her blankets and was still as any animal petrified by fear, self-hypnotized into quiet. Time passed. The plod of those unimaginable feet came again, then once more. In her reverie, the shapes against the stars assumed form, like a puzzle her unconscious kept probing at. Maybe they weren't really that big. Maybe they had like . . . wings. Bats looked a lot bigger than they really were. And birds. Perhaps, in the daylight, one could see that they were quite imaginable, only with wings. If they returned in daylight.

Except that winged things did not plod in that obdurate, inescapable way. Did not stalk across a world as though it were a pasture.

Light flushed the horizon and she squinched her eyes shut against it, refusing to admit the audacity of daylight. It was still night, she told herself. Still safe dark, hiding dark, friendly dark.

Sunlight allowed no such fiction, for she had forgotten to wall herself in. The sequined surface of the sea flashed into her eyes, blinding her. She emerged slowly, cautiously, drew down the branch, and lifted herself to peer above the rimrock across the moor. There was the camp, as she had left it, all the landmarks as she had last seen them. Nothing else. No residue of the disgusting taste. The flatness gone. Sounds once more familiar. Echoes coming from far hillsides and nearby stones. She crawled onto the rim and lay there quietly, waiting. Nothing. Nothing. Whatever it had been, whatever they had been, they had gone. For now.

It took a long time for her to decide to go to the camp, for she knew from the beginning what she would find. A vacancy. Everyone gone. Kane the Brain and slob-lipped Willit and even Susso. No blood. No mess. Not even the feathery ash a disposal booth would have left behind. Nothing at all.

Crumpled blankets on the beds, fallen into body shapes. Here a light left on, where someone had been up, maybe on the way to or from the toilets. And yes, there a pair of slippers, a stride apart, where the feet had been lifted from them all at once, the nightsuit fallen into a heap between them. Living things, human things gone, but their belongings untouched.

Except for the test gardens. There were barren plots. Not all of them. Not all the tests. Just some. This one and that one, apparently at random.

But, of course, it would not be at random. This clean-edged selective destruction could not be by chance. The plots destroyed had been selected; they would have to have something in common!

Snark dug into her pocket for her notebook and dictated into it, listing the plots destroyed, grains type 178 and 54 and 209. Root crops 89 and 102 and 5 and 27. Virtually all the leaf crops, leaving only half a dozen standing. Destroyed because of what? Dangerous? Or merely not nutritious? Or perhaps not smelling nice to whatever the monstrous shadow had been. Or not tasting nice. Or not something nice, some other sense that Snark could not even imagine. Perhaps the destroyed crops made the monstrous shadows itch? Or made their eyes water. Assuming they had eyes. Which one would be wrong to do. The missing crops made their enormous membranous vorticals twinge, that was it.

She found herself thrashing on the ground, laughing hysterically. The sounds she was making frightened her, and she stopped all at once, horrified at herself. She choked the sound with her own hands, terrified at her own panic. She had been conditioned! She shouldn't be able to feel anything of the kind!

Conditioned to be among others, she told herself. Conditioned to be one of a group. Not to be alone. Not like this. She clicked on her notebook once more, setting down her thoughts, her impressions. "The sound was damped, like big curtains hung in open space might do," she said. "Absorbing sound waves." After a moment's thought, she described what she had unconsciously resolved about their shape. "Winged," she said. "I think they must have wings, or some membrane of some kind that covers a wide area. But . . . I got the feeling of shagginess. Of fur . . ."

The laboratories were undisturbed. Her grain furze grew glossily green and spiky in its hydroponic tank. The lights above it were still on. The generator hadn't been touched.

If she were to make changes, would the darknesses notice? If she moved something here, now, would they return and realize someone had escaped their raid?

Who could tell? Better change nothing. Better move nothing. Or, better yet, move some tiny inconspicuous thing and see if they noticed.

She had left a bundle of furze-grain seedling stored in the back of a coldframe. They were in an unlabeled container. Probably the darknesses had not even seen it. In case they had, she divided some other seedlings and put the container back, now holding something else. She would plant the seedlings near her cave, where in time they might stand between herself and hunger.

There were food stores, too, that she could shift, leaving everything looking much as before. When she returned to the cave, she did so heavily laden. Everything had to be swung into the cave at the end of a rope and then tucked away in crannies before she, herself, had room to stretch out. It was late afternoon before she was finished. Too late, that day, to plant the seedlings. Tomorrow she would get them in. Not in rows or patches, but one by one, among the native plants they much resembled. And tomorrow, if the darknesses did not return, she would take more food, carefully, just as she'd learned as a child. Leaving no trail. Making everything look just as it had before.

From my room in the hive, I heard Lutha and Leelson and Trompe talking. It was early morning. They thought I was still asleep, I suppose, for they were talking about me.

"The emotion was shame," said Trompe in an argumentative tone.

"Also anger," Leelson insisted. "She was ashamed, but also angry."

"Wouldn't you be?" demanded Lutha. "My God, gentlemen. Wouldn't you be? The anger part I can certainly understand."

"So can we," said Leelson in a tone even I thought to be patronizing. "It's the shame part we're finding intriguing."

"What they did to her was a rape," said Lutha furiously. "Our persons are in our faces. When we show ourselves to the public, we show our faces. That's what we recognize about one another, those of us who see, at any rate. Our faces portray our personas. Her persona was violated, just as in rape. Rape evokes emotions of shame and anger because of the violation."

"Why was it done?" Trompe asked.

She replied, "We won't understand it until we find out a lot more about this society." She paused, breathing furiously, enraged on my behalf. Even from where I lay on my bed, I could hear her fuming.

"And I *will* find out," she said firmly.

I thought she might indeed, for she seemed a very determined woman. I would have told her what she wanted to know if I could. But could I say, yes, it was my own fault, for sometimes I have doubts, and my sisters in sorrow tell me they, too, have doubts. But, so my sisters say, we are not alone in this! Our mothers, siblings, cousins, our dearest friends, they have doubts. Most of those who emerge unscathed from the House Without a Name, they, too, have doubts. Doubts are not peculiar to those who have been maimed, so why . . . why we? Was our doubt of a particular kind?

More had been maimed lately, so the sisters said. In our great-grandmothers' time, almost no one was maimed, but now it is more than half! Why? What was happening? The sisterhood argued over this again and again, finding no answer. What does one say? I was guilty of doubting. I did not doubt more than others, or differently from others, but I was selected for punishment. My punishment was particularly horrid because . . . because of who did it to me. . . .

Lutha was right. There is no rape on Dinadh, but I can imagine it would be as shaming, as cruel as this. In a way, it was like what the two Fastigats were doing to me, questioning me, searching at me, examining me, bending their Fastigat sense upon me. That, too, was rape. They increased my shame and sorrow for no good reason, for they could not learn something I did not know.

It is better to do as the sisters recommend, to say nothing at all, to admit nothing. Let them seek elsewhere, among others for answers. And if they find answers, let them tell me.

A voice from the door.

"Saluez? Are you awake?"

Lutha.

I sat up, pulling my veil into place. "I was up earlier," I confessed.

"Leelson and Trompe and I've been talking," she said. "We have an offer we wish to make you, in return for your help."

I had heard nothing of an offer. What offer?

She said, "It's possible . . . your face can be fixed. Restored . . ."

"No," I cried, thrusting away with both hands. "No. Do not say that!"

She looked shocked, horrified. "But surely . . ."

"I would have to leave Dinadh," I cried hysterically. "I would have to go away from my people. They would not let me live here if you healed me."

"But . . . but I thought . . ."

"It was my fault," I cried. I who had decided to say nothing! I, who knew it was not my fault! "My face is evidence of my sin. Do you think you can erase my sin by healing me? Do you think my people will let me live among them if I am healed!"

She backed away from me in confusion. Leelson came from the study and put his hand on her shoulder. "What?" he demanded.

She turned and led him into the room, shutting the door firmly behind them. And I sat on the edge of my bed and cried. Oh, if I were healed, Shalumn might be mine again. Oh, if I were healed, I would have to go away. Oh, if I were healed, it would change nothing, it would change everything!

After a time I dried my face, straightened my veil, and went to knock upon the closed door.

"I will help you," I said when they opened it. "But you must not talk of . . . what you said earlier. Not at all. Not ever!" I could not bear it. It set all my hard-won peace at nothing.

They stared at me, all three of them. The boy was curled on a bench beneath the window, playing with his fingers. They cared, but he did not.

"Why?" asked Leelson. "Why will you help us?"

"You say there is great danger for everyone, perhaps for Dinadh too. Perhaps the outlander ghost found something to avert this danger, so I will help you search for the outlander ghost or for what it was he knew."

Leelson ran his hands through his hair. He was a handsome man, Leelson. Tall, bright-haired, with one of those rugged, rocky outlander faces that always seem strange to us Dinadhi, who are round-faced and smoother looking. The boy looked something like him. More like him than Lutha. But he had a big-eyed strangeness to him, something I thought I should recognize.

"Where could Bernesohn Famber have gone, Saluez?"

It was a foolish question. He knew as well as I. "You heard his own voice," I replied. "He spoke of the southern canyon, of the omphalos. You yourself said he must have walked. That is where he walked."

Leelson frowned as he seated himself. "All right, let's take it point by point. Last night you told us certain gods were abandoned on your former world."

I nodded. Unwisely, I had said it.

"And these gods were abandoned for"—he gestured toward the window—"the beautiful people."

"We chose the Kachis instead," I said. "Our songfathers chose them."

"Why?" asked Lutha.

"It is not something we speak of," I told them. "I have already said more than is proper. We chose them, that is all. We abandoned certain of our gods, and chose these instead, and came here to this world."

"Through the omphalos?"

"Through the omphalos."

They looked at one another in that way they have, like grown-ups amused by the fanciful tales of children.

"She believes it," said Trompe, staring at me.

Why would I not believe it? It was true.

"If you'll allow a non-Fastigat a comment," said Lutha in a dry voice. "As a linguist, I've become aware that there are many kinds of truth— factual truths, scientific truths, spiritual truths, psychological truths. It is no doubt spiritually true that the people of Dinadh emerged from the omphalos. That being so, it doesn't matter whether it's factually true or not." She smiled at me, saying I might believe as I liked, she would not question it.

"Why do you say that?" Trompe demanded.

She turned to him, gesturing. "I say it because we can only deal with so many variables at a time! Bernesohn didn't mention emergence stories, he spoke of a place! A geographical location. We need not concern ourselves with what's true or false *about* the place, at least not until we get there."

I bowed my head. Exactly. What was true or false did not concern them. Only their duty concerned them, as only my duty now concerned me. My duty and my child to come. The future, to which life itself owes a duty. "To fit into the pattern," say the songfathers. "Each life owes a duty to fit in."

Even men who know many lies occasionally tell the truth.

"We must go there, then," said Leelson. "To the place."

"It is forbidden," I told them. "No outlanders are allowed at the omphalos. Only Dinadhi without stain may attend Tahs-uppi, and the ceremony will be very soon."

They simply stared at me, knowing what I was feeling. How strange to have people know as these men knew. They knew what I had said was not all I meant.

"But you're going to take us there," said Leelson at last, prompting me.

"I will guide you," I whispered. "If you want to go."

"But I have a map," he said, holding it up for me to see. "Do I need a guide?"

"You don't have a way to travel," Lutha said. "That's what she means."

"You would not last an hour after dark," I said quietly. "There are ways and ways. You need someone who knows the ways."

Not that I knew the ways. I'd never been out after dark, but I'd spoken with herders who had. Leelson moved to the desk, Trompe to the bench, Lutha to her child, all thinking, all deciding, as though this wandering motion helped them think. Perhaps it did.

"They'd know we were gone," said Lutha, pulling Leely into her lap. "They'd come after us."

"How would they know?" I asked. "I am your servitor. I take care of your needs. If I do not report that you are gone, who is to know?"

"They would see we aren't here, see we aren't moving around."

"They don't look at you anyhow," I said. "That's what I am assigned to do. I look at you so the others don't have to. We do not look at outlanders, we of Dinadh!"

"They would know *you* aren't here," said Trompe.

Lutha said softly, "They don't look at her, either."

Behind my veil, my mouth twisted. It was true. If Chahdzi or songfather did not see me for a number of days, they would think I was staying out of sight. The sisters below would know they had not seen me there, in our place, but they would not search for me. They knew I served these outlanders. They would wait until my duty was done and I came to them.

"So they wouldn't know we were gone," said Trompe.

"No," I said. "They would not know. Not for some time. Songfather may not know until he himself arrives at the omphalos and finds you there."

"The ceremony is soon?" Lutha demanded.

"Very soon," I told them. "Within days."

"Can we get there first?"

"Not by much," I admitted. "A few days, at most."

"How do we get there at all?"

"There are wains here in the canyon, wains that make a safe enclosure for people, with woven panels to make a safe pen for the gaufers that pull them. When the songfathers attend Tahs-uppi, that is how they go. We must take a wain and six gaufers to pull it."

"Gaufers?" asked Lutha.

"Woolbeasts. The young are gaufs. Gaufers are the neutered ones."

I could see her tucking these words away against later need.

"How do we get these gaufers down from the heights?" asked Leelson.

"We don't. There are still some here, because all the flocks have not been moved up the trail yet. We must steal them before the flocks are taken up."

"Food stores?" murmured Trompe.

"There is much food here in the dispenser," I told them. "Though it is outlander food, I imagine I can figure out how to cook it over a fire."

They thought about this for some time. Lutha went on cuddling the child. Trompe stared out across the floor of the cave to the canyon. Leelson fiddled with things on the desk, moving them about, here and there. When Leelson turned to me at last, it was not to ask how, but why.

"If this journey is forbidden," he said, "you may be putting yourself at grave risk."

Behind my veil I smiled. "What can they do to me that has not already been done? Perhaps they will kill me! They will not do it until after the child is born, and I do not care if they do it then."

Perhaps it was only what Lutha calls bravado, but I think I was telling the truth.

I am not much practiced at stealing. We Dinadhi do not steal, not much. Oh, children, sometimes, a little dried fruit more than our share. A handful of nuts. A finger dipped surreptitiously into the honey pot. What else? What is there? Only what we make with our own hands.

So, considering how to steal a wain and gaufers was a novel thing for me. It had a certain stomach-churning excitement to it. Leaving the outlanders to mutter and worry behind me, I went out onto the lip of the cave and sat with my legs dangling over the edge. Below me, behind screened openings in the canyon wall, the herds have their winter caves. There before the time of First Grass the females bear their young. When all the gaufs have been born and are steady on their legs, the herds are driven up one of the trails onto the grassy forested lands above. Wains are not taken back and forth. They are too bulky and heavy to drag up and down the trails. So there are wains on the heights for the herders to live in, and there are wains in the canyons for the songfathers to travel to and from the little ceremonies at each other's hives and the big ceremonies like Tahs-uppi.

At the Coming of Cold, the herds come down again, into the caves, where they eat the dried remnants of our gardens, the vines and stalks and even the weeds we have pulled and set aside for them. When they have eaten it all, they eat fungus, as we do, growing as tired of it as we do and becoming eager for the fresh green of the heights. Most of the herds had gone up already, but a few small flocks were left.

Getting six gaufers away from the herders would be possible. Harnessing them would probably be difficult, though I thought I could figure it out. Harnessing them, hitching them, driving them, all that to be figured out and accomplished without being observed. Which meant at night.

"What are you thinking?" asked Lutha, coming to sit beside me.

I told her my thoughts, describing the caves, pointing downward where this one was, and that one, shaking my head at the danger, at the difficulty.

"When we came to Cochim-Mahn," she said, "we left the hostel and started down the trail when it was barely light. Chahdzi said it wasn't quite proper to start before the dawnsong, but we did it, nonetheless. Suppose we take the animals very early in the morning, just at dawn."

"The herders would not hear us then," I agreed. "They sleep in the hive, and they do not come out until the daysong."

"So, if you locate the animals we need, and if Leelson finds a wain, and if we take all our supplies down, a little at a time . . . well, then, in a few days . . ."

"It must be sooner than that," I told her. "There are only a few animals left in the caves."

"Well, we'll begin at once," she said. I heard apprehension in her voice. It would have been surprising if she had not felt it. I did.

"At once," I agreed. "It will take time to carry our supplies down the ladders."

She sighed deeply. "Do you know the way to the omphalos?"

"No. But I have heard the stories of the journey, over and over since I was a child. How the wains go, and what people see on the way, and how the . . ." I had been about to mention what the beautiful people did at Tahs-uppi. That was forbidden. Instead I said weakly, "I've heard how the songfathers draw out the extra days, to balance the seasons."

"What did they look like, these extra days?" she asked, half smiling.

I shook my head at her. "No one knows. All those present hide their faces. It would be improper to look."

"Improper to look at a lot of things around here," she muttered to herself as she rose and went back into the leasehold, to tell the others. I went down the ladders to see if our plan could be made real or would remain only talk.

The herd caves smell only a little, because the droppings are taken away at once to the caverns where fungus is grown, just as our human waste is taken in the hive. So, when I came to the caves, there were herders moving about with their shovels, cleaning the pens and pretending not to see me. Perhaps they did not see me. I tried to remember if I had seen veiled women before I became one myself, remembering times in childhood when adults had whispered to me that it was not wise to look, not wise or polite to see. So I had not seen. Now I was not seen.

So much the better. I could take my time. I could linger. I could see where the stoutest gaufers were, two in this pen, three in that, one in the third. When they are neutered, their horns curl tightly instead of growing out to the sides. That way we may drive them in pairs, side by side, without their bumping. The neutered ones get heavier, too, and tamer, for they are constantly handled. There were seven or eight good ones in the pens, and they nosed the woven panels at the front of the caves, soft noses wrinkling, side-whiskers jiggling. *They* had not been trained not to see me. If I brought tasties for them, they would see me well enough. Well enough to follow me.

Where was the harness kept? I did not see it in the caves, though there was other equipment hung here and there among the bins of dried fungus. I swept dust from my memory, recalling me as a child, riding on Chahdzi's shoulder, being shown the beasts, the caves, the wains. What had the harness looked like? Chest straps, as I recalled, with fringes on them to keep the insects away from the soft, naked hide between the front legs, where the false udders are. And carved wooden buffer bars, to hold the pairs abreast. Wide hauling straps of gaufer leather, and long, light reins of braided bark fiber, the same as our well ropes.

There was nothing resembling a harness in the caves.

Which meant the harness was with the wains. Or in the hive somewhere.

I passed Leelson Famber on the ladders, murmuring to him that I had not found the harness. He nodded and continued downward. Perhaps he would find it.

If it was in the hive, it was in the quarters of the herdsmen, where their families lived. I could not go there when the people were there. Perhaps at the morning song, when everyone was gathered behind the doorskins, waiting to go out. Then I could slip inside to look around.

There was a time I would have hated this sneakiness. Was a time I would have considered it beneath me, beneath any Dinadhi. Now I was no longer a person to be concerned with such things. I was an unperson. I did not exist. Who would point the finger at me when they could not even see me?

I returned to the leasehold. Lutha was there, feeding the child. I offered to do it for her, and she handed me the spoon with an expression almost of relief. She went to sit in the window, looking out at the day while I plied the spoon. It was like feeding a little animal. He was too old for the breast, but I had the feeling he would best have liked to suckle, for he could have done that without thinking at all. Certainly he could not keep his mind on the spoon.

He calmed as he grew less hungry. When we were finished, it took a large towel and a bowl of warm water to clean up the boy and the area around him.

"He has always been this way?" I asked.

"Yes," she said, her body stiffening. She did not want to talk about it. Well then, we would not talk about it.

"There are some good gaufers down there," I told her. "But I couldn't find the harness. Perhaps Leelson will find it in a wain. Where has Trompe gone?"

"He's carrying supplies down the ladders," she said with suppressed laughter. "Or was. Here he comes, very hot looking!"

As he did, out of breath and considerably annoyed.

"Leelson's found a wain," he said. "It's parked out of sight of the hive, around those stone columns south of the cave. He told me to put the food inside it. Otherwise he thinks it won't last until we're ready to leave."

I nodded. He was right. Any food left where the Kachis could get it would be either eaten or fouled past use. "Was the harness there?" I asked.

"I don't know. I didn't look and Leelson didn't say." He collapsed onto a sleeping bench and threw one arm across his face. "Lord, that's a long climb. You Dinadhi must have steel legs and arms, up and down all day as you are."

"Two trips a day is considered much," I told them. "One is the usual. When the farmers go to work in the fields, they go down at daylight and return before dusk. They carry their lunch with them."

"We haven't talked about how long this is going to take," he said. "How much food we'll need . . ."

"All we can carry," I told him.

"Then we'll need a faster way of getting it down there."

Silence, broken by the sound of the door. Leelson, returning.

"Harness is in the wain," he said. "I counted the individual sets, and it looks like enough for six animals. On my way back, however, I overheard several of the herdsman talking. They're taking the animals up tomorrow."

Silence again.

"We'll have to leave before then," murmured Lutha. "Won't we?" She gave me a pleading look, as though hoping I could think of some other choice.

"No time for sneakiness," I said. "Were there panels on the sides of the wain you chose?"

He nodded, his lips pressed tightly together. "Yes. I remembered that part. They make up the pen for the gaufers, I presume."

"Walls and roof, to keep them safe at night," I said. "Tomorrow before light, we'll take all the food from the dispenser, put it in sacks, and drop it into the canyon. We need not carry water. This time of year there will be water along the canyon-bottom trail we'll follow. We'll have to be gone before light." To my own ears, my voice shouted panic, but the others did not seem to hear it. They merely sighed, resolved on the struggle to come but taking no joy in it.

"They'll know the wain is gone," Trompe objected.

"Perhaps not," I replied. "There are extra ones. If the one you picked is beyond the pillars, likely it is one that was not to be used this year. Or, if someone sees it is gone, they may think someone moved it. People are always moving wains around. To store things in. Or to repair them."

"They don't belong to anyone in particular?"

"They belong to Cochim-Mahn. Not to any particular person. Anyone might move a wain."

"Well then," said Leelson.

"I just had a thought," Trompe interrupted. "What about weapons?"

"Weapons!" I cried. "To use against what?"

They looked at me, the two men with those expressions they have, reading me, knowing how I felt. Well, I could read their faces as well!

"No!" I shouted at them. "That is forbidden. You will not!"

The two exchanged glances, then shrugged, both at once, as by agreement.

"They are our . . ." I said, trying to explain, remembering I couldn't explain.

"Your what, Saluez?" asked Lutha curiously.

I could not say. I had already said forbidden things, thought forbidden thoughts. I shook my head at her. Enough. One might do this little wrong thing, or that little wrong thing, but not forever! One could not cut across the pattern over and over again. I had to stop, even though these folk were eager to know more. Let them find out some other way. Let them read it in someone else's feelings. I had said all I could say.

On Perdur Alas, night on night the monstrosities returned to wander the world. Even when Snark did not see them, she could tell they were present somewhere: just over a cusp of hills, in a valley somewhere, at the bottom of the sea, perhaps, for when she stood with her mouth open and turned about slowly, she could taste them, strongly or faintly. At first she would taste nothing, perhaps, but then her tongue would curl at the subtle disgust of them, the cloying rottenness, the foulness that could not be spat away.

One taste was enough. Whenever she detected it, she went to ground. Driven as much by instinct as by prior knowledge, she made herself a dozen hidey-holes around the camp and between it and the sea. She dug upward, into the sides of hills, so the tunnels would drain and the holes would stay dry. She made them large enough to be comfortable. She knew if she was surrounded by earth, the beings could not detect her. If she was in a hole, with foliage drawn over her, they could not tell she was there. She thought someone had told her this, just as they'd told her how to dig holes. She seemed to remember these things from that former time.

The blacknesses, as she called them, did not always come to the camp. Moreover, the blacknesses were not always the same. Occasionally, rarely, they were like the first time, with that same muffled soundlessness, that same trembling of the soil, that same monstrous plodding. More often they were merely shapes against the stars, who brought with them a horrible taste. Very rarely they were both. They came irregularly, once every three to five nights, seldom two nights in a row, always after dark. She wondered if they came to the other side of the planet when it was night there. She dug out the reports and found that the other side of the planet was mostly water, covered by the vast shallow sea that made up nine tenths of Perdur Alas. They came when this side was in darkness, she decided. The other side was not useful to them, or was less useful, or was . . . unimportant, perhaps. Who knew?

Why did they come at all? After that first night, they changed nothing. They took nothing away. They added nothing at all. They merely came and wandered about, black against the stars, occasionally trembling the earth, shaking the hills, shaking Snark herself in absolute terror.

At first she survived on this terror, letting it drive her deep into her cave and keep her there. As time went by, however, curiosity asserted itself, and she found herself speculating more and more about what the presences were, and what their enigmatic business might be. She wanted to see them. She wanted to get a good look! She did not consider that she might have been conditioned to be curious. The feeling was natural to her. She had always been that way. Mother had . . .

Mother had always been that way too. Mother had been here with her, long ago, and Mother had always been curious about Perdur Alas. The others . . . the other people used to warn her. Don't take chances. But Mother had taken chances. The memory came and went, evanescent as a breeze.

It was time to satisfy curiosity. Since the beings seemed no longer particularly interested in the camp, she stealthily removed a number of items to make night spying easier: devices for seeing in the dark; recorders activated by change in air chemistry or pressure, by sound or movement, by temperature change; solar-powered lights, solar-powered reference files. More food and blankets, to make her other hidey-holes warm enough to spend whole nights in, if necessary. The things that wouldn't fit into her cave or into the new hidey-holes, she hid elsewhere. The solar devices she secreted here and there in newly dug holes or among piles of stone, covering them with layers of furze that she could remove each morning to allow the devices to charge. The night eyes she secreted in her hole above the camp. There, lying in the mouth of her tunnel, rolled into a pair of soft blankets and screened by carefully positioned branches, she propped herself in a comfortable position, one she could wake from silently.

They didn't come. Toward morning she roused, tasting them. They were somewhere, but not here, not at the camp. The taste was mild, barely discernible. She stood up, yawned, and made her way to the cave over the sea.

Twice more she waited fruitlessly.

On the fourth night they came. She gagged on her own saliva and knew they were nearby.

She focused the device, propping it in the opening, careful not to move the screening grasses and leaves. She watched them come from the west, over the sea, watched them traverse the moor between, watched them gather south of the camp as though waiting for something or checking on something or, perhaps, merely assembling there prior to departure. Through the device she could see the shape of them, the way they moved. They had no legs. These could not be the earth tremblers; these were the others. Monstrous and shaggy, they floated in air, multiple appendages hanging limply below, a few of them reaching to the sides as though feeling the way.

Snark put down the night eyes and clawed at her mouth, cleaning it out with her fingers. Too much of this and she would choke on her own spit! She put a wad of leaves between her teeth to hold them apart so the sticky saliva could flow—if it would—and lifted the device to her eyes once more.

The shapes had no faces, nothing that looked like ears or noses or mouths. Occasionally two of the creatures would pull in all their appendages, making their bellies smooth and shiny, and would then turn toward one another while wavering blobs of deep-hued color flowed across the smooth integument. The next time two of them paired in this fashion, she took the device from her eyes to see if the color was visible to the naked eye. It was detectable only because she knew it was there. A shifting red shadow, a depth of blue or purple, at this distance hardly discernible without the device.

On Prime, while living in the sanctuary, she had gone with the other children to an aquarium. She remembered a multiarmed sea creature that had changed color, being in one instant white and gray, in another dark, marbled with red, and in another so gravelly that it disappeared into the sandy seabed it lay upon. So the skin on these creatures changed, from dark to light, from pattern to pattern.

One of them had a winy-red patch that repeatedly moved diagonally downward, left to right. Diagonal Red, she named it, turning her attention to the others. By the time night was over, she had named Four Green Spot, Blue Lines, Big Gray Blob, and Speckled Purple, these particular ones because they were at the top of the hierarchy. Diagonal Red was the one who moved first, the one the others followed. Blue Lines and Speckled Purple were next, then Four Green Spot and Big Gray Blob, and after them, a host of others whose characteristics she had been unable to identify. Over their next few visits she counted them, seeing as many as eighty at a time. Her count never came out the same. There were at least eighty. Maybe as many as a hundred, all huge as hills. All truly and unbelievably horrid.

For a time she stopped watching them, too exhausted to do otherwise, but curiosity reasserted itself and she came back to her hidey-hole, back to her blankets, watching. Very late, choking on the taste of them, she wakened from restless sleep. Two she later identified as Diagonal Red and Speckled Purple had returned alone and were moving through the vacant camp. After making colors at one another several times, they separated, one stopping at the seaward edge of the camp, the other stopping on the inland side. There they poised themselves, turned on their sides, settled onto the soil, and extended three or four appendages on each side, these tentacles becoming longer and longer, wider and wider, creeping along the edges of the camp, surrounding it, until at last the tips approached one another and touched.

From her carefully dug hole on the hill, Snark could see down into this squat cylinder of alien flesh, five hundred paces across. The outer surface was shaggy. The inside was bare and shiny. She watched fascinated as colors developed upon the bare bellies of the participants, then moved sideways onto the appendages, moving right to left, onto the

other creature, color succeeding color, shape succeeding shape, an un-
ending flow of luminescence, now bright, now dark, now vivid, now pale,
flowing uninterruptedly from the bare flesh of Diagonal Red across the
appendages to the bare flesh of Speckled Purple, thence around onto
Diagonal Red once more, a slowly whirling vortex of color and movement. She didn't need glasses to see it. It was perfectly visible without!

Despite the strangling taste, the strangeness of the sight, something
teased at Snark's mind, something she should see, should understand.
She strained, trying to think, what was it? Something . . . something . . .

Then it was over. The two shapes darkened, the appendages separated, curled into tentacle shapes, shrank languidly back to their usual
size. The central creatures rose like shaggy, bulbous balloons and moved
away. Propelled, Snark told herself, by thought. Or wish. Or by something else, somewhere else.

A few moments later the taste vanished. Snark scraped her tongue,
rinsed her mouth with water from her canteen, spat repeatedly, getting
rid of it. What had she just watched? What kind of ceremony? Oh, to be
a Fastigat right now! Able to sense whatever emotion had been present,
whatever those two immensities had been feeling!

Something solemn, she thought. Some color litany, some ritual obser-
vance. Or perhaps they had been mating!

If so, why would they pick a human encampment to mate around? No.
It had more the sense of a ritual. Sacrifice, maybe? Explaining to their
weird gods that they had wiped out a few dozen humans as required by
their religion?

Again something teased at her mind. Something she should know! She
held very still, hoping it would come to her. It did not. Merely that
teasing sensation, something she should hold on to and could not get
hold of!

Ah, well. Let it go for tonight. She hid her night-eye device once
more, picked up her canteen, and trudged down the hill toward the
moor paths to the sea. The stars told her it was still some hours until
morning. Still some hours to stay hidden in. She had not known them to
come twice on one night, but this evening's exercise indicated how little
she really knew.

The way seemed longer than usual. When she dropped into the cave
at last, she was in a mood of weary indifference. She wanted to live, but
not much. What she really wanted to do was understand these creatures,

but what she had seen tonight was unintelligible. Perhaps they would remain unintelligible.

She stripped off her clothes and laid them in a pile at the back of the cave. Tomorrow would be wash day. She pulled other clothing from her sack and put it on. She always slept fully dressed except for her boots. One never knew when one might have to move quickly. She checked the emergency pack by the entry hole. Water. Food. Medical supplies. A change of clothing.

"Now I lay me," she told herself, curling into her blankets, knees to chest, one arm cradling her head. "Now I lay me." Outside the surf repeated sea words, over and over. *Shush. Soof. Fwoosh.* Again and again.

She dreamed. She was walking on the moor, coming to the cave by the sea, but she was not alone. Someone held her by the hand.

"We must go very carefully," the someone said. "Try not to go the same way too often. Not to make a trail, you understand?"

Snark jerked her chin resolutely, saying she understood. Things could follow trails. She had to be careful, or the *things* would get her.

They came to the edge of the cliff. "Hold on tight," said the someone.

Snark's arms were locked around the person's neck, her legs around the person's waist. The person leapt, and Snark's stomach came up into her throat the way it always did. Then they were swinging, swinging, then the hole was there, and they were in.

"Home is where the heart is," said someone, kissing Snark. "Home is where my girl is."

Snark looked up at the person. . . .

Color flowing, blotches flowing, making a pattern . . .

The person held her tightly, patting her on the back.

Bright and dim, pale and vivid, colors on the huge fleshy barrier. Shaggy skin outside, bare skin inside . . .

The person smiled.

Shapelessness became shape. Shades flowed into one another. Blotches and colors combined to make a face on the body of an alien monster, a huge face that moved and spoke and smiled and called her by name!

"Sweetheart," the mouth said. "Love."

Her mother's face!

Snark's cry went out over the sea like the cry of a wounded animal, totally alone, infinitely sorrowful.

"Mother," she cried. "Oh, Mother, Mother, come back to me!"

* * *

Night on Dinadh. In the leasehold, Lutha and the two Fastigats had had their evening meal. We had packed the last few things we intended to take with us. Then Leelson insisted that everyone lie down and get as much sleep as possible, promptly thereafter making it impossible for anyone to sleep by getting into a fierce argument with Lutha. I had felt it coming during our evening meal, like thunder just beyond the horizon, a muted mutter, scarcely heard and yet ominous, making one's whole body tense, awaiting the flash of lightning, the crash of riven air!

The flash was Leelson's pronouncement to Lutha:

"When Trompe, Saluez, and I leave in the morning, I want you and the child to stay here, Lutha. Give us a few days to get well away, then ask the people to take you back to the port."

"The hell," she snarled, a thundercrack.

Hurriedly, I left the room. They were so intent upon each other, they did not see me go. Trompe, who had been half-asleep in the neighboring room, had evidently felt the emotional storm going on, for he emerged, blinked at me, and mouthed, "What?"

I shrugged and kept going. While I fully intended to listen, I didn't want to be involved. We mutilated ones are observers of life, not participants. So says the sisterhood. And safer so, so says the sisterhood. And more peaceful.

So I took myself beyond the storeroom door and then shamelessly leaned against the wall while I listened to what was going on. Lutha was saying at great length that having come this far, she had no intention of going home.

"Besides," she cried, "you and Trompe aren't linguists, and I am."

"We are Fastigats," said Leelson.

"Fastigats aren't gods!" she snarled at him. "Much though you like to think so! You can tell how people feel, maybe, but you can't tell why. Sometimes, it takes words to tell why."

It was true that neither Trompe nor Leelson had a really good command of our language. I spoke far better aglais than they did Nantaskan. But then, a lot of us learn languages as children, in order to cater to our leaseholders. Why would they learn our dialect? There are few of us who speak the tongue.

"You will be safer at home," he said, like a father cautioning a child. "You will be better off."

"I'll decide where I'll be better off," she said. "If you'd had the common sense and decency to tell people you were coming here, I wouldn't have been sent. Now that I have been sent, I've no intention of going home until the job is done."

"The boy will be in the way." His tone said she would be in the way, too, which perhaps she noticed.

"Leelson," said Trompe from the doorway. I could see him through the hinge gap at the side of the door I stood behind. "Leelson. Stop talking and think."

Leelson stopped talking. I assumed he was looking at Lutha. The silence had a peculiarly penetrating quality to it, one I have noticed before when he or Trompe reached out. So, he was reaching at Lutha, into her, understanding her.

"Stop it," said Lutha. "Stop digging at me! I'm fully capable of telling you how I feel. I am not a gofer to be sent hither and thither at the whim of any presumptuous Fastigat who gets a burr up his rear! I'm a person. Until the Great Gauphin comes down from heaven and appoints you his lieutenant, I've got the same rights you have. I decided to come here, and I've decided to stay until our mission is finished. Since I had to bring Leely in order to get here, he'll come along, no matter how much 'in the way' he is."

Silence. I saw Trompe make a helpless gesture.

After a time Leelson said calmly, "Have you thought about your career? A lengthy interruption certainly won't forward it."

"Having a child didn't forward it," she said. "Quite frankly, I don't anticipate it forwarding much in the future. About the best I can hope for is keeping my head above water."

"She's bored, Leelson." This was Trompe.

More silence. Then her voice, quieter: "He's right. I'm bored with my life on Alliance Central! I'm bored sick with it! I'm also terrified at the threat of the Ularians. I may mock the Firster assurance that men are the meaning and soul of creation, but that doesn't mean I welcome being slaughtered by something bigger and meaner. The Procurator used fear for motivation, succeeding better than he knew!"

Even I, who am no Fastigat, knew she was not telling all the truth. Later, when the men had gone to sleep, she came to the storeroom door and peered in, looking for me.

"You're still up," she said, trying to be surprised. No doubt she had seen the light of my candle.

"I'm too . . . too something to sleep," I confessed.

She sat on a sack of grain, crossing her ankles, then recrossing them, twiddling her feet, wanting to talk about something, obviously.

"Leelson was right," I murmured. "You would be safer back in your home. And so would the boy."

She looked up at me blindly. "I don't want to be safe, Saluez." There was a sob in her voice, betraying a feeling I knew well. She wanted to die. It is not so much an active thing, this feeling, not so much a desire to kill oneself as it is a desire not to be. An absence of hope. Despite everything she told herself about the boy, she had no hope. She saw herself getting older and older while he got bigger and stronger, his demands got bigger and bigger, more and more difficult. She saw herself victim to a helpless love for him, unable to help him or herself, desiring rather to be dead.

I found myself holding her, cuddling her as she had cuddled me, laying my own fingers on her lips.

"He should get to know his son," she said, taking my hand in her own. "Get to know him."

What was there to know? I wondered. I didn't say it aloud.

"Leely has many . . . many interesting qualities," she insisted.

"Of course," I murmured. "Children do."

"His artistic talent alone . . ."

"Shhh," I whispered, rocking her. "Shhh."

So we sat together in the dark, reaching for light. My sisters tell me so women have done for lo these thousands of years.

CHAPTER 6

In the hive of T'loch-ala, which is *Old Place* in Lutha's language, Mitigan of the Asenagi and Chur Durwen of Collis, being neither linguists nor Fastigats, found that getting information out of the Dinadhi was easier assumed than accomplished. Though they were well served by the two women appointed to the task, one veiled and one barefaced, the women had no more to say than any other member of the hive. True, they spoke a little aglais, as did Chur Durwen, and Mitigan spoke enough Thibegan, which was a Nantaskan tongue, to make his wants known if he used sign language along with it, but neither of the men had any luck whatsoever in finding out where Bernesohn Famber might once have lived and even now held lease upon Dinadh.

"I've told you we don't know," said the barefaced servitor, an older woman whose voice verged upon annoyance. "We would have no reason to know. We do not discuss such things. Until you said the man's name, I had never heard of him. We have our own pattern here on Dinadh. Why would we ignore our own pattern to enter that of some outlander ghost?"

Both men were Firsters of the more primitive sort, accustomed to treating every itch in the groin as though it were divine commandment, and after several days of utter boredom in the hive, Mitigan thought he'd try a bit with the veiled servitor. She had a seductive shape beneath her robes and a pleasant voice from behind her mask. He managed to twitch the veil a little bit to one side before she got away from him, but that little bit was enough to leave him sweating and cold, like a man who had just escaped dropping over a precipice.

"My god, man," he whispered to Chur Durwen. "She looked chewed. Like a viper bat had been at her, or one of those hovolutes they have on Zeta Nine."

"Hovolutes don't leave anyone alive," objected Chur Durwen.

"Well, imagine one of the victims surviving and you'll have an idea what our waiting woman looks like."

Chur Durwen was curious. He kept watch, and one day as the woman bent over to pick up something, the veil fell loosely at the side of her face. He, too, caught only a glimpse, but that was enough.

These happenings were small in themselves, but enough to set both men thinking. They had assumed there were no predators on Dinadh, but now they began assessing certain phrases and silences, certain movements of avoidance, certain rituals of aversion.

"It's them," Mitigan said to Chur Durwen one night as he looked through their barred windows at the pale forms assembled across the canyon. "Those flyin' things that hang about after dark. They're dangerous beasts."

"Small ones," murmured Chur Durwen, unimpressed.

"Chowbys aren't big either," said the other. "Or viper bats. But you get overrun by a dozen of either one and you're dead meat. And ants, they're tiny little old things, but people on Old-earth used to go in fear of their armies. Stingers, those were."

"I'd forgotten about chowbys," mused the man from Collis. "And you're right. There's a considerable mob of those night fliers about. I must've seen several hundred, just last evenin'."

"So."

"So?"

"Puts a bit a crimp in goin' lookin' for Fambers, dunnit? Stands to reason they're not comin' here, we got to go lookin'."

"Must be a way." Chur Durwen stared meditatively at his boots. "Always has to be a way."

Mitigan grunted. What his friend said was true. There was always a way to kill a man or woman. No matter how he hid, how he ran, how he vanished into another identity; no matter how she pleaded, how she bribed, how she threatened. There was always a way. So Mitigan's father's brother had taught him when he was a boy.

"Always a way, boy. Study on the target, make him your book, make him your library, boy, and you'll find the way."

"They say killin's wrong, Uncle Jo."

"They! And who's they? They put power in your pocket? They buy festives for your women? Food for your children? Ha? Who's this they? Not Firsters, that's sure! No Firster ever said such a damn fool thing!"

Which was true. A man who'd recently killed was considered blood guilty, but there was a ritual for erasing blood guilt. All Mitigan had had to do was pay a hefty price to the Firster godmonger in the district where the victim lived. Those who spoke against killing were only do-gooders, reformers, non-Firsters all. They were men who belonged to no tribe, swore allegiance to no hetman. Men who, it was said, would puke themselves inside out if told to go out and get an ear for the hetman, a hand for the hetman, or somebody's head in particular.

Mitigan was born of the Dirt-hog tribe, and Uncle Jo sat on the hetman's right hand. Not quite next to him, true, but no more than three or four men down. Mitigan's pa, now, he'd sat right next to the Dirt-hog hetman, and when the hetman said go, Pa had gone. One time too many, as it turned out, but he died with his name bright, so Mitigan had no dishonor to live down.

It was a good tribe to learn killing in, all the way from elementary mutilations right up to, so Uncle Jo sometimes said, a graduate degree in massacre: an MMA, Master of Mortial Arts. Mitigan studied his subject as Uncle Jo had advocated: studied it and practiced it, and got so good at it that when the Dirt-hogs were ambushed by the Lightning Bears one bloody night at Headoff Hill, only fifteen-year-old Mitigan escaped and survived. He'd sworn vengeance. He could not have lived with himself otherwise.

The Lightning Bears had laughed at him, man and boy, laughed at him and hadn't even taken the trouble of killing him. They hadn't laughed five years later, after Mitigan had taken out the whole Lightning tribe, one man by one man, including every male child. That's why it took so long. That last infant he'd had to wait for, since it hadn't been born yet. Firsters didn't hold with killing babies until after they got born!

A man with that history had his future pretty well laid out for him. There was always a market for assassins, especially assassins who could think. Mitigan could think, though he did not think much about his career. A man could get tied up in his own thoughts, worried over them, or guilty over them, or overly convinced of his own prowess. A man needed a clear head to survive. He had to be careful.

Still and all, if a man really wanted to hit a target, Chur Durwen was right. There was always a way.

It wasn't long before Mitigan put two and two together to come up with the same answer those at Cochim-Mahn had arrived at. The key to traveling on Dinadh was to have a structure or vehicle inside which one could be safe at night. Since the hover cars were controlled from the port city, they wouldn't do. Since any other structure would make too heavy a load for a man, it would have to be hauled by beasts, which meant the beasts themselves had to be protected. Travel on Dinadh required a wain and beasts to pull it. Or the equivalent.

"You think I'm goin' to fool with animals, you got a fool's idea." Chur Durwen yawned.

"Right," agreed Mitigan. "We'll do it our way."

They'd brought certain items of equipment with them, the parts innocuously labeled and packaged as health monitors or retrievers and transcribers or library modules. Several of these items, taken apart and reassembled into a portable unit, would create a protective dome big enough to sleep in. Big enough to live in for a while, if necessary.

"Though it'll be somewhat troublesome," Mitigan told his companion, "I think we'd be wise to take a pack animal."

Chur Durwen didn't argue with him. In a pinch, Mitigan later told me, they could have carried their own provisions, but assassins preferred to stay unencumbered when engaged in their profession. Besides, at T'lochala, spring had not advanced so far as it had at Cochim-Mahn and there were many strong animals to choose from still in the caves.

"So now we know how," muttered Mitigan over his evening meal as he stared out the window at the dancing Kachis. "All we have to figure out is where."

The question plagued him as he ate, as he slept, as he did his weapons exercises morning and night. Chur Durwen, who preferred to get his daily exercise climbing up and down the ladders between hive and valley below, was bothered by the same question. Where?

It was a conversation Mitigan overheard between two women at the well ropes that gave them the clue they needed.

"Will you be going to Tahs-uppi with songfather?" one asked of the other.

"Alas, no," replied the other. She was quite beautiful, Mitigan thought, with black hair that fell in a lightless flow almost to her knees. She was also very pregnant. "Songfather feels it is too near my time."

"He's probably right," said the first, with a delicate shudder. "One should not be far from help the first time. Still, it's sad that you'll miss it.

All the songfathers and their guests will be there, from everywhere in Dinadh. Another such opportunity will not come in our lifetime."

Mitigan went at once to inform his colleague. "She said people would be there from all over Dinadh. Which means there'll be someone there who knows where Famber is, or was."

"Fine," muttered the man from Collis. "So we go to Tahs-uppi. Where is it?"

It took them some days of fumbling questions to elicit the information that Tahs-uppi was not a place but an event that took place at the omphalos, the navel of the world. Plotting a route that would get them there occupied them for scarcely another day. The morning after, very early, they stole a beast from a herd cave and departed T'loch-ala, leaving only one dead body behind them, that of an impertinent herdsman who'd wakened early and gone down to his flock without waiting on Lady Day. Had he waited properly, he would still be alive, a fact the songfather of T'loch-ala would later discourse upon at length.

"Have you never married, then?" Poracious Luv asked the King of Kamir.

Jiacare Lostre reflected. "I saw wedlock as wedded lock indeed, another set of chains binding me fast. Seeing what fate I saw for all Kamir, I did not wish for children."

"You can speak like common people if you like," she said, grinning at him. "You are no longer king."

He flushed, started to say something, then stopped. The slow beat of aristocratic speech had become second nature when talking to any but intimates or servants—in which category he had always included his ministers, just to infuriate them. And yet, he had not spoken like that when he was Osterbog Smyne. Why should he as ex-king?

Enjoying his embarrassment, Poracious thrust her seat back to the limit of the inadequate space the ship provided, stretching out her legs. She felt cramped. She was cramped. Her sleeping cubicle was the size of a disposal booth, and after spending several hours in it, she wished it *were* a disposal booth. One would travel more comfortably as ashes.

Of course, the journey could have been passed in sleep. Most passengers had chosen to sleep until a day or two before they reached their destination, but the king wanted to savor every moment of freedom, and Poracious had thought it wisest to stay with him. On the well-established ground that men like best to talk about themselves, she had led him to discuss his life and times at great length.

"What did you do for amusement?" she demanded. "Everyone has to have amusement."

"One spends one's time—" he began, catching himself. "I spent a great deal of time in the gym. I used to retreat there as a child, and I've rather depended upon it. One is told . . . I'm told I acquit myself well."

"In what sport?"

"Bisexual heptathlon."

She regarded him thoughtfully. He had the build for it, wiry and compact, and no doubt the energy for it, too, since he'd used it for nothing else. Or almost nothing. "I suppose they allow you women?" she said in a silky tone.

"Oh, Lord Fathom, yes," he blurted, unthinking. "Women. Men. Animals, too, one supposes, if one liked. One's father had an insatiable appetite for little girls. So far as one is aware, his desires never went unfulfilled. There are middle-aged women all over Kamir living on pensions from the government. One supposes that's how the ministers managed it."

"That and payment to the girls' families, probably," said Poracious.

He sighed. "I always had trouble imagining what kind of family would . . . would . . ."

"Many kinds," she said dryly. "Believe me, Your Majesty."

"Jiacare," he said. "If I am to speak like a commoner, you must stop calling me Majesty. Call me . . . Call me Jickie."

"Right. Jickie. As I was saying, I've seen families who would sell their children, their grandmothers, their husbands or wives. Sometimes out of desperation, sometimes out of greed, but I have seen it."

"One's own life has been more circumscribed," he admitted. "One has only read of such things, and it is hard to know what is real and what is fiction."

She nodded ponderously. "Most fictions turn out to be real. At least, such has been my experience. I no sooner hear some horrible story, told as a mere tale, than someone assures me it really happens, here or there. Sometimes it turns out the perpetrator heard the same tale and decided to copy it. Massacres, mutilations, murder, mayhem. There are worlds where all these things are everyday affairs. Asenagi, for example. From among whose people you did not hesitate to send an assassin after Leelson Famber. Surely Kamirian law does not countenance such activity."

"Well," he mused doubtfully, "in fact it does. Though only for kings. Kings customarily do anything they like so long as it can be hidden from the public. One's father often said that public officials generally do so.

People want to believe in their kings or presidents or procurators. They gild their leaders with brightest gold, as they do their idols, though both may be but clay. And so long as one does not rub our people's noses in one's filthier habits, one can lead them to the slaughter in war, one can squander their treasure for one's own aggrandizement, one can give preference and immunity to one's friends, children, and kin. One can let the poor starve and the sick die, and the people will still follow so long as they see one smile and wave and seem to be satisfied with the way things are going."

"So long as taxes are kept low," Poracious rumbled.

"That too. But mostly one has only to wear a kingly mask in public while seeming to be interested in the common man. It's easy to do. One simply watches for occasions when common men do something uncommon, then one notifies the news sniffers that one is gratified at this example. One has one's picture taken with the awed hero, who may, in fact, have done a very stupid thing. All his neighbors treat him with reverence for several days thereafter, and a holo of himself rests into perpetuity upon his altar shelf, along with the image of his god."

"Your ministers cooperate in this effort?"

"Oh, yes. Aristocracies conspire to keep their reputation clean. Though they fuss at one for not begetting sons, one has heard them privately say that a bachelor king is less trouble than royal offspring, who are, however one trains them, beset by the passions, ambitions, and rebelliousness of youth. One's own escapades have been minor. One was assured, for example, that word of the previous flight from Kamir never reached any further than the palace walls."

"It reached the Fastigats," she said. "Obviously. May I make a suggestion?"

"Of course."

"It is not customary for commoners to refer to themselves as 'one.' If you are desirous of appearing less—"

"Oh, one takes the point. I, that is. Do." He flushed. "It's difficult. I keep forgetting. When I ran away, I had a role I'd planned on. I'd practiced my speech, my gait, the clothes I would wear. I haven't practiced this." He fell silent, nodding to himself, before saying, "About the Fastigats. I didn't know that Famber's finding me was merely an assignment. I'm afraid I attributed to him some degree of personal malice. To one being pursued, the pursuer may seem motivated by something more than mere duty, and once he had found one . . . that is me . . ."

"If you'd told him you didn't want to come back, he'd have left you alone, as required by Fastigat ethics."

The king flushed. "I didn't ask. He didn't say."

"It's of no consequence now," she said. "So, tell me, do you have a favorite mistress or sweetheart?"

Jiacare smiled slightly. "I did. One or two."

"But you didn't bring anyone with you."

"No encumbrances," he said. "I wish to experience freedom. I've never had freedom before. The other time I was a fugitive, not a free man. By the Great God Fathom, madam, do you have any idea what it's like, being born to royalty? Every action scrutinized. Every word assessed. Every royal bowel movement inspected. Every royal sneeze worried over. I cannot say with any certainty that there were not several pairs of eyes looking through holes in the wall during my acts of sexual congress. The best I could do was draw the bed curtains and stay beneath the sheets!"

"It would have a damping effect," she admitted.

"Indeed. A very good word for it. All that attention put out one's, that is, my fires very well, madam, both physical and spiritual. Believe it."

"I can see why you wanted revenge against Famber."

"Well, yes. But I shouldn't have done it, even so."

Poracious allowed him a moment of reflection before asking, "So, tell me what kind of woman you like? Assuming, that is, you do like women."

"Women, yes." He stared at the curved surface above them as though he saw a picture there. "I have never paid much attention to appearance. My favorite woman—up until the time she married someone else in order to have children—was not at all attractive in a physical sense, though she had great vitality. I admire humor and intelligence. And, of course, patience. It takes a great deal of patience to be mistress to a king."

"In future, perhaps your companions will need less patience. That is, if you are truly resolved to be no more a king."

He shrugged carelessly. "If one went back, they'd have to depose Fenubel in one's favor. Such is Kamirian law. But if one . . . that is, I don't go back . . . Well. I am free not to go back."

Poracious Luv nodded. He was indeed free not to go back. Perhaps he would stay on Dinadh. The Alliance had offered him a vast sum for his help. The former king could live much as he would, if he would.

"I've been wondering," he said. "What happens if we get to Dinadh and find that my assassins have already killed Famber's wife and child? What if they've found Famber himself and killed him?"

She shifted her huge bulk uncomfortably. "Pray they have not. When this Ularian business started, there were four populated systems in Hermes Sector: Dinadh, with one world and a few storage installations; Jerome's system, with several settled worlds and moons; Goan's system, with several settled worlds and a homo-norm team on another one called . . . Perdur Alas; and finally Debair's system, with several settled worlds, one of which, Tamil's world, was wiped clean by the Ularians just before we left Kamir. Or, so I heard. I don't remember how many worlds that makes. Half a dozen or more, totally wiped clean. The losses are in the millions."

He scowled at her, vertical wrinkles appearing between his eyes. "That's too many to keep quiet. You'll have a panic."

"There's already considerable panic in the outlying areas, those nearest Hermes Sector."

"The ship's library says the Dinadhi keep their foreign guests pretty well spread out. Will the authorities let us go directly to the Famber leasehold?"

She grunted, a porcine sound. "They must. I bear letters of demand from the Procurator. All ships of the line are engaged in evacuation, but the Dinadhi don't know that. I'm to threaten them with invasion if they don't cooperate."

"I shall follow your lead," he said carefully. "Lord Fathom, but I've messed things up."

"Not your fault, lad," she murmured. "Not anyone's fault. How can you lay guilt for an enigma like the Ularians? We still have no idea who, or what, or why—"

"Or when," he murmured.

"Or when," she agreed. "All we can do is our best, and do it as quickly as possible."

Among the scattered buildings at Simidi-ala was a small stone house occupied by Thosby Anent, the Alliance agent, and by Chadra Tsum, a Dinadhi woman. The moment Thosby took up residence, everyone in Simidi-ala knew what he was, for everyone knew who Chadra Tsum was, and she was assigned as his housekeeper. Chadra was an agent for Simidi-ala, assigned to find out things, which she did with one hand while busily keeping Thosby's house with the other. All in all, the functionaries of the Edge were thankful that Alliance interference was limited to one elderly individual, known to be addicted to imported tobaccos and liqueurs, who was, even when sober, more otiose than diligent.

Thosby Anent was as blessedly unaware of this assessment as he was of most other real things. He galloped through life like a fifth leg on a horse, always in motion, seldom touching the ground, and to no purpose when he did. Even in childhood he had been far too preoccupied with being other people to learn to be himself. Early on, he had played at being Mysterious Child or Royal-Boy-Raised-by-Commoners. Later he had played Brilliant Scholar and Gallant Lover and Deep Thinker, in each case adapting or even curtailing reality to accord with his current persona. He maintained a little recorder in which he entered supportive quotations from old books and antiquarian records along with lists of tasks he meant to undertake, turning each morning to a new page without ever referring to the old.

All this I was told, in time, by Poracious Luv, who had used all the resources of the Alliance to get a clearer picture of its agent upon Dinadh.

While in his early twenties, Thosby had experienced the biography of an almost legendary diplomat-cum-secret-agent, and this had convinced Thosby that his true talent lay in foreign service. He thereupon invented the role of Sagacious Applicant, performing it so well that the Bureau of Information Services actually awarded him a minor clerical position, which he filled with his customary distracted inefficiency. His supervisors, finding him too ineffectual to retain but too amiable to dismiss, shifted him to another department, whence he was shifted to others yet as successive executives moved him gently along. Thosby misinterpreted their efforts as he did most things. He believed he was being groomed for A Really Important Position, so he flitted from job to job with an air of intent incomprehension, waiting for his true talents to be applied.

Thosby reached the acme of incompetence in the Division of Minor Planets, a department whose charge it was to recruit unencumbered persons to serve as factotums and general mumbleglums on small and unimportant worlds—places like Far Barbary or Finagle-Chump or Dinadh. No one objected when Thosby was sent to Dinadh as covert flunky in charge of routing intelligence from Hermes Sector. The personnel officer who made the assignment knew, quite rightly, that any idiot could route intelligence!

Thosby Anent, however, was not just any idiot. He was an idiot convinced he was being moved into An Important Place! Prior to his arrival on Dinadh, he spent a great deal of time choosing the roles he would play there—the roles, that is, in addition to the one he had been assigned—coming up with two that were no more inappropriate than all his other roles had been. He chose, as primary persona, the role of Master Spy. For this he had designed and rehearsed a conspiratorial manner and a repertoire of winks and nods of great significance. As a "cover" for Master Spy, he adopted the persona of Codger. This required him to smoke a tobacco pipe, wear an eccentric hat, and adopt a manner of gruff but kindly bemusement along with a spraddled way of walking, as though slightly crippled in the knees. In order to avoid "giving anything away," Master Spy was laconic while Codger was obfuscatory, apt to take off in dizzying locutory flights, which left his listeners not only lost but remote from any point of reference.

Between the mystifications of Master Spy and the divarications of Codger, Dinadh-Alliance communication soon dwindled to a muddy trickle. People back at Prime learned to send Thosby's infrequent reports directly into the files, not even feeding them through content analyzers that would have scanned for key concepts, such as *lost contact* or *disappearance.*

Thosby took comfort in the lack of feedback. He felt continued silence from Prime was an expression of confidence in him and his work. Meantime, after one or two feeble attempts at supervision, line functionaries at Prime gave up on Thosby and turned to alternate sources of information: agents for other organizations, rumor mongers who were paid for knowing things, people with relatives or friends on settled worlds in Hermes Sector. It was through these that Prime had learned of the Ularian incursions, almost as promptly as Thosby could have informed them.

One young administrator, who was still naive enough to believe that efficiency was a Good Thing, unearthed Thosby's reports, and after laboriously plodding through one or two, recommended that Thosby be replaced. The recommendation, however, languished on the desk of the aide to the deputy assistant to the subassistant secretary for personnel matters. Everyone was now in a panic about Ularians and much too busy to do anything at all about Dinadh.

All of which, so Poracious Luv told me, explains how the Intelligence Division at Prime, purely on the basis of contiguity and without questioning competence, assigned Thosby Anent the responsibility of monitoring the highly secret work of the Perdur Alas shadow team.

"For want of a nail," the Procurator would say to me, Saluez, as he reviewed this entire matter, with many a shake of the head and furrowing of the brow. "For want of a nail, the horse was lost. . . ." (Our animals on Dinadh do not have nails, so I had to ask Lutha what he meant.)

Thosby accepted responsibility for the shadow team with his usual nonchalance. No one told him how important Perdur Alas was. It would have made no difference if they had. The more challenging and important a task, the more good sense and concentration it required, the more likely Thosby was to ignore it in preference for something else, anything else, that was repetitive and familiar and disconnected from reality.

As a consequence, the shadow team had been gone for some time before Thosby knew it. To give him credit, he did use his equipment to search for survivors, though it took him ten times as long as it should have. He found Snark through sheer luck, and when he set the machines to provide a readout of Snark's sensory data, he found, to his slight discomfort, that it covered a very long period of elapsed time, during which he, Thosby, should probably have Done Something.

Codger was neither honest enough to admit incompetence nor dishonest enough to destroy the evidence. Master Spy, on the other hand, was convinced it was a ploy. Trapped among his several personalities, Thosby chose to do what he had often done in the past with real things that presented real problems: ignore them until they went away.

Perdur Alas didn't go away. The ship that had transported the shadow team stopped subsequently on Dinadh, where, in a drunkenly lugubrious moment, the captain had grieved over the fate of the bait. This was reported to Chadra Tsum, who routinely used Thosby's equipment to find out things that interested her, whether they interested anyone else or not. Chadra knew about Snark long before Thosby did. She told her colleagues, who told other people, with the consequence that, among certain circles in Simidi-ala, Snark was spoken of familiarly and with sympathy as the lonely shadow of Perdur Alas.

Which is not to say that *Dinadh* knew. The people at Simidi-ala, because of their forced association with foreigners, are not considered to be real Dinadhi. They are, so to speak and through no fault of their own, tainted and resented. Though I had not realized it, it seems the resentment runs both ways. They are as suspicious of us as we are of them. So, though the port buzzed with the drama of one lonely shadow upon Perdur Alas, one lonely shadow confronting the might and mystery of the Ularians, the rest of Dinadh remained ignorant.

As did I, and all those with me. We knew only what Lutha had been told: that our worlds were in danger. If my world was in danger, so were my people, so was my child. What more did I need to know?

* * *

It would have been helpful to know a great deal more about driving gaufers! I had assumed they were gentle and accommodating beasts, but then, I had only seen them driven. I may even have seen them being harnessed—without paying much attention—and I'd certainly never done it myself. It surprised me, us, therefore, when the beasts made it clear they did not like being harnessed, did not like pulling, and would do so only when . . . when something none of us could figure out!

Leelson blindfolded them to harness them, only to find that when the blindfolds were removed, they would not move. We were working in the predawn darkness, the sun threatening at any moment to edge the rim-rock above us, and I was having a hard time staying calm.

"They are accustomed to some other order," said Lutha in a perfectly rational, matter-of-fact voice. She stood next to the lead animals, strok-ing their necks, an expression of wonder on her face, as though she had never touched animals before. "Use your skills to find out which ones are leaders."

Leelson and Trompe looked at her in astonishment, the lantern light showing their faces, hard with frustration. Gradually, Leelson's face cleared, however, and he turned his attention to the beasts. "That one," he said, pointing to one of those hitched in the third pair. "I think. Don't you, Trompe?"

"I think so," said the other doubtfully. "And that one, maybe. The one on the right in the second pair."

"Likely they will also have a preferred side," said Lutha. "Right or left. If we are lucky, we will have picked one leader for each side."

I had not thought of any such thing, and obviously the men had not either. Nonetheless, after a few moments of swearing and sweating, they were able to say that the two animals at the front were accustomed to being there and were on their accustomed sides. The animals did not feel affection or longing for the proper side; they merely felt less aver-sion.

"There are probably other refinements," said Lutha, "but I think we'd better get away before it gets any lighter."

The rimrock above us already glowed with gold. Even as we looked up, the first notes of the dawnsong came from above and behind the great stone pillars that hid us, notes falling like water, silken as falling water. Lutha put Leely into the wain; Leelson drove it. Trompe, Lutha, and I walked alongside. The animals pulled, though without enthusiasm, and we went away south as quietly as we could.

"How did you know that?" I asked Lutha. "About the lead gaufers."

"I am a translator of documents," she said. "I read. I read many things from many worlds. I translate documents about crops and water rights and weapons and marriage law and livestock. My head is full of a million irrelevant facts, one of which just happened to be useful." She laughed, somewhat harshly. "Another thing I know, which is more troubling, is that these animals will have to be fed. Since we're not carrying any food for them, presumably they'll have to have time to graze before night, correct?"

She was right, of course. I had not thought of it. Even though this was my world, I had not thought of it. It was not a woman's thing to worry about. Only men did the herding. Only men drove the gaufers. Why would I have wondered about it?

Still, I felt shamed that she had and I had not.

"It's going to cut down on our travel time," said Leelson, his lips compressed. "They'll probably need to graze for several hours."

"One of the middle pair would be less unhappy if it was back by the wagon," muttered Trompe. "It's clear enough, once you know to look."

"Most things are," said Lutha in a dry voice, with a sidelong glance at me. I knew what she was thinking, that I was not clear and that she did not know where to look. "What do they eat, Saluez? Grasses? Leaves? Can we cut fodder for them as we go?"

I didn't know and was ashamed to say I didn't know. We took knives and cut grasses and leaves along the way, for the trees along the trickling stream were coming into leaf, and when we stopped at noon for a brief meal and a drink from our canteens, we soon learned which things the gaufers would eat and which things they would not. By this time we had come along the canyon wall all the way to the place where the five canyons meet. Because of the way the canyon curved, we could not see Cochim-Mahn behind us, but then, the people there could not see us either. We could cross the open place and go to the right around the Gathered Waters and get all the way to the south-tending canyon before anyone could see us from Cochim-Mahn. Of course, if someone were on the trail across the canyon from the hive . . .

"I think that's stretching good sense," said Lutha, when I suggested this plan. "What I think we'll do is camp for the night near the water to give us grazing time. Then we'll get ourselves into that other canyon very early in the morning, when we won't be seen."

Though Leelson showed surprise at her decisiveness, he grunted approval as he went to help Trompe, who was shifting two of the gaufers to their preferred positions. One animal was still out of place, its preferred slot occupied by another with the same preference. Leelson pointed this out. Trompe said the out-of-place one was the lesser opinionated of the two. This made Lutha laugh, a sound I had not heard since she arrived. She had a lovely laugh, like water. I told her so, and she said she had noticed that Dinadhis think most lovely things are like water.

"It is because we are water poor," I said. "We value it."

"Well, it flatters me that you like my laughter," she said. "Sometimes I think I have forgotten how to laugh."

Her eyes were on the boy, and I knew why she had almost forgotten, but I said nothing. She did not want to discuss Leely, and I did not want to offend her. Still, I wondered why. Among the Dinadhi, once we know a child is . . . incompetent to live, we do not insist upon keeping it alive. Sometimes a mother will fight the inevitable, and she is allowed to do so. Mothers are mothers, after all. But eventually, even a mother understands that humans are not immune from nature's error. Some babies are not meant to live. I thought Leely was one such. So did Leelson, and this was the source of the conflict between them. I almost said hatred, but it was not hatred. Not that alone, at any rate, for she loved him too. I am no Fastigat, but I could feel her yearning, and his. It was like wind, or sunshine, or flowing water, an undeniable presence.

It was all very tragic and complicated, and I interested myself with it for all the miles we walked that afternoon, down the long canyon, out into the bare space where the five canyons meet, and across that rocky expanse to the place beside the water where we hid ourselves in a grove of trees and set up our camp.

I had no more idea how to set up the gaufer cage than they did. After a time we figured it out. The pen had the wain for one side, with a narrow panel fastened across the wheels to keep anything from coming under. Two oblong panels hooked onto the front and back of the wain, then onto other panels to make a six-sided enclosure. Then six triangular panels made the peaked roof, all joined together with paran-wood fasteners on the inside.

"Leather lacings would be easier," said Trompe as he struggled with a panel that would not line up correctly.

"The Kachis can chew through leather," I said quietly. "They cannot chew paran, which is sometimes called wood-adamant. It must be steamed a long time before it can be worked, and when it is dry, even metal tools have difficulty cutting it."

"I can see why," he muttered, continuing his struggle.

Eventually, he and Leelson figured it out. Only after they'd done it by trial and error did they find the faded marks on the edges of the panels to show which one went where. Meantime, the gaufers had been watered and allowed to graze in the woody glade. When the sun was almost gone, they surprised us by coming purposefully out of the woods and entering the enclosure by themselves. They milled about uncertainly until we shut them in, then they settled, each to a small pile of the edible growths we had gathered during the afternoon. We were shut in as well, with a tiny fire in the firebox to warm our food and make a pleasant smoke. The Kachis do not like smoke, though they are attracted to fire. Carrying a torch at night is a sure way to bring them by the dozens.

We heard the dusk song, echoes of it from far up the canyons. Only from the southern canyon came no sound, for it is too narrow for men to live in. The days are short inside it, and there are no hives there. Luckily, the canyon itself is not long. We could traverse it, I told Lutha, in a couple of days.

"Will we find enough fodder for the gaufers?" she asked.

"Lady, I do not know," I told her. "I feel such a fool. I should know more about my own world."

"Your world is sexually di-cultural," she said seriously. "Men know one set of things, and women know another. And, I suppose the women are di-cultural as well. Those who are . . . veiled and those who are not."

"No," I said. "We who are veiled know everything the others do. And more, besides."

She opened her mouth as though to ask a question, then caught herself and was still. Trompe and Leelson were murmuring together, but they, too, fell quiet in that instant and we all heard the questing cry from the southern canyon.

At that sound, the gaufers shivered and crowded together, away from the woven panels. They arranged themselves in a circle, holding the same order they had occupied during the day, the less opinionated one hissing and laying his ears back as he took a few moments to decide where he belonged. When they were settled, with their legs folded under them and their heads laid back upon their spines, eyes half-closed, jaws moving, no part of them was within reach of the panels. Whatever was out there could not get hold of them.

"So interesting," said Lutha, looking at the beasts. "You know, gaufs are the first animals I've ever seen."

"There are no animals on your world?" I asked, and she said no, no animals upon Alliance Central. No animals on any world that had been completely homo-normed. "They're all in the files," she said. "If there's ever room for them again."

I thought I would miss animals if there were none. I had a pet cornrat when I was a child. Many Dinadhi have pet gaufs. Weaving Woman is said to favor animals and there were many in Blessed Breadth, the world from which we came. On the other hand, the Firsters teach that the universe was made for man, made for man to use and use up, including all its creatures. We talked of this in desultory fashion while we listened for approaching wings.

Try though we would to keep our minds on something else, it did no good. First a little silence fell among us, then a longer one, then one longer yet. Finally, we withdrew into the wagon itself and pulled the door almost shut behind us. There we each sat in our own ten square feet of space and tried not to hear what was going on outside. They were teasing us. Kachis always do, tease us, try to frighten us. They do it, say the songfathers, to try our faith, to be sure we are strong and resolved. First they flutter. Then come the cries, like hungry children, enough to melt ones heart. They shake the panels, they thrust in their long, stick-thin arms. They gnaw at the panels with sharp, white teeth. They cannot chew paran wood. It is for this reason we call paran the Lord Protector of Trees and never cut a mature one without planting two in its place.

If it had not been for Leely, perhaps we could have slept, but he would have none of it. He wanted to see what was going on. Finally, Lutha took him to the wagon door, cracked it a bit wider, and sat there with him for a long time while he reached toward the white arms, the white faces, the sharp teeth, and cried, "Dananana. Dananana."

I stood behind them, looking out, and Lutha heard my indrawn breath.

"What is it?" she asked, looking up at me.

"So many," I blurted. "There are so many of them!" I had never seen that many in Cochim-Mahn. I wondered if they were following us or traveling to the omphalos. Then I relaxed, remembering. Of course they were going to Tahs-uppi. They were a part of it!

Eventually Leely tired, and Lutha laid him down, shutting the door tightly. Even then, it was a long time before he slept.

When Leelson woke us before dawn in the morning, the Kachis had gone. The ground outside the panels was littered with their droppings. I have a hard time reconciling the mess they make with . . . with what they are. Holy creatures should not smell like that. I was eager to leave, but Lutha insisted we take time to cut fodder, storing it on top of the wagon. Then we took down the panels, stacked them on the racks, hitched the gaufers, and were gone before light. We were, as we had planned, into the southern canyon by the time the sun rose. Too deep to be seen from Cochim-Mahn, which was good, but lost in deep shadow ourselves, which we had not thought on.

Leelson unfolded Bernesohn Famber's map on the seat beside him and traced our route with his finger.

"This canyon branches into another," he said. "One leading southwest. Is that right?"

I rehearsed the way as we children had learned it from songfather. "The Canyon of Cochim-Mahn to the Lost Things Canyon. This canyon to the Burning Springs. Burning Springs to the Nodders. Beyond the Nodders, the omphalos."

He tracked my words on the map. "Burning Springs?" he asked me. "It's printed here, but what is it?"

"Songfather told us it's a flammable gas that comes up through fissures in the rock. There is water that comes also. The gas was ignited at some time or other, perhaps by lightning, and it burns in the water. Sometimes the place is called the Fountains of Fire or Canyon of Fire. There is a superstition that drinking the water from there will keep—"

I caught myself in time. I had not said it.

"Keep what?" Leelson asked.

"Keep one in good health," I said. Masanees had mixed her medicine with water brought from the Canyon of Fire. So she said.

He gave me an odd look. I suppose he read my discomfort, but at least he did not ask me anything more.

"What are the Nodders?" Lutha asked.

"Tall thin pillars of rock. Many of them. With stone tops that move sometimes. Songfather says when the wind blows strongly, they nod."

"If that is true," remarked Trompe, "sometimes they no doubt come crashing down."

"I don't know," I confessed. "Songfather never mentioned that."

"No animals?" Leelson asked. "Nothing dangerous except the Kachis?"

"The beautiful people are as they are, which is as the Gracious One wills," I replied. Who knew what the Gracious One willed?

"No *known* dangers, then?" Leelson smiled, reading my mind.

I flushed. "None."

I was more worried about the known than the unknown. Known dangers were quite bad enough. These feelings were justified at about mid-morning when we began to hear wings. At first it was just a barely heard flutter behind us. When we looked, we saw nothing. The noise grew more frequent the farther we went. I caught Lutha and Leelson exchanging long glances. I felt myself growing pale and sick. I knew the sound. Oh, yes, I knew the sound.

Then we heard the noise from before us as well. Both behind and before. Casting a quick look around, I surprised a pale shadowy movement on the canyon wall to our left. Then I saw them everywhere, pallid shapes slipping behind rocks. More than I had ever seen before.

"They're all around us," I said in a voice that I could not keep from sounding terrified. "They're all around us."

"I thought they didn't," said Trompe. "In daylight . . ."

"But it isn't daylight," I cried.

It was day*time,* but we were still in deepest shadow. The sun lay upon the wall to our right, perhaps a third of the way up, a long line of brilliance that inched downward slowly . . . so slowly.

"We could stop and set up the shelter," said Lutha.

"I read that as a bad choice," said Leelson, keeping his eyes on the trail. "The minute we try it, they'll be on us."

"You can feel them?"

"If it is them I'm feeling, yes."

"Then what? What, Leelson!"

"Keep your eyes on the sun line, there on the right-hand wall. How long would you say until it hits us?"

"I have no idea! Saluez?"

"Not long," I mumbled. "But maybe too long."

"I think not," said Leelson. "I'm getting feelings of slyness, of calculation. They want to be sure of us. They aren't yet. They're cunning."

"You speak as though they were rational beings," Lutha objected.

I pinched my lips shut and said nothing. Trompe looked at me curiously, his brows knit together. I concentrated on the lower pool at Cochim-Mahn, thinking deliberately of its coolness and the lightless depths within the stone. Leelson looked away, perhaps foiled, perhaps merely respecting my desire not to be thought at.

"We'll talk of something else," he said firmly. "Trompe, how were the league championships coming when you left Prime?"

Trompe responded, and the two of them talked in quite natural voices about interalliance sports of various kinds. Their voices seemed normal and casual, but their eyes were narrowed in concentration. I stayed frozen in place, gathered into myself, my face hidden in my hands. I could still hear the Kachis, even above the sound of the men's voices. Lutha put her arm around me and squeezed. I scarcely felt it.

Then, suddenly, "Here," said Leelson.

I slitted one eye and peeked. We had come to a puddle of sunlight, a spot where the eastern canyon wall dipped low to let the sun through. Leelson got down from the wagon and pretended to check the wheels; Trompe joined him, the two of them continuing their discussion. Lutha and I merely waited. Silence. The Kachis were not going to announce their presence. They didn't know about Fastigats. They didn't know we had heard them, that their slyness had been interpreted. It was obvious they didn't yet want us to know they were there.

We waited in the puddle of light until the sun flooded the bottom of the canyon. Only then did Leelson cluck to the animals and we moved on, more rapidly. Trompe buried himself in the map, measuring and muttering.

"There's a turn to the west ahead," he said. "Quite a lengthy east-west arm. That should be lighted for its entire distance. If we hurry, we may make it before the sun drops behind the west rim."

"If everyone who can will walk, we can hurry more easily," remarked Leelson, his voice little more than a whisper.

I had thought my legs wouldn't hold me, but it was actually easier to walk than to sit. Walking gave my trembling muscles something to do. Even Leely walked, all of us except Leelson striding along, and the gaufers moving almost with alacrity. The Kachis kept pace with us, fluttering among the stones at the eastern side of the canyon, more of them every moment. If we had not known to look for them, we might not have seen them. When they were still, they appeared to be only some lighter blotch on the stone itself.

It was not long until we came to the turning, not in actual time, though it seemed endless. The sun had shifted from the west side of the canyon to the center, from the center to the east. We were driving close to the eastern wall when we came to the turn, and now we moved around the corner into the light of Lady Day, she who smiled fully upon us as we moved toward the west.

Behind us in the narrow canyon, one lone derisive cry, faint and far, immediately silenced. If we had been near the sea, it might have been mistaken for the call of a bird, but we have no large inland birds.

"They want to get ahead of us," said Leelson. "There are shadowed ways in and among the rocks along the walls."

Lutha shivered. I swallowed over and over, not to let the bitterness in my throat rise into my mouth. Then, all at once, Leely pulled away from Lutha and began to run back, as though he had been attracted by that lone cry.

Lutha caught up to him and seized him, but he struggled, pulling so strongly that Trompe had to help her restrain him and shut him in the wagon. There he raged incoherently for a time before falling asleep.

Late in the afternoon we stopped, still in the east-west part of the canyon. Ahead of us it turned south again, though the map indicated the southward arm was not a long one.

"That's where they probably expected to find us tonight," remarked Leelson, pointing to the turn ahead. "Instead we'll stay right here, make an extra long halt, and not leave here until that southern arm is in full sunlight. Besides, there's grass here, enough to supplement what we cut earlier."

This time we had less struggle with the panels, we knew how to handle the gaufers. It was they who found water, a tiny spring that seeped from the canyon wall. By the time the sun set, we were safely shut in. The men fell asleep almost immediately, though Lutha and I were still awake.

Tonight Leely showed no interest in the Kachis. They came, as before, to gnaw the panels, to reach through with their long, white arms, but he curled himself into slumber and did not seem to care. Instead it was I who stood at the crack in the wagon door, looking out at them, at the faces of those who crossed the narrow line of light that escaped through the doorway.

Lutha heard me gasp and came to stand beside me.

"What is it, Saluez?"

I was so surprised, I spoke without thinking. "I just saw him, the outlander ghost!"

"You mean . . . Bernesohn Famber?" she asked in an incredulous voice.

"See, see," I said, pointing. "Look, there he is again. The one with the twisted shoulders."

She stared out, turned to me, and stared again. "I see a Kachis with twisted shoulders, Saluez."

"That's him! That's how we know him. He, too, had twisted shoulders."

Only then, I realized what I had said.

I clung to her. "Don't tell," I begged. "Please. Don't tell the men that the Kachis are the spirits of our departed! I'm not supposed to talk about it!"

She pressed my lips with her fingers, a soft pressure through the fabric of my veil. "Shhh. I won't, if you don't want me to, but you must tell me, Saluez. I need to know. When someone here on Dinadh . . . goes, he comes back as a ghost?"

"When people's bodies don't work anymore, their spirits depart the human bodies and find Kachis bodies. We invite them to return to us. We promise to feed them and care for them. The Kachis were made by the Gracious One, just for this purpose, to hold our spirits. And they do come back, where we can see them, and they live for many, many years, staying with us, enjoying the lives of their children and grandchildren, eating, coming to our . . . taking part in our lives."

"All of your people who . . . die, Saluez?"

She didn't understand! "But we *don't* die. Don't you see! We don't die, not anymore. No. We just change our forms, that's all. From human form into Kachis form, but we know who we are, we are still alive."

She mused a long time. "I see," she said at last. "So your mother is out there somewhere, Saluez?"

I could not answer her. She should not have asked that. I turned my face from her and went to my place to sleep.

Halach, songfather of Cochim-Mahn, finished his salute to Lady Day, took the three ritual steps into her light, then fastened his robe and looked around for his breakfast. Someone should have come with it from the hive the moment he sang, "Go forth!"

He grumbled, his belly grumbling with him, missing Saluez. She had never been late with his breakfast. Shuddering, he put the thought aside. It was forbidden to think these things. One could not think kindly of someone who had doubted, who had had heretical ideas. And she had, had doubted, had fallen away from grace, otherwise . . . otherwise she would not be down below with the other veiled doubters and recalcitrants. Lady Day had smitten them, and Weaving Woman had made dark patterns of them, and the Gracious One had turned his back upon them. Praise to the deities who knew the inner hearts of women, darker and more devious than those of men!

Shalumn hastily approached, bearing a bowl and ewer. He held out his hands for the ritual washing. Then Shalumn handed him his food bowl and politely turned away, looking out over the canyon.

He forgave her tardiness with his first bite.

"Only a little time until Tahs-uppi," he remarked. "Would you like to see the ceremony?"

She was very still. What ailed her? He spared her a curious glance before returning to his meal.

"I am better suited to my duty here, songfather."

Was she refusing to attend? For the goddesses' sakes, he hadn't been suggesting anything improper. Surely she didn't think . . .

He made the matter clearer. "Hazini will be accompanying me, along with her father. I thought you might be company for her."

She didn't look at him. "Thank you, songfather. It is a kind thought. But I am better suited to my duty here."

He put down the bowl and stared. "What is it, Shalumn? Something is troubling you."

"Nothing one may speak of, songfather."

He dropped his voice to a confidential whisper. "One may speak of anything to a songfather."

She confronted him, her eyes filled with tears. "I fear Saluez has gone into shadow, songfather."

Confused for the moment, he could not understand what she was saying. Those behind the veil were said to be in shadow, and of course Saluez was among them. "Into shadow? But . . ." Of course those who passed on were also said to be in shadow. Though veiled women couldn't be said to pass on. Because they had doubted the Great Gift of the Gracious One, veiled women truly died. They were not accorded the right of living on in Kachis form. Shalumn must mean something else!

"Tell me!" he demanded in a whisper. "You think she's gone"—he gestured outward, at the canyons, the mesas, the distant glinting mountain peaks, all the faraway that was Dinadh—"there?"

"Yes, songfather."

"What makes you think so?"

"I haven't seen . . . not for days."

He sighed, surprising himself with the realization that it was a sigh of relief.

He reached out to shake the girl gently. "Shalumn. Shalumn, you were her friend. You recognize her shape, her walk. Of course you watch for her, even though you know it is forbidden. That's quite common, my dear, and it is not a severe sin. But it's customary for those behind the veil to spend days below, in their own place, unseen by anyone."

"But she cares for the outlanders! No one else has been given the duty! And no one has seen them, either!"

"Put it out of your mind," he said sternly. "Hear me, Shalumn. Put it out of your mind." Her voice had been too full of grief. She should not feel so about a doubter!

"Songfather," she said submissively, bowing her head. "I will do as you say."

He turned his back on her and resumed eating. So no one had seen Saluez for a few days. Well, that was as it should be. No Dinadhi should see her at all. She was a trash-person. Just as the outlanders were trash-people. Dinadhi didn't look at trash-people, or look for them, for that matter.

Still, it was strange no one had encountered the outlanders. On the ladders, perhaps. Even trash-persons took up space on the ladders. One had to wait. Or step aside. One noticed.

He scraped the sides of his bowl with his spoon. Not long now until there'd be some greens. Early greens, springing up along the streamlets, a welcome addition to the diet. If those gaufers that had gotten loose somehow didn't eat them all first.

Strange, that. Six gaufers had escaped their pens. Songfather had assumed they'd been let loose by someone. Some child, too frightened to confess. But the six missing ones had been a hitch. Almost. Two leaders, right and left, who as mere gaufs had established their right to that position by kicking and biting their herd mates into submission. Two followers, right and left, who did not kick or bite at all, and two middles —though they were both left middles.

Who would steal a hitch? And for what? Some young man who wanted to prove himself, taking the animals onto the heights, maybe finding an unused wagon there. But to do what? To go where?

To Simidi-ala, perhaps? Sometimes young people did run off to Simidi-ala. They grew bored with the Dinadhi way of life. They did not treasure the Great Gift enough. They decided they wanted excitement, and off they went. Hive-reared, they knew the only way they could get there was in a herder's wain. Fully half the population of Simidi-ala was made up of runaways, which was another reason for not trusting those at Simidi-ala. Apostates, all of them. Apostates and renegades.

He chewed the last bite thoughtfully. Young people were always interested in Simidi-ala. When Saluez was young, she had asked a lot of questions about the port city, so many that he'd taken her there himself during one brief visit.

He stared blindly at the opposite canyon wall. Saluez couldn't have taken a hitch. A mere girl? Not strong. Now wounded, though he did not know how badly. It was better not to know how badly. Better if loved ones never knew. Too many questions if they knew. Too many doubts. Saluez couldn't have taken the gaufers. It was physically impossible.

But she had been tending the outlanders. Taking care of the Famber family. Who, so Shalumn said, nobody had seen for a while. Of course, they wouldn't know about a hitch.

But Saluez might!

Halach found himself moving rapidly toward the hive, meantime praying fervently to Weaving Woman, to Lady Day, to all the other deities of the Dinadhi that he was merely woolgathering. Oh, let it be that he was merely making up stories, telling tales. Let him not have happened upon the truth!

The morning wore away in questioning and discussing, with this one, with that one. In time he found we had gone. Consternation in the hive. Much mumble among the elders. Then, finally, days later, what no one had thought to do until then, an inventory of wains and the discovery that one was missing, not from those upon the height but from those in the canyon itself. So, where had we gone?

What other place than the omphalos, for Tahs-uppi!

And the end of that episode was songfather standing at the edge of the canyon, swearing retribution on those aliens who had betrayed the hospitality of Dinadh and on that apostate who had aided them. He would follow them, so he howled to Lady Day as she departed. He would follow them and bring them to judgment. His voice quavered in its rage. His arms trembled. The people of the hive quaked behind the doorskins.

So I imagine the scene, at least. Later, while he was raging at me, he let me know some of it, including that he gave me credit for knowing about gaufers, about hitches, things I'd never even been curious about. He told me he had sworn judgment on me, a judgment that did, in time, come to pass. So, though I visualize the details for myself, in all important respects, that is what happened.

While songfather stuttered and swore, I was trying to sleep in the westerly elbow of Lost Canyon. The gaufers were quiet. Trompe snored, an abrupt, breathy sound, as though he were surprised over and over by something. Leelson slept like a child, radiantly, his lips curved into an angelic smile. Leely had the same expression, but Lutha burrowed, like some little animal, her face buried between her hands. And I lay on my back, urging my sinews to let go, let go, let me not think of my mother, let me merely be.

Eventually the struggle wore me out. The attempt to unthink it did no good. All right, I said to my disobedient mind, I will think of it. Let me remember it all. Let me wear out remembering, until it no longer hurts.

Mother went away when I was only a child. No one ever said how she departed. It wasn't a thing we talked about in the hive. Not openly, at any rate. As a child, I overheard this and that. Putting it all together, I understood she had departed because something had gone wrong when she had a baby. The baby departed also. The circumstances were, as we on Dinadh say of things we should not talk about, "difficult." If Lutha were translating, she might say blasphemous. Which does not mean anyone was at fault, but simply that something happened that was unpatternly and unpleasant. Whatever it may have been, this something happened and my mother . . . departed.

And I wept desperately in father Chahdzi's lap, he petting me and murmuring over and over and over, "We'll get her back, Saluez. That's what we'll do. She's out there, just waiting for us to ask her. We'll beg her to come back. And she will, you'll see." He actually smiled when he said it.

So we prayed her return. There is a chamber on the ground floor of the hive, a place where petitions are made to any of our deities, a quiet place, softened by hangings and lighted dimly by little wax lamps, even at night, for night is the time we most need such a place. Chahdzi and I went there with songfather—he was just Grandpa then—and we petitioned Weaving Woman to tell my mother we wanted her to return, to take habitation among us.

I echoed the words. "Take habitation among us . . ." What did the words mean to me? That she would come home, come back, be there as she had been before. But that wasn't what Chahdzi meant, or songfather. For seven nights we uttered our petition. For seven nights we stood behind a window of the chamber, which, alone of all the windows in the hive, has no shutter. It is glazed with heavy glass so that petitioners may look out upon the beautiful people, the dancers, the Kachis.

Oh, beautiful upon wings, the Kachis. As I child I learned the hymns to the Kachis. *Oh, beautiful upon wings, gift of glory, loveliest of beings, those for whom the night was made!*

The seventh night my father's hand tightened upon my shoulder as he pointed with the other, saying excitedly, "There, there, see, Saluez. See, there's Mother, with the cleft in her chin, just like always. Here's Mother come home again, Saluez!"

He pointed and pointed and I looked and looked, until eventually I saw what he was pointing at. A Kachis with a deep hollow in her chin like the one my mother had had. Though at the time I thought it was only rather like, as I remembered the event over the years it grew more and more like until I was sure it was utterly like. Of course. When the spirits of our loved ones return as Kachis, they always let us know who they are by some little trait. The shape of a nose. The shape of an ear. The way they move. A birthmark. So this was my mother, come back to be with us again.

Why didn't she come in?

Songfather shook his head. Because the spirits of our beloved dead are holy, sacred, taboo. They couldn't mix with ordinary people.

Then why did she come at all?

To see her girl Saluez grow, so Chahdzi said. To see her grandchildren born and watch them grow. To take delight from seeing us, to live among us until that time she would go on, sometime in the far future, to a blessed life that awaited her elsewhere.

I said I would go out and kiss her.

No.

I said I just wanted to hug her.

No, no forbidden. We must not touch the Kachis, even though they are people we love. But we can still care for them—her: feed her, love her, watch her dancing with the other spirits. . . .

"Doesn't she know who I am?" I cried. "Doesn't she want to kiss me?"

Of course she did, but that, too, was taboo. Forbidden. We Dinadhi had been given this great gift, the gift of continued life, continued embodiment, the ability to live on with our families and those we loved. We must keep our part of the bargain. Our part of the choice.

Had I doubted then? Did it seem to me then that this pale winged form was a poor substitute for a warm and living mother? Then, when I was only what? Six or seven? Before I knew the whole story? Before I knew the other reasons it was taboo, or what the other side of the choice had been? Before I knew that songfathers had done the choosing but women had paid the price?

Possibly, without even knowing it, I was an apostate even then. Possibly my mother, even then, looking in through the window at me, saw my thoughts and knew I was unworthy. Perhaps then is when she started hating me for being so ungrateful. How else explain?

How else explain why it was she who led the pack that ate my face away?

CHAPTER 7

I woke first in the morning, and my rising brought Trompe and Leelson from under their blankets. Lutha was a knobby lump beneath hers, and we were quiet, not to disturb her. I knew she must have been wakened during the night, probably more than once, for I had heard the boy moving around. He was sometimes a restless sleeper, a murmurer, given to odd little cries that seemed more curious than restless.

The two men and I had no sooner started to take the shelter apart, removing the pins from the fasteners, than Trompe said in surprise:

"This one is open."

It was open, gaping, the pin removed and dropped onto the ground beneath it. Even with just one pin removed, the panels could be pulled apart, though it took some strength to do so. We turned immediately to the gaufers, looking them over for blood or wounds, but they were as placid as a rain pool on a rock, gazing liquidly beneath fringed lashes, jaws moving in the immemorial rhythm of the cud. So, our songfathers tell us, animals of the long ago twice chewed their food, even back so far as Old-earthian times.

"*Something* pulled it loose," said Leelson, clamping his mouth into a grim line. "One of your beautiful people?"

"They couldn't," I said. "It's made so they can't. We must not have put it in tightly last night."

"I did that side," Trompe objected. "And believe me, it was as tight as it is possible to get it!"

We were still standing there, lost in that kind of slightly fearful confusion that readily leads to contentiousness, when Lutha came to the door of the wagon and asked in a plaintive voice, "Where's Leely?"

I blurted, "Isn't he curled up under the blankets? I thought . . ."

She turned back to rummage inside the wagon, crying almost at once, "He's not here. Trompe, Leelson, he's not here."

"He's only a child," muttered Trompe. "He couldn't have opened—"

"He's strong as the proverbial nox," grated Leelson. "If you haven't seen that, you haven't noticed much. He's stronger than many men I know."

"Oh, God, God." Lutha's voice rose in a shriek. "Where is he. Where's my baby?"

The two men exchanged glances once more, pulled two more pins out, thrust open the loosed panels, and went in opposite directions, one up and one down the canyon, quartering the ground, looking behind stones and among low growths, calling, "Leely. Leely-boy. Leely."

Lutha was out after them in the moment, barefoot as she was, her hair streaming behind her, covering the same ground and lamenting so loudly that the rock walls echoed with it.

"Hush!" bellowed Trompe. "Listen!"

Abrupt silence. Then I heard it. Softly, a little voice, not at all fearful or pained. "Dananana." And again: "Dananana." It came from upstream, in the direction of our travel.

Lutha darted in that direction, soon catching up with Trompe. Leelson trudged slowly back to the wagon and continued disassembling the panels as though nothing had happened. He had about him an air of frustration that had been growing hour by hour since Lutha had arrived at Cochim-Mahn. Everything she did irritated him, but he could not, for some reason, just let her be, so everything he did regarding her irritated him as well. By the time Trompe and Lutha came back, she carrying the boy, Leelson was muttering to himself angrily with the gaufers half-harnessed.

"What are you doing!" Lutha screamed. "My, God, Leelson, don't you care about him at all!"

She lifted the boy in a dramatically hieratic gesture, as though offering him for sacrifice or dedication, drawing attention to his arms. There were several little red spots on the flesh above his wrists, no more than insect bites. Leely seemed undisturbed by them. He wasn't scratching or whimpering, and even as I looked the redness faded. It was like watching a candle burn down, slow but perceptible. So healing was with him.

"He doesn't seem to be hurt," said Leelson in an expressionless voice. "Look at him, Lutha!"

Her eyes were still full of righteous fury, but she did look at the boy, her chin quivering as she kissed and hugged him and looked beneath his shirt to see if he was hurt, murmuring small endearments the while, all of which Leely ignored in favor of churning his arms and legs and caroling "Dananana."

"He's not hurt," said Leelson again. "He woke early, let himself out, and got bitten by . . . what, Saluez? You know your native vermin better than we."

"Jiggerbugs," I said, giving the creature an equivalent aglais name. "Maybe. Or there's a kind of spidery thing we call D'lussm. Both of them bite."

Which they did. A bite from either would leave spots similar to those on the boy, though usually it took a day or two of frantic itching and even localized pain before the swelling disappeared.

"Or it could be something local," I offered apologetically. "Something we don't have around Cochim-Mahn."

"Whatever it is didn't hurt him," Leelson repeated for the third time, reaching out a hand to shake Lutha by the shoulder. "Get him dressed, Lutha. Feed him. Feed yourself, you'll feel better."

She reddened at his tone, which was impersonal and disinterested. It would have angered me had I been she, but then, she couldn't see the look in his eyes. His disinterest was as false as her fury. Both of them were playing at it. Still, Leelson wasn't lying to her. The boy wasn't hurt; the boy was strong; the boy had opened the panels to let himself out. And Leelson was considering all these facts with an appearance of calm while Lutha was wildly splashing about in her own terror and guilt at having let Leely escape. Or, perhaps, wondering if Leelson had not purposely let him out. I saw something like that in her eyes. She wanted someone to blame besides the boy himself; she knew this was silly; so she added guilt to all the other things she was feeling.

After a time she settled down, but the look was still there, in the way she watched Leelson when he wasn't looking, in the hard set of her lips and the wrinkles between her eyes, in the shamefaced flush when she caught me watching her. The travel was hard enough without this simmering away. I went to her, putting my hand onto her arm.

"I heard the boy moving around in the night. No one else, only he. He let himself out, Lutha."

She shook off my hand angrily. "Perhaps," she said, with a grimace. "Perhaps he did."

She didn't want to believe me. Any more than she wanted to believe all those people who had told her about the boy, over and over, for years. She rode her own belief. Sometimes she slipped off its back, for it was a slippery beast, but most times she straddled it steadily, whipping it onward: Leely was human; soon he would talk, he would amaze people, he would be supernormal.

I sighed and set about fixing us a quick meal so we could get on our way. Leelson stood by the lead gaufers, tightening harness straps. His back was rigid. When I moved to get the food bowls, I saw that his eyes were closed. He was reaching at Lutha, feeling her out, deciding how to behave toward her.

When I handed him a morning bowl, his eyes opened and he smiled at me, a courteous curving of the lips with no real camaraderie behind it.

"Give her time," I whispered.

"She's had years," he murmured, this time really smiling, though ruefully. "She's had . . . enough time, Saluez. She simply will not see!"

I knew the saying in aglais. *The blindest are those who won't see.* We have similar sayings in our own tongue. *None so lost as those who will not believe.* Leelson could quote the blindness one to Lutha, she could counter with the belief one. And neither would change their opinion one whit!

We ate in strained silence. I washed the bowls in the trickle of water provided by the spring. We drove on to the end of the elbow and turned south once more, hoping we would come to the end of the canyon before midafternoon, for though it was midmorning, the shadow had only just moved away from the bottom of the western wall.

We had not gone far when Leelson pulled up the gaufers and sat staring ahead. On a huge flat stone, one that the trail veered around to the right, something pallid heaved and struggled. To me it looked like a pile of our cotton underrobes, almost white and softly shapeless. But it moved.

Leelson clucked to the gaufers and we moved forward a little, then a little more.

"It's one of them," breathed Lutha in my ear. "One of the Kachis, Saluez."

In fact it was two of them, tumbled side by side on the flat stone, where they writhed, lips drawn back from their sharp teeth, eyes blind and unseeing. Even as we watched, one of them collapsed, motionless.

The other cried out, a long, ululating cry that made the canyon ring, then it, too, fell into motionless silence.

From somewhere came a distant echo, or an answering call. We waited to see if it came nearer, but there was no more sound.

Leelson got down from the wagon seat. Trompe went with him. I stayed where I was, unable to take my eyes from the place where they were, from Leelson's and Trompe's hands as they moved the wings, the arms, from their faces as they looked curiously at the slender bodies.

"They're dead," cried Leelson. "Do they normally die like this, Saluez."

I could not move. I could not speak. Lutha looked at me curiously, then put her arms around me and held me closely, whispering, "They don't die at all, do they, Saluez?"

I shook my head frantically. Of course not. Of course they didn't die. They couldn't die. They stayed with us, until they went on, at Tahs-uppi. This wasn't the way they went on.

"Leelson," she spoke sharply. "Leave it. We can't afford this delay."

Almost reluctantly, he left the tumbled bodies and trudged back to the wagon. I went inside it so I could not see those bodies when we passed. I was trembling so hard I thought my bones would snap. They couldn't die. Kachis could not die. They never died. No one had ever seen one die, or seen a dead one. That was a fact! Part of the evidence we were taught as children, part of the supporting evidence for the choice.

The wagon moved again, and I heard Lutha muttering to the two men. She wouldn't break the promise she made to me, not to tell them about . . . the spirits of our people. I knew she'd keep her promise, but she would have to tell them something. I didn't care. Just let them leave me alone. I couldn't bear to be questioned.

Later, when she and I were alone, she whispered to me, "Did you . . . recognize either one of those Kachis, Saluez?"

I did not. I had not looked. I didn't want to know if they were dear departed of mine.

During the following hour, I had time to calm myself, time to tell myself it had been something aberrant that had happened there, something utterly beyond belief. Perhaps even Kachis can sin. Perhaps even Kachis can disbelieve and be punished for it. This occurrence might be perfectly understandable.

So I thought until Leelson pointed out another dead one. After that, they were scattered all along the way, like fallen rocks. When we emerged from the canyon a little later than midafternoon, he had counted several score of them dead.

"I'm doing it," I said frantically to Lutha. "It must be me. My apostasy. My evil. My sin."

She shook me. "Don't be ridiculous, Saluez. Are you the only so-called apostate? How many are there? How many women in your sisterhood? Plenty, I'll wager. Back in Cochim-Mahn I did a count. I'd say between a third and a half of your women are veiled. You have an exaggerated opinion of your own importance if you think you can cause something like this!"

I had never counted them. But . . . the chamber of the sisterhood was large. Extremely large. And it was full, too, even on those nights when we had no guests from other places. Lutha was right. When I thought of it calmly, I knew she was right. But knowing and believing . . . oh, they are such separate things. "What's causing it, then?" I cried. "You tell me what's causing it!"

"If I had to guess, I'd guess some virus brought in by one of your leaseholders," she said. "There are new viruses turning up all the time."

"But why *here*! Where we are!"

She shrugged. "Saluez, maybe I'm carrying it. Or Leelson. Or even Trompe. By the Great Gauphin, girl, it could be anyone. We handle the panels, the Kachis chew on the panels and pick up what we've left there. Just be thankful we were away from Cochim-Mahn when it happened. I have a feeling if this had happened while we were under the eyes of songfather, he'd have assumed we caused it and we'd all be dead by now, including you because you'd associated with us. And Chahdzi, probably."

I shuddered. Poor Chahdzi father. "You really don't think I did it."

"No," she said firmly. "I don't think it's you. I don't think it has anything to do with you. I'll go further. I don't think you sinned at all. I don't think your face is the result of apostasy or heresy or whatever you choose to call it. In fact, I don't think you're guilty of anything, Saluez."

"Please don't," I said feebly. "You . . . you disturb me when you talk like that. You take all my . . . all my foundations away."

It was true that when she spoke so, something quaked inside me, as though my heart had torn loose. I couldn't bear it.

She shook her head angrily, flushing and pinch-lipped. "Sorry," she said. "I have no right. Ignore me, Saluez."

But how could I? As we drove across the open space between Dark Canyon and the Canyon of Burning Springs, I could not get it out of my head. Was it better to be guilty of sin while knowing there was a power

Sheri S. Tepper

that had punished you? Or was it better to be innocent and feel there was no power? Was it better to be lost in a horrid storm at sea, knowing there was land, or be sailing peacefully with no certainty of land anywhere?

For myself, I decided I would rather be guilty. I could deal with that. One had only to outlive it. Submit to it. Atone for it. Surely if I helped these people save humanity and Dinadh along with it, that would atone for something!

So I set my teeth together and resolved to listen no more to Lutha the temptress. Not that she was a bad woman; she wasn't; but some people are not good for other people, and I thought then that Lutha was not good for me.

At the port city of Simidi-ala, the arrival or departure of outside travelers is an infrequent occurrence. Days go by with only the wind blowing in from across the shallow sea, tangy with the scent of rushes that grow along the shores and of the fragrant weed that floats on the waves. The people of Simidi-ala are Dinadh's only sailors or fishermen, and the bright sails of their shallow little boats scud to and fro across the placid waters, a pattern of bright dots, continually changing. I have seen them. I was there once, long ago, as a child, with Grandpa.

The boats were the first thing the ex–King of Kamir saw as he stood with Poracious Luv at the latticed gate of the shiplift while it slowly lowered them to the beach. The former King of Kamir said something convoluted and quintessentially Kamirian to her, a lengthy cadence comparing the brightness of the boats to the desolation along the shore. Normally Poracious indulged his poesy games, but this time she didn't answer. Her eyes were fixed elsewhere.

Poracious murmured, "How in hell did he beat us here?"

"Who is he?" Jiacare asked, following her gaze to the stooped figure waiting at the gate, a younger man standing in attendance.

"The Procurator, boy. Things must be in a pickle if he's decided to join us. Pull up your socks. Smile. Make pleasant. He looks like a nice old man, but he can have our guts for garters if he likes."

The Procurator did not move toward them, but waited for them to come to him, murmuring as they did so, "Madam Luv," and to the ex-king, "Citizen Lostre. How do you do, sir. May I introduce my aide, Mikeraw?"

They uttered conventional phrases of greeting as the Procurator led them away across a paved courtyard and into the nearest of the slablike structures that serve Dinadh as hotels or inns or warehouses, as needs must. The ex-king verified a suspicion by scratching a wall with his nails. The place was built of dried mud. He shook his head, wonderingly.

They went up a flight of shallow, curving stairs, down a wide hallway, and through an open door. Mikeraw shut the door behind them, then absented himself, leaving the three together in a sizable chamber lit by a score of glazed openings in the outer wall. They were not the shape Poracious associated with windows, being mostly round or oval, some head-sized, some larger, all randomly scattered from floor to ceiling, from sidewall to sidewall, though sidewall might be a misnomer since the general effect was that of being inside a perforated egg with a flattened bottom. Still, the chamber had a peaceful feel to it, and Poracious rejoiced to see several chairs large enough to hold her comfortably.

"Sit," the Procurator urged them. "I've asked the person responsible for leaseholds to join us, but if you want to eat or drink or wash up before he arrives . . ."

Jiacare smiled his thanks, taking a piece of fruit from the bowl on the table.

Poracious said, "Nothing for me, Procurator. How did you get here before we did?"

"Military ship," he answered. "In and out of holes like the proverbial rabbit. Very fast. Very uncomfortable. I felt there was no time to waste." He fumbled with a case set on a nearby table, removing a dataplat, which he handed to Poracious. "Current situation."

He sat down, leaned back, and shut his eyes.

The former king leaned over the big woman's shoulder as she keyed the plat and scanned the contents.

Puzzled, he asked, "What language is this written in, I don't read—"

"Never mind," Poracious Luv replied with a sigh so heavy it was almost a groan. "All it says is that we've lost several million more people in Hermes Sector. The last populated world has been wiped clean, the attack is continuing. We still don't know who or what or why. Every available ship was engaged in evacuation of the remaining planetary populations and all the ships that were in Hermes Sector are gone."

"Succinct, Poracious," said the Procurator without opening his eyes. "Very succinct. You left out that we are helpless. That we've kept this Ularian business inside our administrative skinnies about as long as we can. That we're going to have panic once it gets out, as it will."

The ex-king stared at him curiously. "You're a Fastigat, aren't you, sir? First among Firsters?"

Poracious made shushing motions, but the younger man shook his head at her.

"I'll do what I can to help, but I want to know! Is there any chance these Ularians are actually human? Somebody out there we don't know about?"

The Procurator gave him a long, level look. "The idea has crossed my mind."

"I should have thought so. If the universe is made for man, who else could be out there?"

"I don't know. If they are men, they are able to do things we cannot do. For purposes of action, I refer to them as Ularians, no matter what they are. I take it you are not of the Firster persuasion?"

"I am not, no."

"May we set the matter aside? May we agree to let our differences alone for the moment?"

The ex-king shrugged. "You mentioned panic."

"There will be panic. Many of the vanishees have friends or associates on Alliance worlds. Once ordinary person-to-person communication ceased, rumor began to spin among the citizenry. It won't be long before they learn the truth. We could make up stories until we're bright green; we could issue silence edicts until our voices fail, but not all the evacuation ships were in Hermes Sector; some of them had returned across the line. The crewmen are going to talk. The evacuees are going to talk. They already have! The newsies are already on it, if the opposition doesn't tell the universe first! In either case, we'll be up to our necks in chowbys." He sighed heavily. "I reflect on my own coming political troubles to keep grief at bay. Some of those taken were my grandchildren."

He got up and turned away, going to one of the windows and standing there with his back to them, his shoulders shaking.

Poracious heaved herself out of the chair and went to him, putting one huge arm around him and murmuring, "Has there been any word from Perdur Alas? From the shadows?"

"None that I've received," the Procurator said, drawing himself erect. "Though we certainly should have had *something* by now, if only a preliminary report on their activities. I don't understand the delay."

The former king ran his hands through his hair. "Lord of all Confusion, I pray I have not added to this woe!"

"Sorrow comes as the seasons," the Procurator answered, wiping his eyes as he returned to his chair. "Inevitably. Being Procurator doesn't make me exempt. But it doesn't make me any better able to bear it, either. Well and well, grieving gets one no fowarder, as my grandfather used to say. There is an immediate task before us. We have to find two men, quickly! With your help, sir"—he bowed slightly in the ex-king's direction—"and that of the local leasehold functionary, perhaps we can do so."

"Mitigan of the Asenagi," said the former king, with a wry twist to his mouth. "And Chur Durwen of Collis. Or is it the Haughneep brothers?"

"The former two." The Procurator wiped his eyes once more and made himself sit tall. "We know they came to Dinadh. Now we need to know where they are."

A discreet rap at the door drew their attention. The man who came in was robed, tassel-bearded, and gray around the temples. "At your service, Procurator," he said, sounding neither obsequious nor interested.

"Do you know of Jerome's system?" asked the Procurator.

"It contains, among others, the ocean world of Hava," replied the Dinadhi, raising his eyebrows almost to his hairline. "It is the inhabited system nearest to our own."

"Your nearest neighbors have gone missing," said the Procurator heavily. "Yesterday, more than a million persons vanished from Hava. The other worlds in Jerome's system had already been wiped clean. It is clear the Ularians have returned. Last time around, every human person in Hermes sector was disposed of except you Dinadhi. One exception does not create a pattern. You may not be immune this time around."

The man simply stared, taking it in, his eyes gradually widening.

"Some kind of jest, sir . . ."

"I would not have gone to the trouble of a painful journey to jest with you, sir. The Procurator of the Alliance does not flit about playing games. The only persons who may be able to help us are now at the leasehold of Bernesohn Famber. Lutha Tallstaff, her son, a helper named Trompe. You recall!"

"I recall, of course." Offended dignity. "I am a rememberer!"

"There were two men who arrived about the same time, Mitigan and Chur Durwen. Assassins. Hoping to kill at least two of those earlier mentioned, Lutha and her son. We have to find them!"

"The men were sent to T'loch-ala," said the rememberer. "Which is a hive remote from Cochim-Mahn, where Bernesohn Famber still has leasehold. We knew they were mercenaries."

"That's all very well so far as it goes," said the Procurator wearily. "Though I'm delighted to hear that you took precautions, you have not told me those precautions were effective. Can you find out whether the assassins are still at this T'loch-ala?"

"We have systems for communicating with the songfathers of each hive."

"Quickly, or at leisure?"

"With some dispatch, sir."

"Then let us stop dancing and do so. Please. And while you're about it, I want to see a man named . . . ah." He tapped his wrist-link. "Name of agent on Dinadh?"

"Thosby Anent," said the link.

"Thosby Anent," repeated the Procurator. "Get him, too, as quickly as you can."

A peculiar expression showed for only a moment, then the tassel-bearded man put on his lofty face once more and went striding away, his robes lashing his ankles in a frenzy of offended motion.

"He hasn't really taken it in yet," said the former king.

"No. Habit tells him to do nothing quickly, but we tell him to act at once. Such people grow defensive when forced into motion." The Procurator rubbed his forehead wearily. "There are disadvantages to being responsible."

The former king considered this. "There are also disadvantages to being responsible for nothing, Procurator."

There seemed nothing more to be said until the rememberer returned. While they waited, as though with one mind, the three turned slightly away from one another and sat, each lost in an individually lonely world.

It was almost dark when Trompe drove us into the entrance to Burning Springs canyon. We camped once more. Setting up the enclosure was getting to be a routine. Cutting fodder for the beasts was becoming habit, as was watering them, hobbling them, letting them graze awhile. While rummaging among the food stocks, trying to decide what to prepare for a meal (on Dinadh, we rarely have that much choice), I overheard a conversation between Lutha and Trompe.

"You want me to sit up and watch Leely half the night?" Trompe asked in a slightly offended voice. "Because he got a few bug bites? Why don't you put his harness on him?"

"Even if I put him in his harness, he might manage to escape. And supposedly, you're here to help me!" she snarled.

Long quiet moment while he stared at her. "Right," he said. "Quite right."

Then he went off muttering and shaking his head while Leelson stared at his back resentfully. It was an interesting muddle. Leelson and Lutha could neither accept one another nor leave one another alone. And, though Trompe had been quite willing to play Lutha's servant so long as Leelson was thought to be missing, he felt it put him at a disadvantage now that Leelson was present and accounted for. He, Trompe, was, after all, as much a Fastigat as Leelson was, and Lutha was, more or less, Leelson's responsibility. Leelson, meantime, felt he had the right to argue with, ignore, or even attack Lutha, but he denied Trompe any such right. What with long hours of either drudgery or boredom plus our restless nights, all three of them were on edge, irritable, ready to lash out at anyone, anything.

So I analyzed the situation, as though I were a songfather setting things to rights in a winter hive, where, as here, everyone is shut up together and irritation mounts. It was an ordinary, irrational human stew, quite complicated enough, even without the sexual feelings that were churning around among them. Among us.

Myself included. I found myself watching Trompe, time on time. Liking the shape of him. Imagining him in other places, at other times. I was not in love with him, but yes, I lusted after him. Lusting after men is a particular pain for women of the veiled sisterhood, because we know it is hopeless, fruitless, foredoomed. Even if some man could overlook . . . overlook our appearance, we are not allowed to have children who might inherit our . . . tendencies. Well. Set all that aside. It was of no importance. Certainly it was of no consequence. It simply was.

Though we had set up the panels, we had not yet fastened the last ones. It was open country where we were, a wide canyon, with no Kachis about, and it was not yet dark, though the sun rested upon the canyon rim above us. Leelson and Lutha had gone away from the wain, he to cut forage and she to a pool in a nearby grove—to wash herself, she said, for she was tired of smelling like smoke. She took the bucket, to bring water when she returned. Trompe was fussing about with the harness, which he seemed to have adopted as his particular responsibility. Leely was asleep and I was restless. I slipped out between the panels and went in the direction Lutha had gone.

The grove was made up of d'kymah trees, trunks no larger than my arm, the first branches just above my head. The trees are not good for anything but smelling sweet and being delightful, for they grow always in company with a carpet of flowering grass we call golden eyes. Lovers' woods, we called places like this. Sweetsong woods. The leaves were just coming out, no larger than the nail of my little finger, a pale green, the purest of all colors.

I did not disturb the quiet but went silently, as Dinadhi sisters learn to do, touching the trees for thanks, smelling the foliage with kindness. These pleasures could not be taken from us, so my sisters said. These pleasures were to be enjoyed. My enjoyment was ended by the sound of raised voices, and I stopped, behind a screen of leaves, peering through them at Lutha, and at Leelson.

She had stripped off her outer robe and had taken her arms out of the inner one, lowering it around her waist. She had loosened her hair so the great wealth of it hung over her wet shoulders and breasts. One hand still held the comb, the other was out, as though to ward him away. Leelson stood a pace away, his hands out, imploring her.

"I can't," he said. "Lutha, I can't."

She lifted her hand. Even from where I was, I could see it tremble. She was like a little tree, shivered by wind. "Oh," she cried. "Oh, Leelson."

They came together then, so swiftly it was like an attack, like a rape, only that wasn't what was happening. Neither was more frantic than the other, loosening, unfastening, ridding themselves of garments so their flesh could lie together. The comb fell with a tiny click onto the stone, unnoticed. The clothing sighed away.

I turned away, my eyes burning. So it had been for me. So it would never be again. I crept away, ashamed, piteous, angry, needing to stand for a long time at the edge of the grove before I could return to the wagon. In time, Leelson returned, his face empty, as though he had purposefully decided not to think of anything. Later Lutha came back. There were still tears in her eyes. So. Passion and pain. Attraction and anger. Two who would not, but must.

When we went to our beds, Trompe propped himself near the slightly open door, saying the night air (and the Kachis, no doubt) would keep him awake while he kept watch on Leely. He was there when I fell asleep. He was there when I woke the following morning, his head lolling on his chest, breathing heavily.

It was barely light. I slipped out past him and went to the panel that had been loose the day before. It was loose again. Even as I stood there I saw Leely coming from among the stones at the canyon's mouth, skipping like a little gauf, arms extended, hands waving, a portrait of perfect contentment. I pulled the panels apart to let him in, and he looked at me as he went past. I have seen that look in the eyes of birds, or lizards. A kind of fearless wariness. A look that says, "I know you could get me —kill me, eat me—but at this moment you are not a danger."

His arms were marked as they had been the morning before, as was his forehead, a dozen small, slightly reddened spots that were already fading. He gave me that lizard look again, then went into the wagon silently, he who was rarely silent! I stood listening, but there was no outcry from within. He had sneaked out; he had sneaked back. Considering how everyone felt at the moment, perhaps it was best that I keep Leely's excursion to myself. If I said anything about it, Lutha—whose emotions were always at the surface of her, quick to erupt, quick to cool —would blame Trompe, who would be angry at her, which would annoy Leelson, which would make Lutha angry at him. Angrier. She who could no more resist him, or he her, than the stone can resist the rootlets of the tree. Even the hardest stone will break, for the tree will grow, despite all.

Far better say nothing.

We broke camp without incident or argument. We drove into the Canyon of Burning Springs, the mouth and throat of which are no different from any other canyon: a trickle of water at the center, water-rounded stones along the sides among a sprinkle of low grasses and forbs and woody plants, then a long slope of rubble piled at the foot of the canyon walls, then the walls themselves, fissured and split, some parts actually overhanging us as we wandered slowly below. The canyon tended generally westward, so we were in light, the sun lying midway between the zenith and the southern rim. We heard no sounds, we saw no living things except ourselves. The canyon curves slightly, so we could not see far ahead, though we could hear the sound of water. We did not realize we had made a considerable change of direction until we were well into what Leelson called a "dogleg." (I called it an elbow. We have no dogs on Dinadh.)

The change impressed itself on us when the light went out as though someone had closed a shutter. Even in a sunlit canyon there are often narrow shadows thrown across the way by protruding boulders on the rims, but we had come to a veritable lake of shadow, thrown by a monstrous monolith we could see black against the sun glare, south and east of us. We blinked and murmured and stared around ourselves, dark afterimages of the sun dazzle swimming across our eyes. Only after we stepped into the shadow and let our eyes adjust to it did we realize we had come to the place of fire.

Songfather had often amused the children of Cochim-Mahn with tales of this place, but I'd never imagined it as it really was. I'd thought there would be small fires here and there, like a gathering of campfires, perhaps. When our eyes cleared, however, we saw a world of flame. Fountains gushed everywhere, up the sides of the walls, along the rubble slopes, in the canyon bottom, beside the steamy stream that trickled along beside us, braided into a dozen vaporous streamlets. We were surrounded by firelight and water noise, by fire roar and water glimmer. The light and the sound twisted and warbled together, so that it was hard to know whether we saw the movement or heard it. There was a mineral smell, not unpleasant, and warm damp upon our skins that turned clammy as we moved.

"Worthy of a tourist's visit," murmured Leelson, an awed expression on his face. "Why have I never heard of this place?"

"Because Dinadh does not want tourists," Lutha said, in a voice equally awed.

I had no words at all. Around us the fountains burst forth from smooth basins they had polished into the stone over the centuries. Some were clear jets like pillars of glass, others were peaks of foam; some were single towers of evanescent light, others were multiple spouts that collided in fans of glittering gems, then drained away through multiple fissures, back into the fiery depths below. The small streamlets beside us carried away only a tiny fraction of the leaping water. Mostly it was recirculated, seeping away, bursting forth again, every shining cascade lit by the changing, evanescent spirits of flame burning within the water. Sometimes the fire topped the foam, sometimes the water leapt higher; no instant was like any other. Together, the plash and burble of water and the muted roar of flame hummed like a giant voice, a great harmonic chord.

"Wow," whispered Lutha, cupping her hands over her ears. An inadequate response, I felt, becoming for an instant very planet proud.

"You could make hard coin bringing tours from Simidi-ala," said Trompe.

I said, "It is a tortuous distance overland, and we will not fly unless it is absolutely necessary." My voice was properly stiff and Dinadhish, but my senses echoed Leelson's pleasure. Why shouldn't people from other worlds see this wonder? I knew the answer, of course, but for that moment it did not seem sufficient.

Our mutual awe and pleasure was quickly lost.

"Uh-oh," murmured Leelson. I looked in the direction of his gaze and saw what the fiery fountains had prevented our seeing until that instant. The pallid wings. The shining forms. Not one or two, but dozens, scores. I found myself counting. There were a hundred of them, at least, sitting around a fountain at the foot of the wall, heads resting on their folded arms or lax upon their shoulders.

We made no sound, almost holding our breaths. A long moment went by. The pale forms did not move. They took no notice of us. One of the gaufers grew impatient and struck the rock with the hardened skin of his foot. It made a rough, scraping noise, quite loud, but it occasioned no reaction.

I was close at Leelson's side. I felt him drawing in a deep, quiet breath before he clucked to the gaufers and shook the reins. They moved, their heads down and forward at the end of their long necks. They are curious beasts. So they greet the offer of some new kind of food or the hand of some new handler. We approached the first fountain and its surrounding forms. The fountain danced and chuckled. The Kachis did not move.

The gaufers drew their heads back, snorting and spitting as they jerked the wain into quicker motion. The next fountain was larger, with even more Kachis about it. We drove by and they did not move. So we went on, four fountains, seven, ten: all of them ringed by Kachis, none of the Kachis moving. Gradually, as our eyes accustomed to the variable light, we saw more Kachis, thousands of them scattered all the way to the canyon walls, up the rubble slopes, behind broken boulders and pillars.

Lutha tapped my arm and pointed upward. They were there as well, high upon the narrow ledges left when blocks of stone had fallen away. Every shelf was edged with them, like white tatting on the edge of a sleeve.

"Are they asleep?" Lutha whispered to me.

How did I know? I had never seen a Kachis asleep. Still, most things sleep, so one might suppose . . .

I shook my head at her. Who would know what Kachis do when they are alone, afar, away from us? Who knows the truth of what they do even with us?

Finally, at the end of the dogleg, Leelson gave the reins to Trompe and told him to drive on. He was going back to examine the Kachis.

"Don't be a fool," said Lutha, yearning toward him, furious at him.

"I lead a charmed life, remember?" he told her, actually smiling.

"Leelson! It's dangerous!"

"I don't think so," he said. "Drive on. I'll catch up with you in a while."

Trompe grunted in annoyance, but he drove on. We kept going for some little time, then, at Lutha's insistence, we stopped. We waited, and waited, growing increasingly apprehensive. At the moment when both Trompe and Lutha had decided to turn about and go back, Leelson appeared at the turn in the canyon, sauntering toward us as though he had been out for a morning stroll around a hive!

"Do you know anything about what we saw back there, Saluez?"

I looked blankly at him. Of course I didn't.

"Very strange," he mused. "They're unconscious. As in a trance."

I said nothing. What could I say?

He shrugged, with an apologetic look at me. "I'm picking up all kind of avoidance signals here. This is evidently something Saluez doesn't want us to discuss."

"Saluez doesn't want to talk about the Kachis," said Lutha.

"Talk," I said weakly, flapping my hands at them. "You talk. I won't listen."

Of course I did listen, even though they used many words I didn't know then, words I only learned later.

Leelson said, "There are a few dead ones back in the canyon, like the ones we saw yesterday. But those gathered around the fountains don't seem to be dead, even though they're totally unresponsive to stimuli. I thumped a few of them. They're rigid. But there's no sign of decay or mummification, so I wondered what Saluez could tell us."

Lutha looked at me from the corner of her eye. I avoided her look.

She said carefully, "I believe . . . at the ceremony of Tahs-uppi, some Kachis go into the omphalos—"

The Kachis, I corrected her mentally. All of them. Our beloved ghosts, going on to heaven.

"—and if this ceremony is dependent upon songfathers getting to the omphalos, perhaps it's a state the Kachis go into at this time. Making the journey safer for people."

"Interesting," mused Leelson, climbing up to take the reins from Trompe.

Not interesting! Holy!

I was amazed to find my eyes wet, to feel that choking sensation that comes with tears. What was there to cry over?

* * *

In Simidi-ala, the rememberer returned to the outlanders, his brow broken by three deep horizontal wrinkles, his mouth twisted up as though he had drunk sour water, his hands flapping.

"Well?" demanded the Procurator.

"Gone!" said the rememberer. "Mitigan and Chur Durwen, they're gone from the hive we sent them to. And there's been a herdsman murdered, a gaufer taken!"

"Chowby excrement," said the Procurator. "The piss of diseased farbles. The sexual relationships of brain-dead bi-Tharbians."

"Now, now," said Poracious Luv. "Cursing won't help."

The Procurator shuddered. "How long ago?" he demanded.

"Several days." The rememberer fell into a chair limply. "There's hardly a chance of their surviving."

"Why?" asked the ex-king. "What dangers does your world afford?"

The rememberer flushed. "We enter upon a delicate area, sirs, madam."

"I don't care if we enter upon you and your wife in the act of holy procreation," the Procurator snarled. "Damn it, we need to know!"

"We have certain sacred . . . creatures upon Dinadh. They are nocturnal. Anyone who is abroad upon the planet during the hours of darkness is almost certain to be . . . ah, damaged."

"Mitigan came from Asenagi," said the ex-king. "Though the Asenagi are Firsters, they are of a sect which does not believe in homo-norming. Have you heard of the viper bats of Asenagi? Or the great owl weasel? Both of them are nocturnal. Viper bats go in clouds of several thousand. Owl weasels are more solitary, but then, they're as big as a man. Asenagi youth spend several years in the wilderness, living off the country, before they're accepted into the clan of assassins. Do you think your nocturnal creatures, whatever they are, will bother Mitigan?"

"Or Chur Durwen," Poracious Luv offered. "Collis, too, is a warlike world. Young men are expected to have slaughtered their first enemy by the time they are seven."

Beads of sweat stood like pearls along the rememberer's brow. "The songfather of T'loch-ala is questioning those who spoke with the two leaseholders. He will determine whether they gave any hint as to where they are going."

The Procurator said something under his breath.

"Meantime," offered the rememberer. "The man you asked for. Thosby Anent? He's waiting to see you."

He hurried out, and after a long moment the door opened only far enough to admit a lean, rather stooped man who moved through wraiths of smoke on legs oddly bowed, as though he were crippled at the knees. He looked at the three who awaited him, and his posture straightened.

"A peculiar time," said Codger, bowing slightly. "One in which we might be led to question the very bases of our existence. A time in which humanity's overwhelming concern with its own affairs must give way to a more general consideration. . . ."

"Anent?" questioned the Procurator.

"Myself." Thosby bowed. "Who has lately been much involved in philosophical musing."

"Can such musings be set aside for the moment?" queried Poracious Luv. "I would suggest that now is not the best time for—"

Thosby interrupted with a grandiose gesture. "But what time is, madam? Is any time *best* for the consideration of ultimate disaster? When we are faced with—"

"What are we faced with?" demanded the Procurator. "That's what we want to know! Intelligence Division tells me you are responsible for forwarding reports from the shadow team on Perdur Alas. We've received no information!"

Thosby was momentarily paralyzed. He puffed furiously, his head disappearing in a hazy cloud. Poracious Luv lunged from her chair and struck the pipe from his lips. It clattered against the far wall.

"Summon your wits, man! The Procurator wants to know about the team on Perdur Alas."

"Survivor," murmured the Master Spy, desperately seeking a role to fit the current circumstance. "Just one survivor."

"One! Since when?" cried the Procurator.

"Ah, well, one doesn't know, does one? They simply, ah, disappeared."

"How long ago?" Poracious barked.

Thosby hum-gargled, deep in his throat. "It's difficult to say. The information received now is sensory, but is it objective or subjective? Does one count time when one is alone as one does when with one's fellows. There's an interesting philosophical—"

"Stop these interminable divagations!" she cried. "When did you know they had disappeared?"

"Well, the equipment says . . . perhaps thirty, forty standard days, though from the low standard of equipment maintenance I have noticed during my stay here on Dinadh, I would be forced to—"

"Do you have any other information?" the Procurator said in a dangerously calm voice.

"No," Thosby said sulkily, retreating into Codger.

"None at all?" asked Poracious, unbelieving. She retrieved the pipe from where it had fallen and held it out to the man, like one using a morsel of food to coax an unwilling animal from its den.

"So far as I know, she hasn't found anything at all interesting," mumbled Codger, snatching the pipe. The last time he had monitored the recording had been days ago, but he did not mention this.

"She?

"She who?" asked Poracious in a silky tone.

"The survivor."

"Who in the name of all the excremental and sexually active deities now or ever thought of is this survivor?" demanded the Procurator, his face gray with rage and frustration.

"This girl who seems still to be there," said Codger. "This XZ51."

The other three in the room exchanged looks of amazement.

"What girl is he talking about?" asked the ex-king.

Poracious Luv sat down and held her hands high, commanding silence and attention. "Let's make sense of this! Anent seems to be saying the entire team on Perdur Alas has disappeared except for one girl or woman designated by the code number XZ51. That one is still on Perdur Alas with a functioning sensory recorder. Is that more or less correct?"

"Said that," muttered Master Spy, biting hard upon his pipe stem, his lips writhing back to disclose a gray-coated tongue and stumpy, smoke-blackened teeth, at the sight of which Poracious averted her eyes. "Already said that!"

"You have the records."

"No," he said between clamped teeth.

"You don't have the records? Where are they?"

"At my house."

"You will provide them?"

"That was the plan." It was a favorite saying of Thosby's, used in reply whenever anyone asked him when he would do something he had said he would do a long time previously.

"Not a plan," whispered the Procurator, his hand at his throat, which felt raw and dry. "Not a futurity, not a possibility, not a matter to be thought over. It is now, an immediate order. Go, at once. As rapidly as it is possible for you to do so. Without doing anything else or going anywhere else. Go to your house, and get the records. Bring them here!"

"I'd better go with him," said Poracious, heaving her bulk from its chair. "He might get sidetracked."

The two got only as far as the slightly open door when a young woman of Dinadh pushed it open, bowed politely, and spoke to Thosby Anent in a cheerfully guileless voice:

"Sir Thosby, when I learned you were on your way to meet with the Procurator of the Alliance, it occurred to me you might want the records you have been so assiduously compiling." She held out several datachips, offering them to Poracious.

Poracious broke the astonished silence.

"And you are?"

"Chadra Tsum, ma'am. I am housekeeper for Thosby Anent." She relinquished the datachips with a significant glance, which said, "I am who and what I am, but this matter is larger than who and what I am."

"You were both thoughtful and correct," the large woman said.

"I believe this room is equipped with retrievers. If the Procurator wants the latest information." Chadra bowed to Poracious, to Thosby, a perfect model of polite servitude.

"Pushy, unpleasant woman," Thosby snarled as Chadra turned away. "Always interrupting me when I'm busy."

"Perhaps she wishes to direct your attention to something important," whispered the Procurator. "Had that occurred to you?"

"Oh, sir," said the Codger with a patronizing smile, "we are too concerned with things we believe are important. When one considers the infinite nature of time, that all races including our own are doomed to live and perish like the candle flame in that infinitude—"

"Good day," said Poracious, taking him by the shoulder and moving him gently toward the door. "We can't thank you enough for your help." She shut the door behind him, then turned, the datachips in her hand, murmuring, "Where's the retriever?"

"What's that beside the window?" the Procurator asked plaintively. "Surely that's a retriever."

The ex-king took the plat from Poracious and inserted it into a wall-mounted retrieval complex that had been designed to look like a landscape sculpture. "Is there a code?" he murmured, stepping politely aside and averting his eyes.

Poracious referred to her wrist-link before entering an activation code. The unit hummed briefly, then the walls of the room disappeared and the three were on Perdur Alas, assailed by sounds, sights, smells. And a taste!

They gagged.

Before them, observed from some distance, through a twiggy growth, monstrously shaggy flesh encircled something they could not see, great cliffs of hair reared high as hills, walls of old dog, of lairs deep in layers of fatty bones, the taste of beast, hot reeking blood, and sour spit. From behind them came the sound of the sea. Between their teeth a twig was jammed to keep their mouths slightly open so they wouldn't gag on the taste . . . on the dreadful taste.

The scene jiggled and moved as they rose laboriously. Their point of view changed. They climbed, up and up, then peered out once more from above, down at the inside of that wall of flesh, seeing bare skin upon which patterns moved, around and around the abandoned camp, memories of slaughter, retelling of the chase.

They raised their eyes. Through the air, from the south, three things came toward the others, reaching out with appendages that seemed to stretch forever, joining others, making other enclosures. In the middle distance, a dozen shaggy mountains moved in a slow procession.

What was it they tasted? Oily, soapy, rancid, bitter, nasty . . .

Poracious Luv, from her vision of Perdur Alas, stretched her arm through the vision to find the reality of the retrieval control on Dinadh. She turned it off. While the other two retched and gagged she unashamedly wiped out her mouth with the hem of her garment.

"Technician!" she said. "Call for a technician to filter out the tastes. We can't analyze this until we filter out the tastes."

"Do it," sputtered the Procurator, heading for the door labeled SANITARY FACILITY. "Summon that rememberer back, and have him find someone. Now!"

From behind a clump of furze, Snark watched Diagonal Red, Four Green Spot, Big Gray Blob, Blue Lines, and Speckled Purple—the ones she'd come to call the Big Five—gather over the camp. Recently these particular ones had been assembling more and more frequently, sometimes only three or four of them, often all five, looming aloft for a while, then descending to encircle the abandoned camp with appendages that seemed almost liquid in their ability to flow together. Peering at them from her hole at the top of the nearest hill, Snark had decided this was either the way they conversed or the way they remembered. Each new picture coalesced on one Ularian before it moved across the united flesh to the next Ularian, where some other details or actions were added. Each Ularian augmented or complicated the picture created by the previous ones, and the event continued accreting finer and finer detail until the sequence was completed. Or until the Ularians got tired of it.

She had watched them kill her mother half a dozen times. Since she had first realized that the color blobs were pictures, she had counted the number of different pictures they shared. The most frequent one was Snark's mother, a huge mother one who covered the whole front of one of the things. Soon Mother would run across the moor, her hair streaming behind her. The shape of running Mother would move to the left, racing along that great wall of flesh. The next Ularian added the shapes of the pursuers. This picture went on, left, farther left, until Snark lost sight of it. When it came into view again, to her right, the pursuers were pouncing, sending Mother fleeing this way, that way, playing with her. Every time the same, the sea coming nearer and nearer, safety almost within reach . . .

Each time Snark had seen it, Mother had almost reached the edge before they caught her.

Why did they show it over and over? Tell it over and over? It wasn't a story one of them told, it was a story they shared. Sometimes Diagonal Red would start it. Sometimes one of the others. And the details were always the same, as though they'd all agreed just how it was, just what had happened, remembering it all the same.

Snark told herself the pictures were not necessarily true. The chase might not have happened at all. Maybe it was something they wanted to have happened. Maybe it was a religious thing, a kind of ritual they went through, like primitives did, counting coup, telling tall tales, even painting lies on their tombs to make their gods think they were better, or bigger, or stronger than they actually were.

Today they weren't telling the mother-chase story. Today they were showing another favorite, a fish story. The picture was of shaggy forms that hung over the sea, dropping their tentacles into the waves, drawing them up again, laden with silvery fish. The detail was so complete that Snark could see the fish flapping inside the tentacles that had caught them.

When they were finished telling stories, they would float away, like monstrous balloons. There was a wrongness to them. Balloons should be festive, not repulsive. Snark put her face onto her hands, waiting for them to finish showing the fish story and go away. Close as they were, she dared not move, though the taste was hard to bear. When she watched them for a long time like this, the taste seemed to permeate her own flesh until she herself tasted as they did, sick of her own saliva, nauseated by the rottenness of her own tongue. When they left, she would lie in the mouth of her cave with her mouth open, letting the sea wind wash around her teeth, cleansing her into humanness once more.

During the past few days, they had been around more frequently and had stayed for longer times. Maybe they were planning a fishing trip. Maybe they'd taken over this whole planet just to go fishing! Though all they'd done so far was talk about it, that is, show pictures about it. They themselves hadn't caught any fish, not that Snark had seen.

She clamped her eyes shut and concentrated on breathing deeply: one breath, two breaths, three, four, the smell of the sea, the sound of the birds, thirty-two, the sound of the waves, eighty, one hundred, a hundred thirty, seventy. . . .

When she raised her head, they had gone. She didn't move. A few days ago, she'd thought they were gone and had been about to move when she realized they were hanging directly above her. She'd come that close to being eaten. Or transported. Or cat-and-moused like her mother. Whatever it was they did. Would do.

She risked a look up. Clear sky. Nothing. Nothing near the camp. Nothing between herself and the cliff. Still, one had to be careful. They could move with horrid alacrity. One minute they wouldn't be anywhere around, the next moment they'd be present.

Maybe they knew she was here. Maybe all this was part of the ritual. Showing her what would happen to her.

She wouldn't think that. Wouldn't let herself think that. If she thought that, she'd run screaming right at them, out in the open, panicked. She couldn't do that. She had to hold on, hold on. . . .

For what? There was no one here. No one to protect, no one to talk to, no one to lie beside, sharing warmth, sharing comfort, even.

Untrue. Somewhere was a monitor. Seeing what she saw. Feeling what she felt. Somewhere on Dinadh was someone watching over her.

Though the monitor might not be the only thing watching over her! Sometimes in the night she woke to that flattened sound, that curtained feeling, that almost subliminal shudder, as though a mighty hoof had touched the planet, moving it slightly in its orbit. What was that? Did *it* know she was here?

"Lonely," she whispered. "God, I'm so lonely! I'm all alone. Please. Help me. Come get me. Please!"

Late Dinadh daylight filtered chill through multiple windows, making puddles of grayed gold upon the floor. Three sat stunned, facing one another, only just returned from Perdur Alas, returned from fear, pain, hunger, cold. From weary loneliness.

"Well," said the Procurator in an exhausted whisper. "At least we now know what they look like."

They did not know whether they had been living Snark's life for a day or two or three. Only when she reached the safety of her cave and curled into sleep had they turned off the retriever and let the Dinadh evening surround them once more. The Procurator's words were the first intelligible ones any of them had made, though their experience had been punctuated by cries and grunts and indrawn breaths.

"Can't we do something for her?" the ex-king asked, his voice breaking. "Send a ship or something."

Poracious Luv arched her brows disbelievingly. "You? The King of Kamir, the practitioner of ultimate ennui? Touched by the plight of another human being?"

"She's alone," he blurted, flushing. "I've . . . I've been alone. It would touch anyone!"

The Procurator rubbed his forehead wearily. It ached from the battering he, Snark, had received. It had ached before, and now it was worse. He had, after all, sent her there. He was responsible for her.

He said, "Touched or not, right now there's no ship to send. Even if there were a ship, we couldn't risk it for one survivor."

"Particularly inasmuch as we now have records of everything she's picked up," said Poracious Luv in a dry, cynical voice. "So there'd be no advantage to rescuing her."

"Advantage," Jiacare Lostre snarled. "Advantage!"

"Would you trade a hundred lives for one?" the Procurator said, looking him in the eye. "Surely you don't think those . . . creatures would let us go to Perdur Alas and simply remove her? We'd have to send a cruiser at least. Would you trade a shipload of men on a gesture?"

"How do we know they wouldn't?"

Poracious sighed. "We know what happened to ships in the Hermes Sector a hundred years ago. Any ship approaching a world that had been stripped was taken. They went, just as the people went. Gone. Whisk. Away. Nobody knew where. That's what has happened to the evacuation ships this time, too."

"I didn't realize," mumbled the ex-king. "Sorry. This is all . . . very new to me. I've tried not to care about anything for a very long time, but this . . ."

"Nothing like a heady dose of danger to wake one up," Poracious agreed. "Well, Procurator? What do we do next?"

"With what we've seen happening currently, there must be dozens of episodes in the record that will warrant perusal by experts."

"Experts." She laughed. "Ha!"

"Well, by people who might have specialized insights, at least. Some other Fastigats than myself should see this. Also some linguists who specialize in sight languages."

"Sight language?" Jiacare Lostre cocked his head curiously.

"There are, or were historically, several sight languages for people who couldn't hear. Now, of course, such languages aren't necessary, but we still have records of them. The girl mutters to herself a lot, so we can pick up clues as to what she's thinking. She said 'telling stories'; she said 'ritual'; both in connection with that pictorial thing they do. I'd be interested in knowing what others think."

"What do you think?" demanded the ex-king.

The Procurator considered. "The episode with the running woman had the feel of a story, didn't it?"

"Was the woman actually her mother?" Poracious asked.

"Each time the woman appeared, she, Snark, subvocalized the word," said the Procurator. "She said the word *mother,* and her throat and mouth sensed the shaping of the word. Whether she actually believes so, we don't know. Her thoughts can't be recorded. Only what she senses."

Poracious mused. "If the woman was her mother, then the girl was a child there, on Perdur Alas. A survivor from the former Ularian crisis?"

The Procurator shook his head. "It seems impossible. She'd have to have been third or fourth generation."

"We've found great-grandchildren of colonists before."

"True." He stared at his hands, surprised to find them trembling. "I've just thought, Lutha Tallstaff is a linguist. One of the best, according to my sources. I don't know if she knows anything about sight languages, but it's worth bringing her from wherever she was sent. What was the name of the place?"

"Cochim-Mahn," said Poracious.

"We should be fetching her anyhow. She's at danger if those two assassins are on the loose. And meantime, we should be bringing in some other experts to experience what this girl is going through." The Procurator stared blindly at his companions. "Think of it. The first human contact with a life-form that speaks, and it speaks a nonverbal language."

The ex-king remarked, "My Minister of Agriculture would say we
don't know that it's speaking. It could be merely replaying things it has
seen. My Minister of Agriculture would deny it thinks. He says the universe was made for man."

Poracious stared at the wall, remembering. She didn't believe it was a
mere replay. There had been too much relish in the retelling. Reshow-
ing. She went to the door and beckoned to the tassel-bearded rememberer waiting outside. He rose, bowing attentively as she said:

"Will you please send word to Cochim-Mahn that we need to get
Lutha Tallstaff here, as quickly as possible."

"And Trompe," called the Procurator. "Bring him as well!"

The rememberer stared at the ceiling, shifted his feet, cleared his
throat.

"Well?" demanded Poracious, suspiciously. "What?"

"Inasmuch as we had determined the assassins were no longer where
they belonged, I took the liberty of communicating with Cochim-Mahn.
While you were . . . occupied."

"And? Come on, man. Spit it out. All this havering merely makes us
itch."

"They're gone," he blurted. "She, the boy, her companion. As well as
Leelson Famber. Also a shadow woman. An eaten one." He curled his
lips around the word, whether in disapproval or disgust, she couldn't tell.

"Gone?" she cried.

"Leelson Famber!" exclaimed the Procurator as he joined her in the
doorway. "When did Leelson Famber come here?"

The rememberer shrugged, looking from face to face as though trying
to decide which question to answer first. "He came, sir, some time ago.
And it is believed by those at Cochim-Mahn that they may all have gone
to Tahs-uppi."

Jiacare Lostre joined the others in the doorway. "Gone where?"

"Gone to what," corrected the rememberer. "A ceremony. Held once
every sixty years or so. At the omphalos. At the sipapu. At Dinadh's
birthplace, the site of our emergence. The songfather of Cochim-Mahn
believes they have gone there, and he is pursuing them. The assassins
asked questions about the ceremony, so we believe they're headed there
also."

"Can we intercept them on the way?" Poracious demanded.

The rememberer turned up his palms helplessly. "Who knows which
way they've gone. If they intended to avoid other travelers, they would
have tried less-traveled ways, of which there are thousands! The canyons

ramify, netlike. They go off into pockets and branches. We'd never find them."

"Well then," the Procurator said. "How long for us to get where they're going?"

"Not long, great sir. I can arrange it for tomorrow. We can fly."

The three shared helpless glances, equally at a loss. Poracious Luv broke the silence, attempting encouragement. "We'll meet them when they arrive," she said, patting the Procurator upon the shoulder.

"If they arrive," corrected the rememberer. "I would be remiss if I did not tell you that their arrival is far from certain."

CHAPTER 8

The first of us to catch sight of the Nodders was Trompe. He was driving the hitch; Leely was asleep inside the wain; and the rest of us were trudging some way behind, cursing every step we made across the curved pebbles that often twisted treacherously beneath our feet. Trompe's *whoof* of surprise brought us stumbling forward to find him gaping, the reins lax in his hands. Gaufers are incapable of astonishment. They simply lay down, snapping and grumbling at one another as they did at every halt. We made no effort to get them moving. There seemed to be nowhere they could go.

It was another place like the Burning Springs, that is, one I'd heard described without getting any idea what it was really like. Songfather had said there were many Nodders, that they were tall, thin pillars of stone, topped with stone heads.

What he'd said wasn't inaccurate; it was simply a ridiculous understatement. Trompe climbed down from the wagon seat to join Lutha, Leelson, and me as we went slowly forward. The first Nodder was like a sentinel, standing a little forward from the rest. As we neared it our eyes were drawn upward, seeing the tower narrowed to a pinpoint against the massive bulk of the balanced stone head. Perspective, I told myself. It wasn't really that slender. It couldn't be. It couldn't be frigidly cold in the vicinity of the stone, either, but we thrust our shivering arms into our sleeves as we backed slowly away. Beyond the first pillar stood two more, side by side, and behind them, hundreds.

Songfather had said they were many, tall, and thin. I also recalled—as we fled in howling panic!—he had said the stone heads moved.

It was impossible to run over that treacherous footing and we collapsed in a confused heap not far away.

"I thought it was coming down on us!" Lutha cried as she scrabbled backwards on all fours, never taking her eyes from the ponderous, impossible nodding of that great stone head.

I still thought it would come down. When it did, it would roll purposefully over us. Behind the three menacing outliers, the great forest of them seemed to whisper to one another in sinister agreement. *Yes, yes, let's roll over on that wagon and squish all the people. Wouldn't that be fun?*

I couldn't keep from saying this, a mere whisper to Lutha, and she laughed, a wild peal of amusement. The two men turned disapproving looks on her, which only increased her hilarity. All the tension she'd bottled up during the journey poured out in hysterical torrents. She put her hands over her mouth and smothered the sound, head on knees, shoulders shaking.

Leelson, with his usual casual disapproval, pointed to the sharp-edged fragments of curved stone that littered the ground, fragments not unlike those that had been troubling our footsteps for some miles. He said pointedly, "It really isn't funny, Lutha. They do come down."

Not the least sobered, she spared a glance for the surfaces around us, then took a quick look at the conspiratorial heads. My eyes followed hers, and the same odd idea possessed us both at once, for we said, as in one slightly echoed voice:

"From where?"

"Why, from . . ." said Leelson, his words trailing into silence.

"If some tops fell down, then there should be some pillars without tops." Lutha giggled. Her voice sounded foolish, like that of a petulant little girl. She heard herself, cleared her throat, and said in a more normal tone, "But there aren't any pillars without tops. So where did they fall from?"

"Strange," mused Trompe. "Very strange. The shape of the heads, I mean. They shouldn't be quite that spherical, should they? Or would erosion tend to round them off?"

When one focused on the shape and not on the streaked and blotched surfaces, the roundness was obvious. Lines and smudges of mineral colors—ocher, brown, red—made them appear more irregular and rugged than they actually were. Except for the horns on top, they were ball-shaped.

"The mass can't be uniform," Leelson remarked in a troubled tone. "The center of gravity has to be . . . where?"

"Doesn't matter," mumbled Trompe. "It'd have to be below the point of the pillar to keep the thing balanced that way. The way they are, the damn things can't exist."

"But they do," I said.

"It would work if there were a gyroscope inside." Leelson strode away in a long arc to examine the nearest Nodder from the side. "Or a central support. Or a gravitic drive."

"Or if they weren't really stone," said Trompe, joining his colleague. The two of them stood there with their mouths open, wearing identical expressions of annoyance. Fastigats, so I had already learned, do not like things they do not understand. Their irritated silence made me uncomfortably aware that I understood no more than they.

Lutha had regained control of herself. "You're not thinking that they're unnatural, are you?"

Leelson took his time before answering. "You've seen Dinadhi children playing ball games. You've seen Dinadhi herdsmen spinning wool. Imagine yourself trying to balance one of the balls on the tip of a spindle and tell me how much luck you'd have."

She gave me a quick look, and I shook my head. As described, it would be impossible. Unless the ball were spinning. We have jugglers skilled in such tricks, but these heads weren't spinning. So. It couldn't be done.

The two men came strolling back, foreheads wrinkled with concentration.

I said, "But if they aren't natural, wouldn't someone have noticed before now?"

Leelson shook his head. "According to you, Saluez, people come this way only once every sixty Dinadhi years, which is about once a century, standard. Since that's a generous lifetime, it's unlikely anyone makes the trip twice. Suppose a traveler *had* noticed. Suppose he'd gone back to his hive and told someone. Would there have been any consequence?"

His superior tone implied there would have been none, and he was probably right. On Dinadh, whenever someone raises a "difficult" question, someone else can be depended upon to mutter, in that particular tone of hushed apprehension people always use on such occasions, "Perhaps it's part of the choice." Once the choice is mentioned, all conversation ends. Only songfathers are allowed to discuss the choice, along with the rest of their arcane lore.

I suppose my thoughts showed on my face, for Leelson said:

"As I thought. No one would have done anything at all about it." Then he shared one of his infuriatingly smug looks with Trompe.

Lutha glanced at me from beneath her lashes, and I blinked slowly in sympathy. We were both thinking that Fastigats were impossible. She took my hand and we walked back to the wagon behind the men. I was wondering if our being here was blasphemous, but Lutha had a different concern.

"From here, they look like a herd of great horned beasts, don't they? If they're artificial, why are they here?"

Leelson stood for a moment in thought, then fetched Bernesohn Famber's map from the wagon, unrolled it on the ground, and put a stone on each corner to hold it down. Kneeling beside it, he pointed with an extended forefinger.

"The important geographical features are all shown on this map, canyons, tablelands, hives, and so forth—even the omphalos, beside this winding river on what seems to be a flat plain. The Nodders, however, are not shown."

"That is, they're not printed on the map," said Trompe, underlining the obvious.

Leelson continued. "No. The word *Nodders* has been written in, probably by Bernesohn himself. He learned about them a century ago. Either someone told him about the Nodders or he himself came this way."

I said, "But Bernesohn Famber wouldn't have been allowed to go to the omphalos. He was an outlander."

"We're not allowed either, but we're going," Trompe snorted. "What would they have done to him if they'd caught him?"

It was not a proper question. It was not a question any Dinadhi should have to answer. "I don't know," I said. "Sometimes the songfathers have people stoned."

Leelson sat back on his heels. "Let's assume he came here himself. Let's even assume he was put to death by the songfathers for that impropriety. Would his property have been forfeit?"

I didn't know what he meant, but Lutha did. She turned to me, asking:

"If a person is executed on Dinadh, what happens to his property. What happens to his clothing, or anything he may be carrying?"

"Everything we have belongs to our families. When someone dies, if the body isn't too close to a hive, it's just left where it is. It's only . . .

flesh. The spirit is already gone. But anything like clothing or tools would be returned to the family."

"Even if the person has been executed?"

"The family is not tarnished for what one person of it does. That would not be just."

Songfather was not tarnished because of me. Chahdzi father was not tarnished because his daughter had failed. It would not be just. I felt my throat tighten, all my sinews strain. Was it just that I had been tarnished? What had I done to deserve tarnishing?

Lutha put her hand on my shoulder, but Leelson did not notice my pain. He was focused elsewhere.

"So if Bernesohn was killed out here somewhere, the map would have been returned to his leasehold."

I brought my mind back to where we were.

"The map?" Leelson demanded impatiently. "It would have been brought back?"

He made me angry with his insistence. "Yes, but the same would be true if he had been found dead. He didn't have to have been executed. In fact, we know he wasn't, because if he had been, no one would have—" I caught my breath and put my hand over my mouth.

I'd been going to say, "No one would have prayed his return if he'd been guilty of blasphemy." Since he came back to Cochim-Mahn as a Kachis, he must have been invited. This is one reason our people are careful to be pleasant to one another, not to be hostile, not to be mean, for if one of us is not well liked, that one may not be invited to return, may not be invited to be part of his former family.

I turned away in confusion.

"What?" demanded Leelson.

Lutha squeezed my hand, saying, "It's one of the things she's not supposed to talk about, Leelson. Simply take it as given that she has reason to believe Bernesohn Famber was not killed by the songfathers."

Leelson glared at her and at me, shaking his head. "It really doesn't matter whether he vanished during his journey or subsequently. In either case the map ended up back at his leasehold with his handwritten notes on it. It's unfortunate he's no longer among us to enlighten us as to the details."

I opened my mouth, then shut it without saying that Bernesohn Famber was still among us. Lutha hadn't believed it. Leelson wouldn't believe it either.

Leelson went on, "Let's assume the songfathers know the way to the

omphalos because they've inherited instructions from former generations, not because they've made the trip before."

Lutha asked, "Where are you going with all this, Leelson?"

"I'm getting there. The map shows a dozen canyon mouths opening
into the area of the omphalos, and assuming the Nodders did not grow
here but were put here, we could extrapolate that there may be similar
installations at the mouths of all the canyons. In which case, what purpose do they serve?"

"I haven't the least idea," she replied in a grumpy voice. "Do you? Or
are you just being rhetorical."

"He's not being rhetorical," Trompe offered. "He's saying there may
be Nodders guarding all access to the omphalos. Controlling traffic, so
to speak."

"Traffic!" She stared pointedly at the emptiness around us. Stone and
more stone. No traffic.

Trompe persisted. "If he's right, timely travelers get through, others
don't."

I said, "It is true that songfathers may not go to the omphalos except
at the time of Tahs-uppi."

"What about leap year?" asked Lutha in a contentious tone. "I
thought an extra day had to be drawn from the navel hole every few
years!"

"Only the big days must be pulled by songfathers," I told them. "The
little days are pulled out by the spirit people who live there, at the
sipapu."

"Monks?" Lutha puzzled in aglais. "Priests?"

I knew those words. "Women too."

"Nuns?"

I shrugged. "Spirit people is what the songfathers call them. Spirit
men, with spirit women to take care of them." In the sisterhood it was
said the spirit people had no House Without a Name. It was said the
spirit women never got pregnant. No one had ever told me how they
managed that. I thought perhaps they were all very holy. Or very old. I
would ask Lutha about it later.

Trompe rolled up the map and put it back in the wagon. "How do the
Nodders decide to let people through? By the season of the year? By
counting planetary revolutions since the previous visitors? By genetic
pattern? Or are they controlled from somewhere?"

"We're going to have to find out," Leelson said. "One of us will have
to try it. You or me, Trompe."

"I can go," I offered. Perhaps this is why I had come, to spend my life, and my child's, for something important. "I want to."

"Your going wouldn't tell us what we want to know," Trompe said kindly, patting my shoulder. "They could let you through, then come down on us. We need to know if non-Dinadhi can get through. Assuming the time is right, of course."

"But that's not all you're assuming!" cried Lutha incredulously. "You're assuming they're artificial, you're assuming they're a danger, you're building this whole scenario out of thin air."

"Thin air! Look at the damn things," Leelson snarled at her. "For the love of heaven, Lutha! Stop living in your gut and start living in your head!"

She went pale with anger as she spoke between gritted teeth. "I'm as thoughtful as you are, Leelson Famber. And as intelligent! It's just that I don't go building elaborate theoretical structures on damned little evidence."

"Really! That hasn't been my observation up until now," he said, with an obvious sidelong look at Leely.

"That's unfair," she cried, storming away from us to stand at some distance, back turned, rigid.

He strode after her. "Lutha, damn it, use good sense!"

"You're talking about Leely."

"Forget Leely!"

"I can't. He's alive! His heart beats. His lungs pump air—"

"Frogs' hearts beat," he shouted. "Sparrows have lungs that pump air. Is that your criteria for humanity? Hearts and lungs?"

"He has brain waves!" she shouted.

"He has the same kind of brain waves as chickens. As a matter of fact, his brain waves are virtually indistinguishable from those of chickens."

"He's not a chicken. He's a human being!"

Leelson's face was very pale, his mouth was hard. "Morphologically, he's a human being. Mentally, he's a chicken."

He came striding back, saying something to Trompe in an angry tone, words I couldn't catch. Trompe soothed him.

"Give her room, Leelson. She's not here because she wants to be."

"She stayed when she had a chance to leave! I wanted her home, safe, out of this!"

"It's no good arguing that point now. She's here. Leely is here. You're here, and so am I, and Saluez. We've got people, animals, and a wagon to get through those . . . whatever they are. You're not going to get

Lutha to think logically about Leely, so let's forget that and concentrate on what we have to do!"

Leelson heaved a deep breath. "You or me, then. We'll draw for it; short straw goes, on foot. Then we'll know if nonplanetary human males can get through. Saluez can come next, to establish whether women are allowed."

Even angry as he was at Lutha, to protect her he would sacrifice himself. And me. But then, I was used to that.

"Then Lutha and . . . Leely. Then the other one of us, driving the wagon."

"Not driving," amended Trompe. "Leading on a long, long rope. That way, if they don't like wagons, or gaufers, the one leading will still have a chance."

They nodded at one another, agreeing. I thought we wouldn't have any chance unless the Nodders let the gaufers and the wagon through. But then, before we left Cochim-Mahn, I was fairly sure we'd be eaten the first night or so. And before I first met Leelson, I thought outlanders would be strange and exotic instead of just ordinary people. And at one time I'd thought the Kachis were invulnerable and all-seeing, but some of them had died and thousands of others had sat like stones around the Burning Springs. And at one time I'd thought Leely was helpless, but he wasn't. He sneaked around like a clever little cornrat. Leelson was wrong about him. He was smarter than a chicken. Of course, I'd never seen a chicken.

Just because Leelson might be wrong didn't mean Lutha was right about him, though she was about some things. She was probably right about the Kachis we'd seen at Burning Springs. If the songfathers couldn't get to the ompahlos, the omphalos wouldn't be opened. If the omphalos wasn't opened, the Kachis couldn't go through it to heaven. It made sense that all the Kachis would find nice warm places and meditate there, awaiting their time of transfiguration.

While I was puzzling over this Leelson had wandered off to the edge of the small stream that we had traveled along since we had left the Burning Springs. He plucked a few lengths of dried grass and came striding back to Trompe, holding out a fist with two straws protruding. Trompe drew one.

Leelson opened his hand to show that the one he retained was the shorter one, and then, without so much as blinking or saying good-bye, he turned and walked rapidly toward the Nodders, leaving Trompe and me with our mouths full of unspoken advice. Leely poked his head out

of the wagon and stared at Leelson's retreating back. Only Lutha, still
angrily facing back the way we had come, did not see him go.

When he came beneath the first of the Nodders, I forgot to breathe.
The Nodder began to sway again, very gently, side to side, like someone
saying no, no, don't do that. Leelson looked up, hesitated only a fraction
of an instant, then went on. The Nodder went on swaying: no, no, no,
and it didn't stop swaying when Leelson went past it, out of its shadow,
and strode toward the gap between the two other outliers. Both of them
began to sway also, saying no, no, no. This time Leelson didn't look up.
He just went on, arms swinging, eyes on his feet.

The great heads were horning the heavens, right, left, right. Lutha had
been right. They resembled a herd of . . . what? "They look like animal heads," I whispered. "What is that Old-earthian animal, Trompe?
Men fought it ritually, risking their lives. Was it a cattle?"

"Bull," he said.

Of course. Bull. Virile and puissant. Mighty bull. I remembered now.

From behind me I heard an indrawn breath. Lutha came running.
Trompe caught her as she was about to pass us.

"Hush," he said as she began to babble. "Don't do anything to foul up
the findings. Or to risk his life more than it already is."

She paused, frozen, one foot still raised, watching as intently as we. A
few moments before, she had hated him. A few hours before, when we
had stopped to rest, I had seen her in his arms again, the two of them
holding one another as though they would never let go. It would be nice,
I thought wistfully, if they could sort it out. Whenever I saw them at it,
loving or hating, it was hurtful to me.

Leelson went between the sentinel pair, then into a veritable forest of
pillars. The great horned heads bobbed restlessly above him, moved by
something. Not wind. It was, for the moment, utterly calm and very cold.

When Leelson moved out of sight among the stones, we all looked
upward, readying ourselves, I suppose, for one or more of the great
heads to fall. Nothing happened but that slight motion, that measured
horning. Jab, jab, jab, they said. No, no, no.

Trompe murmured, "We can postulate it's the correct time to get
through, but only just. The traffic controllers seem to be in some doubt."

That was one explanation. I could think of others, but to no profit. No
amount of thinking would tell us what we needed to know; only action
would do. I took a deep breath and trudged off in the direction Leelson
had gone, hoping the path would be self-evident. One route through
might be passable, while another might be forbidden! The two Fastigats

had not considered that! Behind me Lutha said something and Trompe hushed her. I heard Leely burbling his eternal Dananana. Then I heard nothing but my own blood roaring in my ears.

The temptation to look up was too strong when I came beneath the first one. I staggered at the sight. So huge. So horrid. So heavy. The tops of our caves are as huge, as heavy, but they curve comfortingly down around us, like sheltering arms. These curves went away, the wrong way, and it was like looking up at the shape of some flying monster, diving on me. I shuddered, forced my eyes down, and kept walking. Everywhere the ground was littered with shards of broken stone, sharp edges, curved surfaces, like fragments of eggshells made gigantic. They had fallen from somewhere. At one time or another, they had fallen.

I kept my feet moving, one foot in front of the other. My mouth and throat were so dry it hurt to move my tongue. I gulped at the sight of bones. Not human. Gaufer bones. A scatter of them, as though something had been eating them. Then, as I moved around a great pillar, there were human ones: shoulders and a skull staring at the sky, arms and torso disappearing under a broken-edged stone.

The rock was curved like a fragment of cup and it rocked as I passed. Curve inside curve. Were the Nodders hollow? Were they great stone eggs? With what inside? Were these the remnants of some that had hatched?

Beware, the skull eyes said to me. *Beware. Don't panic. Don't shout. Don't run. Beware!*

I had passed between the Nodder pair. Off to my left the streamlet ran, winding among the pillars, which were all around me now, a thick copse of rising trunks with a multitude of paths among them. How did one keep from getting lost? The stony soil showed no trace of Leelson's passage.

Look up, I told myself. Look past the threatening heads to the canyon rim. Even these monsters are not so high as that lofty edge. Look where the sun is, and where it comes across the heads to make scallop-backed scythes of gray-golden light upon the rocky soil. The rays come from the left. The scythe crescents open to the left. Keep them lying so as you go.

And so I did, while something inside my mind made little gibbering noises and a muscle near my eye twitched as though someone were pulling at it with a thread. The temptation to look up never abated, but it was hard enough to find a way among the fallen fragments without frightening myself more. Turn and turn again. Stop. Look for the light. Turn so the light is coming from the left. Go a little way. Stop again.

Look for the light again. No sound at all but my own panting breath escaping the halter of my throat. Turn and turn again, winding among them, winding around them, to come out of them at last quite unexpectedly!

Leelson stood a short distance away, beckoning with one hand, the other before his lips, urging quiet. Then I allowed myself to look up to see them nodding, nodding, nodding: no, no, no.

Still, they had let me pass. I trudged over to Leelson, bending double to catch my breath. I felt sick. I had half strangled myself.

"Lutha and Leely next," he whispered in my ear. "Is she coming?"

I nodded, supposing that she would. Trompe would tell her she was next; she would take Leely into her arms and start walking in a kind of fatalistic calm. She would recognize the risk. She would tell herself she had never rejected or neglected him, that she had resolutely denied Leelson's assessment of him. Nonetheless, she would risk him and herself. If she allowed herself to think about it at all, she would consider dying with Leely to be an acceptable solution to the problems of their lives, hers and his.

I could read her as though I, too, were a Fastigat. Her longings were mother longings. I knew about mother longings. Sometimes they did not bear thinking on, so I thought instead of her pathway, how she would walk, as I watched the slot from which I myself had emerged. There would be movement, I told myself. At any moment there would be movement.

There was none. Perhaps I was wrong. Perhaps she would not risk herself, or Leely. Leelson gave me a troubled look. I shrugged. I didn't know. We planted our feet and watched, leaning slightly forward, as though to urge her out of hiding.

She did not come, but Leely did, quite alone, face glowing with an almost supernatural light, skipping into sight at the base of one of the pillars, waving his hands, caroling, "Dananana." He was more beautiful than any child I have ever seen. He gave us an enigmatic look, that same look he had given me when he returned from his morning expedition, then he slipped between two pillars to lose himself once more, shining like a little sun.

Beside me, Leelson grunted in surprise. I looked upward as he was doing so and saw only quiet stone heads. Not a motion. Not a quiver. I stepped forward involuntarily to go after the child, but Leelson caught my robe, stopping me.

"No," he whispered vehemently. "Wait!"

We both waited. Everything was silent, still, an interminable stillness. Not a sigh, not a tremble. The first sound we heard was the creak of wheels. Though we'd greased them again and again, they still creaked, a distinctive, irritating sound that might have been near or far, approaching or departing. The echoes and reverberations came at us from all sides, bounced around by the Nodders until they had no point of origin. I swayed with sudden dizziness and realized I'd been holding my breath again. Beside me, Leelson had been doing the same, for he exhaled in a sudden burst as Leely appeared once more.

This time Lutha was behind him, her hands twisted into the shoulders of the child's garment so he could not break away. Her pallor was icy, almost blue, and even from where we stood I could see the rigidity of her arms and shoulders. She was holding the boy in a death grip of which he took no notice at all. His hands waved and his feet skipped and his voice rose in its constant contented comment on the world. I was transfixed once more by his ethereal, marvelous beauty. As one imagines angels or fairies looked in old stories.

Beside me Leelson said, under his breath, "Seraphic." That was the word I'd been wanting. Either Leelson had thought of it, or he'd somehow picked it up from me. He wrenched his eyes away from the boy and held out his hands to Lutha. She ignored him, marching past us.

Trompe appeared next, tugging at the end of a rope. At first I could not imagine where he'd obtained a rope, then I saw he had knotted the reins together. A trivial thought at such a time, for when I looked up, the heads were shaking once more: no, no, no, no. Trompe wasn't looking. He was concentrating on the gaufers. Either they disliked being led or they had picked up our tension, for they were behaving skittishly, throwing their feet sideways as they do when disturbed, bobbing their heads and growling in their throats. With shaking fingers, Trompe put the end of the line into Leelson's hand, threw a glance in Lutha's direction, where she'd stopped a few paces farther on, and then collapsed onto the ground.

"You made it," said Leelson flatly, tugging the gaufers nearer us.

"Obviously," Trompe returned, wiping his face with his sleeve.

Leelson turned to Lutha. "What happened with . . . him?" he asked, indicating Leely with a jerk of his head.

"He just . . . jumped out of my arms," she murmured almost inaudibly. "I should have had his harness on him, but I never expected . . . One minute he was there, and the next he was running off between the pillars. He kept appearing and disappearing. I thought he was lost!"

"Where did you catch up with him?"

"Just there, at the edge, one moment before we saw you."

Leelson shut his eyes, concentrating. Was he trying to reach Leely? Most likely he was, for all the good it did him. I didn't know what Leelson thought, but *I* thought Leely had not been lost among the Nodders any more than he'd been lost when he sneaked out during the night. Leely didn't get lost.

Lutha obviously thought otherwise. Her eyes were full of exhausted tears, and I realized that though Leelson and I had seen how quiet the Nodders were when the boy was among them, she would not have seen it. Not if she'd been running this way and that, seeking the boy at ground level. Would she have felt more or less fearful if she had?

I caught Leelson's eyes upon me and flushed. He turned away, but I knew he was probing at me, trying to figure out what I knew or felt, which, Weaving Woman be thanked, was little enough. I didn't want to know anything. I said so mentally, over and over, a little litany. *I know nothing about Leely. I know nothing about the Nodders. I know nothing about anything. I am an ignorant Dinadhi woman, an unworthy Dinadhi woman, of no possible use to anyone!*

When I finally looked up, Leelson was helping Trompe restore the reins to their ordinary use. Wordlessly, we got moving into the canyon, Leelson driving and the rest of us trailing behind. A few dozen paces farther on, the ground was suddenly clear of curved rock fragments; the footing was blessedly good; we could actually look around us as we went. Still, Lutha never for a moment relinquished her grip upon Leely, even when he began to fuss at her.

The canyon went away in a long, westward-curving arc, and we did not pause until the Nodders were no longer in sight. When we stopped, the ravine was level, widening toward the west, where the sun lay in a shallow notch, like an apple in a bowl, tempting us. That notch was a definite place, discernible, reachable, pulling at us despite our weariness. The temptation to go on was in all our faces, a yearning to be done with this, to be away from the canyons. Even the gaufers leaned into the harness, stamping impatiently.

But Leelson said no. He said the sun was low, we would finish the trip tomorrow. He said we should be well rested when we arrived. He was no doubt right, but it was hard to wait. Beyond that notch was the world's gate, through which the beautiful people would go on their way to heaven. All of them would come, lost children, slain fathers, grandparents dead of age. Bernesohn Famber's outlander ghost, he would be there. My mother would be there. Even now she was probably sitting near a fire fountain in the Canyon of Burning Springs, deep in meditation. Saying good-bye to this world. Saying good-bye to me.

It did not seem fair. The outlander ghost had lived among us for almost a hundred years. My mother's spirit had lived among us for only a few. If she hated me when she went, she would never have a chance to love me again. If this was the choice we had made, shouldn't it be fair for everyone. Shouldn't she be allowed to stay longer? To see her grandchild born?

But then, why would she? Her only child was unworthy of her. If I were one of the beautiful people, would I choose to stay with an unworthy child, or to go on to heaven? Perhaps that is why they meditated, making up their minds.

I looked up to catch Leelson and Lutha watching me. His gaze was intent, hers sympathetic. He wanted to know what I thought; she already knew. Mothers, her eyes seemed to say, always choose happiness for their children, no matter what they or the children have done or not done.

Where was my happiness? Was I less worthy than Leely?

I turned my back on them, pulled my veil across my eyes, and let the tears come. Cry and be done. Soon enough this journey would end and then I might know the truth.

Halfway up the wall of another canyon, one southeast of the omphalos, Mitigan of the Asenagi and Chur Durwen of Collis emerged from the mouth of a shallow cave and stood looking down upon the narrow sea of smoky mist below them. For the last two days they had been traveling in a region of boiling springs, each spring surrounded by multitudes of Kachis, all immobile, all seemingly insensate.

"Quite a change," remarked Mitigan, unwinding a bandage from his forearm and disclosing a nasty-looking bite wound. He smeared it plentifully with reeking salve from his pack, then replaced the bandage. "Damned critters have dirty teeth."

"I told you the thing was behind you," Chur Durwen remarked mildly. "You're getting slow." He examined the line of knives on the stone before him, seven of them, including the ones from his wrist scabbards. All of them needed cleaning and sharpening. Kachis blood was corrosive, and Chur Durwen had bloodied all his knives repeatedly during the earlier stages of their journey.

"If I hadn't ignored the one behind me, you'd have been dead," said Mitigan. "The one I killed would have had you by the throat."

"You're right. Which tells me the throat flap on my battle mask was badly designed. I doubt the Collis Arms Consortium had vampire butterflies in mind when they created it." He took a sharpening stone from his pack and ran it along the edge of the largest knife with a repeated wheeping sound. "They certainly aren't interested in biting now, are they? What do you think they're doing?"

"Could be dead," said Mitigan. "Could be in some kind of hibernation."

"Estivation," corrected the other. "It's closer to summer than winter."

"Why in hell would anything go dead in the summertime?"

Chur Durwen picked up the next knife and peered at it closely. "I think animals do it on desert planets. Where it gets too hot and dry in midsummer. Where the cooler winter weather is actually more supportive of life."

"This probably qualifies as a desert planet. And I can't say I'm sorry they've quit bothering us."

"Nasty, aren't they? Almost human, the way they look, the way they sound. That little whine of theirs. Like a child, or a woman trying to get you to buy her something."

"Or pay her for something," gibed Mitigan.

"Hell, if you have to pay for it, you don't deserve it." The man from Collis tried the second knife with the hardened skin of his thumb. "Come to think of it, though they have very female-looking bodies, every damn one of them has a dingus long as your forearm and pointy as a dagger. Do you suppose the locals . . . ?"

"You'd have to be more than ordinarily stupid," remarked Mitigan. "Or quite irresistibly horny." He turned away from the cave entrance to examine the map he'd pinned to the wall inside. "This canyon, then one more. We'll make it in one or two days if the butterfly bats stay quiet."

"Vampire butterflies," corrected Chur Durwen.

The other muttered, "Vampires only suck your blood. They don't bite your throat out and try to chew on your face."

His companion grunted agreement. When he had finished three more knives, he asked, "You really think there will be Fambers there? At this navel hole?"

"Just a feeling," admitted Mitigan. "A hunch. I've learned to pay attention to my hunches. I think we're going to hit the main vein of Fambers at the omphalos. I think when we get there, we'll earn our pay."

* * *

According to the rememberer in Simidi-ala, the Procurator could not fly directly to the omphalos. He could fly to a point very near. To the very next canyon, in fact. But the last little bit, one had to go on foot.

"And why is that?" demanded Poracious Luv.

"Only songfathers will be allowed to go into the sacred area or to . . ."

To make decisions, the Procurator silently finished the remark.

"Interesting," said Poracious. "Why is that?"

"It's not my area of expertise," said the rememberer, staring over her left shoulder.

"Most interesting," she repeated. "Don't you think so, sir?"

"I think we should waste as little time as possible in conversation," muttered the Procurator between his teeth. "We would not enjoy arriving at the omphalos only a few moments too late to prevent assassinations from occurring."

"Quite right. Fastest way, please, rememberer. On foot or whatever."

The rememberer's "on foot" seemed to include gaufer feet, for both a chariot and a cart, each with its team of gaufers, awaited them near the head of the shallow valley in which they landed. Two servants, who had accompanied them in the flier, jumped down at once and began loading the Procurator's voluminous baggage into the cart while both hitches of animals stamped their feet impatiently.

"I suggested the conveyances would make the remaining distance a bit easier," the rememberer murmured, keeping his eyes resolutely away from Poracious's bulky form.

"For which my thanks," she said, heaving herself aboard the chariot with remarkable agility. She picked up the reins and gave them an experimental tug.

"I must leave you here." The rememberer bowed. "As I've mentioned, those of us from Simidi-ala are not allowed to enter the sacred precincts. Neither are outlanders, of course, and I cannot guarantee an exception will be made for you. We have managed to convince the songfathers it is in their best interest to speak with you. That's the best we can do."

"We understand." The Procurator nodded. "Where are they?"

The rememberer nodded toward the very top of the valley, where several figures stood athwart a shallow col, silhouetted against the sky. "High officials. And I'm afraid we're persona non grata." He beckoned to the servants. "As soon as I've gone, they'll come for you."

He and the servants climbed back into the flier and were whisked aloft in a great cloud of dust.

"He seemed relieved to get out of here," commented the ex–King of Kamir, wiping the dust from his eyes as he climbed into the chariot beside Poracious.

"I can see why," murmured Poracious, peering beneath her lashes at the black-clad men who were approaching. "They don't look happy to see us."

"Please allow me to speak for us," said the Procurator from where he stood beside the left wheel. He had donned an official tabard for the meeting, one glittering with gems and fine gold embroidery. It bore upon the back panel the great arms of the Alliance, worked in pearls and sapphires, and on the front panel a grid, in each square of which was the symbol of one of the Seventeen Sectors. Stitched over the symbol of Hermes Sector was a pall of black tissue, showing it to be under threat.

The symbolism was not lost upon the approaching Dinadhi. They saw it and stopped to mumble with one another before continuing their advance.

"What has this predicament of the Alliance to do with Dinadh?" demanded the foremost, threatening with one clawlike hand.

"All your people may perish," said the Procurator silkily, the words sinuous as snakes, demanding attention. "Dinadh is next in line."

The Dinahdi glanced at one another, only briefly.

The speaker sneered. "We do not believe we are in any danger from . . . the Ularians."

The Procurator blinked slowly. His voice gained both volume and vehemence. "If you are not in danger from them, you are in danger from the Alliance. If you alone in Hermes Sector are not destroyed by the aliens, we must assume you have made common cause with them against the rest of humanity. Is it not written, 'All life is struggle. He who will not stand with me stands against me'? Humanity will have vengeance for such treachery. You will not be allowed to remain here unscathed while others suffer."

The hearers shivered. Even Poracious felt her bulk quiver. Fastigacy at its finest, she told herself, maintaining her composure with difficulty. What actors they made!

"There has been no common cause with aliens," cried one of the other Dinadhi. "Nothing such is needed! We are under the protection of our gods! Our gods are stronger than any . . . aliens."

The Procurator smiled voraciously, his teeth showing. "Then we will have vengeance against your gods, Songfathers. If your gods choose some men to favor, while sacrificing others, then those sacrificed may well cry from beyond the grave for justice."

The third man spoke. "You threaten much. We see only one old man, much bedecked, one fat woman, and one younger man who does not look dangerous. From where will this vengeance come?"

"From the battleships of the Alliance that hang in orbit around your world," said the Procurator, poker-faced. "From persons on those ships who even now listen to our conversation and watch your actions."

"And from the royal navy of Kamir," said the ex-king, "which will extort retribution for any dishonor done its king."

"And from Buchol Sector," said Poracious. "Where my brother is emperor."

The Dinadhi turned their backs and went a little distance away, where they put their heads together in troubled confabulation.

"The royal navy of Kamir?" asked Poracious, without moving her lips. "Since when?"

"Since your brother was selected emperor of Buchol Sector," said Jiacare Lostre.

Only the former speaker rejoined the outlanders as the others straggled away toward the col.

"I am Hah-Rianahm," he said. "Subchief of the Songfathers' Council, Second Grandfather of the Great Assembly. My word binds or looses. It is my decision that you will come with us to the omphalos! We cannot delay to parley with you, for Tahs-uppi approaches, and our presence is required in the eternal circles. When those are broken, however, we will take time to hear what you have to say. This is not a good time for you to have approached us."

"We didn't pick it," said Poracious. "It was picked for us, by the Ularians."

"What are these Ularians?" asked Hah-Rianahm.

"The beings who have destroyed humans on all the occupied worlds in this sector."

"You have seen these beings?"

"We will show them to you," said the Procurator. "We will let you see them, and feel them, and taste them. . . ."

"After Tahs-uppi," called one of the other men urgently. "Even now the circles are forming!"

"At the first possible moment," said the Procurator. "At the very first possible moment."

* * *

In her cave above the sea, Snark lay dreaming. She'd been doing that a lot lately, spending whole days in the cave, dozing, remembering, having imaginary conversations with people she'd never met or never really known. She carried on an animated three-way conversation among herself, her mother, and the Procurator. She discussed life with Kane the Brain. She talked to the mistress of the sanctuary, the one who had labeled Snark a liar when Snark had claimed to come from the frontier.

"Wrong," said Snark in her reverie, holding the mistress in a grip of steel, forcing her to look upon the moors of Perdur Alas. "You were wrong about me, madam! Look upon my childhood, my rearing, the cause of all my woe. . . ."

The daydream dissolved in a spatter of icy spray, and she opened her eyes, startled. Outside on the branch, a large seabird tossed a scaly thing in its beak, preparatory to swallowing it. The scaly thing struggled, not quite fishlike, throwing water in all directions.

"You woke me," said Snark, wiping her face with the back of her hands.

The bird did not reply. The bird didn't even see her. It looked past her in the same way people always had. All those at the sanctuary when she was only nine or ten. All those she'd asked for help later, when she'd been a street rat. All those who'd had business with the Procurator: bureaucrats or military, male or female, foreign or domestic, old or young. All of them had been fully present, completely in the picture, aware of one another and of the world at large, but unaware of Snark. She had always been a shadow, even before they made her one. A mere thing in the background, never quite in focus. One of the unseeables who lived in the alleys of Alliance Prime. Like the brain deads she'd known in the sanctuary, kids born with faulty circuits, not bright enough to be human but still able to be embarrassingly vocal. "I, I, I want, I want!" Like some kind of meat animal suddenly standing up and begging out loud. Too human looking to be killed; not human enough to live. Brain dead. That was the mildest of the epithets the other orphan brats had given her. Snark the brain dead, Snark the liar, Snark the thief.

She wished for them all, wished they were here, fleeing across the moor as the great creatures disported themselves. Let Diagonal Red eat this one, and Big Gray Blob eat this one, and . . . and, and, and . . .

Though eating might not be what the creatures did. Had they eaten her companions? Had they killed Kane the Brain and Willit and Susso? Had they tortured them, enslaved them? What? Would it make her feel better to know they were worse off than she? Not really. Since she'd been alone, she'd longed for them. Even slob-lipped Willit. Especially Susso.

She rolled onto her side, finding the stony hollow that fit the curve of her hip. Near the opening, the jar in the niche stood as it had when she had found the cave. Never moved. Never looked into. Why was that?

"Because you know what's inside," she told herself soberly. "You've always known what's inside."

Mother had made that jar. Mother had painted it, using the rib of a furze plant for a brush, her own blood for the paint. Mother had fired it, so the blood turned black on the white clay. Mother had told her daughter to put her bones inside, in the care of Mother Darkness. If there were any bones.

When Snark had gone looking for Mother, overcoming her fear, deciding to disobey the prime command ("Stay in the cave!"), she'd found bones. She'd been hiding that from herself for many years, but here at the trembling edge of sleep, nothing could be truly hidden. Longings came out, and hates, and loves, and old, old memories that she'd tried to obliterate. Old horror would sprout, old bones would walk, old blood would fountain up.

Though homelier things returned as well. Like the stories of Breadh that Mother had sung.

"Homely Breadh of long ago!"

Snark remembered once when they'd been inside the cave, Mother cross-legged, Snark in Mother's lap. She hadn't been Snark then. Mother had called her Laluzh, Laluzh-love, Laluzh dearest daughter. Laluzh, last remnant of the faithful.

"I sing, Laluzh-love, of our homeworld of Breadh, where we patterned our lives as the weaver the cloth, light and dark, day and night, sorrow-joy, pleasure-pain. On Breadh we were born, on her bosom we grew, there we found our nearhearts, there we danced when we wed. On Breadh's shoulder we grieved when our loved ones were lost. So it was, so had been, for time out of time."

This was story rhythm, a kind of chanting. Mother could do it for hours. Sometimes the story rhythm changed, becoming inexorable:

"But then the tempter came. Ancient and sly was he. Rising from dark of caves. Mammoth with mighty feet. Furred like Behemoth he. Whispered in darkness, he. Telling the songfathers. How they might never die. If they would make the choice. Leaving beloved Breadh. Where even animals. Were kindred souls to us. Leaving behind our gods—"

"And the old men listened to the tempter," interrupted Snark, anything to break that rhythm, that pounding.

Mother nodded, rocking back and forth, resuming the sweet motion Snark loved, like being cradled on the waves of the sounding sea: shush shush shush, to and fro. Mother sighed as she answered, not in story talk but as herself.

"The old men listened. They listened to sweet words and tempting promises. They bowed down before the tempter and called him the Gracious One. Gracious to them, indeed, for the price demanded was not paid by them but by the womenfolk. Godmongers have always found it easy to pay for their beliefs with women's lives. . . .

"So, they chose. Some of the people on Breadh said they would not do what the tempter ordered, they would remain behind, on Breadh, but no one was allowed to remain. Even after they were taken to the new home, the faithful refused the new commandments. Though we pretended to follow them, it was in appearance only. In secret, generation after generation, we remembered the old ways and recited the old prayers."

"For we are the faithful," Laluzh/Snark said.

"We are the faithful, Laluzh-love. And faithful we remained, even when a traitor among us denounced us to the songfathers. Then we were reviled and persecuted, some of us were tortured and killed. We decided to run away, to go back the way our ancestors had come, to return to Breadh."

"Many of us. Many, many of us!"

Mother didn't answer for a long time. There was only the *shush shush shush* of her garment on the floor as she rocked. Her face was wet when she spoke. "There were many of us who came to the gate. Enough of us to open that gate, for it is a heavy gate indeed, made of stone set upon stone. We were many as we came through that gate, but who knows if any came to Blessed Breadh. A few families of us ended here, and only Mother Darkness knows where the others ended."

"And the scourges came. . . ."

"True. When we opened the gate, scourges of the tempter pursued us, coming through the gate with us. Almost before we knew they were here, they had killed some of us. Yet faithful we remained, for in the end, where can even these scourges bring us except to the waiting arms of Mother Darkness and Father Endless, they who were before the Consequential Egg was hatched?"

She rocked Laluzh/Snark, softly *shush shush shush,* singing in her mother voice:

"Ahau, Father Endless, Mother Darkness. Ahau, thou who wert before the stars. Ahau, eternal entropy, refuge of the sorrowful, haven of the weary, salvation of the aged, unlit by grief or pain. Ahau, to lie upon the breast of darkness knowing only peace."

The song was like a lullaby, a hymn to the gods left behind on Breadh, a memorial to those who entered the gate, a plea for those few left on this world: Mother and Laluzh and the four other children, silent Nanees and strong Ehrbas, weepy little Hahnaan and some other little girl whose name Snark couldn't remember. Six of them in all. And Mother herself was gone by the time the ship came.

An Alliance ship, screaming out of the sky, landing upon the moor, where the children ran back and forth like panicked animals. Twenty standard years ago, when she'd been eight or nine. Old enough to remember the questions.

"Where did you come from, little girl?"

"I live here."

"What happened to all the grown-ups, little girl?"

"The scourges of the tempter ate them. Something killed Mother, but I put her bones away safe, in the Mother Darkness jar."

Glances, one man to another. A finger circled beside an ear. Crazy little girl. Out of her head. Must be a survival pod somewhere nearby. Kids must have been boosted off some ship in trouble. Castaways. Couldn't actually have lived here for any length of time. Impossible. There was nothing here: no agriculture, no edible animals, no beasts of any kind. Only seabirds, fish.

"She's gone snarky from the trauma," said one.

"What's snarky?"

"Snark's a kind of a duck thing. From Herangia Five. It goes crazy and drops eggs on people."

The label had stuck. Laluzh became Snark the crazed, later Snark the liar, Snark the thief. Eventually, she forgot Laluzh, forgot Perdur Alas, forgot Mother. Only the cave had remained, a place of safety and comfort. She might never have remembered the other parts if she hadn't been sent here. But now . . . now she recalled everything she had been told of: Breadh, the Tempter, the Choice, the Journey to Dinadh, the Faithfulness, the Persecution, the Flight, and the Scourges.

She had not seen scourges since she'd returned to Perdur Alas. Mother had said they'd died soon after arriving, screaming in the night, crying like lost children, hungry and cold. So it wasn't scourges who'd killed Mother. Something had. Something had killed her and chewed on her bones. Was it as Diagonal Red and the others had shown her? Had they done it?

She didn't know. There was no way of telling. Nothing was left of that former time. Nothing but monsters. Monsters and Mother's bones.

CHAPTER 9

Saluez had thought to grieve a little and then to sleep, but it was not to be. There was a stir of discontent eddying among us travelers, and its name was Lutha Tallstaff. She would not settle. Trompe fell asleep. Leelson fell asleep. Even Leely was quiet, with none of his usual restless little murmurs, but Lutha moved and sighed, sighed and moved, wearing herself out with trivialities. She went out and checked the panels not once but a dozen times. She put Leely's harness upon him and fastened the end to her belt. Though Leelson had already referred to Bernesohn Famber's yellowed map when he said we would finish our journey on the following day, Lutha unrolled the map once more and sat perusing it by lamplight. When she tired of that, she wedged the door shut, leaving me gasping for air.

"I'll go outside," I said. "There are no Kachis tonight." It was true. There were none at all, and I desperately wanted to be by myself.

I did not escape. She came after me, to the limit of the cord that bound her to Leely at any rate. Obviously, I was to have no privacy on this particular evening. I sighed and sat myself up within my cocoon of blankets, seeking some topic of conversation that would distract her from this hectic activity.

"How did you and Leelson ever meet?" I asked.

She sat down upon the step of the wain. "I met him while working in the Greinson Library at Prime."

"Such places must be interesting," I said politely.

She laughed under her breath. "Or deadly dull. I was trying to make sense of some knotty old document written long ago in a dead language, memorializing a contract between peoples who don't exist anymore."

"Dull, but no doubt important," I murmured.

"I suppose. It was one of those documents universally acknowledged to be 'precedental,' so I struggled mightily, trying to extract something my client could use in a court of law, glumming, as one does, writing down and crossing out. Then I had this odd feeling, as though I was being stared at, and when I looked up, Leelson was there. I knew at once he was Fastigat."

"How did you know?"

"Oh, they have such absolute confidence, a stunning savoir faire which puts mere poise to shame. Still, I'd dealt with Fastigats before. One does tend to get a bit short of breath when they turn on the charm, but up until then I'd considered the effect manageable."

"Until then?"

"Until he began to speak, yes. 'Something called me down from up there,' he said. The document niches are all up and down the towers, and the whole place was dotted with little scholars on their lift plates, zooming up, dropping down. He said, 'Perhaps it was your perfume.'

"I wasn't wearing perfume. I made some remark about being generally in good odor, and Leelson laughed. We introduced ourselves. I thanked him for his compliments, and the whole time I was gasping for air, sort of mentally, you know?"

I said yes, I knew. I'd been doing the same all evening.

"I resolved with every fiber of my being not to return to the library and to stay away from Fastigats. My kind of people, that is, Mama Jibia's kind of people, the non-Fastigat professional class, consider Fastigat men unsuitable for women who are serious-minded."

"You are serious-minded?" I wanted to laugh, but did not. Despite Lutha's undoubted intelligence, she was constantly exploding like fireworks, laughing or crying, passionate about every trifle. On Dinadh, we think of such behavior as typical of children, not serious adults.

"Don't you think I am?" she asked, surprised.

I told her exactly what I thought, hoping she would go away.

When I had finished, however, she only said thoughtfully, "It's the way we were reared, Yma and I. If you'd ever met my Mama Jibia, you'd understand. She was a singular person, of extremely forceful mien, a faithful follower of the Great Org Gauphin, who preached logic and good sense in all things. Mama Jibia was dead set against Yma or me getting tangled up in feelings we couldn't express or understand. Starting

at puberty, she had us experiencing sex through sensurround, so we'd
know about that. Then, twice a year she had us vetted by the mental
health people from the Temple of the Great Org Gauphin. We had emotional and stress inventories and sessions with a behaviorist, and I'd wager we knew more about the human animal at fifteen than most of our
contemporaries ever learned."

I murmured, "It sounds quite . . . rigorous."

"Well, she was trying to make us immune to romance or sentimentalism. Of course, many of our friends came from Firster families, and
sentimentalism is one of their largest stocks in trade. They use it to
excuse all kinds of nasty behaviors. If Papa beats you, it's because he
loves you, you know the kind of thing. . . ."

I did. I knew more than that. Probably far more than she!

She went on, "Firsters don't approve of pragmatism, self-analysis, or
sexual sensurround for anyone, much less virgin girls who should be, so
they claim, innocent, by which they really mean susceptible to any self-
serving lie that's going around! So, Yma and I saw our friends being
romanced and falling in love and making babies they weren't at all ready
for, and we thanked our stars we'd been raised differently." She sighed.
"How did this conversation start?"

"You said you were so passionate about everything because of the way
you were reared."

"Yes. Mama thought feelings should be expressed. Whatever they
were, it was healthier to have them out in the open, and neither Yma
nor I could do it quietly. It's our sense of drama, you see. We inherited it
from a scandalous ancestress who was well-known in her day, as Yma is
now. Yma made a career of it. I merely play at it."

"You play very intently," I said. "You and Leelson. I saw you that
time, at the pool. I've watched you. Like magnets, one minute pulling at
each other, then turnabout and you're pushing at each other."

Lutha flushed and gave me a half-angry look. I had no business com-
menting, and I was slightly ashamed of myself for being rude to her.

"It's always been that way," Lutha admitted. "Like some kind of
shackle we didn't know existed until then, tying us to one another. The
relationship was never suitable. Not at all."

"You don't like his mother?"

"She's . . . contemptuous. Of me. Of Leely. Fastiga woman are that
way, just like Fastigats. She wanted Leelson to have children with one of
his cousins—Fastiga is quite inbred, though they deny it—and of course,
I'm far from being a cousin. She used to send some of the relatives over

to look at Leely. I'm sure she did it to infuriate me and so she could say 'I told you so,' to Leelson."

"What about Leelson's father?" I asked, before I thought. I had opened a new floodgate!

"Leelson's father disappeared. Grebor Two, his name was. And his father disappeared, too. Grebor One. They each fathered one son and then disappeared. Leelson's mother was afraid Leelson was following in their footsteps."

"Twice doesn't make a habit," I said, giving up rudeness in favor of letting her talk.

"Three times," Lutha said. "There was a granduncle, too. One of Bernesohn's twins. He did the same thing Leelson did, got some unsuitable person pregnant."

"Who?" I asked politely, not caring who.

Lutha frowned for a moment, then came up with an answer. "Dasalum Tabir."

I laughed, intrigued despite myself. "D'ahslum T'bir! That means *skeleton*. That's not a name you'd forget."

Lutha said the words over to herself, this time with the Dinadhi accent. The root words were for *bones* and for *ladder,* or *tree*.

"She was famous for more than her name, or infamous, depending on how you look at it. A cradle robber, according to the Fastigats. Twice Paniwar Famber's age."

I heard disapproval in her voice. "Maybe she couldn't help it any more than you can. Try pretending you were hit by lightning. You can't feel guilty about being hit by lightning."

"It is rather like that," Lutha confessed with a half smile.

Without meaning to, I said, "I know about that kind of lightning." I spoke then of Shalumn, and Lutha responded with stories of her own life, of her own family.

"Was your mother pleased with you?" Oh, such a pang I felt when I asked her that, but I wanted to know.

"Yma and I have always felt that she'd have been pleased with us, that we had done well for her. Thank the Great Org Gauphin she was gone before . . ."

"Before Leelson?"

She spoke between gritted teeth. "Oh, Saluez! I swore I wouldn't get entangled with him. I swore I wouldn't, but I kept . . . feeling him. Smelling him, tasting—foretasting—his skin, seeing parts of him that I hadn't realized I'd noticed, like the lobe of an ear or the way his hair grew at the base of his neck.

"Yma said I was smitten. She laughed at me. Of course, she hadn't met Leelson. As events conspired, perhaps luckily, she never actually met him."

Now I was really curious. "How did events conspire?"

"Leelson showed up at my door a few days after our chance meeting. He looked oddly subdued, and I felt . . . oh, I felt as though I were being pumped full of sunlight. He stepped inside and took me in his arms before he said a word. I don't think either of us said anything that evening. Words would have been . . . misleading."

"That's how you were for each other? Made for each other?"

"That's how. He said never one like me before. For me it was never anyone before and never one since."

"It's like your edges are dissolved, and you feel yourself spreading out. . . ."

"Gossamer thin," she said, giving me an astonished look. "Feeding on starlight."

We stared at one another. "I know," I said at last. "I know."

She dropped her head, scowling at her shoes. "After a while Leely was born. Not long after that, my former self reasserted itself. And then Leelson left me."

"Did he leave you? Or Leely?"

"He wanted me but not Leely. I wanted them both. I wouldn't let Leely go because he needs me."

Hearing those words, I accepted that she was a serious person. There was something implacable in her voice. Something rigorously dutiful. Leely needed her. I thought it possible that until Leely, Lutha had never known herself truly, and Leelson had never known her. Likely he had known only a soft and corrupted creature who dangled from his lips like fruit from a vine, sweet and yielding, rotten with juice. That woman had laughed and cried and tempted. That woman had been sensual and mindless. But finally she had remembered herself and became Lutha Tallstaff again, saying no, no, I will not send Leely away.

"You can't help yourself, can you?" I asked softly.

"I can't," she snarled, half-angry, half-amused. "The only way I can resist him is by being furious at him. The only way I can stay furious is to remember what Leely and I came here for. We're not going to be disposed of just because Leelson would prefer it so! I will do my duty!"

"Yes," I murmured. "Yes, of course, Lutha."

"I promised," she said. The words had the feeling of old familiar sounds, worn smooth by repetition. I looked up to see tears.

"What?" I demanded.

"When Leely was almost lost, back there in the Nodders . . ." She gulped, fell silent.

"You were frightened?" I suggested. "Panicky?"

She shook her head, a quick motion, a denial she could not admit even to herself. I read it.

"You thought he was gone. You felt . . . relief."

"How could I!" She leaned upon her knees and wept, her shoulders heaving. "How could I?"

How could she not? How could she not feel as though a window in her soul had been cracked open upon joy. A gigantic relief, as though the solution to some painful problem had unexpectedly presented itself! As it had for me, to come on this journey.

"It was the shock," she said firmly, raising her head and wiping at her eyes. "It was only the shock."

So she slammed the door shut on her feelings, despite all Mama Jibia's teachings. She would not allow herself to want him gone. No matter how she sagged beneath the burden of him, no matter how wearying his needs and demands, no matter the evenings like this when she wearied herself with minutiae so she could sleep, the deep heedless sleep of exhaustion, lying so drunken with sleep she could not worry over days to come; no matter all this, he was her son and she loved him!

So she said to herself as she rose to go within and be with him, leaving me at last in peace, now that I no longer wanted it.

The night was without incident. Trompe roused us at daybreak. By early afternoon we emerged from the last canyon onto the winding plain the map had shown as the site of the omphalos. Since leaving the Burning Springs, we had had on our left a small stream that occasionally surged over its banks in response to the rain that fell far away, upon the heights. I thought we would need to cross it between surges, but this proved to be unnecessary, for once out of the canyon, the stream relaxed into a gurgling, shallow brook that meandered in silken loops across the plain to join a considerable river flowing toward the south. According to the map, this river was the Tahs Ahlai, which is a Dinadhi way of saying, the future, or time to come. All waters, we say, run into the Tahs Ahlai. All lives run into the pattern.

We crossed the smaller stream with only minor difficulty. Gaufers do not like wet feet, and they had to be blindfolded to be led over. They could no doubt feel the wetness as well as see it, but evidently feeling it and seeing it were two different things. Lutha brought the last one across, pausing beside me to say, "It seems so natural to have them here."

"Why wouldn't they be here?" I asked, surprised.

"They are the first living animals I have ever seen, Saluez. The first I have ever touched!"

"There are no animals on Central?"

"None at all. No animals. No trees. No grassy meadows. No water running freely. It is a very different place from here."

I gaped, unable to imagine it.

"Like one big building with many, many rooms," she said softly. "Even the seas are covered over, for that is where our food is raised."

I considered the gaufers, really seeing them for the first time. They smelled warm and earthy, their muzzles were soft and their bodies sleek. What would it be like never to see any living creature but one's own kind?

"They think," she said. "I was surprised at that."

"Of course they think!"

"On a homo-normed world, we never consider that. We don't consider animals at all, and certainly we don't consider that they can think. But the gaufers . . . they have their own order of precedence, allowing them to interact without constant conflict. They have their own habits of alertness, one keeping watch while others eat, one standing apart, head high, while others drink. They have even a kind of sympathy, for when the lead left one injured his leg slightly, the others gave way and let him have the best spot to lie down."

She had noticed more than I!

"They like to be scratched just behind the ears, for it's an itchy place they have difficulty reaching for themselves. They do it for one another, turn about. They know each one of us. They don't like Leelson and Trompe. Every time one of the men comes toward them, they make whuffing noises with their nostrils. They like you and me, Saluez, for they butt us with their heads as they do one another when they are content. Leely, they ignore. He climbs all over them and they seem not even to notice. Perhaps that's the way they treat their own young."

As we went on I thought about what she had said, for there had been something wondering in her voice, like a person under enchantment. Not that I have had much experience with enchantment, but our old stories are full of it.

We moved onto peaceful meadows where a soft wind tossed the grasses into long rollers of shaded silver, a placid, utterly beautiful land-scape. This wide valley was green, all green, and I, too, began to feel enchanted at the wonder of it. I had never seen so much grass! It beck-oned to be embraced, and I did so, pulling a plumy clump toward me, smelling the fragrance of it.

I turned to find Lutha beside me, holding out her hand. I took it. We stood so, smelling the grasses, while the wagon moved on. Her hand was warm in mine, and comforting. Finally we had to run, hand in hand, to catch up with the others.

We followed the river until it entered a steeply walled channel through a shallow rise, and there we turned a little eastward to climb the hill. Our view southward was blocked until we reached the top, but once there, a new world opened out. Canyon walls retreated on either side, leaving room for endless emerald meadows. The river curved first left, then right, and beyond this scribble of flowing silver was yet another loop in which a building stood.

"How artful," said Leelson.

"How appropriate," murmured Lutha.

"It's a temple, isn't it," said Trompe.

The building was circular, made of wood and plaster. The pillars sur-rounding it were the trunks of great trees, smoothed and ringed with gold. The shallow dome was ribbed with wood and gilded with gold, as was its central pinnacle. All around the building were smoothly plastered pediments, aisles of huge wooden columns, and shallow flights of wide, smooth steps that descended to a surrounding plaza from which paving led in all directions, an enormous spiderweb of narrow roads. It was like nothing else on Dinadh. I might have been on some other world!

"The omphalos," I breathed. "This is the house of the omphalos!" Then I saw a hive at the foot of the cliffs, east of the temple. "That must be where the spirit people live. Songfather says the omphalos is guarded by spirit people."

Far to the south, the canyon walls, diminished by distance, thrust in from the west over a diamond glitter, where the river Tahs Ahlai turned eastward toward the sea. Leelson pointed in that direction.

"Something moving."

Trompe, meantime, had spotted movement in the west, and when we all stopped marveling at the view and concentrated on people, we found traffic in every direction: lines and clumps of people and gaufers on the spiderweb of roads, wagons of all sizes and types crossing meadows, all of them moving toward the common center we looked upon.

"Drawn to Tahs-uppi," said Lutha. "Like moths to a flame. Unable to resist, no matter how dangerous the way."

"Commanded to come," I murmured. "Some of these wagons have been on the way since early winter. It takes a long while to come from the far side of Dinadh. The delegation from Cochim-Mahn is probably not far behind us. Songfather will soon be here, and he will be very angry with us."

He would be angry with me most of all, for he expected obedience from me. Lutha put her arm around my shoulders and hugged me.

"You're such a little thing," she said. "But you're stronger than I." She said it to be comforting, knowing how apprehensive I was. She took my hand, and we continued our inventory of the travelers coming toward us.

One particularly impressive procession had come over a saddle in the cliffs southwest. It included a chariot, several wagons, and files of marching persons, one of them glittering as though dipped in jewels. Above this line of march a long banner floated, like a superscription.

Lutha said, "That flag has a familiar look to it."

Trompe reached into his pack for glasses, and looked again.

"What in . . ." he blurted. "It's the Great Flag of the Alliance."

"The Procurator?" she questioned. "Here?"

"Doesn't have to be the Procurator," murmured Leelson. "Could be an envoy."

I looked up to see that Lutha had gone red in the face. Her lips were tight, her nostrils flared. She was furious!

"What?" I whispered.

"I came all this way! Unwillingly, at considerable danger and discomfort! Then Leelson turned up, out of nothing, trying to send me home, trying to get rid of me and Leely, but I stuck to my duty, and *now,* before I've had any chance to do what I was sent for, here's the man who sent me, or his envoy! Why was I needed at all? Why disrupt my life? This person has probably come directly from the port! *He* has not been forced to endure a hover car for endless wearying days, plus a strenuous canyon climb, plus the danger of being maimed by the Kachis!"

I touched her cheek. She dropped her eyes, seemingly ashamed.

"Drama," I whispered.

"I'm ridiculous," she agreed. "As the Gauphin taught, people *are* ridiculous! We have language and history, we have technology and philosophy, and we still have not achieved good sense and self-control! And those of us who pretend to, as Fastigats do, are so damned smug about it!"

I patted her, evoking a smile. I smiled in return, though she could not see it. She knew there was nothing to be gained by being annoyed with the Procurator, or with Leelson. No gain from lying sleepless over Leelson. No gain from weeping over Leelson. No gain remembering that time at the pool, before the Burning Springs . . .

"Shhh," I whispered. "It'll be all right."

Her eyes said it wouldn't be all right. "The next few moments will be all right. That will have to do. I must live from one set of moments to the next."

"Shall we go down?" Trompe asked, nudging Lutha impatiently.

"Of course." She and I moved off in a purposeful manner, ignoring the sidelong glances Leelson and Trompe cast in our direction, feeling for our feelings.

She snorted, saying under her breath, "One's feelings, one's lovemaking, and one's letters should be strictly private! In my opinion, when these things are dragged out and displayed to strangers, affection is corrupted and destroyed. It is what bad biographers do, this digging into what might have been intended, what possibly had been felt. See here, she feels; see there, she says; look here, she promises! Even I do not always know what I feel or what I intend. What arrogance for these Fastigats to presume to know me better than I know myself!"

"Perhaps they should spend their time analyzing themselves," I suggested, receiving a smile of agreement in return.

We had no time for further conversation. We had come about halfway down the slope when a crowd of black-clothed figures swarmed out of the hive near the canyon wall and came hastily along a path that intersected our line of travel. Lutha moved up beside the left-lead gaufer to translate as necessary, and I saw her start with dismay when they came near enough that we could see them clearly.

They were like me! Like the members of the sisterhood! Missing ears, riven lips, tattered eyelids. It was not only faces with them. Fingers and hands were missing, as were feet. Bodies were contorted and thin as saplings. The one in the lead shouted in an out-of-breath voice, in a sort of dialect that was not clearly understandable, at least not to me. I took them to mean something on the order of "Halt, stop, come no nearer the sacred land." Since we were already halted, his commands seemed superfluous.

Lutha held out her hands, empty, the universal gesture of peace.

"We have come to save the lives of the Dinadhi," she said. "There is a threat from outside the planet."

They began shouting fervently at one another. I gathered that one faction wanted to kill us immediately, while another, slightly larger faction was reminded that blood could not be shed near the sacred precincts without the gravest consequences. These antiphonal shouts went on for some time—during which Lutha muttered fragmentary translations—before the shouters reached a solution that all could agree to. They would pen us up during the ceremony, which was about to begin. After Tahs-uppi, they would take us somewhere else and kill us. Not one of them had paid attention to the threat Lutha had told them of. Either they didn't believe her or they didn't care. They were frightening in their single-mindedness.

I went to Lutha's side.

"Are these your spirit people?" she asked me.

"I don't know," I whispered. "Nobody ever told me they were . . . like this. Why are they like this?"

My words drew the attention of one of them, who darted forward, twitched my veil to one side, then screamed as he turned and fled. The others chattered among themselves, backing slowly away. Lutha took hold of the left-lead gaufer's halter and tugged him forward. The other gaufers leaned into the harness, and the wain creaked after. Trompe and Leelson dropped back to walk beside it.

"I am unclean," I told her as we slowly pursued the spirit people, who were limping and stumbling away from us as fast as they could go. "He says the beautiful people have rejected me, and now that he has touched me, he must go out of the valley and cut his hand off at once."

"You sound quite calm about it. Do you think he means to do it?" she asked.

"I don't care if he does," I said angrily. "They're all men, Lutha. They're eaten worse than I, but *they're* not unclean! What right have they!"

The fleeing bunch split before us, creating an open aisle that led toward a stout pen set upon a small rounded hill.

"Gaufer pen," I said, sidetracked from my annoyance. "They're always set high like that, so they drain well and don't cause a muck."

Whether intended for gaufers or not, the pen was now to be used for us. There were already a dozen spirit people arrayed outside the fence, muttering angrily to one another over the bulk of several large and shiny weapons.

"I hope those fusion rifles are not charged," Leelson said to the air.

One particularly clumsy guard (not his fault; he had no fingers on his right hand) chose that moment to drop his weapon.

Lutha said, "I've had arms dealers as clients, and I've seen diagrams of that weapon. It looks to me like an Asenagi product, but he had it set on standby. If it had been set in firing position, this whole place would be gone by now."

Leelson paled. Trompe gulped, "We are probably the first outsiders they've ever seen. They've obtained weapons for protection against intruders, but they have no idea how to use them."

The idea of novices with deadly weapons was not cheering, and the others turned their eyes elsewhere, not to seem threatening.

"Let's not bother them with talk," Lutha suggested. "If that's really the Great Flag of the Alliance coming down the hill, let the envoy or whoever deal with the problem."

Our willingness to be penned up seemed to have quieted some of the panicky gestures and voices around us. The clumsy guards backed off a little, allowing us to concentrate on the view of the omphalos our low hill afforded.

The temple was now surrounded by several nearly complete concentric circles of kneeling men, some spirit people, and some songfathers, distinguishable by the colors of their robes, black for spirit people, hide brown for the others. Each had his own cushion, and each knelt at an equal distance from his fellows. The circles were neat and perfectly regular, and as new men arrived they filled in the gaps and started new circles concentric to the old ones. I saw no women anywhere near the temple.

Lutha laid her hand on my arm and jerked her head toward the eastern cliffs. There were other black-clad forms huddled at the base of the buildings and in the windows. She borrowed the glasses from Trompe and gave them a good looking over before passing the glasses to me. They were the female spirit people, all of them disfigured or maimed and as thin as the men.

Lutha said, "They're too thin for childbearing. Starving women don't get pregnant. They don't even menstruate."

"But this valley is fertile!" I told her. "The soil is wonderful. And they have a river! They should have lots of food! More than we can raise in the canyons!" Perhaps it was significant that we had seen no sign of cultivation anywhere in the valley. The grass was of a different sort than I knew. Perhaps it too was sacred and farming was forbidden.

"Look at the temple," urged Leelson. "At the floor!"

The temple was in the form of a circular dais made up of three concentric steps. The first was below the pillars. The second formed the base for the circle of pillars that supported the roof. The third was inside the pillars and made up the floor of the temple itself. The south half, a semicircle of this inner circle, was one step higher yet, with massive metal links protruding at both the east and west ends of the low step. A long and heavy rope had been attached to the eastern link, then threaded around the golden base of the northernmost pillar, back across the raised floor, around the southernmost pillar, then back to the north again, making a Z shape.

"It's a tackle," said Trompe.

So much was obvious. We used similar gear to get water from the deepest wells. The loose end of the rope lay stretched along the ground to the north, and it was now being tugged at by a few dozen songfathers. They managed to pull the east end of the semicircular floor a hand span closer, rotating it on its diametric center, then nodded in satisfaction at one another as they dropped the rope and departed.

"Those golden rings around the pillars are metal sheaves," remarked Leelson, who was looking at them through the glass. "What are they moving the floor for? And what's it made of?"

"It is made of one great block of stone," I told them. "It was brought from the cliffs by the Gracious One, who, having created the great gate, then opened it unto us. The stone covers the navel of the world. The sacred sipapu. The gate through which we came. Now it will be uncovered and the beautiful people, those who carry the spirits of our beloved dead, will depart through this gateway to heaven."

Leelson threw Lutha a startled glance, and she gave him a look that meant "don't ask." He glared, but he clamped his lips shut. I had just revealed the holiest secrets of our religion. It didn't matter now. There would be no secrets soon. He would see, as I would.

More songfathers arrived. There were other brief episodes of rope tugging with nobody trying very hard. Groups came and went, rehearsing separately, accustoming themselves to the feel of the rope. It was as Leelson had said at one point during our journey: every participant was here for the first time. They knew what was to be done, but not precisely how to do it. They had to practice.

By midafternoon there were tens of thousands of wains filling a shallow valley south and west of the temple, a good distance away. The ordinary men and women who had accompanied the songfathers fringed every slight rise of ground, none of them close enough to get a good view and none of them equipped with glasses. Evidently these laymen were to view Tahs-uppi only from a distance.

During the afternoon, groups of songfathers came up the hill to the pen to take a look at us. Late in the afternoon, one came who was well-known to me. Hah-Hallach, songfather of Cochim-Mahn. He summoned me to the fence.

"Foolish woman, what have you done?" he demanded in a soft voice full of suppressed rage.

"I have come to say good-bye to my mother," I replied.

"You have led strangers here! You have blasphemed the Gracious One. You have risked our immortality!"

"So, let the Gracious One deal with me," I said. "He can cause me little more pain than he has already done."

"Because you doubted," he said, cursing. "Because you doubted!"

I shook my head. "The sisterhood knows better than that."

"All heretics. All doubters. Why you?" he shouted.

I turned my face away, not answering, sobs welling up inside me. Lutha came to me, put her arms around me, and said across my head:

"If you're asking her why she came here, it's because she believes what we have told her. Your people and your world are in danger. She does not care for herself, but she is going to have a child. She wants that child to have a future!"

He turned his glaring eyes upon Lutha and spoke from a mouth contorted by wrath. "There is neither future for blasphemers nor children for those who doubt," he said. Then he turned on his heel and went back down the hill. Lutha's arms held me while I wiped my eyes.

"Thank you for trying to help me," I said. "But there is no help against . . . them."

"Them?" she whispered.

"Old men who enslave us, then rebuke us when we rebel, calling us disobedient daughters, doubters, even heretics. I told him the sisterhood knows better. He did not like it much."

We had no time for discussion. The crowd of songfathers and spirit people around the temple had grown larger and noisier, and now it erupted with shouts and waved fists as the Great Flag of the Alliance came bobbing and wavering toward us through the mob. The kneeling circles of spirit people opened up with some difficulty to let the flag come through, and I saw that each man had attached himself to a metal eye set into the ground. Now, what was that about? I scanned the temple, finding more such metal eyes set into the semicircular stone inside the temple.

The flag jounced up the hill, carried by a youngish, long-faced man who walked beside the Procurator, he all aglitter like a fish just out of water. With them was a huge red-faced woman driving a chariot, and behind that a stolid Dinadhi driving a cart loaded down with heavy packs. Leelson opened the gate for them.

The Procurator greeted us with a nod, then said to the woman, "Madam Luv, this is Leelson Famber."

"Who has much to answer for," said the big woman, in a disapproving tone.

Leelson took no notice of their disapproval. Fastigats, Lutha was to say, often don't take notice of others' disapproval, even that of other Fastigats. While the bearers stacked their burdens in a pile near the pen gate, Leelson made introductions as though we were at tea. The long-faced man was the ex–King of Kamir, who seemed embarrassed at seeing Leelson, though I could not imagine why. The large woman was Poracious Luv, an Alliance councilwoman, flamboyant, but with good sense, so Lutha said. I gathered she had been visiting the king when both of them had been dragged into this business more or less accidentally. Or, if not accidentally, for some reason they did not, at the moment, choose to explain.

As the cart driver shut the gate on us and clomped off down the hill, Poracious joined Lutha and me at the fence while the three Fastigats went to the other side of the pen and put their heads together. They were looking at a small, hand-sized mechanism that the Procurator had taken from the baggage. A retriever, said Lutha, asking Poracious what it was they intended to retrieve.

Instead of answering, the big woman took her by the shoulder, saying, "So, Lutha Tallstaff, what's happened thus far? Have you solved our problem?"

Before Lutha could answer, Leely appeared suddenly at the door of the wain, totally naked, his skin darkly and oddly blotched with chill. I went quickly to him, leaving Lutha to deal with the demands of Poracious Luv. I could hear them from inside the wagon.

"Your son?" asked the big woman in a kindlier voice. "No doubt he likes the feel of air on his skin. I did, when I was smaller. Now I have rather too much skin for the air. I understand your son is an amazing artist."

"Where did you hear that?" Lutha asked, surprised.

"I heard of it in Simidi-ala," Poracious said. "I was told he did some excellent portraits there. There is one on the wall of a women's convenience. They have framed it and put Perspex across it. They say he is beloved of Weaving Woman."

I glanced outside, to see Lutha much discomfited, digging her toe in the dirt.

"I know all about him," Poracious confided. "You needn't be diffident or defensive with me. We are both women. We understand our feelings, whether these men and Fastigats do or not."

"Leelson doesn't think Leely's human," Lutha blurted.

"My, my," Poracious said. "He is exclusionary, is he not?"

Exclusionary was an improper word in the Alliance, so Lutha had said, more than once. The Alliance likes to think of itself as an egalitarian organization.

Lutha said, "That's not quite accurate where Leelson is concerned. His prejudice is limited to his own children. His family has certain well-defined expectations for its posterity, that's all."

"Oh, my, don't we all know that," Poracious murmured. "I've met his mama." She winked at Lutha. "Don't take me for a fool, lovely girl. We fat old things have not laid aside our brains with our silhouettes. We put on flesh for as many reasons as others make love, have you ever thought about that? Out of lust, out of habit, out of greed, out of ambition. Out of time, too little or too much of it, or too little else doing in it." She sighed. "The flesh does not represent the spirit, for which observation one can thank the Great Gauphin. Though one wonders, sometimes, what the purpose is of either spirit or flesh."

She gave Lutha a kindly pat, ignoring her confusion, then beckoned to the ex-king, who had been standing diffidently to one side, looking rather lonely.

He came over, hesitantly, asking, "Has your group been threatened at all?"

It seemed an odd question. Lutha said, "Threatened by the Kachis, certainly. Not particularly by anyone else until we came near the omphalos."

"Have you learned anything?" asked Poracious.

Lutha said, "We found a voice recording that Bernesohn Famber left in Cochim-Mahn. It was old, fragmentary, not at all clear. It mentioned three things—the abandoned gods of the Dinadhi; the omphalos, which is why we came here; and finally a few enigmatic words about the rejoinder of his posterity."

"Abandoned gods?" the ex-king asked with an intent and eager look. "Tell me?"

"The Dinadhi claim they came here from somewhere else, or perhaps were sent here from somewhere else, after being commanded to leave certain of their gods behind. In return, they were to receive"—she paused, glancing through the open door of the wain at me—"immortality?"

"You don't sound sure," said the king, still in that intent voice.

"I'm not. The whole matter's complicated." She led them away from the wagon slightly, and when I heard the king ask, "What's a Kachis?" I knew she was telling them about our beliefs.

They talked quietly, then Poracious's voice rose:

"These Kachis must have a lengthy life span if one of them has been around since Bernesohn's time!"

Even Lutha forgot to keep her voice down.

"I have no idea whether there's been one or a succession of different ones. Saluez believed the Kachis cannot die, but we saw dead ones during our trip, which has sorely tried her faith."

Tried, but not defeated, I said to myself as I fastened Leely's shirt.

"Does this relate in some way to the Ularian problem?" the ex-king asked.

I came out of the wagon, bringing the now clothed Leely to stand beside his mother as the king went on:

"I see no connection. These Kachis may be nasty, but the Ularians are . . . quite inexpressibly vile!"

I looked at him across my veil, asking, "Have you seen the Ularians?"

"I've seen them. And tasted them. I've heard the sound of the waves on the world where they are now, heard the scream of seabirds and the weeping of the girl who's there watching them." He shook his head, making a face. "They're . . . horrible beyond belief."

"What do they look like?" I asked.

The ex-king gestured. "Big. Big as one of your hives. Shaped, oh, like any old thing at all. A massive middle, rather shapeless, with a lot of appendages or tentacles hanging beneath like a fringe. They float. Or they sit like mountains. Or they build themselves into rancid walls of flesh that can surround an encampment! On one side, their skin is bare, and they are able to show pictures on their skins."

I felt my eyes widen. It was an unbelievable description. Leely slipped loose and started purposefully toward the fence surrounding us. Lutha caught him just as he was climbing through.

"Dananana," he cried, struggling to get away from her. "Dananana."

She pulled him into her arms and asked me to get his harness from the wagon. He hated it, but sometimes it was the only solution. I fetched it and we buckled it behind him, fastening the tether tightly to Lutha's belt.

He looked at the harness, decided he couldn't get out at the moment, then opened his pants, peed onto the dirt, and sat down to make a mud picture on the bottom board of the fence. I saw Lutha flinch, but Poracious Luv watched him with lively interest and no discernible disapprobation.

About this time the three Fastigats concluded their conference. Both Leelson and Trompe spat over the fence and then wiped their mouths. The Procurator said something to them, then calmly let himself out the gate and went off down the hill. The spirit people and songfathers had left an aisle open all the way from the pen to the temple at the bottom. He was confronted almost at once by one of those who had accompanied him up the hill in the first place.

"Hah-Rianahm," Poracious whispered. "Lord high-muck-a-muck among this rabble."

The Dinadhi's voice was strident. I could hear him clearly, though he spoke from some distance.

". . . must return to the pen!" he howled.

". . . must take time to experience this record," shouted the Procurator in stentorian tones, overriding the other, no small achievement considering how the skinny old man was screaming.

"No time! Tahs-uppi!"

"Until Tahs-uppi!"

Gabble and shout, pushing and shoving, the Procurator was thrust back up the hill and through the gate that Leelson opened for him. The three Fastigats exchanged wry looks that said the result of the foray had not been unexpected. Then all three of them began dragging items from the baggage pile, opening sacks and cases, sorting out items of equipment. When they had unpacked and assembled the first half-dozen elements, Lutha said:

"Isn't that a wide-range retriever? The kind entertainers use?"

Lutha was looking questioningly at Poracious, but the large woman was preoccupied with what was going on at the temple. There the circles of kneeling men were completely filled in and various ritual personages with towering headdresses had taken up positions atop the raised semi-circular section of floor. As we watched, songfathers manned the entire length of the pull rope, and half a dozen black-clad spirit men were pouring the contents of large jars upon the northeast quadrant of the temple floor—oil, I presumed, to make easier the moving of the great stone lid across this lower stone. When their jars were empty, they departed. One of the hierarchy shouted a command. Though we could not see musicians from where we stood, the sounds of their instruments came to us clearly: drums, gongs, trumpets, panpipes, and several sonorous stringed instruments.

First a blaring fanfare, then a *whomp, whomp, whomp* of drums and deep-toned plucked strings, then a shouted command, and those along the rope took up the slack. They began to tug, grunting with each pull. The arrangement of the rope allowed a one-quarter turn of the semicircular stone, and I held my breath, awaiting what this displacement would reveal.

At first it was only a darkness. A darkness within darkness. A circular blackness. A pit, perhaps. A pit smeared with cloudy concentric lines to represent a . . . I struggled to find a word. A vortex.

A blotch spun past, appearing at the edge farther from us, disappearing behind the edge nearest us. Well then, it wasn't a representation of a vortex, it *was* a vortex. A . . . maelstrom. Though it didn't look like water.

"Not water," said the ex-king doubtfully. "It doesn't look like water."

Leelson cursed briefly behind me. He had dropped some part of the device and now knelt to attach it once more. The loose parts were almost all attached; I assumed they were finished with it. Trompe knelt beside Leelson and they thrust a record file through a narrow slot.

Poracious followed my glance.

"A record from Perdur Alas," she murmured. "Unfiltered, if I don't miss my guess!"

I only half heard her, for the ex-king made a muffled exclamation, drawing my attention back toward the temple where the steadily grunting line, *ungh-ah, ungh-ah, ungh-ah,* had moved the floor the entire quarter turn the tackle permitted. Now the whirling darkness was fully disclosed. The music stopped. We heard a shouted command. Then trumpets again, and a quicker tempo from the drums. The rope went slack. The ritual personages unshackled it from the eye, hauled it in, and carried thick coils of it away eastward to the accompaniment of panpipes and gongs. The members of the orchestra marched onto the northeast quadrant of the great stone lid and fettered themselves, facing north, while over their left shoulders the vortex whirled with hypnotic force. The musicians' hair whipped in the rising wind.

"Look away," demanded Poracious. "Don't let your eyes get sucked in. Observe—the musicians are wearing blinkers, and none of the people are looking at it."

As indeed they were not. The temple stood on a slight rise; almost all of the observers were on lower levels, where they couldn't see the vortex; if any were higher than we, they would see only the temple roof or the processions of spirit people and songfathers who were marching hither and yon, waving banners and censers while drums pounded, gongs sounded, trumpets brayed, and panpipes tweedled breathily. When the music stopped, no one looked toward the temple. All eyes were searching the far canyon edges, where they opened into the valley.

"The beautiful people are coming," I cried, hearing both the pain and the joy in my words. "Oh, they are coming. They will see us one more time before they go to heaven! Perhaps . . . perhaps . . ."

Oh, perhaps. The crowd stirred. At first I did not see what they saw, then I detected the pale movement at the canyon entrances, like a flow of milk. It did not come closer. Not then.

At the same time Leelson said something in a self-satisfied tone, there was a click, and I was elsewhere.

Before me, observed from some distance, through a twiggy growth, Diagonal Red and Four Green Spot floated over an abandoned camp. I heard the sea, at some distance behind me. A twig was jammed between my teeth to keep my mouth open as I drooled filthily. From the south, enormous shapes bobbed toward me, and my throat formed the words, Blue Lines, Big Gray Blob, and Speckled Purple. In the middle distance, a dozen more shaggy Ularians moved in a slow procession.

I was tasting . . . what was it I tasted? Soapy, rancid, bitter, nasty . . . Over the sound of the sea I heard retching; through the view of the moorland, as through a transparent picture, I saw the valley of the omphalos, filled with people who bent and twisted as they tried to get rid of that filthy taste. Abruptly, the effect lessened somewhat, becoming no less nasty but less overwhelming.

I heard Leelson's voice. "I've put in a partial filter." Whatever he had done, it did not prevent the experience continuing . . .

. . . showing pictures on their bodies! Each newly pictured thing coalesced on the body of one single being. "Ularian," my throat said. The picture moved on to another Ularian, and more detail was added. Each

*Ularian augmented or complicated the picture created by the previous ones,
and the event continued rotating. . . .*

I shut my eyes, held my breath, refused to smell or taste anything. No
good. It was not an experience one could evade.

The woman fleeing. Fleeing. The monstrous beings coming after her.

I heard indrawn breaths. Not from the vision; from reality. There were
murmurs of denial in the valley of the omphalos. Shouts of anger. I shut
my eyes and made myself listen for sounds from Dinadh. What were the
spirit people doing while this went on? The music had stopped. What
were they thinking?

*Huge, those beings. Great shaggy walls. Shapeless, amorphous, threaten-
ing, with dangling tentacles. Now the huge bodies began a new sequence of
pictures, a detailed sequence playing over and over and over again:*

*A place near the ocean. A strangely shaped stone. A twisted tree. The
hammered sea sparkling under the sun . . . A note of . . . anticipation?
And then, all at once, an explosion of shapes from the face of the cliff, like
puffs of thick smoke that separated into individual things, a horde of shaggy
little floaters, miniature likenesses of the huge Ularians, countless numbers
of them, spewing out of crevasses, out of caves, pouring into the sky . . .*

*The huge ones sit, unmoving, bands of bright color dancing upon their
skins as the little ones fling themselves outward, pursuing the seabirds,
catching them, gulping them down! Oh, they are hungry, so hungry!*

And the experience stopped, all at once, like waking from dream.
Leelson had shut down the machine. Before me, Poracious Luv wiped
her mouth and spat across the fence. Beside me, Lutha and the ex-king
did the same. At our feet, Leely, unbothered, still painted upon the
fence. He, too, had seen what we had seen. His painting was of them,
the little shaggy things that had come pouring from the cliff wall. He had
seen but he hadn't tasted.

Across the pen from me, the three Fastigats stared down toward the
temple, waiting. Everywhere in the valley people stood up, shaking, wiping their mouths. Afar, at the openings of the canyons, movement began
again, a milky flow made of countless white forms floating from the
canyon mouths, streams of them, coming through the tall grasses, con-
verging upon the omphalos.

From somewhere below, a shaky command. Then again, louder, more
vehement.

I am lost in anticipation! A drum pulses, trembling. Voices shout. Music resumes, unsteadily, out of tune, out of tempo. The milky streams
come nearer.

Kachis! Floating wide-eyed, arms and legs spread wide, only their wings moving them, rivulets of them, becoming rivers, becoming pools, becoming a surrounding, foaming sea! Oh, our people. Oh, our ancestors. Oh, our loved ones. So many! Could there be so many in only one hundred years? And how would I find *her* in such a mob! Millions of Kachis swirling in creamy eddies, nearing the omphalos, twirling more and more rapidly as they are caught at the edges of the vortex, as their wings . . .

As their wings rip away! Glassy fragments flying! A sigh from the songfathers assembled, from the spirit people. Was this expected? Was this the way of things? Would they not need their wings in heaven?

Perhaps not, for the Kachis are changing. There is a stripe of darkness up their fronts, from groin to chin. A widening stripe of darkness. At first I don't understand, then I see what it is. The pale delicate skins have split. Whatever is inside shows dark against the pale integument, thrusting outward, fighting its way out of the tight white casing in which it has been trapped. Arms split from wrist to shoulder, legs split from toe to thigh. Translucent pearly coverings curl away, and what is inside heaves out.

New forms. Different forms. Forms we had just seen, as recorded upon another world, shaggy ravenous hordes of creatures, miniature Ularians . . .

I hear my own voice howling, no, no, no.

Trompe screams. Why is Trompe screaming? I turn. He is lying beside the fence, blood-covered. Leelson is down behind him, and above them bright ruby lines cut the air into deadly polygons of cross fire, pulses of force coming from downhill, southwest and northeast. Someone is firing at them, at us!

I hear the ex–King of Kamir, shouting. "Mitigan. Stop! Don't! Chur Durwen, no!"

At the bottom of the hill shaggy, fringed shapes pour into the omphalos like a foaming tide. The air is full of Kachis ghosts, split-skin phantoms, half faces, single wings, shed skins whirling on the wind, clattering softly against one another like fallen leaves.

Leelson runs toward Lutha, seizes her up, tied as she is to Leely, who grabs my arm and holds me in a grip of iron, so I must run alongside. The ex-king pursues us, trying to shield us from the weapons fire. We five are fleeing down the aisle while the spirit people rage around us. Faces, I see, mouths, I see, wide mouths, shouting, furious faces. They are tied down. They cannot stop us, for they are belted to eyelets set in the stone, tied down against this dreadful wind!

Oh, but they scream. Blood has been shed. Violence has been done. Worse than that! Worse than that! They have seen, oh, they have seen . . .

Leelson stumbles. He is attempting a tangential course, one that will carry us to the west, around the omphalos, but by this time the force of the whirling vortex has built into a tornado, a hurricane spinning uncontrollably, a maelstrom of wind! We run through air, legs churning space. We fly!

Beneath us I see musicians held in place by stout straps, kneeling circles of men chained to their eyelets. We are not chained and we spin, sucked down after the shaggy creatures, sucked down as the ghost-white skins of the Kachis are being sucked down. . . .

Leely, Leelson, Lutha, the ex-king, and I, and as we go screaming down, in terror of the darkness below, our heads twist to keep sight of the light, the light, where other dark forms fly after us like the shadows of doom.

"MI . . . TI . . . GAN . . ." I hear the ex-king shout. "NO. NO. NO!"

Then only darkness and howling and shed skins making a horrid rustling sound and shaggy things with tentacles and sucking mouths all around us.

Then blackness, and pain, and no more story of Saluez. For a time Saluez is gone from the pattern and the weaving goes on without her.

They did not know how much time went by. Lutha seemed to recall going in and out of consciousness, in and out of places, always borne on that terrible wind, unable to move except as it moved them. There were momentary pauses, as though the maelstrom had to switch gears or decide where to go next. During one of these, Lutha hauled on the tether between her and Leely, pulling him close, and with him Saluez, who clutched him tightly. It was then she realized there was light where they were, for she saw Saluez's face, eyes rolled back, only the whites showing. Then the wind grabbed them up again, and they were away.

The next thing they felt was the crushing impact of hitting something solid and hard, of being dropped with enough violence to drive out their breaths and cause pain. Then was the sound of cursing and sobbing and fighting for air. Lutha was on top, with Leely sandwiched between herself and Saluez. For a moment she simply lay there, so thankful for the quiet that she didn't care whether anyone else was there or had survived.

Leelson's voice rose, cursing, then that of the ex–King of Kamir. Then another male voice, raised in challenge.

"Leelson Famber! Stand and die!"

"Don't, Mitigan!" cried the ex-king.

"What are you doing here?" snarled the stranger voice in a tone of furious surprise.

"Come to stop you doing what you're trying to do," the king gasped. "I was wrong."

"I swore an oath!" trumpeted the other. "We Firsters honor our oaths!"

"Oath or not, you won't get paid if you kill anyone! Take a new oath. I was wrong. I hired you to do it, I'll hire you not to do it. It wasn't his fault."

Lutha pulled herself gingerly erect. Saluez was not conscious. Leely was simply asleep. He did that sometimes when things were confusing. Lutha pushed herself away from them both and struggled to sit up. At least one rib had something wrong with it, for it hurt to breathe. Light pouring through a jagged opening at her left disclosed a room-sized cavern, the rugged walls streaked with white, the floor leveled by deposits of gravel and stones and a million years' worth of bird droppings. Translucent membranes waved from a dozen places, and it took a puzzled moment before Lutha identified them. Kachis wings caught among the rocks, brought here by the winds. Leelson lay slightly above the others, prone in the slanted opening, feet kicking against the sky, mumbling about wormholes. Somewhere nearby the sea swallowed and sucked, the stone vibrating in tidal rhythms.

The ex-king leaned against the back wall of the cave, facing the savage stranger. Jiacare winced as he rose to his full height and moved to put himself between the savage and Leelson.

"There's still the matter of my oath," said the savage, curling his lip.

"Mitigan of the Asenagi, I will compensate your bruised honor," snarled the king with equal force. "By your blood and mine, man! We've been sucked through a wormhole in space; we don't know where we are or when we are, and it's a poor time in my opinion to argue about honor!"

The man addressed as Mitigan did not put aside his bellicose manner, but at least he took his hands away from his weapons. Saluez moaned and put her hand to her head. Leelson went on cursing under his breath, the same words over and over. Lutha looked around for Trompe and then remembered.

"Was Trompe killed?"

"Yes," gasped Leelson. "He was. For which someone will answer . . ."

His voice failed. Lutha blinked. Trompe had been a faithful companion. She wept into her cupped hands, regretting that they had not always seen their duty alike, that she had been impatient with him.

It was then that she heard another voice, sharp though rather plaintive, pitched to be barely audible over the sound of the sea. "Hello?" And again: "Hello?"

Leelson, startled by the voice, slithered down from the opening in an avalanche of gravel. Lutha detached herself from Leely's tether and crawled up into the space he'd left. Above the ocean the transformed Kachis were furiously feeding, dropping long lumpy tentacles into the sea and pulling up fish after fish, spreading their tentacles into nets to capture seabirds, meantime bobbing, weaving, spinning as they increased the spaces between themselves, all the time gobbling voraciously. They stretched away in a level plane, a flat grid of bodies that met the flat surface of the sea at the horizon. Lutha risked sticking her head out of the hole just far enough to look along the cliff face. She saw nothing but rock and more rock, all of it splotched with salt and bird droppings and streaked with black ropes of what could only be seaweed.

"Hello," she called. "Where are you? Who are you?"

"I saw somebody's feet!" cried the voice. "I'm Snark. Did you come to rescue me?"

What a question! Turning toward the sound, Lutha saw light-colored movement, something waving, a scarf or shirt, then a face peering down. The person was above them, almost at the top of the cliff, her head and shoulders protruding from a hole. Some other cavern, Lutha thought as she glanced out at the transformed Kachis, still busily eating.

"What place is this?" she called.

"Perdur Alas," the other cried.

At the moment the name meant nothing to Lutha, though she was sure she had heard it recently. She rubbed her head fretfully, calling, "Don't go away."

She squirmed back inside to tell the others there was a human being nearby and the name of the place. Leelson's and the ex-king's exclamations reminded her where she'd heard the name recently. Poracious Luv had said the sensory recording was from Perdur Alas.

Leelson felt his arms, groaning. "No doubt the woman who's calling to us is the observer whose senses we experienced."

"Don't you find that unbelievable?" Lutha asked.

The ex-king said, "Those who encounter chains of events at two disparate points, without observing the connections, think they have observed coincidence when they have, in fact, seen only consequence."

Lutha's mouth dropped open, and he grinned.

"I was a figurehead, yes, but I was allowed tutors."

Leelson started to laugh, cut himself off in midamusement, and rolled over so he could feel tenderly along his ribs.

Mitigan stepped over Leelson's body and looked out the entrance, then he helped Leelson up so he could do the same. The ex-king didn't bother.

"I'm no good at practical things," he said. "I've had no experience."

"You can keep watch, then," Leelson directed him. "Sit in the opening there and tell us if any of those things come back this way."

The ex-king obediently sat, throwing Lutha a good-natured glance as he pushed by her to get at the opening.

"How's the boy?" he asked.

"He's fine." Leely was fine. She had no worries whatsoever about Leely. He had just wakened and now sat happily arranging bits of gravel while Leelson and Mitigan talked about getting out, and Lutha turned her attention to Saluez.

At some point in the wild journey, perhaps when they were dumped from the vortex, Saluez's head had been injured. She had a large bruise above her left ear, and as Lutha felt gingerly around the edges of it, she opened her eyes.

"Have we come to heaven?" Saluez murmured.

For a moment Lutha couldn't answer. Had they come to heaven! Hell, more likely, but she hesitated to say that, not knowing how badly Saluez was hurt.

"Dananana," whispered Leely, laying his face against Saluez. "Dananana." He pulled her veil aside and kissed her face moistly, repeatedly.

Lutha looked away. Just another of Leely's little habits. She took a deep, painful breath and turned to meet Saluez's terrified eyes. She'd had time to realize it wasn't heaven, which saved Lutha from having to break the news.

"We're not dead?" Saluez asked, sounding strangely disappointed.

"Not so far," Lutha told her glumly. It would do no good to delay telling her the truth. "If the Kachis don't come back, we may even survive for a while."

"They went to heaven," Saluez cried, her eyes wild with pain and confusion.

"They went out there to eat fish," Lutha said as matter-of-factly as she could manage. "If the big creatures we saw are Ularians, then your beautiful people are baby Ularians. Or maybe Ularian larvae. Or nymphs."

"Imagos," corrected the ex-king from the opening.

"Whatever." Lutha shrugged, gasping at the pain. Shrugging was not a good idea.

"Mother," Saluez cried, her eyes wide. "Mother."

Lutha leaned forward to take Saluez into her arms, and for a moment Saluez clung to her before slumping into unconsciousness once more. The men stopped their talk long enough to cast a sympathetic glance toward the women. Leely scrambled up to the cavern entrance, crawled into Jiacare Lostre's lap, and stared out across the waves, waving his hands and saying over and over, "Dananana, Dananana," at which the king looked rather more intrigued than Lutha thought appropriate.

After a time Mitigan took the king's place in the cavern opening and carried on a shouted conversation with the person in the other cavern, who identified herself as Snark. By this time it was becoming obvious to all those in the cavern that they could not simply climb up or down from where they were. The cliff was sheer below and overhanging above. Snark tried to get a rope to Mitigan, who leaned widely from the entrance, gripping the stone with one hard fist while he flailed unsuccessfully at the windblown line. After a time Snark shouted that she would go up on top and try it from the other side, but by this time Leelson had made a rope of Leely's harness, all the belts and sashes, plus some strips torn from the bottom of the robes, and had weighted the end with a stone.

Mitigan succeeded in tossing the stone over the tree that protruded from the cliff just above Snark's hole and turned to the others with an expression of triumph. Then, inexplicably and simultaneously, they all gagged.

"Get in!" demanded Leelson.

Mitigan dodged back into the hole and lay flat.

"Ularians," breathed Leelson, unnecessarily. Those who were conscious had already figured that out. They lay on their bellies, drooling onto the cave bottom, waiting for the taste to pass. Lutha was nearest the opening, and she actually saw one of them go by, like a hairy whale sailing out over the sea, long, tangled tentacles hanging like a tattered drapery beneath it. It should have seemed balloonlike, she thought. It should have seemed airy, but did not. Instead it breathed ominous cold, horrid intention, ghastly power. She felt the tears start and barely kept herself from moaning.

After a lengthy hiatus, the taste dissipated and they got shakily to their feet once more. When they looked out, Snark had already attached her rope to the makeshift line. Mitigan hauled it in. Snark made an amazingly acrobatic leap out from her cavern to the tree branch, squirmed up and onto it with the rope between her teeth. Shortly afterward she called, and Mitigan went up the line like an ape. Leelson went next, though with rather less agility, and the two of them raised the rest, one at a time. First Leely, then the unconscious Saluez, tied into a kind of rope sling, then Lutha, her head reeling from the height, the immensity of the sea, the nearness of the Ularians. The ex-king came last, looking around himself delightedly, his cheeks pink with excitement.

The entire process, though lengthy, took place in virtual silence, bouts of strenuous, grunting effort interrupted by periods of frozen stillness when they tasted even the remotest presence of the great Ularians. Each time it was only a hint of taste, a momentary awfulness.

The sun was setting by the time all were assembled at the top of the cliff. Saluez lay wrapped in warm blankets—provided by Snark—while the rest hunkered down with their heads together, telling Snark how they had come to be with her and watching the sun set in a bonfire of reds and pinks and oranges against a purple sea and lavender sky. The shaggies had spread themselves evenly, a plane of blobby black shapes cutting the red orb of the sun into a knife edge of light.

"So you haven't come to rescue me." Snark laughed. It was a harsh, self-mocking sound. She looked directly at Lutha. "I guess I knew that as soon as I saw your face, Lutha Tallstaff."

"Why?" Lutha asked, puzzled.

Snark laughed again, like a cock crowing, half jeer, half boast. "I hate you, Lutha Tallstaff. And him, Leelson. Not that I can do anything about it. Prob'ly learn to hate him, too, the one that was king. Not her, though." She jerked an elbow in Saluez's direction. "She's like me. Life ate her up and spit her out, din it."

Lutha was both offended and mystified. "Have we met before?"

Snark told her where, and when. Lutha flushed. She had known the shadows were . . . people. Hadn't she? Or had she?

Unexpectedly, Leelson came to her defense. "Lutha doesn't know anything about shadows. None of the ordinary people do. Only the Procurator's people knew about them."

"Likely." Snark sneered.

"True," he said. "I am well connected in the bureaucracy, and I knew next to nothing about them until the Procurator told me, there on Dinadh."

Lutha added, "And if we've offended you, we're sorry."

"I killed you. I got even."

This required explanation, and Mitigan was much fascinated by Snark's description of a simul booth.

"Sensurround doesn't work that way! It has built-in censors," he said. "You can't kill anybody in sensurround. You can't do anything to a person that's against his will!"

"Shadows can." She sneered again. "Simuls let you do anything you want, and they let me kill her, more than once." She cast a ferocious glance in Lutha's direction, making the other woman pale and draw back.

The ex-king intervened. "As I've mentioned to Mitigan, we have no time for hating or killing, for our survival must come first. So tell us, Snark. How do we survive?"

She gave him the same up-and-down look she had given Lutha, though a more approving one, as she said offhandedly, "I've got me a few holes dug here and there, but they're only big enough for me. I don't know whether the big Rottens know I'm here or not, but I do know they like to play games."

"Let's take it one thing at a time," said Leelson. "Food, first."

"There's all you'll ever need in the camp. The Rottens don't seem to care if I take stuff. They don't seem to notice, I mean."

"Warmth?" Leelson asked.

"So far it hasn't been very cold. The team records say it doesn't get really cold. If you're out of the wind, all you'll need is a few blankets. There's both blankets and solar-heat storage units at the camp. 'Course, they'll have to be recharged at the camp, where the collectors are."

"And, finally, shelter?" asked Mitigan.

"Well, that's it, isn't it?" she agreed, with a lopsided, rather desperate grin. "That's what it's all about. Either they don't know we're here, the big Rottens—"

"Why do you call them big Rottens?" queried Leelson.

"Because it's descriptive, damn it! Call 'em Ularians if you like, I don't care. Like I was saying. Either they don't know we're here, or they know damn well we're here and are playing with us. If they don't know, then we got to stay hid, don't we? If they do know, it still makes sense not to tempt 'em."

"We can't stay in the camp?" asked the ex-king.

"Well, I'll tell you. Used to be the Rottens just came out at night. Lately, they've been coming daytimes, too, and they all the time hang over the camp. That's a favorite spot, that is. An it's not all that secure. Wasn't built to defend. 'F it was me, I'd go back behind the ridge north of the camp. There's a big rockfall there, pillars and blocks all tumbled down with spaces between. You'd be close to food stores and the solar collectors, and likely there's a place in there big enough for all six of you. Not real smart, to my mind, but then—"

"Why not?" Lutha asked.

"If the Rottens go after one of you, they'll get all. Spread out, maybe they won't get you all. That's the way my folks did it."

Mitigan smiled approval and she flushed. She was not accustomed to approval.

"Am I right in thinking you were here before?" Lutha asked her. "You were one of the 'survivors' the Procurator mentioned?"

Snark nodded, responding unwillingly. "Me. Yeah. There were five of us, all kids."

"Why were you . . . ?" Lutha didn't know how to ask the question.

"Made a shadow?" She laughed harshly. "Yeah, well. Things just happen to some people. Runnin' from scourges, you get what they call antisocial."

None of them knew what she meant by scourges, but they did not interrupt her as she went on:

"I'd had a few years of running before I was rescued. Makes you quick. Makes you—what you say—crude. Guess I didn't adapt real well to civilization."

This time Mitigan grinned admiringly at her. Snark returned the grin, a quick feral flash, no more used to humor than to approbation.

Lutha watched the two closely, thinking them a good pair. She, brown and lean, with muscular shoulders and calves, high, strong cheekbones, and a rounded but stubborn jaw; he wide as a door, his almost white hair drawn up into a tall plume atop his head, wearing a hide vest, a beaded crotch piece, and not much else besides a bandage and his many scars. If he'd ever worn Dinadhi dress, he'd dropped it before attacking at the omphalos.

Leelson peered down his nose at both of them, the aristocratic Fastigat sneer Lutha found so infuriating. Snark didn't bother to notice. She had seen so much of Fastigat superiority at Alliance Prime that it ceased to impress.

"What's happening back on Dinadh, do you suppose?" Lutha asked Leelson. "They must have seen what happened to us. Are you sure Trompe's . . . dead?"

Leelson looked at his boots. "I'm sure. The other . . . assassin was aiming at you or Leely, and Trompe jumped in front of him." He glared at Mitigan. "You had no reason to kill Trompe!"

"We weren't aiming at Trompe," said Mitigan, unmoved by Leelson's anger. "As for what's happening back there, your Procurator will be stirring dust. As will Chur Durwen. We are sworn to cover one another."

Leelson nodded. "The Procurator will mount a search immediately. He'll send probes through the vortex."

Lutha wondered, briefly, why Leelson hadn't noticed that the vortex was no more. She started to say so, but was cut off by the ex-king:

"Poracious Luv is on Dinadh. She will also put her considerable talents to the problem. And perhaps the songfathers of Dinadh as well. Though they won't want to admit they were wrong about the . . . Kachis."

His words made the hair rise on the back of Lutha's neck. She could infer from various things Saluez had told her that the songfathers wouldn't want to admit they were wrong. In fact, if what had happened at this Tahs-uppi was what usually happened at the ceremony, they *would* not admit they'd been wrong. Every hundred years they would be disillusioned, and each time they would swear to hide their disillusionment in order to retain their power. "We won't tell anyone," they'd say. "We won't let anyone know. We'll deny it. We'll defend the traditional teachings!"

Such things had happened before! Men in power had made mistakes or foolish claims and spent the rest of their lives and their successors' lives defending the indefensible, or hiding it. And arrayed against the impenetrable wall of the songfathers was only one big woman, one old man, and one warrior who might or might not take sides.

"Whatever they do," Snark remarked, "they're not going to do it tonight. Those little shaggies, they came out all along this cliff."

"Not just one place?" Leelson demanded.

"Hell, no. They spurted out from where you were, and from south of me a dozen places. Some of 'em even came out of that island out there."

She pointed westward, where a stone point jabbed the glowing sky. "Doesn't matter where they came out, you still got the same problem. You need cover. You need food. You have to put that pregnant woman somewhere safe if you're going to try to keep her. Right after dark still seems to be a good time to move around. The Rottens haven't ever come over the camp right after sundown. I keep a kind of chart. When they come, how many, where. Then I try to stay away from the worst places, the worst times."

All of them were exhausted, but they could not argue with the local expert. They got wearily to their feet; Mitigan put Saluez over his shoulder with surprising gentleness; Lutha was less gentle with Leely; and they went in a weary straggle through the dusk. Before it was completely dark, they arrived at a shallow swale halfway up the slope north of the camp.

Mitigan rolled Saluez under a windrow of dried brush, and Lutha was appointed to keep watch over her and Leely while Snark took the three men down among the buildings. Leelson left her with a lingering stroke along her cheek and the remark that it might take them a while to find everything that was needed.

Lutha didn't care. She could have slept atop a volcano, so she thought, struggling to stay alert until they returned. The last of the dim purple along the sea horizon was being sucked into a black throat of night. Stars blazed on the moonless sky, like paper lanterns, their light diffused. Strange. Down in the camp small lights moved about, not radiating as one would expect, not making star shapes in her vision, but softened, dampened. She blinked, assumed the air was foggy, or that perhaps her sight was affected by fatigue. Then she realized it was not only sight that was affected but also sound. She shook her head, swallowed, twisted her head from side to side, trying to unplug ears that suddenly weren't working properly. All sounds were flat, with no resonance. Damped. Someone had lowered a curtain over the world.

Which trembled. Beneath her. Only a little, as though some large creature had taken a step near me. And another. And another yet. Three steps. Something. Something huge enough to make the stone backbone of the ridge tremble like a leaf.

She swiveled her head, silently, scanning the darkness, trying to see something, anything against the sprinkled star field. There . . . across the camp. To the southeast. On the horizon, the stars winking out, and those above them, and those above them, and those above . . . By the

Great Gauphin, halfway to the zenith, the stars winking out. Something huge close up? Something even bigger far away?

She put her hands over her mouth and breathed quietly. The sound of the sea came as a series of flat slaps, no susurrus, no following hush. The world trembled again. She counted the steps, one, two, three, four. Five, six, seven. Eight, nine. Coming or going?

And then the stars bloomed in heaven and the sound of the sea was there once more, the soft rolling shush of waves on the gravelly beach. Down in the camp, the lamps made sparkling stars of refracted light.

Lutha was wide-awake when they returned laden with blankets, charged solar stoves, and camp lights plus a number of prepacked emergency kits full of food and other necessities.

"Did you hear?" Leelson whispered to her. "Did you feel?"

Snark said, "It's happened before."

"How often?" demanded Leelson.

In the light of her lantern they saw the shrug, the twisted mouth, the fear in her eyes. Still, her voice retained its usual offhand manner.

"A few times. Just a few times."

Deeply troubled, they straggled off again, uphill to a ridge spiked by stone fragments, scraggy as broken teeth, where—so Snark said—a natural dike had fallen. The remnants lay behind the ridge in a tumble of chunks and pillars, like a child's blocks dumped from their box. Among this rubble were the clefts and shelters Snark had described, places where the hunted could go to ground.

They found a room deep inside, roofed by huge pillars that had come to rest across a dozen rounded boulders, the floor cushioned by a few centuries of dust but no bird droppings. It was large enough for all six of them and their stack of provisions. Snark, very subdued, was nearest Lutha when they variously knelt or flopped or fell onto spread blankets.

"Really, have you counted how many times that thing happened?" Lutha asked her quietly, wanting to know but not wanting a general conversation about it.

"Once just before the first time I saw the Rottens," she said through her teeth. "And maybe three or four times since. There were times I thought it was maybe happening, but I wasn't sure."

"So it isn't the Rottens that do it?"

"You didn't taste Rottens when it happened, did you? So, if that means anything, it means they don't do it." She gave Lutha an almost friendly look. "You wanna know the truth, I'm glad it happened with you here. Those other times, I thought I was losing what little brain I've got left."

Mitigan approached them, his mouth full of questions about the Rottens. While he and Snark talked Lutha went to wrap Leely against the chill.

Snark said, "I'll hang around close. I got a hole up the hill there. You sleep. You all look like hell."

And with these helpful words she departed while Mitigan stood looking admiringly after her. At least Lutha assumed it was admiration that kept him standing there in the dark while the rest of them settled in like so many marmots, gathering close together to share warmth and wishing at that moment only to be safe, at least for a time.

CHAPTER 10

They slept restlessly on the rocky floor with a fair share of grunting and turning—all but Mitigan and Leely, both of whom were able to sleep anywhere, under any conditions. By the time enough gray light pried its way through the stone pile to make a few dim puddles on the floor of our shelter, they were all awake, aware of the morning's chill, coveting the warmth of the stove and something hot to drink.

All, that is, but Saluez, who had lain closest to Lutha during the night. At intervals she'd moaned softly, but she had not responded to Lutha's touch or voice, any more than she responded to Leelson, who bent over her in the early light, shaking his head.

"She's lost in something fearful and ugly. I sense feelings of betrayal and guilt. Hard to say what it may be."

Lutha thought that Saluez's feelings of betrayal were much the same as her own. Even now Leelson went past Leely as though the child did not exist.

"How cruel," said Jiacare Lostre.

Lutha turned, startled, but he wasn't talking to her. He was kneeling beside Saluez, holding her hand.

"A cruel joke on all of us," he said with a grimace, gesturing at the rocks around them. "Perhaps Saluez simply prefers to be out of all this."

She was lying supine, the melon swell of her belly rising above the slackness of her body.

Lutha said, "She's never mentioned how long she had left in her pregnancy. Poor Saluez."

"Why say 'poor Saluez'?" Mitigan demanded angrily from his corner, over the *wheep, wheep, wheep* of his sharpening stone. "She will soon have a child. All women want children. Bearing is what they are good for!"

"Thus speaketh a Firster," Lutha growled, deeply offended. "I suppose your god came roaring out of a whirlwind to tell you the universe was made for man, and so were women!"

"I received the visitation from the Great Warrior, yes! At my coming-of-age." He glared his disapproval, then went scrambling off among the stones in the direction Leelson had gone a few moments earlier.

Lutha muttered, "Why is it all Firsters have to talk about their visitation. Even Leelson does it, though he dresses it up in philosophical language."

"And what did Leelson's god look like?"

"Like a Fastigat." She laughed grimly. "Of course."

Jiacare drew the blanket closer around Saluez's shoulders. "Mitigan was right about one thing. We can't assume she regrets her pregnancy. Most of us humans seem to find one excuse or another for increasing our numbers."

"Oddly enough, that didn't seem to be true on Dinadh. Trompe and I were surprised to see how many vacant hives there were. Dinadh's population is evidently decreasing."

He thought about this, his mouth pursing, his eyes squinting. "That would fit the pattern. The Ularian reproductive cycle would start with a growing human population and few Kachis, and the proportions would reverse by the end of the cycle."

Lutha shuddered. "Through predation?"

"It is a kind of predation," he mused. "If Saluez is an example. She's a young woman with an unimpaired body, but as I understand Dinadhi culture, she'll never have another lover or another child."

"Why maim her? Why not just kill her?"

"As she is, she can still work in the fields to produce food. Late in the cycle the Kachis probably get the biggest share of what food there is."

"If it's cyclical, then some Kachis must have remained on Dinadh to start the process over. Also, we've assumed the Kachis are the young of the Ularians. Where are the Ularians on Dinadh?"

He shrugged. "Being offspring of Ularians doesn't preclude multiple parthenogenic generations. Or even sexual reproduction as immature imagos—"

He was interrupted by Snark, who darted from the tunnel through which the men had departed. "You oughta go up and watch the show. The little shaggies that came blasting out when you folks came! They're blowing each other up, like balloons!"

The lure was irresistible. Lutha tucked the blankets close around Saluez's shoulders and tied Leely's tether around a stony knob nearby, putting the knot above his reach and jerking it to be sure it would hold. He settled down next to Saluez, curling into the curve of her body, his eyes half-shut, while Lutha and the ex-king went out after Snark.

Beyond the cover of the stones, they got their first daytime look at their hiding place: a dark cleft gaping between enormous, rain-rounded boulders beneath a jackstraw tumble of huge basalt crystals, so dark a gray they were almost black. Gap-toothed shards of similar crystals fanged the ridge.

From beyond that toothy ridge came a thin shrilling, rising and falling in volume, punctuated by explosive sounds. Mitigan and Leelson lay prone at the top of the slope, and the others joined them to peer through the scraggy scarp. They saw a seething caldron of shaggies, great globules of them rising and falling, tentacles whipping like strands of flung lava, the whole punctuated by eruptions in which one or more shaggies were blown apart. The cacophony was underlain by the sodden gulp of the sea, its waves flattened beneath a mat of floating body parts. The slender crescent of rocky beach was piled with clotted, squirming fragments, and more were washed ashore with each vomitous surge.

Lutha averted her eyes from the beach and focused upon the battle. There was a certain horrid fascination in the relentless winnowing. The rain of dead and injured was continuous. Gradually the deafening noise abated. Much of the detritus was sinking. The height of the waves increased, showing patches of clear water and making a more surflike noise.

Snark said, "It's brood aggression. Sibling murder. Happens with a lot of creatures. Supposedly it maximizes reproductive output. All the rearing effort will go to the strongest."

Jiacare muttered, "How many will they leave alive?"

"Too many," said Mitigan and Snark, as with one voice.

"It's hard to believe they changed shape that much," Lutha murmured, half-hypnotized by the continuing massacre. "They looked almost human on Dinadh."

Snark turned slowly, her eyes very wide. "What did they look like. On Dinadh?"

"Small. That is, slight. Very thin, but human in form, with wings—"

"And sharp teeth," she said. "Right? And their teeth was really poisonous! And they come out at night!"

Lutha nodded.

"We called 'em scourges," Snark muttered. "When my people ran off from Dinadh, some of the scourges followed 'em through the gate."

"Kachis? In their original form? What happened to them?"

She made an aimless gesture. "There weren't very many. Mother said our people hunted and killed some of 'em. The others starved, I guess."

Above the sea, the carnage had come to an end. Some few ragged forms still floated on the waters, gradually disappearing beneath the waves, while above, the uninjured ones separated and arranged themselves in an orderly grid that stretched to the horizons. By counting how many body diameters would fit in the previously crowded but now empty space, Lutha estimated one out of a hundred of the original number had survived.

She was about to mention this when she gagged, sickened by a sudden, horrible taste.

"Down, quick!" Snark spun her around. "It's the big Rottens!"

They made it down the ridge and into the rocks before the creatures appeared—though barely. When they came to the sleeping chamber, each of them found a water bottle and a wiping rag and sat down well away from one another, each careful to look away from the others as they drooled and wiped. The few pale rays of sunlight that penetrated the piled stones now stood almost erect, disappearing one by one. All scarcely breathed as the rays reappeared.

"No clouds today," said Snark unclearly but matter-of-factly. "That was a big Rotten goin' over. Floatin' and danglin'."

"Is there a place we can safely watch from?" asked Leelson, wiping his lips. "I'd like to see a big one."

Snark dug her heel into the sand and twisted it as she considered. "This rockfall piles higher the farther east you go. Clear at the east end, it's right on the ridge. We can try working through in that direction."

Lutha had stacked the provisions in a neat pile, away from the stove. Disregarding these efforts at order, Mitigan tumbled the stack, tore open one of the personal kits, and burrowed inside it to find a full water bottle. Snark wiped her filthy face with the back of one hand and went scrambling off with him in pursuit, looking from the rear more like four-legged creatures than two-legged ones.

"Be back," said Leelson as he followed them into the dark.

Jiacare Lostre shook his head, muttered fragmentary phrases of fastidious annoyance, and set about picking up the scattered contents of the personal kits.

"This isn't a kit knife," he said. "Whose knife is this?"

"What knife?" Lutha asked, swiveling toward him.

He held a knife into the light of a slanting beam. Lutha saw it, and saw beyond it, where the severed end of Leely's tether hung white against the gray stone she had tied it to. The knife belonged to Saluez. She carried it in the pocket of her underrobe and Lutha had seen her use it dozens of times. So had Leely.

Lutha scrambled across the sand toward Saluez's recumbent form, feeling frantically along her blanket-covered body. Leely wasn't there. Saluez hadn't moved. Only her covers had been shoved aside to gain access to her pocket. Leely had been lying there when Lutha and the ex-king had gone out!

"Your boy," said the ex-king. "He did it?"

Lutha nodded, rigid and cold with tension. She hadn't thought of his using a knife. Why hadn't she thought of that! Now what? The Ularians were out there, and Leely was wandering around in this warren, or outside it. Maybe out in the open. What could she do? What dared she do?

Jiacare Lostre put his hand on her shoulder, forced her down, sat before her, taking her hands in his. "Be still," he said.

"Got to—"

"Don't. Don't do anything. If he's inside, he's as likely to come back here as we are to find him. If he's outside, anything you do might endanger him more."

"I could go to the entrance and call to him!"

"If you did, would you want those creatures to hear you? Listen to me, Lutha. The best thing you can do is nothing. Just wait. Besides, the others are looking out. If they see him outside, they'll come back and tell us so."

She thought that Leelson wouldn't. Leelson wouldn't give it a second thought. She shivered. Jiacare put a blanket around her, then his arms around that, and they sat so for a long time.

Time went by. The patches of sunlight shifted nearer the stone, crawling amoebalike on the sand. The taste went away, but Leely hadn't returned.

"What?" demanded Leelson from the edge of the cavern.

"Leely," said the ex-king. "He's gone."

"Oh, tsssss." Leelson hissed, grimacing at Lutha, at the world. "How long?"

Jiacare said, "He was gone when you left. We just didn't notice until afterward."

Lutha put her face in her hands. He meant that she hadn't noticed. She would have, if it hadn't been for that horrible taste. . . .

Leelson was suddenly beside her in the ex-king's place, his arms tight around her. "Oh, damn it, Lutha," he whispered. "Why did you have to come out here. Why."

He wasn't asking for information. She gave him none.

"I have to find him."

"No. Not until it's safe. Snark says they haven't really gone. I came back to tell you to be careful."

"Leely could have gone out there!"

"He could have. But likely he didn't."

Saluez moaned. They looked up. She had lifted one hand to her forehead as she made whining, hurt noises. Leelson got up and went to her.

"Saluez?" Leelson raised her up.

Jiacare had already filled a cup, and Leelson put it to her lips. She drank, only a little.

"Hurt," she said, putting her hand on her chest. "Hurt."

Leelson laid her down once more. She breathed deeply, experimentally, her expression unchanging. "Not broken," she whispered. "Don't think it's broken."

It was not clear what she had decided wasn't broken. A rib, perhaps. Her collarbone. Her heart.

"Maybe you got a bump on the head," Lutha said, forcing herself not to scream. It wasn't Saluez's fault that Leely had stolen her knife.

"Not in heaven?" Saluez asked, one side of her mouth twisting in a pathetic attempt at a smile.

"Not noticeably, no," Lutha agreed, tucking the blanket back around her shoulders. "Are you cold?"

She ignored the question. "Who's here?"

"You and me and Leelson. And the former King of Kamir, Jiacare Lostre."

"Your servant, ma'am," said Jiacare, with a bow.

Saluez tried the smile again. "Where's Trompe?"

"Gone," Lutha said flatly, tears starting in her eyes. She had been trying not to think about Trompe.

"The other one who's here," Saluez said faintly. "That warrior. He killed Trompe."

"Mitigan," said Leelson. "Yes, he's here, too."

"Leely?" she asked.

Lutha tried desperately for calm. "He seems to have gotten himself lost."

"No, no," Saluez murmured, squeezing her hand. "Can't get hurt. Can't get sick. Can't get lost." Her eyes fell shut. She was gone again.

"Why?" Lutha demanded. "Why does Leely keep doing this?"

"Doing what?" asked Mitigan, emerging from the shadows with Snark close behind him.

"He's disappeared," said Leelson.

"He's gone exploring. Kids do that," Mitigan said offhandedly.

"I've suggested we not draw attention to ourselves," the ex-king offered.

"If we go looking, we'll have to be careful," Snark said, nudging Lutha, not unsympathetically. "It'd be dangerous to go running around out there. Sometimes they come out right on top of you."

"Stupid to go out at all," said Mitigan, with a warning glare at Lutha.

She felt a scream welling up! They were full of what they could or must do, which was everything but go out and find her son!

Leelson picked up on her panic. He tightened his hold on her and said, "We're not at all certain he is outside. Let's search the rock pile first. I'll stay with Lutha and Saluez. If he isn't found in a reasonable amount of time, we'll decide what to do next."

Lutha knew he was staying to keep an eye on her so she wouldn't do anything motherly! She was so angry the blood hammered in her ears.

"We're being sensible," said Leelson, his forehead wrinkled in apparent concern. "We really are, Lutha."

"I know you think you are!" she cried at him, hating him. "Stop feeling at me!"

He only held her closer. "I can't stop feeling you. I do feel you, Lutha. I've felt you since the moment I first saw you. I was high up in that library, all by myself, quite contented, and I . . . heard a summons. I tried not to answer it. And when I'd met you, that first time, I went away, fully intending never to see you again."

She laughed shortly, wrenching herself away from him. "You did? I did too. When I told Yma about you, we both decided you were like a case of the plague, better avoided and very hard to cure!"

"More or less what my mother said."

She flushed angrily. "Damn your mother."

"She's a product of her heritage. If you damn her, you'll have to go on damning former generations, all the way back to Bernesohn's time or earlier."

"You're just like her! You and Limia are so much alike I can't figure out why she can't understand about . . . about us."

He shook his head. "Why should she understand? I don't. I've been with other women. I've loved some of them. But when I've decided to go, I've always gone."

"You went from me! Damn it, Leelson, you went!"

"I went." He laughed in wry amusement. "But I wasn't gone. Or rather, you weren't. You were there, love. Every morning when I woke, like an invisible rope, tying us together. Every night when I was alone, I felt it tugging. Even when I wasn't alone, you were there, between me and whoever."

She tried to laugh, tried to pretend he was lying, knowing all the time that Fastigats didn't lie. It was one of the infuriating things about them. They might not see the truth the way others saw it, but they really couldn't misrepresent what they thought was true.

"Why? Why did you go?" she demanded, a question she'd been wanting to ask for years.

"I told you why. In the note."

"You call that a note? Five words! 'I can't get to him.' "

"I couldn't get to him. And I couldn't . . . couldn't bear to see you . . ."

"See me what?"

"Wasting all that caring."

"Wasting? On my own child!"

He threw up his hands. "That's why I went, Lutha. This is why I'll go again, when this is done. If this is ever done."

"Don't say it." Lutha banged her fist against the stone, hurting herself. "We can't change each other. We can hammer and hammer, and in the end we'll be the same. Things happen. We can't go back and make them unhappen."

Lutha saw Leelson's lowering expression and laughed out loud. "This is ridiculous! We're marooned, we're in danger of death, we're sitting in a rock cavern with nothing but a few blankets and a rather modest stack of food, my child is missing, and you and I are—"

"Are doing exactly what I wanted to avoid," he said firmly. "But you're right. We won't change our views in this matter. The more we talk, the more pain we'll cause, but we won't change."

"But he's—"

"Lutha!" Leelson glared at her. "Don't talk about what Leely is!"

Then a voice from among the stones! "Dananana. Dananana."

He danced into the cavern as though Leelson had summoned him, shining as brightly as one of those vagrant rays of sun.

Lutha gasped. He was bleeding! Round wounds on his arms, on his face. No. Perhaps not. Not wounds exactly. There was blood, but not . . . not so much. "He's been bitten," she cried.

Though maybe he'd only scratched himself on the stones. His little shirt was torn, a fragment of the striped fabric missing, his skin abraded beneath. But already the redness was paling, the rough edges of skin were smoothing.

"Can't get lost," breathed Saluez, from some great distance.

"He's not hurt," Leelson said in an ugly tone. "Look at him, he's not hurt."

"Can't get hurt," said Saluez, her voice fading into silence.

Lutha held Leely close, he waving his hands, kicking his feet, caroling the way he did when he was contented. "Dananana."

Leelson turned his back on them and slowly moved in the direction the others had taken. "Be back," he said, the same words, the same tone as before. Definite. Dismissive.

Lutha heard the sounds of his going away, the tumble of small stones, the crunch of his feet.

"Poor Lutha," breathed Saluez.

"My own damned fault," she mumbled. "Maybe you're right. Maybe Leely can't get hurt, or lost. People used to believe strange ones like Leely were protected by the gods."

There was no response. Saluez was gone, back to wherever she'd been since the omphalos. Lutha tucked the blankets around her once more, then sat quietly by while Leely drew pictures in the sand, saying over and over, "Dananana. Dananana." When he tired of this, he curled up beside Saluez and went to sleep.

Eventually the others returned to the cavern and, unaccountably so far as Lutha was concerned, set about making ready for an excursion.

Now, Leelson said, they would go out and look around.

Lutha stared at him in wonderment. He didn't notice. Mitigan raided the supply pile once again for mottled gray-green overgarments he said would hide them among the bracken. Snark suggested that they smudge their faces with dust so as not to show up pale or dark against some contrasting background. Lutha went along with all this for a time, though all the preparations seemed rather melodramatic, but finally she could stand it no longer.

"Will someone please tell me why we're going outside?"

Leelson cast her a lofty glance. "Anything Snark experiences feeds back to Simidi-ala, where the Procurator is no doubt even now planning our rescue. The feedback includes not only what Snark sees and hears but anything she sees us do or hears us say. We've had no chance to look around in daylight. One of us might come up with some insight that may be useful in planning the rescue attempt. Even the scanty information we have now is more than the Alliance has known previously!"

Mitigan, busy checking his own armament, raised the subject of weapons for the others, and Snark suggested they go first to the camp to pick up heat guns like the one she carried. These were tools used by the shadow team to sterilize soil before planting homo-norm crops, but they would serve to discourage attack as well.

While Snark demonstrated this device to the others Lutha checked her arrangements for Leely once more. Saluez's knife was put away in Lutha's own pocket so he couldn't get at that. His tether was tight—she checked it for the third or fourth time—so he couldn't get loose. While she did this Snark was instructing the others: ". . . turn it on . . . press the button." Even distracted as Lutha was, she thought she would be able to manage that.

They went down the slope into the camp, exploring from building to building, Mitigan, Leelson, and Snark half-crouched, looking in all directions at once, the ex-king and Lutha shambling along, feeling faintly ridiculous. Lutha was reminded of the vacated world the Procurator had showed her, where Mallia had lived. Here, as there, was clothing out of which bodies had been stripped. Here, as there, were artifacts, tools, games left behind when their users had been taken away. Through open doors the wind keened softly, a chill murmur that never ceased. In a window a tuft-eared, short-nosed animal sat quietly, staring at us interlopers.

"Is that a live cat?" Lutha asked, disbelievingly.

"Left behind when the real team was evacuated," Snark said. "Her name's Zagger. There's another one somewhere. Zigger."

"Animals? Real animals? Left behind? The Procurator told me the Ularians left nothing alive!"

"I know what he said," snarled Snark. "I was there, pouring your damn tea!"

Lutha fell silent. The cat jumped down from the window and came to rub itself against her legs. A strange sensation. It looked up intelligently. Lutha realized that it, like the gaufers, knew things. Not as humans knew them, but in its own way. She saw language in its movements. Not her own language, not a spoken language, but . . . Smells, maybe? A combination, perhaps, of smells and gestures and sounds.

"You're right about what the old Proc said." Snark leaned down to stroke the cat. "He talked about all life being gone. But you remember that world he showed you—there was a little pet animal crying along the fence. And there was trees and plants and birds. It was only the humans gone. It's just, the old Proc, he's like a lot of people spend all their lives in Class-J cities, with only humans around—he gets to a point of thinking *life* means *human*. People like that, maybe they got a flower in a pot and a clone fish in a bowl, but they get like Mitigan, so set on humans being the top of the heap, they don't give anything else credit for living."

"What do the cats eat?" asked the ex-king.

"I put out food for 'em," said Snark. "They'll eat fish. I used to catch 'em fish. Now I dunno. Won't be many fish left, the way the shaggies're gulping 'em down."

Though they had come to the camp for heat guns, Lutha took the opportunity to do a superficial inventory of supplies available. She was looking particularly for a medical diagnostic unit for Saluez. Such a unit should have been a standard item in any human-occupied area, but there was none in any building they visited. Lutha didn't mention the omission to Snark, considering that Snark had quite enough to be angry about already.

With the heat guns in their pockets, they left the camp and walked down the narrow vale to the pebbly beach, the only place for several days' walk in either direction, said Snark, where the cliffs did not close off access to the sea. They stopped in what Snark called a storm hole, a hollow eaten out by storm waves above the usual high-water line. From this cover they stared at the shaggies from a new angle. The shaggies took no notice.

After some little time Mitigan strode down onto the beach and strutted back and forth to see if the shaggies would react. When they did not, Leelson joined him in his stroll, then Snark and Lutha. Still no attention from the fishers. They walked the length of the beach, not a great distance, noting that the long wave-washed piles of shaggy body parts had much diminished. The remainder was liquescing, trickling into the gravel in inklike runnels.

"You'd think this would smell, or taste, or something," said Snark.

To Lutha, it looked disgusting, but it did not smell or taste, and the shorebirds took no notice of the remains. Neither did the shaggies, who merely hung like lumpy balloons above the sea, their amorphous, knotty tentacles reeling up and down, the fringed tips stirring the water. Whenever a fish was encountered, the lines twitched and drew upward by a process of gradual thickening, becoming a bulbous extrusion from which the catch was drawn into the main sac. Each shaggy had at least a hundred appendages of various lengths, some coming down, others going up, some quiescent, just hanging. Lutha thought them clumsy looking, as though they had been botched or left unfinished. They seemed uncommitted to their present shapes, as though wearing an expedient disguise.

She started to mention this to Leelson, when Snark looked up and said, "Whoa . . ."

Lutha smothered a shriek. While they'd been staring westward one of the shaggies south of them had floated to a spot between them and their cover. It was far larger than Lutha had estimated. Very wide. With many tentacles.

"Split up," said Mitigan. "Spread out. Start inland."

Lutha's instinct was to stay close to someone else, but Mitigan gestured her away, so she moved obediently apart from the others, a full shaggy diameter away southward, swiveling her head to look in all directions above. The shaggy was hanging roughly between Mitigan and Leelson, tracking them, its underside bulging with incipient filaments and with others already partway extruded. The two men were to Lutha's left, and though they moved rapidly, the shaggy had no trouble staying above them.

Snark was nearest Lutha, on her right.

"More of them, moving in from the sea," she said, breaking into a trot.

Lutha ran beside her, realizing that she had no idea where the nearest bolt-hole was.

Snark saw her confusion. "The rocks just ahead," she said. "Aim for the shadow to your left."

There were several shadows. As they came nearer, Lutha saw the one Snark meant. A hole with space behind it. She hurried, hearing Snark's feet racing away toward another hole, one farther south. Out of the corner of her eye, Lutha saw tentacles at her side, left and right. She leapt toward the shadow, making it under cover just in time.

A slithering sound came from behind her. She turned to see a tentacle slide down the rock behind her, its end plopping onto the ground she had just left.

"Safe," shouted Snark.

"Safe," shouted Mitigan.

Then Leelson's voice shouted the same word. Lutha breathed easier.

"Lutha!" shouted Leelson. "Jiacare!"

Oh. "Safe," she cried breathlessly. "I think." She heard no responsive shout from the ex-king, but then she had other things to worry about.

The plopping tentacle had fallen on a rootlet that led inward. Now it had wrapped itself around the rootlet and was pulling itself slowly into the shallow shelter where Lutha crouched. The tip explored, feeling its way, reaching out for the next thing it could get hold of. Each time it stretched thin, a bulbous thickening somewhere behind it moved up, allowing the slenderer tip to move forward again. The tip was fringed all around with cilia that moved independently, giving it an odd sort of expressiveness. As though it might be thinking.

Could it smell her? Hear her?

She held her breath. The tip quested, erect, turning this way and that, cilia up. Almost she saw it raise its eyebrows, almost she heard it say in a grumpy voice, "Now, where did the thing go!"

She could hold her breath no longer. She gasped. The questing tip turned toward her. "There she is!"

Damn it, she told herself hysterically, the thing was not talking and she could not go forever without breathing!

She picked up a pebble and tossed it away, toward the entrance.

The questing tendril turned that way.

She tossed another pebble, breathing as quietly as possible. Then another one. The tendril was moving faster, extruding blobs of itself forward, then pulling itself toward them, moving across the rocky floor like a lumpy snake.

She heard a blatting, a muffled roar.

"They burn!" cried Snark.

The Lutha-seeking tendril stopped, its end waving, as Lutha heard what the tendril evidently also heard, a high-pitched weeping noise, a whine, not quite organic sounding. The sound of a wounded one?

The questing tendril went into a fury, lashing itself against the ground in a circle. Finding nothing, it grew longer, lashed again, and grew still longer. It was in a temper, no longer willing to spend time to find Lutha. If it went on doing what it was doing, it would touch her.

Reluctantly, she took out the heat gun and pointed it. When the lashing tendril came closest, she pushed the button.

Nothing. She stared at it in disbelief. Pushed it again. Still nothing. It bore an indicator dial just above the button. A red dial, *charge level minus*. Nobody had bothered to check.

No. Not nobody. She. She hadn't bothered to check!

She thrust the useless thing into her pocket to free her hands. There was something else in the pocket. Saluez's knife. She took it out, her hands trembling so that she almost dropped it. Not a big knife. Sharp, though. Sharp enough, maybe, to cut through that questing tendril. If she could hold it down with something while she cut it.

Knife between teeth. Large rock in both hands. Person, not herself, some other idiot, making small noise. Tendril turning purposefully in her direction. Sneaking, sneaking. End up, questing. Another small noise from idiot. Tendril coming faster, extended, thinner and thinner.

Then, smash down rock. Kneel on rock. Saw at tendril, fast, bulges coming down it in this direction, quick, before bulges got there!

Put foot on rock to hold it down on severed tendril. Decapitated tentacle slithering outward, making weeping noises . . .

Something else screaming louder somewhere. Lutha?

Leelson saying, "You did that very nicely."

Lutha, idiot Lutha, making stupid noises with tears all over her face, flinging herself at the man.

"What did she do?" asked Mitigan.

"Cut the tip off the thing," said Leelson with equal parts accusation and admiration. "She forgot her heat gun."

"Did not!" she screamed. "Damn thing hadn't any charge." She took it from her pocket and threw it at him.

He looked at the indicator, pressed it. It turned blue. "You have to turn it on first," he said. "Then you press the button."

"Snark said—" Lutha said.

"I said," Snark said, "you turn it on then press the button."

Maybe Lutha hadn't been listening, Lutha thought.

Snark shook her head wonderingly, then crouched over the chopped-off tentacle tip, scraping it into a collection bag. "I got samples of the body parts along the shore, but I was wondering how we'd get a sample of a live one," she said. "Like they used to say at the home, fools rush in."

"You did very well," Leelson assured Lutha. "Heat gun or no heat gun."

"How many of them came after us," Lutha murmured.

"One each," Snark said. "And there's a shaggy dying over near where I was. I want samples of that one."

Of course they went to look, at the shaggy and for the ex-king, who seemed to be missing. This time they did not talk, they did not make noise, they did not breathe loudly. They sneaked, insofar as it was possible to do so. The dying shaggy lay behind the south end of the outcropping, its tentacles spread around the end of the stone, almost to the hole Snark had taken cover in. The tentacles quivered as they approached. Each time they moved, they quivered anew. All up and down the tentacles, ragged little holes had appeared and the same inky runnels they had seen bled away from the thing.

Mitigan reached down and picked something up from beside a tentacle. He held it out to Lutha.

A fragment of striped fabric. Her eyes refused to see it.

"This your kid's?" he asked.

"Maybe this shaggy picked it up from outside the cavern. Leely might have lost it there." Snark said it. She didn't believe it, but she said it because believing anything else was insane.

Lutha took the scrap and turned it in her hands. On one side was a series of circular impressions, made up of small, individual eaten or burned dots.

Mitigan had already rolled the tentacle with his boot heel, exposing the line of circular structures beneath, made up of individual pores. He took the scrap and held it close. They matched.

"Can't get hurt," whispered Leelson, his eyes on Lutha. "Can't get lost."

He was quoting Saluez, of course, but his eyes questioned Lutha. What did Lutha know?

Lutha told herself she didn't know a damned thing!

"He's pure poison to these," said Mitigan thoughtfully.

"And to Kachis," Leelson mused. "That's why they died."

Lutha screamed at him. "You don't think . . . ?"

"Hush." He gripped her arm, glancing upward. "Don't yell. I don't know what I'm thinking. Not yet. Keep your voice down."

They stayed where they were for a few moments, watching the shaggies to see if Lutha had alerted them. Evidently not. Even the one she had wounded had returned to its place and was fishing, unconcernedly.

They went in single file along the limp body, for the first time getting an accurate idea of its size. Even flattened as it was, the creature had an ominous bulk. Snark knelt beside the mantle and began cutting at a puffy area, which collapsed with a whoosh of escaping gas and a momentary stink.

"Hydrogen," murmured Snark, carving off a piece of the body before turning to the tentacles. "I'm betting it uses bioelectrics to separate hydrogen from salt water. The analyzer in the lab at the camp will figure it out."

"Jellyfish," said the ex-king, who at that moment came from behind a brush pile and wandered over to them. "It's a huge, aerial jellyfish."

"I thought they got you," Leelson remarked to the ex-king.

Jiacare shook his head slowly. "No, actually I dallied a bit behind you when you all went down to the shore. You seemed to be moving rather precipitously. And then, of course, you were making a foolhardy amount of noise."

He nudged the dead or dying shaggy with one toe. "What killed it? It's too far up the slope to have washed in."

Leelson handed him the scrap of cloth; Snark displayed her flesh samples; there was a consequent babble babble. The ex-king looked shocked, then intrigued.

Lutha refused to join in the talk. What they said wasn't true. It couldn't be true.

"It doesn't make sense," Leelson said. "Evolution takes countless generations to come up with things like this. Poisoned leaves that dissuade leaf-eating insects. Thorny seedpods that are not eaten, allowing them to germinate. Poisoned flesh, brightly colored, that warns off predation."

"Might not be poison," said the ex-king. "Might be . . . oh, a virus."

Lutha blurted, "Leely's been examined by experts. He doesn't have a virus."

"He doesn't have a virus harmful to him, you mean," said the ex-king. "I doubt anyone looked for viruses harmful to other things. Especially exotic things."

Lutha admitted to herself he was probably right. Why would they? Leelson had hired people to analyze Leely, and she'd fought them every step of the way. She'd let them inventory Leely's genetic material, but she'd stopped there. No one had done a complete cell inventory.

"How could he have a virus I don't have?" she demanded. "The two of us are always together."

Leelson shushed her. "Leely went off alone and touched them. You didn't. Maybe you have it, too, and don't know it."

"Fine," she snarled. "Next you'd be suggesting I be staked out as bait, just to find out!"

In this mood of mixed apprehension and annoyance, she followed the others to the camp, where Snark put the specimens into the analyzers, and then back to the rock pile. They had been under cover only briefly when the Rottens returned. Everyone but Lutha went to spy upon them, but she remained in their sleeping chamber where Saluez and Leely were sleeping. Though Saluez drooled unconsciously, Leely did not. He did not respond to the presence of the Rottens in any way. He just went on quietly sleeping while Lutha bent her head over the sand and waited for it to be over.

As, eventually, it was. Lutha was washing her face when the others returned.

"There were five big Rottens," Leelson told her. "They found the dead shaggy. It seemed to upset them a good deal."

Lutha turned, the wet cloth still in her hand. "Why be upset at one dead one? Millions of them tore each other apart this morning!"

Leelson made an equivocal gesture. "I know. The Rottens paid no attention to the piles on the shore, but they did hover over the dying shaggy. One of them touched it, then they all drew in their tentacles and made pictures at it."

His voice held a hint of strain, of puzzlement.

"What is it, Leelson?"

"They grieved, Lutha. I could feel it. The one there on the slope, it has an identity. It has a name. They called it by name."

"Maybe it wasn't a name as such," she suggested. "Maybe it was a classification. A label, like *little one,* or *child.*"

"It was a name," he said. "I could feel the grief, the pattern in it, singularity addressing singularity. If it wasn't a name, what was it?"

Lutha folded the cloth and put it away. "How could it have a name? There were millions of the damned things in the vortex; there are still hundreds of thousands of them. Do ants have names, or bees?"

"Numbers aren't really the issue," said the ex-king. "There are billions and billions of men. We all have names."

Lutha flushed. He was right. Given the Firster attitude toward animals, however, how awkward for them to have names!

A point that Leelson made at once. "They aren't men, damn it. I suppose it's possible there might be a kinship with some sensory way of identifying members of their own group. I wonder how we'd . . ."

Lutha sat down on the nearest rock. "You said the Rottens made pictures to the dying one. It would help to know pictures of what?"

"We couldn't see," Snark replied. "We were looking down at the beach, and the angle was wrong. I just knew that's what they were doing, making pictures at the dying one."

"If you could have seen the pictures, you might have caught some clue to the language."

"Ants and bees communicate," said Mitigan. "But we don't call it a language. Only men have language!"

Jiacare Lostre challenged this in his usual mild manner. "Oh, mighty warrior, it has to be a language." He put up a hand as Mitigan growled. "Hear me out! Didn't the Ularians arrange this world for the benefit of the shaggies? Don't we assume the shaggies are the offspring of the Ularians? Wasn't it a Ularian who went to the people of Breadh to tempt them away from their former home? Didn't that tempter need language to do so? Am I the only one here surprised at our not having been killed or transported by the Ularians, since, according to the Alliance, that's what Ularians do."

Snark disagreed. "The tempter wasn't the same! If Ularians are the same as the tempter on Breadh, then the Rottens are not Ularians. The tempter was mighty and mysterious, wonderful and terrible, so my mother said. He wasn't a blob that made people drool all down their chins while they listened."

Leelson murmured, "Or, if both Rottens and tempter are Ularian, then tempter is some kind of ultimate Ularian, some other race, or evolved type."

Jiacare rubbed his hands together thoughtfully. "An ultimate Ularian. Interesting thought. And both you and Saluez are sure about this tempter?"

Snark nodded in vehement agreement. "The sisterhoods on Dinadh kept alive a lot of the old forbidden stories and songs. The original sisterhood, so my mother said, was made up of women who actually remembered what happened on Breadh."

"So"—the ex-king threw his arms wide—"if the Rottens aren't Ularians, where are the Ularians?"

"Don't ask me," said Lutha. "If Snark is right, then the ones here are just . . . nannies. Caretakers. They fret over a sick or dying shaggy; they come and go, minding the young; but they don't or can't clear planets or transport humans. What we call a Ularian crisis, from our point of view, may be just nannies tidying up, from the Ularian point of view."

"We've got three layers of beings already, and you're extrapolating another?" Leelson at his most supercilious.

As usual, Lutha found his tone infuriating. "I'm extrapolating from what Saluez and Snark have told us and what we've found out, Leelson! We don't know for sure that the Rottens even know we're here, and neither they nor the shaggies have been proven capable of vanishment. Therefore, as Snark says, there's a chance that our local Rottens are not Ularians, or at least, not the 'ultimate Ularian.' Besides, Snark says she's seen . . . how many big Rottens all together?"

Snark made a face. "A hundred, maybe. Mostly I just see the same ones, over and over, about thirty or forty of 'em."

Lutha nodded grimly. "Millions of Kachis came through from Dinadh. Ninety-nine percent of them died in the brood struggle; there are still hundreds of thousands of them out there in the grid; but Snark has seen only about a hundred big Rottens. What happened to the rest of the previous generation? The ones that came through a hundred years ago. They must have gone somewhere. Where are they?"

Puzzled silence until Snark broke it, saying:

"There's the thing. You know. The thing that happened the night you got here. There's that."

They shifted uncomfortably, each recalling the occurrence, the strangeness, the occulted stars, the dampened sound, the odd effects of air and light. Mitigan made a furious gesture of rejection, as though about to burst out in anger, but Leelson quelled him with a look. The ex-king smiled, very slightly, a mere quiver of lips that seemed to say, "Ah, yes, well, there was that." Snark and Lutha exchanged questioning looks, and Snark nodded firmly.

"That wasn't nannies," she said. "That was a different thing, that was. And if that was it, the ultimate Ularian, we don't need to ask where IT is. Part of the time, anyhow, it's here."

CHAPTER 11

The question of whether the Rottens knew there were humans on Perdur Alas was answered during the early-morning hours when they woke choking in the dark. Gray dawn disclosed besiegers all around them. Portieres of tentacles encircled the rockfall, closing off every doorway to the outside world and most of the sunlight as well. While the others stayed miserably huddled near the stove, Mitigan and Snark went scrambling through the stones, trying to find an escape route. There was none. The tentacles were too closely spaced to get between, the tips resting on the ground preventing anyone's going under. The only option seemed to be to outwait them, though as the day wore on it was clear that time meant little or nothing to Rottens. Midmorning came and departed. Noon came, status quo. They forced themselves to drink, to rehydrate bodies depleted by the constant salivation. Eating was out of the question. Early afternoon came and went. Though the Rottens made no effort to infiltrate the rock pile, they seemed prepared to stay forever.

All of them but Mitigan became increasingly worried about Saluez. She remained comatose; only her chest and belly moved; breath came and went almost inaudibly while her belly quivered and jabbed sharply beneath the blanket. How close to the time? Snark wanted to know, receiving shrugs as reply. It could be today, Lutha thought, or much later. Even if they knew when, it wouldn't help. No baby could nurse with this going on! And a dehydrated mother couldn't provide milk.

When Jiacare said he was going to one of the peek holes to get a good look at the Rottens, Lutha offered to go with him, partly from curiosity, but mostly just to stop sitting, spitting, worrying about Saluez. Snark joined them, though Mitigan and Leelson sat immovably, each in his own drool corner.

Lutha had thought the shaggies quite large enough—they were hundreds of times larger than the Kachis—but the Rottens were enormously bigger yet. They shared the same form, even to the bulgy, lumpy tentacles that looked as though they contained bones or hard chunks of something rather than being the sinuous flow of flesh one might expect. Lutha mentioned this to Snark.

"It's a scleroprotein," Snark replied indistinctly. "It's got a lot of silicon in it, and I'm guessing it's the lining for the hydrogen ducts. I think the ducts fold up when the tentacles contract. Probably the gasbags contract, too, so the hydrogen can be pressurized to reduce buoyancy."

"Weird," offered the ex-king.

"Odd," Snark replied, shaking her head. "What's weird is their genetic pattern. Pieces of it are similar to a lot of creatures we have records of—"

She stopped, her words arrested by a break in the thus-far-unchanging view through the crevice. Far to their right the curtain of tentacles was disturbed. A dozen of the lumpy lines thrashed in agitation and began reeling in as the shaggies did when they caught fish. The observers craned, trying to see what had caused the disturbance, seeing nothing at first but stones and bracken. Then came a flash of pale color.

Lutha's throat knew before her brain did. She heard herself shouting, "Leely!"

He was out there! Stark naked! Skipping along the line of tentacles, letting them run over his body, thrusting his hands into them. Damn Leelson! Damn him. He'd let her baby go!

She turned blindly toward the exit, but Snark grabbed her in a devil's grip. "Look," Snark demanded. "Don't go running off. Look!"

Unwillingly, Lutha turned her head toward the crevice. The tentacles Leely touched were withdrawing, reeling in quickly, more quickly than they'd seen even the shaggies do while fishing. The dangling appendages didn't grab at him as he skipped by; it was he who plunged in and out of the ropy curtain, moving right to left along the arc of tentacles, up the ridge.

A few—four or five—of the Rottens didn't reel in when touched. Instead they dropped the touched tentacles, severing them near the body, then drew in all the others, sucking them in as though slurping noodles.

This unlikely sight distracted Lutha just long enough that when she looked back to the left, Leely was over the ridge, out of sight.

Once more she tried to get away, struggling with Snark.

"Wait!" demanded Jiacare. "He's not hurt, and he's following the circle. He'll probably come around again."

She stared outward with a feeling of sick impotence. The Rotten circle was at least four or five hundred paces across, fifteen hundred paces around or more. And Leely was moving in a skipping, sidling way, not in any hurry. It would take him a long time. She counted: One pace, two, three, four. If he moved as she counted . . .

She lost her place twice and was up to eight hundred something, long past hope of seeing him, when he appeared as he had at first, far to the right, still skipping, still touching, though now there were very few tentacles within his reach.

Only when Lutha saw he was safe did she look elsewhere, following Snark's jabbed finger toward the Rotten directly above. It was one of those that had withdrawn all its tentacles before being touched. The bottom surface was smooth, shiny, like the surface of a balloon. Colors flowed across it.

"That's Diagonal Red," slavered Snark.

None of them could have missed the pulsing scarlet blot, edged on one side with misty violet, on the other by deep wine and vivid yellow.

Lutha wiped her mouth. "Do they all have individual patterns?"

Snark nodded.

"No two alike?"

"Not that I've seen." Snark spat onto the dirt with an apologetic shrug. "I don't think we can see all of it."

Despite the difficulty of talking, Lutha persisted.

"Couldn't that be what Leelson sensed as a name? An individual pattern?"

Snark shrugged, raised her eyebrows, mimed possible agreement, all the while choking and hawking.

Lutha gave up. She would pursue the question later. For now, she'd assume each of them had an individual pattern that might extend beyond visible wavelengths, a pattern of which humans might see only a part. For all they knew, the terrible taste might be part of the creatures' titles!

The one to the left of Diagonal Red was probably the one Snark called Four Green Spot. It, too, had drawn in its tentacles and was repeating its pattern. If their patterns were their names, then they were saying their names, over and over.

Lutha tried it silently: "My name is ——. My name is ——." Why were they telling the humans? A nice point of linguistics! Under what circumstances do creatures announce their names?

Perhaps when they want others to know they have names? Perhaps when they want others to know they are not bees or ants but beings? Or perhaps even to say that ants and bees *are* beings?

Leely had returned to a point opposite the peek hole. Now he stood facing the rock pile, looking up, his bare little body mottled with chill.

Not mottled. Colored. On his smooth chest and belly a patch of bright scarlet bloomed, bordered on one side in violet and on the other side by deep wine and yellow.

The enormous being above him made a roaring sound, so thunderous and terrible that those who were watching cringed. Colors fled across its underside. Pictures of Rottens, pictures of Leely being grabbed, drawn in, his bones falling from the sky.

And on Leely's belly, nothing but the colored pattern. No pictures.

"Tell it back," cried Snark out the peek hole. "Oh, little boy, tell it back! Tell it you'll kill it dead!"

But Leely made no pictures. Just the pattern, then another Rotten's pattern, then another's. Lutha pressed her face into her hands, not to see, oh, not to see. Leely had never made pictures that moved. To send a message, he would need motion, but his art was a static art.

It wasn't even art, blared a voice in her mind. *It's no more art than an echo is art. Or a reflection in a mirror. It's reproduction, not interpretation.* Leelson's voice, too well remembered.

"He can't," she said brokenly. "He can't answer it."

"What's happening?" demanded Leelson from behind them.

Lutha stood aside to let him see.

"They're hurt!" exclaimed Leelson. "Or they're scared! By my lineage!"

He plunged off among the stones with Lutha at his heels. They erupted into the open inside that monstrous, fleshy chimney where all the tentacles were raised, all the bellies smooth, all showing pictures of Leely dying, of Lutha being devoured, of Leelson's violent demise.

Unaware they were doing so, they cringed at the sight. Farther up the hill, Leely stood unmoved, staring up at all the colors, waving his hands and singing, "Dananana, Dananana."

Then the great circle fell apart. Rottens sluggishly sagged away toward the sea, pieces of themselves bulging, almost detaching, then being tugged back with lurching effort. These were the ones Leely had touched, now barely coherent as they bobbled awkwardly down the valley. Some barely made it past the beach; some went a little farther out before they fell and floated, amorphous balloons, black bulges against the bright sky and brighter sea. The shaggies took no notice as the Rottens moved out like sinking ships, wallowing out under their own erratic power, out and down, lower and lower, the waves breaking over them at last.

Those few Rottens that had severed their tentacles moved in quite another direction, straight up, dwindling in distance, vanishing at the zenith. . . .

And beneath the watching humans, the world trembled, shivered, rang like a gigantic bell, the vibration dying away to leave them sprawled, deafened, only half-conscious.

Silence, then. A long, disapproving silence.

Who? What? They could not tell. Over the sea, the grid of shaggies remained quiet, all tentacles withdrawn. All around, the moor was soundless, no branch quivering in even the slightest breeze. No seabird cried. No fish splashed. They looked at one another, themselves silent, mouths open, eyes wide. Nothing.

"Dananana." A fretful cry.

Lutha staggered toward Leely where he spun on his bare feet, staring at the sky, still calling, "Dananana." His mouth pushed out, pouting. He had liked all those pretty colors. He had been having fun. Lutha watched him, possessed by a sudden and terrible disorientation. Who was he? What was he?

And she stumbled to a halt, hand to mouth to muffle the sound she felt boiling from her throat. She knew what he was! She knew who he was!

Snark stumbled past her, knife in hand, single-mindedly set on taking samples of dropped tentacles. Lutha saw her sawing away at the great, lumpy coils while beyond her Leely danced in and out of the furze, waving, giggling. Lutha didn't follow him. She was incapable of motion. After a few moments he tired of playing hide-and-seek by himself and came to put his hand in hers. She made herself close her hand, turning like an automaton to follow Snark as she rejoined the others.

They approached Leelson where he stood leaning against a stone, the glasses at his eyes, searching the land around them.

"What was that?" Leelson asked Snark. "That earthquake?"

"Like what's happened before," she said softly. "Only closer. Angrier. Something here's not liking us much."

Everything here didn't like them, Lutha thought. The whole world was arrayed against them, and with good reason.

"How . . . how did Leely get out there?" she demanded, barely able to speak over her sick certainty.

"I sent him," said Leelson with a level look. "And I would do the same again."

It had not occurred to her that he would simply admit it.

"He could have been killed," she said. "He could have been . . ." This was foolishness, and she knew it, but her tongue went on making words her heart did not believe!

"I thought it unlikely," he replied.

"You had no right—"

"Saluez is in labor. She would have died had this siege continued. She may die regardless. And her child."

Lutha opened her mouth, but nothing came out. He would have sent Leely out if there had been no Saluez. Saluez was only an excuse, but she was a good excuse, one Lutha could not argue now.

"Dananana." Unhelpfully.

"I'll go to her," Lutha said stiffly. Later she would deal with Leelson. When she had more time to tell him a terrible thing. When he had time to hear.

"I'll go with you," said Snark, with a glance at the zenith, where the Rottens had vanished. "I guess they're gone! Who'll take this sample down and put it in the analyzer?"

The ex-king took the packet from her and trudged off toward the camp.

"Come on," she said, nudging Lutha. "I know a bit about baby taking."

"I didn't know shadows—" Lutha murmured.

"Before I was a shadow," she interrupted with an exasperated look. "When I was a street rat. Street rats get pregnant like real people. But they don't have *responsible sponsors* to sign for their babies. Who'd sign for a street rat's kid? So they can't go to a registered birther. They have 'em unofficial, like." She shook her head. "Street rats don't eat too good, they get beat on a lot. Sometimes they have a hard time! Let's hope Saluez won't."

They scrambled back into the cavern, where Lutha harnessed Leely to his pillar once more, fastening the latches of the tether, making a sound she was surprised to hear coming from her own throat, half a snarl, half a moan.

"What?" demanded Snark, turning a surprised face.

Lutha pressed her eyes with her fingers, shutting down the frenzied, ugly thoughts that possessed her. "Not now," she said. "We have other things to do now."

Besides, she told herself, trying to calm her frantic mind, the matter didn't concern Snark. It concerned Leelson. Leelson and Limia, and their damned posterity!

Snark didn't pursue the matter, for one look at Saluez was enough to push other concerns aside. Saluez's labor was proceeding without her, so to speak. Her body heaved and pushed, but her mind had gone elsewhere.

"Jiacare," said Snark. "She's filthy. So are we. We'll need some wash water."

He picked up a bucket and went out. Snark knelt beside Saluez, a strange expression on her face. "Dinadhi," she said, as though to herself. "It's her first birth and she's Dinadhi."

"Of course she is," Lutha said impatiently.

Snark nodded to herself, rubbing her forehead fretfully, then went across the cavern to busy herself among the emergency kits.

"What are you doing?" Lutha asked.

"Making a catch bucket."

"What in . . . ?"

Snark stopped, staring at the wall as though puzzled at Lutha's question. "Saluez is Dinadhi. My mother, she . . . said, have a catch bucket, with a lid."

Lutha pursed her lips and forbid herself to say anything at all. Some cultures made quite a ceremony disposing of the placenta and umbilical cord, and perhaps it was for that reason that Snark had emptied the contents from a folding emergency kit, had resealed the sides and top, and was now cutting a narrow opening into it. Whatever Snark's reason, she needed help less than Saluez did.

The floor beneath the unconscious woman was a sodden mess. Lutha dragged Saluez to a drier spot, removed her filthy robes—little filthier than Lutha's own—and covered her with clean blankets. While she was doing this the ex-king returned with a full bucket, put it near the stove, and departed with a nervous look in Saluez's direction.

Lutha scrubbed her hands and arms, then bathed Saluez as best she could. Snark finished her self-imposed task and rejoined Lutha, bringing her "catch basket" with her: an emergency kit with a hand-sized opening surrounded by latches cannibalized from other kits.

Snark set it down with a thump. "The lid," she said, adding a thick slab roughly cut from another kit.

Lutha was muttering over the lack of medical equipment. Had it been oversight? Or had it been purposeful? Had those who sent the shadows to Perdur Alas not cared that they might be hurt or ill? Or had they simply not thought about it?

Snark tapped her. "Stop fuming. There's antibiotics in the kits. We'll make do with those."

Growling, Lutha went to fetch them while Snark dug out several of the unused overalls and ripped them up to make a dry bed between Saluez and the floor.

"She's sucking that veil in every time she breathes," Snark said. "Let's get it off her."

Lutha removed it and set it aside, turning back at Snark's exclamation.

"Her face!"

Saluez's face was a whole face. Like Lutha's. Like Snark's. No bone showing through. No mutilated lips or eyelids. One ear was still slightly battered looking, but even that flesh was smooth.

"How?" breathed Snark.

Lutha had no idea. The woman between them moaned, a remote, careless sound. Her eyes stayed blank. She wasn't there. She didn't know what had happened to her.

They propped Saluez's knees on folded blankets.

"What else?" asked Lutha.

"We wait."

"I'm tired of waiting."

Lutha stared at Saluez, her face, her form, the skin of her legs. She'd never seen a natural birth before. Leely, of course, but there had been medical people there, able to handle any emergency. What would they do if Saluez was in trouble?

"What?" asked Snark.

"Just . . . my mind, pestering me. I need to think about something else."

Snark grinned ferociously. "Think about this. I hated you, you know?"

Lutha swallowed. "So you said."

Snark squirmed, settling herself, her eyes on Saluez. "I got to thinking about that. Truth was, it wasn't just you. I hated ever'body. Ever since they called me a liar and thief in that home, I hated 'em.'"

She scowled, lines of concentration between her eyebrows. "Thing is, I got to figuring, it wasn't just me! It'd been the same for any female. If it'd been a boy and they'd called him a liar, he'd have said so what and who wants his nose flattened over it?"

"Probably," Lutha said, intrigued.

"Boys get in a fight, nobody thinks much about it. Boys tell a few stories, or thief a few things, boys'll be boys, an' nobody says civilization's coming to an end. Do they?"

"Not usually," Lutha agreed. "But you think it's different with girls?"

"Girls go for somebody, they're out of control! People at the home said that; justice machine said that. Snark, you're out of control! I never done anything men I knew didn't do, and they're still back on Central, scavenging and telling lies, just like always. Men a lot like Mitigan, killing folks right and left. Men like Leelson, doing whatever he wants . . ."

Saluez moaned. Snark's voice trailed off, waiting. The moan didn't go anywhere. It fell off into quiet, and Snark resumed her discourse.

"It's different for women. And for some men. Men like the old Procurator, I guess. And for the king too."

"Jiacare?"

"Him, yeah. Old Proc and the king, they're more like Saluez, trying to be in control all the time. More like you."

"Like me?" Lutha was astonished.

"Yeah. You carry on—crying, laughing. Flapping around sometimes like a bird. Lotsa drama, you know, but down at the bottom of it, you're like Saluez too. Trying to hang on."

Lutha laughed, a hollow sound. "Drama," she said. "My family does have a tendency toward . . . drama."

Snark accepted this. "What I think is, men, they can rape and ruin, maim and murder, kill each other off in dozen lots, so long as there's one left, he can make babies enough for the next go-round without even working very hard at it. If you're a woman or a king, though, you got more invested than that, right? You got yourself invested in civility, 'cause that's what's safe for people. You get invested like that, you got to be righteous and do the looking out for other people. There's the young ones, the old ones, the sick ones. Got to stay in there, hoping for something different . . ."

Saluez moaned again. Snark wrapped several folds of her shirt around her hands, like clumsy mittens, watching intently while Lutha wet a cloth and wiped Saluez's sweaty face.

Lutha asked, "You think that's what Saluez is doing? Hoping for something different?"

"Saluez says she wants to lie in sweet grass, eating apples," said Snark. "That's different. That's paradise. Like it was on Breadh."

"Were there many people on Breadh?"

Snark laughed, abruptly joyous. "Hardly any! That's what made it paradise! I told Kane the Brain about Breadh. He said we all make up an Eden. Some old-time place. Some never-never place. Someplace just over the hill, maybe, where things're the way things used to be, ought to be, the way they never were."

Lutha caught her breath, aware of a sudden pain behind her breastbone. Not her heart. Lung and stomach, probably, contending for the title of chief dramatist. It hurt, nonetheless. "Can't there be a real Eden?" she gasped, astonished at the pain the question evoked. "Somewhere? Can't there?"

Snark shrugged. "We could make one here if we wanted. We could make one anywhere, if we would. Instead it's apples and sweet grass, long gone, long past. Kane said we ate them all—"

Saluez shrieked abruptly, a senseless sound that accompanied a seemingly endless convulsion. Her teeth ground together. Her belly heaved and clenched.

"Why is she unconscious?" Lutha demanded. She hadn't been unconscious when Leely was born. Women who chose to give birth usually chose to experience it.

"She's Dinadhi," Snark replied, as though this meant something. Then she shook her head in momentary confusion. "I think I remember what Mother told me. I hope I haven't forgotten. I think we have to do this thing first. . . ."

"Do what first?"

The question was answered, but not by Snark. Saluez shrieked mindlessly. Out from between her legs came a white thing, a bloody white thing, a small head with closed and bulging eyes, a wide mouth that showed the tips of sharp little teeth. The moment the head came into the light, the eyes opened and the teeth began snapping, snapping at them, the eyes glaring.

"Quick!" shouted Snark, grabbing at the thing with her mittened hands, wrenching it from Saluez's body, and thrusting it through the narrow neck of her recently manufactured catch bucket. Despite the wrappings of cloth, the thing brought blood from her arm, leaving a nasty gash.

"Watch out," she cried. "There may be more!"

There were two more. Snark got one, and Lutha got the other one, while one part of herself gibbered mindlessly and some other part demanded that she should not behave stupidly in front of Snark. The creatures were slimy and pale, they shrieked and gnashed, and the gaping slits along their backs quivered like gills as grim-faced Snark thrust them into her bucket and fastened the lid down tight.

When the contractions stopped and it was clear there were to be no more of them, Snark tied the catch bucket top with line and put it inside one of the larger supply cases, which she also lashed closed. The entire bundle rocked and shrieked at them as they returned their attentions to Saluez. She had expelled the afterbirth. With it was what remained of the infant she had carried.

Snark wrapped the bloody fragments in the clean cloths they had intended to receive a living child.

"Did you get bitten?" she asked matter-of-factly.

"A little," said Lutha faintly. "What . . . ?"

"It most always happens," Snark said, her eyes wide and unfocused. "Mother said it's a rare thing that a first baby lives. Sometimes it does, if there's only one scourge inside, but usually there's at least three or four of them."

Lutha trembled, unable to get any words out. Now she knew where the next generation of Kachis were on Dinadh. Even now they were being incubated and born.

"They didn't have wings," she said stupidly.

"Those slits down the back," Snark replied. "As soon as they dry, the wings pop out. They can fly almost right away." She shook her head. "These looked sort of not ripe, though, didn't they?"

Lutha had no idea what a ripe Kachis would look like. "How does this happen?"

Snark made a face, a spitting sound. "It's the Dinadhi way. It's part of the choice the songfathers made. First time a woman's pregnant, a helper takes her to the House Without a Name. They take food and water so the scourges won't be hungry or thirsty. And the helper ties her down on the table and then rings a gong, and maybe one or two scourges come and lay eggs in her. They've got these long pricky-looking ovipositors. But sometimes instead of one or two coming, lots of them come and eat on the woman's face. Only the face, though. No other parts."

She wiped at her cheeks with the back of one bloody hand. "And when comes time for the woman to have the baby, the scourges get born first. The midwives take 'em and feed 'em and turn 'em loose as soon as their wings're dry. And then, if the scourges didn't eat it, the baby is born."

"But why do the Dinadhi do it?" Lutha screamed.

"I'm tellin' you! The songfathers *command* it, so's there'll be *beautiful people* to hold all the people who die. Places for their souls to go. The women are supposed to have this duty so the people can live forever."

Snark took a deep breath. "If the baby's messed up but alive, they take it away somewhere."

"By the Great and Glorious Org Gauphin," Lutha said fervently. "Knowing all this, why does any Dinadhi woman get pregnant!"

Snark shared a bitter half smile. "They don't know it. It's taboo to talk about it. All the girls know is there's a kind of a trial they have to go through to become a woman, but they don't get told about it until after it's happened."

Saluez shifted and groaned.

"What shall we tell her?" Lutha demanded.

"How about telling her the truth. That she had scourges inside her. That we've got 'em in a box. That her baby died."

"That her baby never developed. That's true, too, and it'll be easier for her."

Snark shook her head, mimicking Lutha viciously, "Oh, yeah, by all means, make it easier."

"Snark! Why not?"

"I was just thinking of my flippin' life," she growled. "That nobody was much concerned about making easier."

"Your mother was! Whatever else happened, she saved you from this!" Lutha waved at the shrieking box, the supine form, the bloody rags. "You didn't have to experience this!"

Snark flushed, then her eyes filled and she sobbed, once only. "Yeah," she whispered. "Yeah." She sounded so sad that Lutha reached for her, but Snark evaded the embrace, ducking her head and stepping away.

They bathed Saluez again and wrapped her warmly. She began to breathe more easily.

Snark said, "She'll wake up anytime now. Once the scourges have time to get dry and fly away, then the mother can wake up."

Saluez's eyelids fluttered.

Lutha said, "You're all right, Saluez."

Saluez murmured something, about a baby.

"Rest," said Lutha, helplessly.

Snark shook her head disapprovingly, saying in a firm voice, "You didn't have a baby, Saluez. It never developed. You had scourge . . . Kachis eggs in you and they kept the baby from growing."

Saluez made a lost, lonely sound. She was not truly there, had not truly heard.

Lutha held her, whispering, "They're gone, Saluez. The things are gone. Snark knew what to do."

"Sad," murmured Saluez. "No baby. So sad."

"No baby, but a miracle," said Snark. "Feel your face, Saluez. Feel your face!" She took Saluez's hand and thrust it almost roughly against her cheek, the one that had been riven so the teeth showed through. "It's healed, Saluez."

"It's a miracle," said Lutha. "Weaving Woman did it."

". . . not," breathed Saluez. "Leely. . . ."

"He's safe," said Lutha. "He's fine."

"Has to be fine," Saluez whispered. "Nothing else for him. . . ."

Then she shuddered and was gone again, her breast moving gently, her face calm.

"Now that's normal sleep," said Snark, wiping her face again. There were bloody streaks on both cheeks. "And she needs it."

Behind them the lashed box rocked and rustled.

"What do we do with them?" Lutha asked.

"Drown 'em," said Snark. "I'll do it."

"Drown what?" asked Jiacare from among the stones. He came into the entrance, water still beaded on his skin, his hair streaming down his back.

Snark went to him and they muttered together, his voice rising angrily. Lutha went to the stove to heat more water. She was filthy. She smelled to herself like a tidal flat. She resolved to wash her hair, at least, while she kept an eye on Saluez.

The ex-king came to fetch the lashed box, his face hard and furious. He started to speak to Lutha, then merely shook his head, making a gesture of frustration. Lutha gulped, getting hold of herself. Jiacare felt as she herself did. As Snark did. Angry at . . . what? The songfathers? Much good would that do Saluez. At the Kachis, the Ularians, the whatevers? Much good would that do anybody!

She poured water over her head, surprised that it didn't go up in steam, then set about soaping and rinsing, interrupting the task whenever Saluez made a sound or changed position. She was stripping the water from her hair when Leelson arrived.

"Leelson . . ."

"Snark told me," he muttered as he knelt beside Saluez and closed his eyes. After a long moment he said, "She's not grieving."

"I think she knew," Lutha replied, combing her wet hair with her fingers. "A secret like that can't be kept. No doubt there were whispers, even on Dinadh. I think she knew, but she didn't admit it to herself. I'm so thankful Snark was here."

"She says you were bitten."

"It's really only a scratch." A scratch that burned like fire. She rummaged among the odds and ends, looking for a comb, finding one at the bottom of a personal kit.

"Jiacare and Snark went to drown the things."

She grunted angrily. Good for them!

He drummed his fingers, a little rat-a-tat to accompany thought. "Do you have any explanation for what happened?"

"To Saluez?"

"No. Snark explained that. I mean with Leely. How he is capable of . . . doing what he's done?"

So here they were at last, at the subject of her revelation, at the answer that had come to her, finally, when it was too late to solve anything between her and Leelson!

She put down the comb, folded her hands in her lap, took a deep breath, found a knob of stone over Leelson's left shoulder, and fixed her eyes on it intently. She would not be bellicose. She would be calm.

"You used to talk to me about your great-great-grandpop. You told me he was the biochemist to end all biochemists, a genius, a savant, a polymath. We both know he went off to investigate the Ularians and ended up on Dinadh. We can assume he saw Kachis on Dinadh, and they raised certain questions in his mind. There was an analyzer among his equipment at Cochim-Mahn. Just as Snark has fed pieces of the shaggies into her analyzer, Bernesohn no doubt fed pieces of Kachis into his. Then Tospia visited him. She went home pregnant. One hundred years later, precisely when he is needed, a boy of Bernesohn's lineage, *your son Leely,* turns up with this trait deadly to the Ularians. . . ."

She paused, shifting her eyes to his face. He had gone rigid, eyes staring at nothing, in that moment resembling Limia, feature for feature, his expression of rejection and repudiation exactly like hers. Limia and her damned Fastigat lineage! Limia grieving over Leelson's posterity!

Oh, by the Great Gauphin, Lutha prayed, let me live long enough to tell her!

She couldn't keep the anger from her voice. "What part of that do you find hard to understand?"

"Impossible!" he growled, very red in the face. "That's impossible. Ridiculous!"

Well, well. In all the time they had been together, she had never seen Leelson truly dismayed until now. How marvelous!

"How would you know?" she cried, boiling with five years' fury. "You're only an ordinary Fastigat. Bernesohn was out of your class, or so you've told me."

"But none of the family . . . not my father, not his father, and not me, certainly . . ."

"So? Somehow Bernesohn arranged this talent to lie low for a few generations. Until it was needed!"

"I don't know how he'd do that."

A new speaker heard from! Snark, leaning against a pillar at the entrance of the chamber, where she'd obviously been listening for some time. "They force-fed me a pretty fair technical education, and I don't know a way this could happen all at once, out of nothing."

"Maybe the trait emerges only if the taste of Rottens is in the air," Lutha muttered.

"Then I'd have it," said Leelson. "I've tasted Rottens."

These were mere quibbles. "I don't *know* how Bernesohn did it, but I'm damned sure it's not coincidence. It happened because he's your son!"

"Dananana," caroled Leely, waving his hands and plucking at his trousers. "Dananana."

Oh, marvelous anticlimax! "I need to take him out," Lutha said furiously. "Is it safe to go out?"

Snark shrugged, her go-to-hell shrug, but her eyes were wary. "Safe as it ever is, but don't get careless, Lutha. I've had a bath at the edge of the water, and you look like you could use one, but keep an eye out."

Lutha did not reply. She stalked out past Leelson, Leely trotting along at her side, sometimes moistly kissing Lutha's wounded wrist, sometimes petting her arm. They passed Jiacare Lostre as he returned empty-handed from the sea, and Mitigan, who sat quietly on a rock, his face flushed with sunset, both of them looking like shiny new people. Lutha lusted for water, much water, and for clean air after all those hours of tasting rottenness in the claustrophobic stone chamber. She wanted to wash it away! She wanted to wash Leelson away!

Leely tugged at her hand, leading her over the ridge and down toward the scarlet shine of water and sky. The first line of shaggies seemed a safe distance away. At the shore, Leely peeled his trousers off and waded into the water to do his business. He liked to do that, whenever water was available. He'd been born able to swim. She watched him paddle, sometimes diving, feet in air, taking mouthfuls of water and spurting them like the legendary whale, he all silver and rose like the waters, like the sky. She took off her filthy clothes and waded in far enough that she could dunk all of herself. The water was cleansing, not very salty, but chill. She scrubbed at her body with handfuls of the powdery bottom sand, then waded out and sat like a monument on a pedestal of stone, letting the soft wind dry her while her filthy clothing soaked in the nearest pool.

Leely came up a good way out, clutching a fish, laughing. Not far beyond him, a shaggy lowered its tentacles. Leely took a bite out of the flapping fish, then threw the remainder into the lowered tentacles. Lutha shuddered, again aware of her son's surpassing strangeness. For years this uncanny presence had shared her days, clear as noon, while she denied and refused to see that he wasn't just a little boy, not just a child, not just her beloved son. She had been like Saluez, facing the unbearable, rejecting it.

"You're very beautiful."

Leelson was standing behind her, staring at her, looking wistful. Leelson never looked wistful!

"You used to say so," she said, swallowing deeply as she grabbed up the sodden robes and draped them around her shoulders, trying to put revelation and seduction both aside. She didn't want to talk, not about the two of them, not about Leely, not about anything.

Fastigats paid no attention to that! With them, nothing could remain unsaid, undefined, unfulfilled. "You really think Bernesohn Famber designed . . . that?" He gestured toward the splashing child. "Why isn't he intelligent?"

His expression was very much like Limia's had been. Stubborn. Dismissive. Lutha swallowed again and said stubbornly, "We don't know that he isn't."

It rang false, even to her. Why not say it? Why not get it over with?

"It's because Bernesohn had the same expectations as your mother,

Leelson! He expected you to beget with a woman from Fastiga, not some
. . . outsider! If you'd had a Fastigat woman, Leely would have been all
right." The bitterness boiled to the surface, shaming her. She couldn't
control it. It wasn't fair. None of it.

He ignored her tone. "I wonder if Tospia knew? When she left here,
when she had the twins, Tospiann and Paniwar, I wonder if she knew one
or both of them had been *designed* by Bernesohn."

"If they were, he forgot to plan on redundancy. Twin children, one of
whom—was it your great-grandmama?—had only one child. And your
grandpa, and your father."

He nodded. "It's true Great-grandmother Tospiann had only one
child, but Paniwar had an acknowledged son and a number of daughters,
in addition to at least one . . . escapade."

"Improper fathering," she said, quoting the two dowagers in Fastiga.

He made a rueful face. "An early dalliance with a member of a traveling troupe. On one of the Nantask planets. He was little more than a
boy at the time, and she was twice his age." He was watching Lutha
closely, digging at her.

Déjà vu. She herself had told this story, as Leelson had told it to her
before. She wanted to change the subject, but he wouldn't let her.

"Her name was Dasalum," he said. "She was a celebrity, a superb
actress. It was her fault Paniwar committed improper fathering. She
went off in a temper and the Fambers never did find out what happened
to the child." He watched me, waiting.

A long silence. She could feel him, probing, probing. He'd brought
this up for a reason. She resisted, resisted, then cracked, letting in the
light. Her revelation hadn't gone far enough. And she couldn't lie to
him. He'd know if she did.

She said, "In Nantaskan, her name was D'ahslum T'bir, which means
bonetree. Skeleton." She looked at her hand, surprised. All on its own it
was drawing a lineage chart in the sand.

"And?" asked Leelson.

"She bore a daughter whose name was Nitha Bonetree."

"How do you know?"

"I didn't until just now. But it's the only thing that makes sense."
Lutha looked away, willing him to let it alone, willing him to stop!

He wouldn't stop. "And why is that?"

"Because Nitha Bonetree was my great-grandmother."

He didn't change expressions. She had told him all about her family when they were together. In the last little while he'd figured everything out, everything she hadn't put together until now. She looked down at the chart she'd drawn:

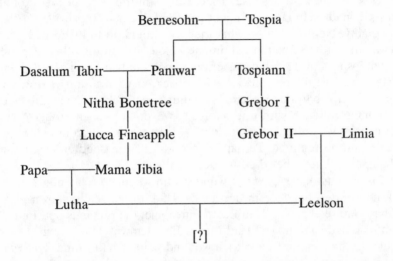

She didn't add Leely's name. He was out there splashing, making bright fountains. The sun bulged on the sea, a fire blister, scarlet veins bleeding along the horizon. The shaggies reeled in fish, flapping silhouettes against the glow. She wanted to scream, yell, throw things, but the moment was too precarious. Not as she had thought. Not as she had thought at all.

"Now we know how Bernesohn managed to do it," Leelson said at last. "That's why he fathered twins. On that old chip we played, he didn't mean 'rejoinder' in a legal sense. He meant 'rejoindure.' Rejoindure of his lineage. Half the virus in one line, half in the other. A virus made from Kachis, from Ularian life. One it would have no antibodies against."

What could she say? What was there to say?

He stared at the dying sun. "Tospia must have known! She was supposed to tell the twins. 'Daddy invented a weapon, children. Daddy didn't want to lock it away in a laboratory somewhere, where it might be lost or forgotten or misused—' "

"Why lost or misused, necessarily?"

"In Bernesohn's time, the government was . . ."

"Mostly non-Fastigat," she supplied bitterly. "Your great-grandpop didn't trust us ordinary people."

Leelson went on as though she hadn't spoken. "Actually, what he did makes a certain kind of sense. There were still things he needed to find out on Dinadh. He knew he might be killed. He had to provide for that eventuality. He didn't know what the virus would do to its host. He had no way to test it. So he put half in one zygote, half in the other, depending on Tospia's pride in her posterity to keep the twins well guarded and protected. If he wasn't killed, he'd be back on Central long before the twins grew to reproductive age. If he didn't get back, he knew the twins wouldn't reproduce with one another! We don't even reproduce with first cousins very often, so it would be at least two generations before the virus could be reunited. Perhaps Bernesohn had learned enough about Tahs-uppi to know they'd be needed by then. . . ."

"Tospia must have known. I wonder who forgot to tell whom?"

Lutha buried her face in her hands. Had Tospia really known? Had Nitha Bonetree known? Had Lucca Fineapple, the religious nut, Lutha's grandma, had she known? Had Mama Jibia known? Unlikely in the extreme. Lutha's mother hadn't known, and neither had Lutha. Five generations back to Paniwar Famber, and nobody had known.

"How did the strain stay pure?" she asked from a dry throat. "It would have been diluted."

"Not if it were carried quiescent in the reproductive cells. A virus is just a machine for making more viruses. We're still carrying around viral fragments from prehistoric times. They merely inhabit, reproducing themselves from generation to generation but not . . . doing anything."

"Until it met up with its other half," she murmured. "But there's only two in my family, Yma and me. And there's only one of you. Surely that was depending a great deal upon fate."

This line of thought didn't delight him, obviously. He scowled. "Bernesohn assumed there'd be lots of descendants from both sides, well spread out among the rest of humanity. Bernesohn himself was prolific. He had half a dozen Fastigat mates and children by all of them; he'd have expected the twins to produce a horde."

"But that didn't happen. There was only you and me. Our meeting was accidental. No one planned it. Almost too neat, Leelson!"

"Too neat to be believed, Lutha. Bernesohn no doubt built in some kind of attractant. Something that would gain effectiveness in each generation." He frowned at the sea. Dirty. Unhappy.

"You're filthy," she suggested, wanting desperately to be let alone. "Why don't you at least wash yourself!"

He wandered off toward the water and began stripping off his clothes. She stared into the sunset, trying not to think of anything at all. Until now she'd regarded their affair, Leelson's and hers, as the summit of her life, the single most exciting and marvelous thing she had experienced. From the day he'd come to her door, she'd kept a journal, just to memorialize the wonder of it, so the episodes would never fade, never dwindle. Since he'd left, night after night, she'd reread it, reliving their time together. Certain expressions, certain words, certain actions. They'd been made for each other, she had told herself.

Yes. Well. So they had. Not quite as she had imagined. It had not been the inscrutable stars that had brought them together. Instead they'd responded to one another like any two moths or frogs or beetles. Leelson was right: Bernesohn had made sure of bringing his great-grandchildren together. He'd built in some attractant. Perhaps a pheromone, growing more potent with each generation, some chemical lure that wafted for great distances, bringing them both to that library. A time bomb in their reproductive cells, set to go off!

How dared Bernesohn Famber do such a thing!

"Don't be angry with him," said Leelson, standing naked at the water's edge, following her thoughts as though she had spoken them aloud.

"Leave me alone, Leelson."

"Think of Saluez's face, Lutha. Look at your wrist. Bernesohn was trying to save the human race." He entered the water, scooping it over his shoulders and body in ruby showers, watching her all the while.

She looked at her wrist. Healed, of course, By Leely, her son, their son, no one's son. Leelson was right. Bernesohn's task, as he'd seen it, was to save the human race. To create a magic bullet that would ricochet around among humanity. One that would kill off the enemy and heal the afflicted at the same time. Or perhaps the healing power was simply a side effect. Serendipity.

Tospia probably *had* known. Maybe Paniwar and Tospiann had been told, as soon as they were old enough to understand it. Which was probably *after* Paniwar had fathered her great-grandma. "You can't screw around like this," his mother had no doubt said. "You're too important. You carry the secret weapon. You're the possessor of our heritage, our survival."

"Don't romanticize either," Leelson cautioned her, standing tall as he stripped the water from his golden head.

She could barely keep from screaming at him. "Please, Leelson. We've done our genetic duty. Now can't we at least leave one another alone." It took all her willpower not to weep hysterically.

"I don't think he invented a way to turn it off," he said helplessly, returning to her with arms open.

She tried not to respond. Oh, she tried, but it didn't work. Leelson was right, of course. Bernesohn had made them for one another, and he hadn't included a way to shut it off.

They had only just lain down that night, all too weary to extend the evening beyond the bare necessities of food and shaking out the blankets, when they came up off the floor as though alerted by some bone-deep klaxon.

Lutha felt a surge of adrenaline, then that stopped-up-ears feeling she sometimes got when swimming, that muffled, gurgling-in-one's-head effect. She yawned widely, momentarily surprised to see the others yawning too. Obviously, it had affected them all. Snark had her fingers in her ears; Mitigan was gaping like a fish; they all looked apologetically at one another as they tried to clear a way for sound that should be there but was not. The sea was a shush, and the wind a hush, and the birds a shrill *tee-tee-tee*, all flat, muffled, without resonance.

"It's happening again," mouthed Snark, grasping Lutha by the shoulder. "Like the night you first came!"

Flinching at the strength of her grip, Lutha nodded. It was very much like what had happened before, only more so. There was a panicky breathlessness along with the soundlessness. They gathered around Saluez's recumbent form while the effect went on, still with no discernible cause. Mitigan's hands were busy with his weapons, which rather increased their apprehension.

Far off, a muted thunder. Though Lutha considered it an odd-sounding thunder, it was more like thunder than it was like an avalanche or a volcano. She shared significant looks with the others, looks meaning more or less, "Did you hear what I heard?" mouthing the word "Thunder?" following this with agreeable nods. Yes. Thunder.

None of them really believed it. First Leelson grimaced, then the others, for it *hadn't* been thunder and they all knew it. Through the cracks among the stones the stars shone clearly in an unclouded sky.

Again the stones around them shuddered, the soil beneath them trembled. This pulse repeated at long intervals, two, three, four, five times. Then nothing. Still the flat sound, the muted uncanniness, the breathlessness. Saluez gasped, her eyes still closed. Lutha felt as she had at the Nodders: terrified of something without knowing what. As the Nodders had been unnatural, so this was unnatural.

"At his feet the mountains skip," whispered Saluez. *"At his step the worlds tremble. See him treading down the star trails, the Gracious One, potent and victorious."* Tears were running beside her nose, at the corners of her mouth, dripping from her jaw. Lutha apprehended her words clearly, though she had no sensation of hearing her.

"What?" breathed the ex-king, falling to his knees beside Saluez.

"A songfather hymn," whispered Snark, her hand on Jiacare's shoulder, her eyes fixed on the stone above them. "From Dinadh."

Songfather hymn or not, Lutha couldn't stop the words from repeating in her mind, over and over. *At his feet the mountains skip.* As on a screen, the letters moved right to left, then started over as her body tensed in rhythm with the thudding of those feet. As her lungs gasped for air, so her ears gasped for something to hear, inventing sounds where there were none, creating them, labeling them, recognizing them though she had never sensed them before:

Touch of hooved feet upon mountains, crack of horn upon horn, rasp of battle breath, slow drumbeat of heart and sinew, final bellow of supremacy. Pad of soft toes through jungles, herb scent slipping between parted jaws to flow across the tongue, night-tasting, prey-finding, huff of soft nostrils flared, whisker tips tracing the night, spotted hide sleeking like silk among the grasses, low rumble in the throat like a bass string bowed, ominous, peremptory. Shuffle of nailed feet below mighty legs, thewed as a tree grown up with vines, billowed dust blown over hides thick as boards, ears wide as doors, massive movers, a trumpet call across tree-bowered stone-speckled savannas. Water surging along slick hides, flick of fins, eyes in the depth turned upward toward liquid-trembling gray light. Beaks cleaving air, chill along the quills, knife edge of wind-buffeting wing, steel grip of talons, amber-slitted horizon-compassing eye.

Blood on the stone. Whether from the deep or the height, whether from mountain or jungle, whether from claw or talon, beak or fang, blood on the stone, rising up to live again. The very soundlessness was their sound—its sound—and all the other senses as well. They stretched, reaching for being. In silence, sound. In darkness, sight. In nothingness, touch.

The sacrifice, it says. *All living is by sacrifice. For one creature to live, another one must die. What will you give me? Where is mine?*

It speaks to her! It says: *Oh, feel how you have unvoiced us. See how you have cut us down. Hear our silent cries! Our worlds were full of the murmur and clatter of being, now listen to the silence we inhabit, all our spirits, still!*

"Lutha?" Leelson, holding out his hand.

"Nothing," she said in a voice she didn't recognize as her own. "It's nothing."

What was it? Not nothing. What were these visions? Things she had seen as a child in sensurround? Fairy tales? Stories of olden times? Creatures out of dream? Creatures come out of time?

Silence, silence, silence, even while the voice spoke, saying: *So you may remember, we give you silence. Where we should be, but are not, there is silence.*

What was this listening? Attenuated, the sense stretching itself outward, begging for something to fill it? Feeling one's own eyes rattling in their sockets, twitching every way, seeking an out, an escape. Why were they here, shielded from the sky? Why was this stone all around them? Why were they not there, at the sea's edge, crawling out of that salty womb onto the shore in company with the creatures of their common birth?

"Lutha!"

"Nothing," she cried again.

He shook her. "Lutha."

Lutha saw him then. Felt his violence transmitted to her own body as he ragged her to and fro, not gently.

"Leelson!" Urgently she called him, from great distance.

"Shhh," he replied, eyes suddenly aware of some outside presence as he leaned against her, pressing her equally into himself and into the stone.

All of them were pressed into the stones, clinging to them, even Saluez, edging toward the crevices and cracks they'd made their own. A stupid place to choose when skies came down. As in a dream, they saw all the great stone slabs falling, obdurate shadows piercing reverie to become horrible reality, crushing them before they knew they were in danger. Little nutkins in the mighty vise of what? And yet, what other choice? They could be beneath the stone or beneath the sky, the vengeful sky, hearing that quiet!

"Listen," Lutha whispered.

"No," said Mitigan in a horrified voice.

"Don't," cried Saluez. "Don't listen."

They were children afraid of ghosts, pulling up the blanket to cover their eyes, pulling themselves into the stone and huddling there. Even Leelson! Even Mitigan! Where is your courage, Fastigat? Where is your honor, Asenagi? Why are you huddled with the rest while this silence goes on and on and on.

Slither of scales upon stone; scutter of hairy legs, silk filament trailing the wind; hear in the silence what is not there. Cry, cry, cry, a bird who hungers; cry, cry, cry, a bird seeking her young, who will never be again. All is desert, all is dry, all is dead and gone, not even a memory. All that is left is a set of symbols, a list of bases, a pattern stored away. The machine knows them as the machine knows everything, dryly, without blood or breath, but humans do not know them at all!

Leely came drowsily naked out of some crack or crevice where he'd been sleeping, cast them a sidelong look, and went past them toward a tilted arch of starlit stone, a window onto the night, where he stood waving his hands.

Lutha didn't move. Lutha was lost among the animals. Oh, the colors of them. Oh, the sounds they make. The eyes of them, bright and quick and full of accusation. Who was Leely in the face of this . . . this!

Too battered by sensation even to be curious, she watched open-mouthed as he turned, again, again, wearing his Leely face, swaying and waving, a familiar and aimless activity. Then his face took on a new expression. Not his usual quiet satisfaction. Not his hungry look or his chilly look or his sleepy look. Not any expression she had seen before. This was something else. A kind of wakefulness.

He opened his mouth very wide, his tongue quivering in the midst of that round, red hole, deep as an abyss his throat. He screamed a sound that went endlessly out into the world. Not any sound they had ever heard him make before. Not a sound any child should be capable of making, a sound that fled unmuted across the moorlands like the shadow of a cloud, sweeping across the world, south, away: a trumpet, a roar, a shriek, a cry, a whistle, a bellow, a blast . . . They could almost watch it go!

Leelson grunted, "By my manhood!"

Mitigan shook Lutha by the shoulder. "What?"

She couldn't tell him. She didn't know!

And normal sound came back all at once, as though a finger had been snapped.

In the window Leely sucked his fingers, murmuring, "Dananana."

He had exorcised the ghosts. He had driven them away. What right had he to do that?

They breathed deep into oxygen-starved lungs.

"Lutha!" Leelson demanded. "What is this?"

"Why ask me?" she cried. "How would I know?"

"You're his mother!" he shouted.

"Bernesohn Famber was his mother and his father," she yelled back. "Bernesohn designed him. Too bad Bernesohn isn't around to give us the operating instructions."

While babble broke out all around, she sat down and wept, feeling her face smart from the salt, feeling her nose swell and turn red, that familiar pain behind her breastbone like a swallowed stone. Obviously, Leelson hadn't told them what they'd figured out about Leely. Well, neither had she. They were both . . . what? Ashamed of it? Probably. How can one tell friends and acquaintances that one's great passion, one's world-shaking romance is no more than a mating dance between ephemerids, that all one's achievements count to nothing in the face of a biological destiny hoicked up by a runaway Fastigat in a makeshift laboratory on a very minor planet!

She wept while Leelson explained, as Fastigats do, unemphatically but in great detail and with all possible inferences.

It would have bored anyone. It bored Lutha. He talked so long she tired of sniveling and began wiping the wetness from her face.

"But what is he?" Jiacare Lostre demanded.

"A virus," said Leelson, without emotion. "To all intents and purposes. Morphologically, he's human, born of a normal zygote that carries a lot of something else—something Ularian. He's a hybrid. He has enough brain to get along at the level of a . . ."

"A chicken," Lutha said bitterly, feeling a new gush of tears. There were no chickens left, but the word remained. One of those sorts of words that did remain.

"Something like that," Leelson admitted.

"Whatever he's carrying, it gets around the Ularian immune system," Snark supplied. "I found disrupted cells in the dropped tentacles, and in the dying shaggy."

Leelson nodded heavily. "He's also carrying an agent or genetic program that promotes rapid healing in humans. It's in his saliva. Probably in his blood. Maybe he had to have that to retain human shape with all that Ularian stuff in him."

"Or it was purposeful, so people would value him," offered the ex-king. "Maybe Bernesohn was looking ahead. He would want his . . . virus to survive. He knew people would value something that could heal their ills." He furrowed his brow, continuing in a doubtful voice: "Of course, that would have depended upon people knowing about it."

"He prob'ly meant 'em to know," breathed Snark. "Meant 'em to know about the whole business. He sure wouldn't depend on it bein' found out like this! By accident!"

Mitigan hoisted Leely high and presented his wounded arm, still festering and red.

"Dananana," Leely caroled, giving Mitigan's arm several wet kisses.

"Me," said Snark. The wound she'd sustained during the Kachis birthing was also inflamed. Leely kissed the bite marks. Lutha had seen dogs lick wounds like that, in old nature chips. She shook her head, ashamed. She had known about Leely's healing ability the day before. She should have told Snark. And Mitigan.

Saluez noticed her pain. She took Lutha's hand, peered into her eyes. "Lutha. Lutha, sister." Her eyes filled and Lutha turned away, unable to bear her compassion. By the Great Gauphin, Lutha didn't want anyone to share her feelings. Her feelings were her own, singular, unique!

Which was bosh. They were the world's woes, as Mama Jibia used to say. No matter what the world, the woes are the same. Pain and loss. Hope dimmed. Ambition quenched. Love becoming an unfunny joke on the lovers! Body saying aye; mind saying nay; now saying can; future saying can't.

Lutha felt Leelson reaching for her, and shook him off, surprising on his face a reflection of her own. He felt miserable. She'd planned his misery, but she hadn't realized she'd be in it with him.

And why should it be so upsetting? She'd guessed the biggest part of this. What had changed since then? Nothing, except the knowledge that she was as responsible as Leelson. Leely himself was as he had always been. Only her hopes had changed. Her hopes and whatever was out there at the edge of the world. The trembler. The world shaker.

She took Leely from Snark, settling him on her hip. It was time they went back to sleep. If they could sleep.

Leely patted her face, opened his dreadful mouth, and said quite clearly, "Lutha Lutha Tallstaff Lutha sister mother love."

It was a person's voice, totally unfamiliar, not a child's voice.

Silence. Shock. Indrawn breaths.

Leelson cleared his throat, a scritch like iron dragged on stone.

Leely turned, cocked his head, said, "Leelson Leelson Famber damned Fastigat darling."

No one even breathed.

Leely said, "Saluez of the shadow. Snark love Laluzh. Mitigan Mitigan of the Asenagi." He smiled. "Exking exking of Kamir Jiacare Lostre. Leely baby Leely love Leely yourson myson."

"He's naming things," said Leelson in a hollow voice.

"Pee—peeeple," said the ex-king, awed into virtual incoherence. "People."

Lutha had been holding Leely pressed against her, but now she felt it was safer to set him down.

"Lutha Tallstaff Lutha Lutha sister mother love," he said, making a mirror likeness of her on the skin of his chest and belly. He showed her as she was, dressed in her gray-green overall.

"Why now?" cried Leelson in petulant, almost horrified surprise. "Why *now*!"

"He's never been out among people before," whispered Saluez. "Not since he was a baby."

It was true. From the time Leelson had left them, they'd lived almost alone. Those who came and went were seldom repeat visitors. Those who came to see Lutha often did not see Leely. Only since this trip began had Leely heard Lutha's name used by this one, that one. She recalled Leelson's outraged, "You're his mother." So now she was Lutha Tallstaff Lutha Lutha sister mother love.

"When he made the pictures back to the Rottens!" she exclaimed. "That's when he made the connection. They have color titles. We have verbal ones."

"That's a title?" Leelson bellowed at the top of his lungs. "Leelson Leelson Famber damned Fastigat darling?"

"Hush," she hissed, pointing through the tilted arch at the shaggies floating against the stars. "Leelson, damn it, don't yell at me. It's not my fault; I didn't do it; I'm not responsible for it. Will everyone just please remember where we are and shut up."

As they did quickly enough, for they felt once more that tremble in the core of the world, heard once more, though briefly, that flattened sound.

Even Leely was silent as Lutha sat down upon her blanket, cradling the child against her. He looked thoughtful. Mitigan and Leelson whispered together, but Lutha was too drained to care what they were talking about. Joy and hopelessness and fear were all fighting for supremacy. If something had harmed Leely as he had been, she would have grieved. But, oh, to be in this danger with him changed! Now if something happened to him! Her child, her son, if anything happened to him now!

"You always said he would talk," Saluez reminded her.

Yes. She had. She had thought he would say Mommy and Daddy and the other things babies say. She had not thought he could tremble worlds with his voice.

All such thoughts were cut short. She saw Mitigan's head come up, alertly, swiveling as he listened, his hands going to his weapons belt. They all heard it then, a sound like rain, like a pouring of sand, an endless hissing. They twisted, searching for the source. . . .

Which slid onto the sand of the cavern like a runnel of dark blood, scaled from its gaping mouth to the darkness in which its body was still hidden, serpent king, snake lord, mighty monster, thick through as Mitigan's body, and all around it, its children, its kindred, the small ones of its kind, striped and mottled and jewel-marked, sinuous and horrid.

"Out," cried Mitigan, something very like panic in his voice. "Out!"

They stumbled to their feet and ran, out and away, Saluez supported on either side by Lutha and Snark, Leely running beside his mother. Mitigan's voice shouted battle cries while Leelson and Jiacare urged him to run. They did run, with snakes all around them, striking from crevices, dropping from holes, slithering across their feet as they struggled on, bruising themselves on the jutting rocks, scraping themselves on the rough stones until they came out under the sky. Leelson erupted from the rock pile, dragging the ex-king behind him. He had thought to bring one of the survival packs with him, and a lamp.

"Mitigan?" cried Snark.

"Coming," said Leelson, dragging the ex-king toward us. "Here, Jiacare's been bitten!" Lutha stood stupidly, not realizing what he wanted.

"Leely," Leelson cried. "Come see the bite."

The ex-king pulled up a trouser leg, displaying puncture wounds that seeped a yellowish ichor. The flesh around the wounds was green. "I fell on it," he said. "I don't think it meant to bite. . . ."

Leely ran to him, hugged the bitten leg, effectively tripping the ex-king, so that he fell heavily and was unable to get up. Leely kissed the bites, then hugged the ex-king once more.

"Jiacare Lostre, ex-King of Kamir," cried Leely. "Poor Jiacare!"

"Can you walk on it?" demanded Leelson, heaving Jiacare to his feet.

"If I have to." He stood up, took one experimental step, and groaned.

"Mitigan!" demanded Snark once more.

"He's either coming or he's dead," grated Leelson.

"Where are we going?" Jiacare smiled as he asked the question, a thin, fatalistic smile.

"Wherever we're allowed to go," Leelson muttered.

Mitigan appeared at the entrance to the rockfall, staggering toward the others. His face and arms were covered with bites. "Hard to kill," he muttered. "Oh, they're hard to kill."

He fell. Leely looked at his wounds, then at Leelson. "Dananana," he said, uninterested.

Leelson thrust his fingers into Leely's mouth, then rubbed the wet fingers onto Mitigan's wounds. The assassin gasped, as though in sudden agony.

"Mitigan Mitigan of the Asenagi," Leely said in a tone of disapproval. "Mitigan fought the snakes."

Where Mitigan had emerged from the rocks was now a darker shadow. They stared at it, trying to find in it the coils of a serpent, the twining shape of the snake. It wasn't a snake. Something deep inside them told them that. Snakes to flush them out, but something else to drive them.

Eyes reflected the light from the lamp Leelson carried. A wavering howl split the air.

"Wolves," Lutha breathed. "It's wolves." How many times had she seen them, recreated in story, remembered in myth? How many times?

As though answering to their name, lithe forms spewed from the rock pile. Some of them loped up the slope toward the camp, others made a line to the north. The way was open south or west, but in no other direction. They were not all wolves. Some of them were other things, shamblers, gigglers, mutterers, throat growlers.

Mitigan stumbled to his feet. He and the ex-king staggered up the slope, the rest following. As they went the bitten men gained strength. They crested the ridge, walking almost normally, then stopped. Across the narrow valley the wolves had made a line barring the way to the south. The only open way was the valley, the crescent of gravel that was the beach. They were being forced toward the sea.

"Make a stand," muttered Mitigan. "Get into one of the storm caverns and make a stand."

"No," said Leelson. "Let's just go along for the moment. See what's intended."

Lutha stared blindly into the dark. Even Leely could not live in this place without food, without shelter. What was intended was eradication. What was intended was that no one of them should return to Alliance to tell men what they knew.

CHAPTER 12

The stories of Old-earth are shared among the people of Old-earth. Even I, Saluez, can identify elephant and whale, ostrich and eagle, serpent and wolf, though they exist no longer. I know that they were and now are not, because of mankind. So, when I wakened under the stone on Perdur Alas to a terror not dreamed but real, I recognized the creatures bringing it upon us.

Snark and Lutha heaved me up, one on either side, and they supported me as we fled. Lutha seemed lost in some apocalyptic vision, concentrated on senses I did not share. Not so Snark. Nothing quenched her insatiable interest, or her avid commentary on each thing it touched.

"Old Tempter," she said as we fled down the valley toward the beach. "Old Tempter sent 'em. Wanted to be sure, he did, we knew what was coming. Righteous vengeance, that's what they're after!"

Her words rang like the gong by the House Without a Name, awaking dissonant echoes, evoking monsters! The Kachis had also been sent by the tempter. They, too, had been a cacophony of bestial noises and the gleam of fangs!

"You notice Mitigan?" Snark muttered. "Mad! That man is so rageous he's about to kindle. Sure never figured he'd get beat by snakes! High-and-mighty Asenagi, with Leely spit all that's keeping him living. Has to be hard for a proud man!"

The fact that she could notice such things while we fled for our lives cut through my panic. If Snark could keep her senses during this wildness, then so could I. I concentrated all my thought and energy on calm, on focus, on breathing slowly, moving deliberately, on noticing what was happening.

It actually helped. It took me out of myself to look at the others, imagining what they felt. Mitigan, as Snark had said, was blazingly angry. So was Leelson, though probably for a different reason. Fastigats like to make sense out of what happens, but Leelson couldn't get beyond his Firster viewpoint to make sense of this! Jiacare Lostre wore a thin smile, like a seer who knows what is happening, perhaps, or someone who thinks it doesn't matter. Lutha, of course, wasn't with us at all. She stared into the distance like one ensorcelled, an inhabitant of some other world.

We halted on the beach, hemmed in on three sides by creatures, on the other by ocean. There we gasped, waiting for what would happen next. I drew the night air deep into my lungs, amazed at the feeling of it, the scent of it! Like the air of a new world! The wind came wildly fresh, with a keening mist and a bluster of cloud.

Snark leaned close against me, supporting either me or herself. Her face was ecstatic as she murmured, "Oooh, they're lovely. Like flowing gold, snakes."

She meant it! Inexplicably, she was enraptured!

She nudged me, pointing. "And see the wolves—it's like I can see them better in the starlight than even in full sun. Look at their fur, Saluez! Soft as clouds, full and sleek. Teeth silver sharp in those laughing jaws. Eyes two smoky mirrors full of what ought to be. Oh, you can see Eden in those eyes! You can see a world stretching away, all green and misty! You can almost hear 'em, nose up, hollering the moon! They make me feel guilty, like Old Tempter meant 'em to, but they make me feel more than just that!"

Lutha came to herself abruptly. "Is this your paradise?" she gasped. "Are you finding it in the eyes of wolves?"

"Maybe so," said Snark. "Are you scared?"

"I'm past being scared," Lutha replied with a shivery giggle, half-hysterical, that built into a spate of wild laughter, quickly hushed. "Long past!"

Snark laughed with her. "Me too. This is sort of mazy, isn't it. Like a dream where you're in deadly trouble, but you go along, kind of floating, and the thing coming after you is monstrous terrible; its eyes fall on you like a horrid light; but it's righteous! You know how it's going to come out and all you can hope is you'll wake up in time or it won't hurt too much. Like that."

I saw new shapes among those surrounding us. Wolf and serpent, yes, but other creatures as well.

"Animals," I said to Lutha, under my breath. "What is it you've been muttering about animals?"

She hoisted Leely into her arms and stared at me over his head. "For days, over and over, I've found myself thinking of animals. They pad through my brain at night; they howl in my ears and climb my flesh with sharp claws. Is it really animals, Saluez? Or is it the ultimate Ularian, pretending?"

I didn't know. It might be the big Ularian, the tempter of Breadh, but I'd have sworn the animals were real.

That interchange was all we had time for. One wolf howled, then another. Something shadowy and immense growled deep in its swollen throat; something shambling giggled; we were stalked by ramified darkness, full of eyes. They pushed us toward the sea. Crawlers and trotters came after, chunky creatures, close to the ground, others sleek and thin, each bone showing through their dappled hides, strung with muscles like taut cable. Sinuous tails whipped; eyes lit like lanterns; tongues licked at jaws with a rasping sound, as at our bones, scraping them clean!

We were not driven into the waves, but onto the path at the foot of the cliffs. The creatures behind us kept their distance, not pursuing us closely enough to make us run, only closely enough to make us move. There was no space to walk abreast as we went southward along the sea. Mitigan was first, carrying the lamp, then the ex-king, with Lutha carrying Leely after him. I came next, then Snark, then Leelson. Only the waves spoke as we went, but when we came around the first curve, we heard howls and growls and hisses from the beach behind us, a cacophonous laughter, as though someone had told a funny story. No doubt who the joke was on.

From behind me, Snark announced, "There's caves along here. Sea caverns. We're headed where you folks come out, where the shaggies come out."

"Toward the vortex entries?" Lutha asked in a far-off, toneless voice. "Does it mean to herd us into the vortex again?"

Leelson ignored her question. "Tide's going out just now," he muttered. "It won't go out forever. Do they—does it mean for us to drown?"

"Probably one or the other," said the ex-king, turning to glance at us over his shoulder. "If I were they, it, I'd want to kill us without touching us. Touching us—at least touching Leely—seems to be fatal."

Though I hadn't seen any of the creatures come onto the path behind us, I felt there was something there, following us. I had no sense that we were escaping. We were only moving in nightmare, not waking from it. Perhaps fortunately, we weren't able to get into a panic over it, for our footing required complete concentration. The sea shelf was narrow, uneven, littered with slippery clumps of sea grass and shells and stones that rolled beneath our feet. And, of course, Leelson was right about the tide. When it came in, the water would come up to the path.

Snark was thinking along the same lines. "Hey, Saluez? Maybe there'll be something in it, somethin' swimming there under the rub and ruckle of the sea. Something else we'd know from olden times. Sharks maybe?"

I was spared the possibility of reply.

"Someone ahead," cried Mitigan. He stopped, holding his lamp high to throw light on the way ahead. "I hear someone."

We all heard it then, a woeful sound. It sounded almost familiar to me, and I remembered when we fell into the vortex. Jiacare had been right behind me, but after him had come at least three others. As we stumbled around the next curve the sound came louder, a solitary weeping over the plaint of the sea, where it fingered in, pestering the cliffs.

"It's Poracious Luv," said Lutha.

It was she, huddled upon the path, her clothing in tatters, a muddy heap lying beside her.

"Dirty as a street rat," Snark murmured from behind me. "Not a high-muck-a-muck now. Just a fat old woman crying."

As she was, next to the limp sprawl of the old man. So were the mightiest brought to nothing.

"The Procurator," I said. "That's the tabard he was wearing at Tahs-uppi."

The path was too narrow to get to him, but Mitigan scrambled down onto the slippery seaside stones to get a look.

"Dead," he said in an angry, wild-sounding voice. "Dead for some time."

Leelson said hard words, striking his forehead with his open hand.

Snark whispered, "All this time they been depending on the Procurator and Poracious Luv to come to the rescue! Now they know it's not gonna happen!"

As was his custom, and as though we were unable to draw the same inference, Leelson spelled it out for us.

"Of all those who knew we had gone through the omphalos, only your colleague remains, Mitigan. He and the songfathers."

The songfathers would do us no good. It would be easier for a gaufer to go through the eye of a needle than a songfather to admit to telling lies.

"There's my recorder," cried Snark. "Somebody's looking at my recorder!"

Poracious raised her head and stared at the ex-king. He began to laugh and so did she, neither of them truly amused.

"By Lord Fathom," he said hopelessly. "We rely on Thosby Anent."

She repeated the name as though it were an obscenity. "Old Thosby! He had a watchword. What was it?"

"Vigilance," said Lutha. "Vigilance was his watchword. Chosen more for its brave sound, I'd wager, than for its requirement of diligence."

Snark was as puzzled by this exchange as I was, but no one took time to explain it. Mitigan and the ex-king hoisted Poracious to her feet, and we went on, stepping over the body of the Procurator. We could not carry him with us.

"Poor old man," muttered Snark. "All his excitements is over! He wasn't such a bad old boss."

We said nothing after that as we struggled endlessly on. Each step became harder. There was pain in my belly, pain in my groin. I felt wetness seeping down my thighs. I wept out of weakness and weariness, wiping ineffectually at the tears. I let myself lapse into dream, making up visions, placing myself back on Dinadh, sitting with Shalumn beside the fire, holding her hand in mine while our children slept warm in the hive.

The vision was ended when I bumped against Lutha, almost knocking her down. Our progress was halted. The sky had lightened. Before us, across yet another of the ramified inlets we had stumbled along through the night, a cliff ran seaward to thrust its rocky jaw into the waves. It looked no different from the dozens of others we had passed, but this particular protrusion seemed to be special. Mitigan was gesturing with the lantern and calling Snark to look where we were.

"We sure didn't get much forrader," snorted Snark as she climbed around me. "That's my own particular tree up there on the rim. All around here's the caves the shaggies come out of."

When she reached Mitigan's side, they mumbled together. I saw her wave her fist at him, and she cried, "There's food up there. There's blankets and a stove. There's stuff we need."

Mitigan's scowl was plain in the light of the lantern. "I can climb it," he admitted.

In the predawn grayness, we could see a faint shadow trail that laddered across the cliff face. Handholds, perhaps. Foot holes. Something arduous and impossible for any normal being.

"You'll never get me up there," said Poracious Luv.

"We don't need to get you up there," Snark said. "When me and Mitigan can get up there, we'll lower the stuff down."

"The tide's coming in," said Leelson wearily.

"There's cover," replied Mitigan irritably, pointing across the narrow finger of sea at the cliff wall opposite. There was a gap there, a black hole at the top of a rockfall, one layer atop another, almost like a wide flight of giant stairs.

No one moved. We merely stood, staring. Like gaufers, I thought.

"It's above the tide line," Snark said impatiently, her tone urging us onward. "Get on! The seaweed tangles don't go but halfway to the cave door. It's as safe and dry as anyplace we're going to come to."

"I might manage that," said Poracious in an uncertain voice. She was limping badly, footsore from her many long days on the cliff path. Nonetheless, it was she who led us toward the gap, all but Snark and Mitigan. By the time we'd staggered around the cove and come to the cavern, we could see them far above, like spiders clinging to the cliff face. Day was coming. If there was something following us along the path, we would soon be able to see it.

It was not long before Mitigan came swarming down a rope and Snark began lowering bundles. The last thing down the cliff was a large jar, not unlike some of the pottery made in Dinadhi hives, followed by Snark herself. When she arrived at the bottom, she picked the jar up tenderly and carried it into our cavern before she brought anything else.

"My mother's bone jar," she said to me, noting my curious look. "Likely I'm not going back up there. Likely there's room enough in there for me, too."

Lutha looked up, startled. I kept my own face expressionless, though I knew our thoughts were the same. It was unlikely there would be anyone left to put our bones anywhere in particular. We, like the Procurator, would probably be washed by waves, dismembered by sea creatures, dispersed by the tides.

Snark brought us blankets and one of the little stoves, which gave us a welcome warmth and light. We huddled around it, all but Mitigan, who remained at the entrance to keep watch for whatever was coming. Something was, we all knew that, and all our eyes shifted to the entrance, then away, then to the entrance again. All we saw was the warrior sharpening his blades, a vague silhouette against the gray spread of a chilly dawn.

Poracious Luv subsided onto the sand with a moan of exhaustion, her head on her knees. I thought she'd fallen asleep, but after a moment she lifted her head and said plaintively, "I wonder if Behemoth is out there, waiting. . . ."

Lutha glanced at the opening, as though someone had sounded an alarm. "Behemoth," she said in a wondering voice. "An odd word for you to use, Poracious."

"Why so?" asked the older woman. "A behemoth is a great beast, isn't it? An old word for some kind of hugeness that lived a long time ago?"

Lutha nodded. "It's an old word, yes."

It was a word I'd heard somewhere. "Is it a real word? I mean, does it mean something real?"

Lutha nodded. "It isn't what it means so much as what it denotes. It means beasts, actually. Plural. But it conveys something more than a mere animal. The connotations are of intractable mightiness, of inexorability and fatefulness."

Poracious nodded slowly as she slumped, the heavy lines of her body seeming to me inexpressibly weary and dejected.

"Fatefulness," she said. "I said the same to the old Proc while the world shook around us. That was after we'd had the vision, you see."

Lutha's eyes came back to us. She raised her eyebrows.

"I say vision, though maybe it was only old minds playing tricks on old bodies. The old Proc and me, we'd stopped a bit, to rest. He was gray, holding his arm across him as though it hurt. We'd found this place where we could sit. . . . So, we were looking out to sea, and suddenly there was an ark, a great primitive sort of boat, rocking against a wrack of cloud, rain slanting across it like a curtain, wind driving it. It was made out of wood, don't you know. We could see the marks of tools on the sides, and it was loaded with animals. . . . Well, you know the old story, only this was real! And one of the animals put back its head and howled words! 'Beware,' it cried. 'Was it not commanded that each kind should be saved?' "

Leelson had been listening. Now he frowned down his nose at Poracious, slowly shaking his head. Thus did Fastigats reject the fanciful. Poracious took no notice of him.

Jiacare, on the other hand, was intrigued. "The ark story is from an ancient literature, isn't it? What was the book called?"

"It was called, simply, the Book," Leelson said in his usual didactic manner. "It was supplanted by the doctrines of Firstism in the late twentieth and early twenty-first centuries of the predisperion era."

He rose, brushed himself off, then went to join Mitigan at the cave entrance.

The ex-king nudged Poracious. "Did you see anything else in your vision?"

She shook her head. "Leelson thinks I am hallucinating, but I did see it, and I heard the voice so very clearly." She sighed, dropping her head once more. "Of course, I hadn't eaten for a long time, and we'd been walking endlessly. I know people who are very hungry and tired can see things. . . ."

Her voice trailed off as though she'd lost the strength to speak.

Snark said, "Suppose Firsters are wrong. Suppose the universe was made for all kinds of creatures." She took Lutha's hand and gripped it. "Suppose, Lutha!"

"I don't know," Lutha murmured. "Instinctively, it seems to me First-ism is illogical, but even now it's hard for me to imagine living with creatures. There are no creatures on Central. In my whole life I've only seen two or three other kinds of creatures. Gaufers. And the cats . . ."

"You must have seen birds in Simidi-ala," I said. "And we had corn-rats in the hive. And little fishes in the streams. You must have seen them!"

"Perhaps I did. I don't remember. Of course, I've seen Kachis and shaggies and Rottens. Are they animals?"

Poracious sighed. "Isn't everything alive either a plant, a human, or an animal?" She rubbed at her head, dragging her hair up in dirty spikes. "When I was a child, there were still a few animals on my home planet. I remember horses. I remember—"

"Horses," said Jiacare Lostre. "Oh, weren't horses wonderful? So shiny, so majestic, the way their necks arched, the way they pranced, high and proud. I remember seeing one running across a pasture, tail high, with her little one running beside her. Oh, on Kamir, we still had horses in my father's time. And dogs. We used to ride. . . ."

His voice faded into nostalgic silence. Poracious Luv drew her blanket more tightly around her, extending one hand from this cocoon to stroke the jar Snark had brought down from her cave. She followed the design with her fingers, asking, "Who are these?"

She was pointing at curvilinear patterns that seemed to make eyes and noses and mouths.

Snark replied, "Father Endless and Mother Darkness. And the carri-ers of souls."

"They have not human faces," Poracious commented. "Why is that?"

"They are mother and father of all things," I whispered. "Why should they have human faces?"

"Did your tempter have a human face?" Poracious asked Snark.

Snark cast a look over her shoulder, to be sure Leelson and Mitigan were still some distance away, before saying, "The songfathers claimed the Gracious One was male and had a human face and a male . . . body. Considering how the songfathers lied about other stuff, maybe it's just a story they made up."

Poracious moved slightly, looking at the jar from another angle. "Most gods of most worlds have human faces."

"Because men make them in their image," Lutha remarked, somewhat bitterly. "To grant mankind license to do what we would do anyway." Her eyes went back to the entrance and she gasped abruptly.

Snark followed her gaze. The two cats had somehow sneaked by the watchmen. They stood well inside the chamber, crying at us as they rubbed themselves against the stones. Whatever we might have expected, it was not cats. Snark went at once to find a food packet among the store she and Mitigan had lowered from above, and while she opened it the animals arched their backs and wound in and out between her legs. Mitigan and Leelson joined us by the stove, and we all watched while the animals ate. From Leelson's expression, I think he was expecting the cats to speak or go up in a puff of smoke. No one said anything at all until they had finished and departed.

Mitigan snarled, "Maybe they're spies. For whatever's out there." He stalked back to the entry.

Leelson joined him, saying, "What *is* out there? And what's it waiting for?"

"Poracious says it's Behemoth," said Snark. "Whatever it is, it's more like the cats than it's like us."

"How?" Poracious demanded. "How like."

"It's part of something," Snark replied.

"So are we!" Mitigan asserted angrily.

She shook her head at him. "No. Not on any homo-normed world. On Central, we didn't depend on anything, and nothing depended on us! We didn't respect anything, and nothing respected us. On natural worlds, life makes a loop. Birth and life and death are all parts of it, and all the parts respect one another. There's no top or bottom. There's just this . . . honorable dependency. But on homo-normed worlds, no flesh lives but man-flesh."

"Because we don't need animals!" Leelson asserted angrily.

"You say we don't," Lutha protested. "But one could argue they need themselves. One could argue that their creator may have purposes for them."

"Do you have any idea how ridiculous that sounds?" He waved a forefinger in her face. "We can be their creator. We have specifications for every species stored away. They can be reanimated anytime."

Snark jeered, "Stored away? Like old chairs, in a cellar somewheres? Would that satisfy you, Leelson Famber? Or you, Mitigan. Not living, not breathing, not moving. Just a pattern, in storage. Suppose before they did it to you, they told you, 'Don't worry. We can reanimate you anytime.' How'd you feel about that?"

"Humans are not animals," Mitigan said angrily. "You can't compare them. The universe was made for man."

"So you say," Snark crowed, with an outrageous snicker. "Now maybe whatever's out there is remaking the universe. Repopulating it, anyhow."

"Snark . . ." Lutha murmured warningly.

Mitigan's hands twitched toward his weapons; his eyes were hard and slitted. Snark wasn't noticing, or she didn't care.

"Well, yeah, but look! Look at this world. Look how it's set up. Doesn't it look like a nursery? Some place all clean and ready to multiply life on, and lots of it?"

"You're saying the world is *it*-normed?" asked Leelson, incredulously. "*Shaggy*-normed. *Rotten*-normed." He was almost as angry as Mitigan.

"That's it!" she crowed, a rapscallion, happily infuriating larger and quite dangerous opponents. "Maybe this world is Ularian-normed! Wouldn't that be a joke on us?"

Mitigan and Leelson were not amused. Before she could say anything else, the ex-king put his hand on Snark's shoulder, calming her, drawing her away. There was enough danger, his eyes said, without causing more among ourselves.

I sat down beside Lutha and Leely. The boy was busy drawing in the sand, and she watched him, her thoughts written on her face. They were old thoughts, ones she had spoken of: love warring with pain, pain warring with love. Leely was uncanny, a changeling, yet flesh of her flesh, fruit of her love for Leelson—which was perhaps something else, not love at all. Leely smiled meltingly up at her. She reached out, and he crawled into her lap to curl up there, playing with her hair. His mouth made silent words. He was trying names for things, silently working them out.

Poracious reached over and tapped me. "Look," she said, pointing out toward the sky. It took me a moment to realize that day had come and the sun shone in vast emptiness. The night before, the sky had been full of shaggies. Now there were none.

"Where'd they go?" Snark demanded.

We went to the cavern opening and looked out. No shaggies. No Rottens.

"The sea!" Leelson exclaimed.

It was alive with swimming things. Great fishy creatures, huge as houses. Monstrous shelled things. Eels that squirmed among the rocks along the shore. Various and multiple, fecund and furious, life beat upon the shores of Perdur Alas. We were so awestruck we did not even see the enormous tentacle that reared out of the water and lashed toward us, missing us by a finger!

We scrambled back, getting out of the way. I had felt this same emotion at the Nodders, when I had known they were capable of killing us easily and quickly, with no one to see or mourn or care. So, too, this great welter of living things could drag us down and drown us, leaving no trace. We were not masters here! This world was not made for man!

"Eagles," said Poracious.

We craned our necks to watch eagles for a while. They were as unexpected and marvelous as the other creatures, soaring in splendid spirals against the cloudless sky. Poracious stuttered and muttered, trying to attach a name to every living thing she saw, but Lutha said not a word.

"Where did they come from?" Leelson cried.

"The shaggies went," said the ex-king. "The animals came."

I turned to Lutha, the question in my face.

She shrugged. "I agree with him. The shaggies bred all kinds of creatures. This life is mutable. It will be what its maker wills."

"What the hell is 'its maker' playing at!" demanded Leelson, outraged.

We felt the earth shake, just a little, like a heavy footstep nearby. Poracious put her head on her knees and shuddered. Leelson pointed out into the sea, far, far, where the sky came down on the horizon. An island there, which had not been there before. It became larger while we watched.

"What's it doing?" demanded Mitigan in a tone almost as furious as Leelson's had been.

Lutha remarked. "Why so offended, Mitigan? You weren't this offended by the shaggies or by the Rottens."

"Animals," he said. "Why bother being offended at animals?"

"So what's coming out there isn't an animal?"

He scalded her with a look, before turning back to watch the blob grow larger. It had horns on top. Even at this great distance it was ineluctable, numinous, but familiar!

Lutha had the same idea. "Did you see Nodders on your way to Tahsuppi?" she asked Mitigan.

"We climbed around them," he grated. "Such things have no right to be."

The ex-king smiled. In some terrible, fatalistic way, he was enjoying himself. "Perhaps this creature feels it has every right to be alive and moving. Perhaps it has judged our storage vaults and found them wanting. Perhaps it has some more immediate destiny to attend to."

"We will soon know," said I, from my position atop a boulder. "It's coming nearer."

It was very tall. The head was massive. The horns on top showed clearly. This was the reality of which the Nodders were only a symbol. This, whatever this was—had the same proportion of height to horned top, to the great bulk of the nodding head. I had no time to consider the effect, for sound changed, the world shuddered, a peculiarly dreamy sensation overtook me, as though all happenings were inevitable and I did not greatly care.

Leely pushed past me and went out of the cavern. He plopped down on a shelf of wave-rounded pebbles and stared outward, his lips making silent words.

"By all that's holy," breathed Poracious. "Look, low down, against the water."

We saw. Light. Shadow on one side, shadow on the other, shadow above, and light under, between.

"Legs," I told them in my dreamy, languorous voice. "We only saw its upper part before. Now we are seeing between its legs."

The Nodders had been only busts, then? Only heads and necks of Behemoth? There was more to the creature than that? Well, yes, my dreaming mind assented. Well, yes. Time went on. Eventually we saw its wings, which had until then been folded along its back. Eventually we saw its marvelous face, its wondrous eyes, its great adamantine teeth.

It stopped when the ocean was no deeper than its knees. Whales leapt around its legs. Gyring eagles made its aureole, and the wind of its breath pushed us to and fro, like little flags.

"I've seen it before," whispered Poracious. "Somewhere."

"Ancient earth," Lutha replied. "Was it Babylon? Was it Ur? Mighty winged creatures were carved upon its walls."

"Winged cattle," said Poracious. "But that is mythology."

"This is not myth." The ex-king smiled. "And this is no kind of cattle."

Lutha clung to Poracious as she backed into the cave, they two pulling me with them. Anything else was past doing. Past believing. Past thinking on. We were ants, crawlers between the hairs of immensity.

Leelson dragged Lutha into his arms and held her close. I saw sweat on his face. I saw fear.

"Come forth," said a voice out of the whirlwind.

There was no place to hide. Stones shattered into powder. The cliff danced. Great boulders skittered through the cavern roof and bounced between us, close as a hair!

Lutha grabbed me by the arm and dragged me back against the wall, but it did no good. Dust rose from the floor in clouds, boiling upward, threatening to smother us in stone ash.

"We must go out," I cried at them. "We can't stay under here." I broke away from them and ran. Lutha came after me. We stopped in the entrance. Leely and the ex-king hadn't moved when the rest of us had retreated. Leely lay where he'd been before. The ex-king clung to a stony pillar, his back to us, staring up at the great face that floated above us like a thundercloud.

The head bent; a mighty hooved forefoot withdrew from the sea, rivers running from its fetlock, alive with silver fishes. The foot stamped down.

The world shook to its roots.

"Come forth," said the voice once more.

There was no denying that voice. There was no hiding from it. All of us shambled out into the open air, where we stood like drunken, tethered creatures, unable to move unless the voice commanded us.

We didn't have to move. It came to us, jarring the world with every step. We fell and got up. It took another step. We fell again, and got up. We leaned together, like floppy dolls, holding each other erect. Leely lay on the ground where he had stayed all along, waving his hands, saying nothing, nothing at all, his eyes fastened on that which came.

Beyond the hugeness was a sky full of birds, a million pairs of beating wings, a whirl of white terns, a swerve of black-backed puffins, a spiral of silver gulls rising on the wind. I knew their names. They all had names. Before each mighty foreleg, a bow wave of life rushed upon the shore to wriggle, to stride, to fly, to crawl. I tasted a sweetness of mown grass and a salt-clean tang of the ocean wind.

In the end, we stayed on our knees, unable to get up again.

"Is this your tempter?" Leelson asked me, through trembling lips.

The stories had not said it was so huge. The stories had said it was male. This was not male. It smelled like flowers and spices and fragrant smoke. It tasted of . . . marvel. It wore a high crown. It spoke to us in thunder.

"Will you go home again?" it asked. "Will you go to your proper place? To Dinadh, where I had placed you?"

I saw Lutha's head move. Nod, nod. There was Leelson, nodding. Mitigan nodding. I felt what they felt. How tempting to go home once more. To Dinadh. To the winding canyons. To the sweet songs of the songfathers.

"Will you go home again?"

Would I go home again? To the lies the songfathers told? To the pain of the House Without a Name? To that terrible destiny for my daughters? To connivance at that evil by my sons? To sell truth and wisdom short in order to buy the false hope of immortality?

Somehow I got to my feet.

"No," I cried. My voice was the cry of a small bird against that mighty thunder. Still I cried, "No. I will not!"

"Not me, neither!" trumpeted Snark, as though my words had wakened an echo in her.

I felt Lutha's eyes, and Poracious's. They didn't understand. Ah, but they hadn't known the House Without a Name. Their wombs had not held what mine had held.

The mighty head bent above us like a cloud descending.

"You were given worlds to share," it whispered in a voice like an avalanche. "But you would not share. You were given life to treasure, but you did not treasure. You counted your own lives holy and all other lives expendable. All my creations you have subverted, all my wonders lost and slaughtered and betrayed. I made a garden to receive you. To make clear my intention, I set my creatures around you to be your companions; you have made of your habitation a termite mound, and of that garden a desolation!

"So now I have made your world suitable, a place where you can serve my creation. What more do you deserve than that?"

I couldn't answer. There was no answer.

"Now I have drawn a bowstring around all mankind, and in the fullness of time, I shall leash him with it. He who will not share shall serve instead.

"Will you go to the place I have allotted you?"

Somehow I kept upright. "No," I cried, my voice breaking. "Mankind deserves no more, but this woman would rather die, knowing the truth, than go back to live that lie! I choose truth! We are not immortal. My mother wasn't immortal. She died. She did not eat my face; she died!"

The face faded. For a moment it was not there. The place it had been was blank. Then the earth shook again mightily, tumbling us about, and a face returned, a lion's face, an eagle's face, a face of leaves, of fruits, of fishes, a woman's face, terrible and pitying. I knew that face. A mother's face!

Leely was up, running toward the sea, the rocks, the tidal pools, the squirming eels, the tentacles, the quivering, hammered surface of the sea, toward the great creature as he made the same noise he had made that other time: the scream, the command, the roar, the whatever it was! And the ex-king went after him, calling out some wordless warning, trying to catch him, trying to get him back.

Too late! Too slow! The great head bent down. It was coming at Leely, but the king got in the way so it caught him first. Oh, he never made a sound, not a sound. I heard him crush between those teeth and I heard the soft sound of his body hitting the stones. The huge head tossed, making a great gust of wind, a buffet that knocked us all away as it withdrew with the child!

It crushed him. He screamed. It drew him up. Lutha went past me like a wind. She leapt. I ran, I jumped. Snark was beside me, even Poracious, all of us, jumping, trying to reach Leely where he hung between those mighty jaws, between those great teeth, screaming all the way.

"Lutha Lutha Tallstaff Lutha sister mother love!" he cried, a terrified voice, a voice like every child who ever was abused or frightened.

"If you choose truth, will you live by it?" cried the Great Beast. "Reflect!"

Blood rained around us. An arm. A leg. Oh, by all the gods of man, by all merciful deities, a baby, a child, falling around us, torn into bits . . .

Lutha screamed as though rent apart, a sound of such pure and utter pain that it pierced us all. Leelson seized her and pressed her face against his chest so she wouldn't see, so she wouldn't hear! Oh, I wished I hadn't seen Leely's blood on its jaws, on the ringlets of its mane. Leely's blood on the stone. Leely's blood falling on the raised knee, the mighty foot that came down and down and down, to shake us like dice in a cup and cast us away into utter darkness. I wished I hadn't seen, but I could not do as it commanded.

We came to ourselves after a time. A day. A moment. Who knows? We crawled into our cavern, dragging Lutha, who lived, and the king, who did not. Him we rolled in blankets against the back wall. Her we put near the warmth of the stove, and I held her head in my lap while I wiped bright blood from her forehead where she had fallen against the stone. Snark was beside me, her hand in her pocket. I knew she held a weapon. Like her, I watched Mitigan and Leelson where they raged in a corner, not at one another. Now they were allies in this matter. Now Snark was their enemy, I was their enemy. We had refused the bargain. We had denied the word of the tempter.

Lutha moaned.

"Don't leave him like that!" she whispered at me. "Oh, don't leave him like that. Leely-baby."

I hushed her.

"My baby."

Oh, yes. Baby. All our babies. All our wealth of babies that we had worshiped more than life itself.

"Nothing there," whispered Snark, shaking her gently. "Listen, Lutha. Maybe it wasn't real! We got Jiacare's body, but there was nothing there but him. I looked ever'where."

I hadn't seen her go out, but she wouldn't lie. Not Snark.

"But there was blood," Lutha cried. "Blood falling . . ."

"Not even blood. Me and Poracious've looked real careful, over and over again. There's no blood."

"Where did Behemoth go?"

Snark shrugged, looking at me.

"I don't know," I said. "I'm not sure. If I had to guess, I'd say it's still there. It hasn't gone anywhere."

"I thought it went down into the waves," said Poracious in a little-girl voice. "I thought I saw it go there. We can't see under the water."

"We couldn't see it now if it was right outside," Snark said. "It's getting dark."

She was right. The day had gone as in an instant while we cowered.

"Was it also the tempter?" Poracious whispered to me.

"I believe it was," I told her.

"Your ultimate Ularian," said Leelson, from the shadows.

"That's not who it is," whispered Lutha. "Why can't you see who it really is?"

"If it's Ularian, we'd taste it," Poracious objected.

"No," Lutha whispered again. "That was for us. It is disgusted with us. It is simply disgusted!"

Poracious stared at her as though she were crazy. "What are you saying?" she demanded querulously. "I don't know what you're talking about."

Lutha closed her eyes, refusing to answer. Her face was agonized. I remembered our talk, on that other world, the night before we came to the omphalos. She had spoken of the guilt she had felt when she thought Leely was lost among the Nodders, wondering if she would grieve. Now he was lost, utterly, and she grieved. I held her, rocking back and forth, unable to forget that dreadful rending.

"Why?" cried Poracious. "Oh, why . . . ?"

Yes. Why. I stopped listening to the others. They went on talking, mostly Leelson and Mitigan, asking each other questions that neither could answer: What might we do to help ourselves? Should we stay where we were or go elsewhere?

After hacking each alternative to death, they decided to stay where we were, a simple decision considering that none of us was in any condition to do anything else.

And Lutha lay in my lap, hurting. Grief is not only in the mind. A spirit does not agonize in separate space. It takes the body with it!

"He called my name," she wept. "Oh, Saluez! He called my name!"

Eventually she wept herself into exhaustion. Despite everything, all our capacity for wonder or outrage or grief wore itself out. No one had the energy to weep another tear, to ask another unanswerable question. I made tea. Snark brought me some herbs to put in it, soothing things, she said. Her own face was wet and weary, but when I offered a cup, she would not take it. She would keep watch, she said, though what good watching could do she did not say.

In the night I heard Lutha moving. I said her name. She mumbled something about a stone in her bed. In a moment she was quiet again.

Gray light came and I woke. Around me on the sand the others lay in blanketed hummocks, Snark among them. Evidently she had decided it would do no good to keep watch. Against the far wall, another hummock showed where the ex-King of Kamir had been laid. Beside me, Lutha moved uncomfortably, whining again about the stone beneath her.

Quietly, thinking to ease her, I reached under her covering to remove what troubled her, encountering instead a warm softness, not Lutha, something else alive.

My first thought was the cats. I had never felt a cat, but presumably a cat would feel soft and warm and alive. Then I had a less pleasant thought, something to do with the serpents that had driven us from our rock pile.

Shuddering, I drew it away from Lutha's side, waking her. Her eyes came open as I held the thing at arm's length, thrust it into the light. . . .

And dropped it as Lutha screamed, a sound that might have waked the bones in Snark's jar. It waked all those around us, who within moments were babbling as wildly as I.

It was Leely! Leely, the size of my foot! Leely no bigger than a small cat, a whole Leely in miniature, exactly like himself but tiny, tiny.

Mitigan cursed, brushing his hands across his blanket, bowling another Leely onto the sand. Two Leelies, three, four. A dozen Leelies from among our blankets, all piping in reedlike voices, "Dananana."

Poracious held Lutha while she came apart. I, too, felt the seams between reality and madness fail, felt myself rip into pieces, then saw all the pieces, a row of them on the edge of a precipice, teetering into hysteria, ready to tumble!

"Lutha!" Leelson, who had taken Poracious's place. "Lutha, Saluez, think! It's all right. It's all right!"

There was Snark beside the stove, holding out crackers to the Leelies. There were dozens of them. Some no larger than my thumb.

What was all right? This? This was all right?

"It's the healing," Leelson shouted at us, slapping Lutha gently to get her attention. "It's regenerative, that's all. A whole organism from any fragment. Lutha. It's all right."

"It's not," she howled. "It's not all right."

Several of the Leelies came running across the sand to stand pulling at Lutha's trousers, caroling, "Dananana," over and over, then running back to the others to make a bird twitter of tiny voices, among which we heard, "Lutha Lutha mother love."

I think perhaps Lutha fainted. Or perhaps she simply abdicated responsibility for living. She let go, fell down, and stopped, quit even being aware that life was going on around her, ignoring all our attempts to arouse her.

Leelson said, "Let her alone."

"Good. Let me alone," she agreed in a far-off voice.

We did let her alone. The Leelies didn't. They liked her. She was their Lutha Lutha mother love. They liked me. I was their Saluez of the shadow. They wandered all over both of us, like tiny explorers setting out across a new land, while I sat there, my hands twitching as I tried to decide whether to pick them off or let them be. Hysterically, I told myself to await the jab of a flag driven into my thigh, a voice claiming this new continent!

Under her breath, Lutha was counting. She stopped at the count of one hundred ten.

"One hundred ten?" I asked.

"That's how many of them I've counted," she said in a high, cracked voice. "One hundred ten."

More had come in from among the stones. The smallest ones were half the size of my little finger. The largest was three times the size of the one I had found first. I found myself saying, that one is leg-sized. That one is arm-sized. That one grew out of a few drops of blood. They clustered around us like grapes, dangling from Lutha like pendant fruit, eager, joyous. They felt no pain. They knew no fear. They had no worry about what had happened to him, them. It didn't matter what had happened to him, them, or how they had come to be.

Lutha said brokenly, "God, what kind of mind could have designed such a thing!"

After a time they seemed to find new centers for their attention. A dozen broke away to cluster around a slightly larger one, and that group wandered off. Then, gradually, another dozen, or a score. The groups wavered across the floor, disappearing into holes, reappearing again, vanishing at last. Finally there was only one left. The largest one.

"This is how big he was when he was born," raved Lutha, "this big. Just this big. The same size . . ."

Leelson sat down beside her, his face very white. "Are you all right?"

"I suppose," she said.

"You understand what's happened here."

Her face twisted. I knew she was cursing him, cursing all Fastigats who would not assume anything, who had to spell everything out, letter by letter. Still, she shook herself, gripped her hands tightly together, and answered his stupid question with reasonable self-control.

"I understand it intellectually, Leelson. Not in any other way. I will never understand in any other way."

"It might help if you consider that . . . thing that tore him apart. It's in for a surprise, isn't it?"

She cast me one incredulous glance, then closed her eyes and refused to speak.

"It's the big one, Lutha. The prime Ularian. The chief Rotten. And whatever venom Leely spreads, that creature is now awash in it."

Laughter welled uncontrollably from her throat. She roared. "You're such a fool!"

He drew away, deeply offended.

"You Firsters! Suppose your Firster god came calling on you. When he arrived, would you call him a Ularian? Would you expect him to resemble you even in your frailties? Would you expect him to catch your cold. To get a bellyache? To sneeze?"

He was rigid, pale, not following her.

She whispered. "You would expect God to be above all that, no? So, if a deity appears who is deity not only of man but of *all* living things, will you really expect it to die from mange or distemper or an attack of the Leelies?"

He still didn't understand.

"Bernesohn didn't understand what's really happening any more than you do."

"What are you saying?" he grated. "What do you know that I do not?"

She glared at him. "There is life in Hermes Sector, Leelson. Life breeding here. Life that uses humans as incubators, infinite, wonderful life. Life for old planets that man has ruined and left barren behind him. As mankind seems always to do, we have stumbled into it and contaminated the process, for which we will be punished."

"No!" he said hoarsely, reaching for her. "No."

She jerked herself away from him. "And your ultimate Ularian is not merely some alien life-form! It is Behemoth. Creation made manifest. Primordial life. Great Beast. Ruler of some large chunk of the universe. So far as we're concerned, it's name is God."

"You're mad!" he exclaimed, turning away from me. "Quite mad."

She shook with hysterical laughter. "We'll see."

Snark seized one of her arms and I the other, putting my hand over her mouth. Lutha wasn't noticing their faces, Mitigan's and Leelson's. Both of them were ready to explode. Snark had pushed them, the ex-king had pushed them, now Lutha had pushed them. They were becoming dangerous.

"Enough," said a voice.

We turned to confront a ghost that rose from the base of the stones.

Jiacare Lostre. Ashen, cadaverous, but alive. From around his feet, beetle-ish things bumbled away, tiny Leelies, who did not stop at healing, but also had a sideline in resurrections.

"You were dead!" cried Mitigan in angry disbelief.

"So I was," he replied. "And if I was killed as a representative of mankind, deservedly so. And if what I heard may be believed, all mankind may soon share my fate, or that of Dinadh, to be incubators for all eternity."

"It'll die!" cried Mitigan. "The way the Rottens died. The way the shaggy died. It touched Leely. It'll die."

Poracious said, "I think not. Look there!" She pointed to the opening of the cave, where one of the Leelies was dueling with a crab among the stones. He touched it repeatedly, but the crab didn't seem to care.

Lutha wept. "Behemoth has vaccinated its creatures against our plague. What is breeding here now is Leely-proof."

The largest Leely crawled into Lutha's lap, climbed her chest, and put his tiny arms around her neck.

"Lutha mother love," he whispered. "Don't cry, Lutha mother love."

She went on crying, and so did I.

"We should go back to the camp," said Mitigan in a stiff, unnatural voice. Poor Mitigan. All his world astray, and him lost with it.

No one had anything else or better to offer. Poracious wanted to stay where she was, but Snark wouldn't let her.

"It's not a good idea for you to be alone. Not a good idea for any of us."

After a time of aimless delay, we went from our cave in a wavering line, much the way the Leelies had gone, each of us wrapped in a blanket or two. Lutha carried the largest Leely. Snark carried her jar, taking the lead when we reached the path. I followed after her, then the others, with Mitigan bringing up the rear, his face hard and angry as it had been since Behemoth had appeared. As we went north along the ocean trail we caught glimpses of the smaller Leelies, jumping into tide pools, dodging behind stones, disappearing down holes in the ground. Several of the larger ones greeted us in tiny voices. "Dananana."

We rounded a corner and confronted a lioness. That is, it was similar to pictures I had seen that were labeled lioness. We scrambled onto the slippery rocks while she passed us by. On her side was a vivid patch of scarlet, bordered by misty violet on one side, by deep wine and bright yellow on the other. Behind her came a train of cubs, each with its own color pattern.

"They are not hungry," Leelson said in an expressionless voice. "At the moment."

The lioness was only the first. There were huge almost birds running on the trail, darting their beaks into the tide pools to spear wriggling, silver things. Each of them bore its own pattern of stripes or mottling or moving blotches of color. There were shelled things, clattering on the stones, turtlelike, crablike, strangenesslike. There were small, furry beings with fluffy tails and piping voices that whistled as we passed. Every corner brought a new creature, each one with a new pattern, and each one bringing a new outburst of rage from Mitigan. Their very existence was an insult to him.

We passed the body of the Procurator in late afternoon, and it was evening when we came out onto the beach. There a snake slithered at Mitigan's feet, and he mouthed impotently, his fury mounting. He saw me cringe, so he turned and began to say to me the kinds of unpleasant things men of his kind often say to women, working himself into yet greater rage.

Snark tired of it. She shouted, "Use your head! *This* world was not made for man, Asenagi!"

"Then why didn't he kill us?" he howled. *"He should have killed us!"*

We stopped where we were.

"Who did you see?" I asked Mitigan, when I could form words again. "When you saw *it*, what did you see?"

"A winged bull with a man's face," he cried. "It carried a bull's pizzle and it wore a great beard!"

"We know," said Leelson. "That's what we all saw. Let's move along, shall we?" He took Mitigan by the arm and tugged him away from us, trying to calm him while the rest of us stood dumbfounded, wondering if we had gone mad.

"I did not see a man's face," said the ex-king, quietly. "But some can see no farther than their mirrors. What wears another face must go unseen."

"It was a good question, though," said Snark. "Why didn't it kill us?"

"It hasn't decided yet," said Lutha.

"How do you know?" I asked her.

"I just know. If it had decided to kill us, it would have done it there, as Mitigan expected." She jabbed her chin toward the south. "But we, too, are the offspring of Behemoth. It has uses for all its creatures and would rather not kill us."

Snark stopped dead. "That's what the justice machine said to me. It would rather not kill me. It would make me useful as a shadow instead."

"As the sisterhood of Dinadh were shadows," I said.

"As all women become shadows," said Lutha. "Where men have their way."

Leelson dragged Mitigan back to the rest of us. "We've been talking about Chur Durwen," he said. "Mitigan believes Chur Durwen will send help."

"How'll he do that?" asked Poracious wearily.

Mitigan glowered at her, his mouth working.

"Through the officials at the port?" suggested Leelson.

"Who control nothing. Who are suspect because of their association with outlanders."

Mitigan growled, "He'll take ship for Alliance Central. There will be someone there."

Poracious nodded, saying calmly, "When we came to Dinadh, shipping in Hermes Sector was already a very iffy thing. Suppose Chur Durwen does get through, how will he reach anyone in the bureaucracy? I assume he is a registered assassin? Such folk are not routinely solicited for unusual information about unheard-of situations."

"He'll go to the Alliance agent in Simidi-ala," said Mitigan.

Poracious smiled grimly. "Much good may that do him, or us. Thosby Anent's information routes are secure, but he won't get around to making use of them!"

The ex-king laughed, almost inaudibly. "There's his servant. The woman. Chadra Tsum. We might offer audible prayer, several times a day, to Chadra Tsum."

With a look of hectic gaiety, Poracious fell to her knees on the sand, held out her arms, and prayed to Chadra Tsum. The ex-king joined her, and they concluded their prayer with a repetitive chant: "Vigilance. Vigilance. Vigilance."

Lutha and I turned away, overtaken by a fit of hysterical laughter. We leaned on one another, tears running down our faces. Mitigan stood stony-faced, eyes glaring, but Leelson pulled Lutha away from me, into his arms.

"Oh, Lutha." He sighed. His own face was wet. I had not seen Leelson weep ever before. Had things come to such a pitiful pass that even a Fastigat could weep?

"Why?" she asked, touching his cheek. "Why tears, almighty Fastigat?"

"Guilt," he said with a grimace. "It seems I may have been, may be wrong about a number of things. I blamed you."

"You blamed me?" she asked.

"For not seeing reality. My reality. And Limia blamed you for not seeing hers."

"And I blame you now for not seeing what is," she said, almost whispering. "This is real, Leelson. This is not philosophy. Pray with Poracious that someone comes, that Behemoth will let us go, for someone must convince the Fastigats at Prime that this is real."

"Little chance of that," he murmured, looking around himself.

"But Behemoth might let us go," I offered, more loudly than I intended. "We could pray to it. . . ."

I had not seen Mitigan edge up behind us. I didn't know he was there until I heard his howl of rage:

"Make prayer to an animal?"

"Mitigan." I faltered, stepping back, away from him. "I meant it only as a suggestion. Perhaps if we offered . . . repentance, self-sacrifice . . ."

It was the wrong thing to say. Perhaps anything would have been the wrong thing to say. He had been teetering on the edge of rage and frustration for too long.

"You think it would accept a sacrifice?" he bellowed, grabbing me by the arm, lifting me with one mighty hand, and flinging me across his shoulder. "Well then, let us make sacrifice!"

It happened so quickly that we were halfway up the slope toward the scraggy ridge before I could catch my breath and cry out. Any sound I made was drowned by his fury.

"We will build us an altar! We will make blood sacrifice!"

All the breath was driven from my lungs when he dropped me at the crest of the ridge. He took a thong from his belt and lashed my feet and hands together with one quick motion while I gasped and struggled. Dimly I saw him heaving great slabs of stone, stones too heavy to lift, stones no man could have lifted.

I rolled my head to one side. The others were halfway up the hill. Leelson. Lutha. Above me Mitigan held a huge boulder aloft.

"Want to join her, Famber? Come closer and you will!"

"Mitigan!" cried Leelson. "This isn't the way—"

"I've had enough of this heresy, these devil beasts," Mitigan howled, casting a manic glance in my direction. "Enough!"

He backed toward me, holding the great stone aloft with one hand while he fumbled for a weapon with the other. Something to kill me with, kill them with. Almost he could have killed them with his eyes, so berserk he was.

"Why me?" I gasped. "Why sacrifice me, Asenagi?"

"Why not you?" He dropped the stone and jabbed a contemptuous thumb toward Lutha. "She belongs to Leelson Famber. And the other one is of some use. But you are no use and you belong to no one but your devil god, so let it have you!"

"I didn't create it!" I cried. "I only saw it, listened to it. I only sensed what was really there, Mitigan. As you did—"

"Lies," he cried, heaving a huge slab of stone into place upon his pile, now waist-high. He tossed me onto the stone like wood onto a fire, effortlessly. My head hit, and I felt myself go limp, dazed. I couldn't struggle, though I could feel him lashing me to the slab. "The Gracious One warns us against your kind! Animal-lovers! Devils! Mistresses of lies!"

He licked at the spittle that ran down his chin. Past him I could see Snark on her belly, worming her way up the slope, and behind her, Lutha struggling with Leelson, trying to get free from him. It was all happening too quickly and too slowly, both at once. There was time to be terrified, not time enough to do anything. I prayed, begging Weaving Woman to let my pattern end cleanly, swiftly, without pain. Surely there had been enough pain!

"Not nearly enough," Mitigan jeered, and I knew I had spoken aloud. Now his hand was aloft, already reddened by sunset, glittering with the blade it held. That was for me.

Far off, as though in another world, I heard Lutha and Snark shouting, not pleading. There was a strangeness in their voices, something inappropriate. I had time to think that. Why did they sound that way? I squeezed my eyes shut, clenched my teeth tight, waiting for the knife to come. . . .

It didn't come. Instead Mitigan bellowed, harshly, horrified.

I opened my eyes against a dazzle of light. Mitigan stood with his back to me, his head thrown back. Beyond him was Behemoth, up from the sea, serpent-necked, dragon-jawed, caldron-eyed.

"No," it said in a voice of wind.

"But she refused you!" Mitigan howled. "She deserves to die. She refused you!"

"She has that right," said the wind. "Do not all my beings have that right? Even you? You may ruin yourselves by your choices, still I will not take them from you. . . ."

Mitigan turned frantically, lunging toward me, the knife aimed at my heart, but the wind came after him, raising him, taking him up as the vortex had done, twirling him, spinning him, up and away, away, glittering with weapons, howling with rage, away. . . .

And all the while, for that tiny eternity, Behemoth looked me in the eye until I felt I had drowned in that look. Willingly. Forever. I did not want to come away.

"Still your kind may choose," it said in a fading whisper. "Choose truth; choose lies; still you may choose, even now."

I saw sunset. Only that. Behemoth gone. That rough beast gone. That enormous glory gone. That terrible beauty, gone. Leaving only its purpose evident all around us.

"Saluez," cried Lutha, her fingers busy with the lashings. "Oh, Saluez."

Far above us in the dusk, a sudden star bloomed and moved, swimming toward us through the evening.

"A ship," said Leelson disbelievingly. "It's a ship."

The ship hung above us for some little time while we stared and mumbled. It had grown quite dark before it broke into two glittering parts, one of which descended. When it set down beside the camp, we saw it was a tender. It was from the *Vigilance,* as it turned out, a battle cruiser of the Alliance.

We stood slack-jawed while the lock opened, the ramp came down, and a woman alighted.

"Chadra Tsum," said Poracious wonderingly. "Just as I saw her in Simidi-ala. And there behind her, that's old Thosby Anent."

He was a crooked man, with a lopsided walk. "Ah," he cried as he hobbled toward us, his eyes scrunched almost shut with delighted self-importance. "Ah, *Vigilance!* See the ship's name? Ah? I've been watching, waiting. *Vigilance!"*

He went on past us to stand upon a small hillock, looking about himself like a conqueror of worlds as he drew deep, dramatic breaths and tapped himself upon the chest in self-congratulation.

"Let me guess," whispered Poracious to Chadra Tsum. "You told him we were here, expecting rescue, but he had to think it over. He couldn't make up his mind to do anything about it?"

Chadra Tsum nodded, murmuring, "After some time had gone by, I asked if he would attempt to rescue you, and he said, 'That's the plan!' Days went by, however, and he did nothing at all. So I commandeered an Alliance ship in his name. Then, when it was the *Vigilance* that showed up, he assumed he had done it himself."

"Quite a coincidence," Lutha murmured.

"Not really," said the woman. "It's the only battleship assigned to this sector. That's where Thosby got his password in the first place."

"I'm surprised you've come so quickly," I managed to say. "Poracious and the king only prayed to you this evening!"

"You mean you really did that?" the woman breathed. "You know, I've felt something for days, as though you were speaking in my mind. Isn't that strange?"

Poracious took her by the arm and led her a little aside, where they spoke animatedly to one another. Leelson joined them, and then others from the ship. Leely watched them for a moment, his face intent, then he wandered away toward the sea. I stayed where I was, with Lutha. In a few moments Snark joined us, then the ex-king, none of us making a move to join the general rejoicing. It was as though the four of us had been pulled together.

"Why did it let the ship come?" whispered Lutha. "Why?"

"Didn't you hear what it said?" I murmured. "We have a choice. We've always had a choice."

"Between what and what?" asked Snark.

"What choices are there?" Jiacare counted them off on his fingers. "What truths we choose to see. What lies we choose to ignore. Whether we become Firsters . . . or something else—"

He was interrupted by a raised voice from the group down the slope. Someone said loudly that ships were still disappearing in Hermes Sector and the captain wanted to get away quickly. Someone else reinforced this, but Poracious demanded, loudly, that the Procurator's body be retrieved. There was a muttered argument, then general assent. The group broke up, with individuals going busily off in different directions.

"They'll want to leave soon," I said.

"It will be good to be at home," said Lutha. It was a statement, but it sounded like a question.

"I have no home," said Snark.

"Nor I," I said, as softly. "In any case, that is not why the ship was allowed to come. It did not come merely to take us home. Remember what Behemoth said when it spoke to us first."

"What did it say?" asked the ex-king. "I don't remember."

"You wouldn't remember," said Lutha in an expressionless voice. You were . . . dead. It was after it tore . . . tore Leely into bits. It asked if we would live by truth. It told us to reflect."

"Such violence," he said distastefully, as though it had happened to someone else.

I broke the long silence that followed. "The violence wasn't arbitrary. The question wasn't rhetorical."

Lutha did not look at me. I knew she had heard me, but she didn't meet my eyes. She was watching Leelson, who had broken away from a small group near the ship and was striding up the slope toward us.

He put his arms around Lutha, hugging her joyously.

"We can go home," he said. "We can take . . . our son and go home."

She turned toward me, her eyes spilling tears. I knew what she was thinking. She had wanted him to say that, something like that.

"He'll be of great value in Fastiga," Leelson assured her, stroking her hair. "For his healing power alone."

My throat was dry. I cleared it, painfully. "Yes, he'll be of great value. For his healing power alone."

The ex-king looked off toward the horizon. "Fastigats should be able to live almost forever, with all the Leelies around."

Leelson frowned, shook his head, stepped away from Lutha. "But . . . I hadn't . . . I thought we'd only take . . . just the one, Lutha."

"But they're all . . ." she cried, her hand to her mouth, not finishing the sentence. She was right, however. They were all.

"As you say, they'll be enormously valued," repeated the ex-king, "for their healing power alone. Not to speak of raising the recently dead. Extending human life spans for how long? Increasing human population by how much? All Firsters will be delighted, of course. It shouldn't take long for there to be a profitable market in Leelies."

Leelson recoiled as though he'd been slapped.

"Later," Lutha said in a voice that was almost a scream. "We'll discuss it later."

"But the ship's leaving. . . ."

"They've sent men to get the Procurator's body. The ship won't leave until they return. Leelson! If you love me, let me be. Give me a moment!"

He backed away, uncertainly. Poracious called his name, and he went off toward her, glancing at us doubtfully over his shoulder, unable to decide whether to be hurt or angry. Poor Fastigat. Even he could not read this tangle!

Lutha turned away from us, her shoulders shaking, wiping her face with the backs of her hands. She shuddered, drew a deep breath, then wept again. In a moment she stopped trying to control herself and simply walked away toward the sea.

Snark said to me, "Go after her, Saluez. She talks to you."

The ex-king nodded, nudging me, so I went after her. By now it was starlit evening, with just enough light to see by. She wound her way among glistening pools with me trailing after, and when we came to the beach, I wasn't surprised to find Leely already there, perched on a rock. He was her destination, after all.

"Lutha mother love," he called in his small voice, sliding off the rock to hug her leg and look happily up at us. "Saluez of the shadow."

She lifted him, hugged him gently, then sat on the rock where he'd been perched.

He settled into her lap. I leaned against a boulder, being invisible, watching the stars come out.

"Tell me about home," he said.

I saw her throat tighten, as though she choked. She swallowed deeply. "Isn't this home, Leely?"

"No. Home home I remember. Alliance Central home."

Who would have thought he would remember Alliance Central? And yet, why would he have forgotten.

"What do you remember?" Lutha asked, looking helplessly at me.

"Everything! My room. My paints. All the nice places you put on my window scene."

"Do you miss those things?"

He leaned back against her with a little squirm of pleasure and comfort. "I like it here. Window scenes are nice, but you can't touch them. You can't be in them. I like real fish. But you want to go back and I want to be with you."

There were tears in my throat. Stars fragmented in my sight. I blinked my eyes clear.

She asked, "How do the other Leelies feel?"

"Most of us don't remember. I'm the only one who *really* remembers. You know."

"I don't know. You tell me."

His little voice was matter-of-fact as he said, "It depends on how big a piece we got made from or maybe which piece we got made from. I got made from Leely head. That's why I remember. The other ones, they were made from Leely legs or Leely blood or Leely guts. They've got good brains, but they don't remember some old things like I do."

He turned to hug her, then went on. "I remember lots of things, Lutha Lutha Tallstaff sister mother love. I remember Trompe. I remember when we met Saluez of the shadow, and how we got here. I remember Behemoth."

She took a deep breath. "You'd probably be fine here, all you Leelies, whether I was here or not."

His face clouded. I had never seen him wear that expression before, though it was one common to other children. The look of a child fearing loneliness. The look of a child afraid.

He put his hands to her face, whispering, "I'd be lonesome. I need somebody to talk to. I want to be with you."

After a time she rose and walked back to the camp, Leely riding on her shoulders, his arms wrapped around her head. Snark and the ex-king were standing outside the dormitory, waiting for us. Lutha took no notice of them. She went on by, as though she would go on walking forever, the child smiling and kicking his heels, his tiny hands clasped around her brow.

The journey from Perdur Alas to Dinadh was not a long one. It brought me, Saluez, almost full circle in my journey. I arrived as outlanders do, through Simidi-ala.

So much had changed.

So little had changed.

Poracious asked the people at the port about the Kachis. The people at the port furrowed their brows and asked in return: What about the Kachis? Had something changed about the Kachis?

What about Tahs-uppi? Poracious asked.

It had been successful, they told her. Additional days had been drawn from the omphalos and time ran once more in its accustomed course. I heard all this, though the people of Simidi-ala were talking to Poracious, not to me. I was veiled and silent before them. They did not even see me.

"What are you going to do?" Poracious asked me when we were alone once more.

"I'm going to make my way to the nearest hive," I told her. "Where I will talk with the sisterhood."

"And what good will that do?" she asked.

I grimaced behind my veil. "Perhaps none. Perhaps a good deal. A few years will tell. What are you going to do?"

"I will do as Snark and Jiacare have said I must. Return to the Alliance and become a preacher. A prophet. A doom crier."

"What good will that do?" I mocked.

She shrugged. "Perhaps none. Perhaps a great deal. I may be of some help on Prime. If things are going to change, it will have to start there. I will do what I can."

"Did you learn what happened to Chur Durwen?"

"He made his way here, to Simidi-ala, and from here went back to Collis." She smiled a strange, harsh smile. "Have you heard of the recent occurrence on Asenagi?"

I raised an eyebrow and waited.

"Asenagi has had a visit from the Gracious One. It—he has spoken to their tribal leaders. They have been promised immortality. . . ."

I took a deep breath. "In return for?"

"In return for mounting a holy war against nonbelievers, which they readily agreed to do."

"War!"

"The Gracious One has promised them a very fierce, unstoppable animal to assist them in their battles. This animal will be born from the women of Asenagi and nurtured by the Asenagi themselves. The animal will fight beside the warriors and will carry the souls of warriors killed in battle directly to . . . well, one assumes Valhalla." She stared out again at the sea. I saw her eyes were wet. "A tempting tale, tailor-made for the Asenagi culture."

"As Lutha once said, it is disgusted with us. I wonder if any of us will manage to choose aright."

"We will try," she replied. "We will do our best."

She kissed me and left me then, alone as I had been before the outlanders came. Later, I saw both her and Leelson being lifted up into the ship that would take them back to Central. He was very pale and focused looking, very set upon his task, his duty, his enormous and quite terrible responsibility. Being a Fastigat, he assumed it was not beyond his capabilities.

And I? I gritted my teeth and set my feet upon the path of righteousness.

Thus was the loom rethreaded.

Thus was the pattern determined.

Thus the shuttle wove.

* * *

Dawn on Dinadh.

Deep in the canyonlands shadow lies thickly layered as fruit-tree leaves in autumn. High on the walls the sun paints stripes of copper and gold, ruby and amber, the stones glowing as though from a forge, hammered here and there into mighty arches above our caves. Beneath those arches, the hives spread fragrant smoke, speak a tumult of little drums, breathe the sound of bone flutes. Above all, well schooled, the voice of Shalumn, songmother, soars like a crying bird:

"The Daylight Woman, see how she advances, she of the flowing garments, she of the golden skin and shining eye . . ."

Years have come and gone since Perdur Alas. I speak often now with Daylight Woman, the Revealer, and with her companion, Behemoth, guardian of all-living. I revere them as I do Weaving Woman and Brother and Sister Rain and the Sisters of Soil. Each morning as my friend Shalumn sings the welcome to day, I pray: *Oh, Great and Gracious Ones, see the choice we have made; do not destroy us but keep us in righteousness. Dinadh shall become as a paradise; and we will share it and treasure it as is your will.*

Each morning before first light, songmother comes to the lip of our cave, raising her voice when the sun touches the rimrock above. Each morning I stand behind her among the sisterhood, they with their faces exposed that all may see the ugliness that comes from seeking more and longer human life at the expense of life itself. Behind us are the other inhabitants of the hive, all joining the song, all hearing the great warp and woof of sound that follows Daylight Woman's eternal march westward. Dawnsong still circles our world endlessly, like the belt that runs from the treadle to the wheel. So much is as before.

Other things are changed. Both Mother Darkness and Father Endless are with us again. They are welcomed with dancing each evening when Daylight Woman departs. Though it is the nature of children to fear the darkness, adults know there can be no light without it. Hah-Hallach and his brethren have been deposed, not for listening to the tempter—for any creature might do that—but for lying to their people after they knew the truth. We have songparents now, mothers and fathers both, as we did on beloved Breadh.

This morning, when the dawnsong is over, Shalumn and I will go to the House Without a Name. In our hive an old woman named H'Nhan died some time ago, leaving an empty place in the pattern. Now a new H'Nhan may be born, to fill that place, and a certain woman has been given the privilege of bearing that child. Today she will lie upon the table, imagining the terror of those who once lay there. There are no Kachis now. The songparents teach that the Kachis were our punishment, but thinking creatures may choose repentance and restitution instead. Now, instead of Kachis we have the reanimated ones from the files on Central: fish and otter; eagle and squirrel; fox and mouse; all manner of creatures to be woven together with us.

We tell the story of Perdur Alas to our children when we teach them the commandments of Dinadh: "Do not wish to live forever. Do not believe that every man-shaped thing is holier than something else. Do not look into the mirror to see the face of God. Do not weave your life only in one color, for Behemoth will not bless you if you do."

Now the morning song is almost over. One of the sisterhood offers the bell. Shalumn accepts it. She rings it, once, twice, three times. Quiet falls. Heads are bowed. All in Cochim-Mahn are saying a silent prayer for Lutha Tallstaff, and for all the Leelies, too. May their shuttles carry brightness; may they be comforted in their choice.

Whenever I say the words, I remember our parting:

The ship was slender and white and still, like a tower, all its crew aboard, all its people waiting. At the bottom of the ramp we few gathered in the light of the rising sun. From the bottom of the valley the sea threw the dawn into our eyes. There was not a sound except our voices, as though the world held its breath.

I hear Lutha repeating what she had said over and over during the long night:

"Leely can't go back, Leelson. He mustn't, not ever."

I hear Leelson:

"Then let the Leelies stay. . . ."

And Lutha again:

"I will not leave my child."

He reached for her then, and she backed away, blazing at him through her tears. "Don't tell me you'll stay, Leelson! The Fastigats will listen only to one of themselves. You have seen what happened in Hermes Sector! Do you want it to happen to all mankind?"

She took one step, then another, her hand lifted in farewell. Yet still he reached for her, tears streaming down his face.

Then Jiacare's voice:

"Go, Leelson. She won't be alone. Snark and I are staying with her."

And finally, Snark:

"Kings and women, Leelson. Kings and women! We gotta do stuff like that!"

Lutha and Leelson and Leely. They are with me always. Leelson left her once, because of Leely. He left her at last, because of Leely. If their love was not really love, their courage was surely courage. Heroes have been adored for less.

The sun is upon Shalumn's ankles now, and her voice ascends the sky. She holds her arms wide, inviting us to enter into the pattern, to go forth into a world that was not made and is not kept for man alone.

And we of Dinadh step into the light.

About the Author

Sheri S. Tepper is the highly acclaimed author of the novels *A Plague of Angels, Sideshow, Beauty, Raising the Stones, Grass, The Gate to Women's Country,* and *After Long Silence. Grass* was a *New York Times* Notable Book and Hugo Award nominee, and *Beauty* was voted Best Fantasy Novel by the readers of *Locus* magazine. Sheri Tepper lives in New Mexico, where she is at work on a new novel.